TOUCHED

THE CARESS OF FATE

A novel by

Elisa S. Amore

Translated by

Leah Janeczko

To my husband Giuseppe and little Gabriel Santo
Thanks to you I'm a better person.
You mean everything to me.

What are you willing to sacrifice when the only person who can save you is the same one who has to kill you?

PROLOGUE

Detroit, Michigan
March 17, 1:45 a.m.

The shadow of fate was waiting, hidden in the night, wrapped in its coils of darkness that were at times protective, at times menacing. Cold, like the heart of he who ruled it.

It would continue to wait, because he would arrive.

An ice-cold wind blew from the north, filling the streets with an ominous hiss. It carried with it the pungent odor of vice that seeped through the cracks around the windows, slipping past the thick curtains drawn to conceal the secrets within: a lost paradise veiled by a lethal cocktail of white powder and sated appetites.

The roar of a car engine mingled with the muffled sound of the wild, rhythmic music coming from inside. A Ferrari pulled up to the opulent entrance, its red body gleaming in the dark night.

Icy, liquid-silver eyes glimmered in the darkness, sharp as a knife, the eyes of a feline that has spotted its prey, as an arrogant-looking man with coppery hair got out of the car.

The wind blew harder as a sly smile hid in the semidarkness.

"Hey!" the man barked, beckoning with two fingers to the valet in the gray suit. "I mean you."

The valet immediately obeyed, walking toward the man and bowing his head with reverential courtesy before catching the car keys tossed at him. "Mr. Mason, welcome back to Royalty Pleasure. It's an honor to have you with us again."

Without bothering to reciprocate, the man ordered, "Take care of my lady." He ran a finger over the car's polished body. A mocking smile lit up his face. "I'll already have far too many other ladies on my hands tonight." He opened the passenger door with a smirk.

Two long, bare legs swung out from behind the red door and a woman clad in a scanty black dress stepped out. To snub him for the insult, she ignored the hand he held out, striding past him and leaving him with his hand in midair.

The man blinked, his pride wounded, and closed his mouth a second before shutting the car door. He walked over to the valet who was staring at him, back straight and chin raised, and grabbed the nametag on the young man's chest, leaning over to scrutinize it in the dim neon light coming from the club behind him.

"Byron Sullivan," he read slowly, as if having difficulty making out the writing. He straightened the valet's lapel, smoothing it down carefully as the young man continued to stare at him, expressionless. "Make sure you bring her back without a scratch," he warned, nodding at the car. "I bet all your worldly possessions wouldn't be enough to pay for it," he sneered, perhaps wanting to take the woman's slight out on the valet.

"Jasper! Are you coming or do I have to go in alone?" the woman whined, standing near the entrance.

The wind blew harder, forcing her to hold down the wisps of cloth that skimmed her legs. A sudden shiver made Jasper's blood run cold. The spine-chilling sensation made him look over his shoulder. Just then, an old lamppost flickered and went out. His eyes ran past the empty sidewalk to the opposite side of the street, partially hidden in darkness, as if the danger he sensed were coming from there, but was only the wind. He frowned and shook his head, chuckling. "Weird. I haven't even started partying yet," he mumbled to himself. "No more than usual, at least. Must be this place, that's all."

"For crying out loud, Jass! I'm freezing!" the woman insisted.

Jasper shook his head to drive the strange thoughts away and wrapped his arm around the woman's neck as he tucked some rolled-up bills into the pocket of the tall, brawny man who towered over them at the entrance to the nightclub. The muscle-bound bouncer barely reacted, as if he hadn't even seen them.

"Finally," she snapped. "I was starting to think you already had far too many *ladies* to remember me."

Despite her reproach, Jasper detected a note of sadness in her voice. He snorted and brushed it off, squeezing her waist. "Don't be silly, babe! If that were true, why would I be here with you? You aren't going to pout the whole time, are you? It's St. Paddy's Day, we're here to party! And dawn is a long time away," he added, pressing the door handle. The noise coming from inside was low and muffled until the door swung open. "Let's let this hellhole take us away!"

The frenzied rhythm of the deafening music hit them full blast, sending a rush of adrenaline through their veins. The door closed behind them, swallowing them up.

3:49 a.m.

The clang of a metal door opening broke the silence of the night as Jasper staggered out into the darkness of the back alley, pulling a young woman in a red dress behind him.

"Mr. Mason! Let go of me! I told you, I do not want to go outside!" The woman's slightly accented voice revealed her dismay as she tried to break free from the man who could barely walk, his brain clouded by a range of substances illegal even in a club like this.

The alley absorbed every sound, suffocating it in the foreboding darkness that shrouded the narrow walls of that godforsaken place like a thick black mantle. A layer of dust covered the surfaces, mixing with the stench of the trash on the sidewalks, turning the air into a stifling sarcophagus.

"C'mon, little flirt . . ." Jasper continued to yank on her arm, trying to overcome her feeble defenses. Although he was wasted and barely able to stand, he easily overpowered her. One more tug on the woman's arm and the door slammed shut, allowing the night to swallow them up completely.

"You cannot . . . you cannot make me stay out here with you!" Her voice came out in a desperate gasp. She grew even more panicked as he pressed her back against the wall with his body. "Let me go!" she whimpered, on the verge of tears. "Please," she cried, close to giving up. A glimmer of hope struck her, like a light at the end of a tunnel. "That woman! I saw you, you came to the club with a woman. What will your girlfriend think if she sees us?!" she said in a last-ditch effort.

He buried his face in the young woman's hair and snorted with laughter, making her blood run ice cold. It hadn't worked; he was mocking her.

"My girlfriend? How could she? She thinks I'm in bed already! Ah, you mean Jasmine. Good-looking, sure, but just a whore. Like all the others." Jasper shifted to look at her face. "Just like you. Don't worry, nobody's going to see us."

She shook her head, terrified, but Jasper rested his finger on her lips. "Tell me your name."

Frozen with fear, the woman didn't reply.

"Careful, babe, I might decide to stop being such a nice guy—"

"Vanessa! My name is Vanessa."

"'Nessa," he said, staring at her. He seemed to like the name. "You're not from around here, are you? You speak good English but you've got this gorgeous accent . . . French, is it? Got to admit it's turning me on."

"Please . . ."

"Shh . . . I don't want to hurt you," he whispered in her ear, lowering his voice as he ran his nose down her neck. "I just want to have a little fun with you. You'll thank me later." He licked Vanessa's earlobe, making her squirm with disgust. "I promise," he whispered, his excitement growing.

"Please, I beg you, I—"

"You'll enjoy it," he panted.

He grabbed her buttocks, hoisted her up against the wall, and shoved his body against hers, beside himself with lust. "You think I didn't notice you staring at me all night long?"

"No, no!" she said quickly, almost as if she'd seen a possible way out. "You . . . you misunderstand. That's my job. It's only my second night here. Let me go, please. They just told me to be nice to customers while they gamble."

The man grunted with desire at the sound of her voice. "You see?" He pushed her hair back over her shoulder. "*That's* what you're going to do for me—you just have to be nice. I'll take care of all the rest." His lips grazed the base of Vanessa's throat as she trembled, her body shaking from the sobs she was holding back. "Besides, I'm no ordinary customer. I'm a very powerful man, you know. You wouldn't want me to have you fired, would you?" he whispered against her skin while pulling her panties down to her knees.

"No! Don't! Please stop!" she begged him, helpless as a child.

With one hand the man unbuckled his belt and undid the button of his jeans while running his other hand up her thigh under her skirt. Stupefied with pleasure, he let out a groan as a hot tear slid down Vanessa's cheek. She braced for the worst.

"Stop making such a fuss. You know you're all just whores here," Jasper moaned.

Suddenly a deafening explosion interrupted their moment of forced intimacy, its ominous noise filling the alley. Jasper whipped his head around, his heart thumping uncontrollably.

The fleeting distraction was enough for Vanessa's survival instinct to kick in. She pulled back with more force than she knew she had and wrenched herself free from the man's grip.

A few yards away, a manhole cover spun on the asphalt, ignoring the laws of physics.

"What the . . . " Jasper gasped. Almost hypnotized by the sound of the heavy, wobbling disc, he only realized Vanessa was gone when he heard the furious click of her high heels as she ran out of the alley.

Just then, a mangy cat leapt onto a dumpster, making him jump. "Freakin' cat!" he cursed, freeing the air trapped in his lungs, his heart still in his throat. The drugs began to wear off, leaving him shaking. "Freakin' women!" he snarled again into the darkness. "Go on! Run! I just came out here to piss anyway!" he shouted as the clicking of the woman's heels faded away in the distance.

"Whore," he growled through clenched teeth. "I never should have come to this hole. They're all crazy here." He turned toward the wall and drenched it with his piss. The sound of his jeans zipper echoed eerily through the alley.

A shudder ran through Jasper's body, but he wasn't sure it was caused by the drugs. Something buried deep within him was waking up, putting him on guard. He looked around, suddenly worried, with the strange feeling that he wasn't alone, that someone was watching him. "Who's there?!" he shouted, panicking. Slowly, cautiously, he moved forward, his footsteps echoing. The door creaked behind him, making him jump, but when he spun around, his heart in his throat, he saw it was closed.

"What the hell?"

Every nerve in his body was tensed and his heart was pounding so wildly his veins felt like they were about to burst.

A gust of wind passed over him and his eyes followed it wildly as if it were a physical presence. "Who's there?" he shouted again.

He was startled by a loud noise behind him as something at the end of the alley tumbled from the foul-smelling dumpsters onto the ground. Instinctively, Jasper reached behind him and wrapped his fingers around the grip of his gun. Five rapid shots pierced the night before he could control his reaction, echoing over and over before fading away. His breathing grew even more stifled, his body racked by tremors.

All around him, silence.

Slowly, Jasper walked over to the spot he'd just shot at, squinting to make out what the darkness was concealing from him. With his foot, he turned over a large, dark form that lay on the ground, but discovered it was only a bag of trash. A mouse squeaked, making him jump. "You piece of shit rat!" He raised his gun to shoot the rodent but the haunting howl of a wolf somewhere in the distance rang out like the lament of an infernal beast, echoing through the alley, and his heartbeat raced like a pacemaker gone haywire. Jasper rubbed his eyes, his forehead beaded with cold sweat.

"What the fuck? I gotta remember not to take this stuff any more!" he said, his hands trembling.

A light blanket of fog crept in through the darkness, making everything eerier than before. Jasper knew he had to get out of there. He felt a bone-chilling presence breathing down his neck, like a ghost that had come to haunt him, and decided to go back inside.

Silence had returned to fill the night as he struggled to regain control of his breathing, but for some reason he couldn't move. Cold shivers continued to run through him. Maybe he'd overdone it tonight. He wondered how much longer his body could withstand his extravagant lifestyle.

Some remote corner of his consciousness whispered that the drugs had nothing to do with it. Another shiver gripped his skin. He swallowed hard, detecting a sound that seemed to come from nowhere. It was in the air, the earth, or maybe inside him—he couldn't tell—but the ominous noise made the blood freeze in his veins. Sweat trickled down his temples as an inhuman growl made him shudder. He got ready to pull the trigger again. "What the fuck?!"

A deafening clatter came from behind him. He whipped around. An excruciating pain tore through his chest, ripping the breath from his lungs like a plant violently uprooted. For a second, his eyes went wide with terror as they beheld the long, rusty iron pole that had impaled his body at the level of his heart.

A moment later, his eyelids drooped, surrendering.

Scarlet life gushed down the pole, dripping onto the damp pavement in a dark red puddle. The fire escape ladder still shuddered, its flaking paint dripping with blood at the point where its wild, uncontrollable descent had driven it deep into human flesh. A final spasm, and death tore the man's life from him, his face frozen in a stifled scream of silent terror.

His jaw dropped open and his head slumped at an unnatural angle as his last breath escaped him.

The wind rose again.

Icy, liquid-silver eyes glimmered in the darkness, sharp as a knife, the eyes of a feline that has captured its prey.

Spectral silence shrouded the corpse. The man's lifeless eyes held the reflection of a shadow, an Angel of the night: the shadow of Fate.

So the Lord God caused the man to fall into a deep sleep,
and while he was sleeping he took one of the man's ribs,
closed up the place with flesh, and made a woman from the rib.

Genesis 2:21-22

Death, if it comes unexpectedly, may be cruel, but it isn't frightening, because you don't have the chance to realize what's about to happen.

Knowing your own fate in advance, on the other hand, is a terrifying form of torture, maybe even worse than death itself. A prelude to madness.

Fearing the shadow of death with each breath is an agonizing countdown that leaves you exhausted and saps your will to fight until its echoing whisper fades into an icy silence that deprives you of everything. It's like a deadly poison that takes effect silently, draining your energy, battering your mind's defenses until you ultimately want to give in to its comfort, letting it shroud you in its dark mantle so the fear itself won't kill you . . . slowly.

The Angel of Death was there for me and soon he would come to take me, because one way or the other I had to die. It was my fate, and who was I to defy it?

1

A BURST OF LIGHT

The remains of famous soccer player Jasper Mason arrived in Los Angeles today. Mason's body was discovered lying in a pool of blood in an alleyway behind a Detroit nightclub of dubious reputation. The body was impaled on the pointed rail of a fire-escape ladder. Born and raised in California, Mason had been playing for Rotherham United, a British team, for several years. Although there are no known witnesses, police discovered a gun lying near Mason's body, and shell casings found at the end of the alley have suggested gunshots moments before his death. Mason's distraught girlfriend told investigators she hadn't heard from him since the afternoon of the incident when he called to cancel their date.

The body was found by a young woman named Jasmine Boulanger, with whom the victim had gone to the club for a St. Patrick's Day celebration. Alarmed when she was unable to find him inside the club in the early hours of the morning, she asked for the entire premises to be searched. The autopsy revealed substantial amounts of narcotics in Mason's system, which may have played a decisive role in the incident, although it remains unclear whether . . .

I glanced at the clock and switched off the TV. I'd already cleaned up everything from lunch but I was still shaken by what Mom had said. Did Peter really feel something like that for me? How could I not have noticed?

Lately I'd had an incredibly hard time concentrating on anything that wasn't printed and bound, as if nothing except books existed or was even worth thinking about.

I climbed the stairs and went to my room at the end of the hall. When I opened the door, Iron Dog—the plump, tawny pug I'd had for ten years—plodded over to greet me, tail wagging. One look at his huge dark eyes always made me forget all my sorrows.

I'd named him Iron Dog—Irony for short—because my parents had surprised me with him during the Ironman competition, an important triathlon held in Lake Placid every year with competitors from all over the world. Basically, he was another one of my mom's attempts to fill the void left by her constant absence.

I put on his leash so we could walk to the lake and enjoy the nice weather. I'd brought along my SLR camera, a gift from my parents for my seventeenth birthday. I'd always loved photography, maybe because of my longing to capture and immortalize every little detail I could. Every inch of my bedroom walls not covered with shelves full of books was plastered with snapshots.

My neighbor and best friend Peter had texted, asking me to meet him on the dock on Lake Placid. Mountain Mist, which was nearby, served the best ice cream in the county, and it was the only sweet treat Peter indulged in from time to time. I couldn't imagine life without burgers, candy bars, and French fries, but Peter took good care of his body; he worked out hard every day and was a real health nut.

After contemplating the lake and taking some snapshots, I sat down at the end of the dock, my feet dangling over the water. It had been one of our hangouts ever since we were little and we'd made a bunch of memories there over the years. In the summer we liked to lie there in the sun and stare up at the sky or dive off the edge and go swimming.

A group of canoeists glided by, making waves that rippled over to me, growing smaller and smaller as they did. Once the boats were gone, the movement faded and the lake again became a perfectly still mirror of water. I opened my English book, which I'd packed in my backpack, and Iron Dog curled up beside me.

I found I couldn't read more than a few lines before completely losing focus. What my mom had said at lunch continued to whirl around in my head, cancelling out the text about the use of the term *irony*. She seemed to be convinced Peter had a crush on me, but it was ridiculous. I couldn't imagine Peter and me together, not in that way. I had no experience with boys. I mean, sure, I'd had dozens of 'book boyfriends,' crushes on characters in novels, but he was real and besides, he was Peter.

Exasperated, I closed my eyes and stretched out on the wooden planks, surrendering to the comforting birdsong coming from the trees. Sunlight touched my eyelids. That sweet torpor was so soothing. A soft breeze gently caressed my skin. The leaves on the trees stirred, chasing each other, speaking in a hushed rustle while I, lost in the quiet, could make out each sound: the rippling water, the squirrels chattering in the branches . . .

Beneath my eyelids the world suddenly grew dark, as if someone had turned off the sun. I opened my eyes. Like a faceless shadow, a dark figure towered over me from behind, standing between me and the light. I barely recognized the outline of his shoulders.

"That you, Pet?" I asked without moving. I was the only one who called him that. It was a sort of nickname I'd used ever since I was a little girl and had spelled his name wrong. Our friends had teased me about it for days, but I didn't care what other people thought. I'd decided that from then on, to me he would be Pet, even if he was Peter or Pete to others.

Although he was upside down and standing against the light, I could still see the dimples shyly appear in his warm smile. I'd never noticed how much sweetness they brought out in his eyes. Nor had I ever thought about how his dark complexion brought out the color of his short dark curls.

"Get any good shots?" He sat down next to me, picking up my camera.

"Photography lets others see things through your eyes, so you'll have to judge for yourself."

"Nobody sees what you see in things," he said casually, flipping through the photos. I stared at him, surprised by how profound his remark was. His hair was still damp. After lacrosse practice he must have taken a shower in the locker room. I ran my eyes over him. Even physically, he suddenly seemed better built. Or was I simply unable to see him in the same light any more? After all, Peter had always been athletic, like most of the boys in Lake Placid.

Peter raised the camera and snapped a closeup of my face. "Quit it!" I protested. A strange warmth spread across my cheeks. I blushed, finding him, for the very first time, attractive. *Was I really blushing because of Peter?* Embarrassed by the thought, I hoped he wouldn't notice.

He showed me the shot. My big, dark eyes stared back at me from the photo, framed by my long brown hair. "Gemma, why are you turning all red?"

"What are you talking about?" I blurted. "It's just the sun." I rubbed my cheeks. "I must . . . I must have fallen asleep. God, my face is burning!" I said, trying to curb my embarrassment.

"Let me feel." He smiled as he leaned over me, clearly intending to personally check the temperature of my skin. I pulled back almost brusquely, avoiding Peter's touch.

"Hey, what's wrong?" he asked, surprised. I could see how my strange response could confuse him. Nothing had changed since the last time we'd seen each other just a few hours earlier. I just couldn't see him with the same eyes any more. My mom's warning came to mind. I didn't want to do anything that might get his hopes up.

"Nothing's wrong! Why?" I tried to make my voice sound natural. "How about some ice cream?"

Peter reached over and tousled my hair as he stood up. It was something I couldn't stand, but he continued to do it regardless. "You've never been good at changing the subject," he said, amused, catching me off guard yet again.

"Have I ever told you you're unbearable?" I asked, narrowing my eyes.

He looked back at me, squinting slightly and thinking aloud. "Let me see . . . Maybe when—? No, wait. Or maybe that time—? No, I'm almost positive you've never told me that to my face," he drawled as his mouth curved in a gorgeous smile that lit up his face.

I forced the trembling in my stomach to stop and kept my tone cheerful. "Then this will be the first time: Peter Turner, you're utterly unbearable!" I bit my lip, unable to keep myself from smiling. *Unbearable and adorable*, I thought as I watched him take a few steps back without turning around.

"I'll be right back, sourpuss. What flavors do you want?" he asked, still backing up. "No, wait! Don't tell me. Strawberry and chocolate." He knew I wouldn't correct him. "Anybody know you better than me?" It wasn't a question. Even he knew the answer.

No, nobody, I thought.

Peter was the first to show up when I needed someone. He could tell what I was feeling just by looking at me. I'd always thought the same thing went for me . . . until that afternoon. We'd once been inseparable, but then—I don't know how or when—it was like something between us had changed. I couldn't explain what, even to myself. One thing, however, had never changed: what I felt for him. Peter had never been just a friend; to me, he was a brother.

As I watched him walk away, a huge burst of light exploded in the cloudless sky above his head, just over his shoulder. I instinctively ducked, my eyes popping open wide, my heart in my throat. The wind grew stronger and a gust of freezing cold air ran down my spine like a silent warning. The birds shot up into the sky, startled.

"Whoa! What was that?!" I stammered, electric shivers running down my arms. Adrenaline filled my veins. I didn't know whether to feel excited or scared. My breathing was out of control, thrown off by the pounding of my heart.

"What was what?" Peter asked, perfectly calm. The only thing that had shaken him was my reaction.

"W-wha . . . You mean you didn't see it? Come on, Peter! It was *huge*! And so close!" I exclaimed, surprised by the look on his face. "You can't not have seen it!" Even Iron Dog wouldn't stop barking.

"What the heck are you talking about? I didn't see anything!" he said even more firmly.

"A giant . . . *thing* . . . like a lightning bolt passed right over your head!" I insisted, hoping to convince him I hadn't lost my mind.

Peter threw his head back and laughed. "Lightning? There isn't a cloud in the sky!"

My fear began to give way to irritation. "I'm telling you I saw something! I saw it with my own two eyes!"

"Ah." Peter nodded slowly, as if he'd finally understood, but something in his gesture made it clear he was about to make fun of me. "Was it by any chance . . . saucer-shaped?

Lit up with lots of colorful blinking lights?" he asked with a grin, moving his finger in a circle over his head.

"Cut it out, I'm being serious!"

"Wait here, I'll go get that ice cream," he said as he stifled a smile. "Oh, and don't get kidnapped by little green men while I'm gone!"

I hugged my knees to my chest, worried, as Peter disappeared. The possibility that I'd actually imagined the flash of light began to creep into my thoughts like a termite boring its way into wood.

Could it have been a plane crash? I quickly ruled out the idea. It was ridiculous—someone else would have seen something. I looked around, studying the faces of the few passersby, but no one seemed to have noticed anything unusual.

No doubt Peter was right. It had probably just been the sunlight playing tricks on my eyes. I relaxed and tried to calm Irony down, but he wouldn't stop barking. It was strange—I'd never seen him so worked up before. In fact, he was always so lazy, I'd never even known he had all that energy inside him. "Hey, what's up with you, huh? Take it easy, Irony." He was starting to make me nervous.

Suddenly he turned toward the forest and let out a low growl that sent a shudder of terror down my spine, then went back to barking like crazy. It was like a demon had possessed him. Another shudder gripped my spine, this time spreading to my heart as it occurred to me that Irony had never acted this aggressive before.

"Calm down. Shh . . ." I whispered, but he ignored me, his barks growing louder and shriller as he continued to yank on his leash, almost imploring me to take him over to that dark patch in the forest that he continued to stare at ferociously.

The forest had never made me feel uneasy before. Quite the opposite—I would often seek its comfort. It had been my favorite place to read since I was a little girl. But now I couldn't get over how nervous it was making me. For the first time, it felt like something dark and sinister was lurking there, with all those roots that twisted up from the ground as if to reach out and trap or devour me.

"That's enough, Iron Dog!" I ordered. I tried to keep my voice firm, but what came out was a frightened squeal he probably didn't even hear. "Irony, calm down! You're scaring me," I whispered in a tiny voice. I'd probably read too many paranormal stories. "How long is Peter going to take?" I murmured, looking around, my eyes full of concern.

In a split second, Irony yanked hard on the leash and it slipped from my hands. He darted away so quickly I couldn't grab the end of it. A moment later he'd completely disappeared among the trees.

Panic filled my throat. If Irony got lost in the forest, some wild animal would have him for dinner before nightfall. Torn between fear and worry, my breath short, I shot off after him but came to a halt at the edge of the thick grove of trees. Summoning up a courage I didn't know I had, I left the warm sunlight behind as the darkness of the forest swallowed me up.

2

ATTRACTION

"Iron Dog . . . Irony, where are you? C'mon, sweetie, come on out." My voice echoed shyly through the humid forest as my breathing, agitated by desperation, covered every other sound. Or maybe it was because of the unusual, sinister stillness of the trees. I forced myself to keep moving as I searched for Irony's trail. I called his name over and over but the forest had claimed him. My heart pounded harder and harder as my panic grew with every step I took across the steep, damp, forest floor.

"Hey! You lost?"

I whirled around. A bald man had suddenly appeared behind me. I'd seen him someplace before but couldn't remember where.

"Need help? I could give you a ride home."

"I'm looking for my dog," I was quick to reply.

"Sorry, I haven't seen him."

"Thanks, I'll keep looking," I said, backing away. All alone in the forest, it was better not to be too trusting.

"All right then, but be careful. It'll be getting dark soon and it might be hard for you to find your way back."

Nodding, I quickened my pace. Hidden behind the trees, the lake had totally disappeared from sight and I wasn't entirely sure where I was. The silence had grown even deeper, as though the forest had fallen asleep. But it wasn't a peaceful silence. Instead, a mystical, foreboding, almost surreal hush hung in the air, as if the entire forest were holding its breath in fear of something . . . or someone. Even the wind had suddenly died down.

I looked up at the tops of the maple trees. They were perfectly still, as if someone had frozen them. My heart was about to break at the thought of never seeing my dog again when a frenzied rustling of leaves made me jump. I stood there, paralyzed with fear, and stared at the spot from which the noise had come. Maybe it was Iron Dog.

Or maybe it wasn't.

"Irony?" I whispered, squinting at the patch of greenery, which moved slightly. A big, shiny, black snout poked out from the leaves, and I could breathe again. "Irony!" I rushed to him as the tension gripping my chest eased. "What were you thinking?" I scolded him. "Never play a trick like that on me again! Where were you hiding, anyway?" I whispered. I knelt, picked him up, and hugged him to my chest.

Another sound—sharper, not far away—put me back on alert. My eyes shot open. Something moved behind me, making my heart stop.

Someone else was there with us in the forest. Racked with shivers, I felt the blood drain from my face. Out of the corner of my eye, I barely made out a blurry figure. Another shiver, one of warning, ran down my spine. I turned swiftly, hoping it was just a trick of light and shadow.

That's when I saw him.

His penetrating eyes captured mine like a magnet as a devastating jolt of electricity swept my skin. Everything around me disappeared, obliterated by his presence. I felt physically incapable of taking my eyes off him, somehow aware that the dark, dangerous energy that gripped my heart would drain away if I even tried.

His body was athletic. His muscles flexed as he clenched his fists at his sides as though haunted by some enigma. Dark, unruly hair hung over his forehead, giving him a wild look. He wore jeans and a tight, dark, short-sleeved shirt that displayed his muscular chest. On the inside of his well-toned forearm, a tattoo caught my eye, an indistinct patch of ink that encircled his arm. It wasn't at all flashy but it did give him the air of a warrior.

The sight of him took my breath away. My heart began to beat wildly, stealing the air from my lungs, as his gaze drank in mine. I'd never experienced anything like it before.

There was something about his face, some sort of energy that reached out with its tendrils and touched my heart. An invisible aura. I *sensed* it, like a spark had suddenly ignited somewhere inside me. No, not a spark: a bell, which was suddenly sounding an alarm, urging my instincts to react. Why? Was my being there just then a mistake? How could it possibly be a mistake if every part of me was utterly captivated, against my will, by those eyes?

The emotion was as powerful as it was unexpected—and sinister. Part of me tried to ignore the warning bell. It was impossible that such an angelic, magnetic face could harbor danger. I was sure that in my entire life I'd never seen anyone so bewitching.

Why was he staring at me so intensely?

His eyes. They'd enchanted me like a dark spell, carrying me away to their fortress dungeon. As clear as crystal, as ardent as fire, they stirred up a whirlwind of uncontrollable emotion inside me. I watched them narrow, sharp as ice, as he stared at me in astonishment, but there was no trace of coldness in his gaze. It was *warm*, comforting. Like a mystical connection, it drew me to him and wouldn't let go.

We stood there staring at each other. The moment seemed to last forever, long enough for me to touch the stars and return. The intensity of his eyes had torn me from the world, connecting me to him with an invisible cord, making me unaware of anything but him. I couldn't break free, even if I wanted to.

And I didn't want to. I'd never been so certain of anything in my whole life. In this moment of madness, I didn't care who he was. I had to stay here with this wild stranger, our gazes interwoven for eternity.

Who are you? And why do you have such power over me? I was sure I'd never seen him before, and yet the emotion was so intense, so . . . *familiar.*

"Gemma!" Peter's worried voice snapped the invisible cord connecting us. "Gemma, where are you? C'mon, I'm sorry I made fun of you. I was just kidding! Answer me!"

"I'm over here!"

A moment later, I saw Peter fight his way through the prickly tangle of bushes. As soon as he saw me, he rested his hands on his knees, exhausted. "Finally, I found you," he panted, reproach in his voice. "You almost gave me a heart attack! Are you crazy? I've been looking all over for you!"

For a minute I couldn't even reply. I stared at him, dazed and shaken by the encounter, my heart longing to restore the connection Peter had just severed. But when my eyes darted back to the mysterious wild boy, I was disappointed. No one was there. In his place, only trees and the wind stirring the leaves, as if freed from an ominous presence.

I peered around, bewildered and suddenly concerned. There wasn't a single trace of his presence, not a scent, not a footprint, not the sound of his footsteps on the path covered with fallen leaves. He'd vanished like a ghost.

"Where'd he go?" I gasped involuntarily.

"Where'd *who* go?" Peter asked.

I was surprised by the irritation in my voice. I felt broken-hearted. How could a perfect stranger make me feel so complete when our eyes were locked and so empty when he was gone?

"Gemma," Peter said, frustrated, "what are you talking about?"

I stared into empty space, at the spot where he'd been until a moment ago. "There was a boy . . ." I murmured, pointing distractedly.

"Gemma," he said gently, "there's nobody here but us. *Nobody.* And while we're at it, what are you doing here all alone? What on earth is up with you today anyway? You're seeing weird things everywhere! First you say you saw a flying saucer and now some mysterious guy suddenly vanishes into thin air. Shall we check around those trees down there? Maybe he jumped six whole yards over that way and out of sight. You sure you're feeling okay?"

At this point I wasn't sure if he was genuinely concerned or just making fun of me. "I didn't see a flying saucer!" I snapped. "It was a—oh, forget it."

"Let's go home," Peter suggested. "The sun's about to set. I don't know about you, but the forest gives me the creeps after dark."

I nodded, lost in memory, my gaze empty. I turned around one last time to scan the trees, but it was no use. The mysterious boy had vanished. Suddenly, another jolt of energy ran through my body, tingling beneath my skin as if to contradict me. It was the same feeling I'd experienced just minutes ago. The same warning. I still felt his gaze on me, as if he were still there, somewhere among the trees, watching me. I shook my head, confused, and quickened my pace to catch up with Peter.

As we walked home together, I could tell he was still concerned. Convinced I was overstressed from studying too much, he told me several times to get some rest. No matter how hard I tried, though, I couldn't focus on Peter's babbling. My mind kept going back to the encounter, as though a piece of me was still trapped in that gaze. For the first time since I'd known Peter, I found the sound of his voice annoying. I didn't want to be torn away from that memory, and his going on and on about my 'crazy hallucinations' only made it more difficult. It was ridiculous. The boy was real. He had to be. I couldn't have imagined it all.

Or could I?

3

DAZED

Like a nail driven into my skull that I couldn't pry out, that bizarre afternoon was stuck in my mind. That burst of light, the forest, his look. No one had ever told me a gaze could have such power over someone.

I turned the TV on to Channel 5 News, hoping to see a report about a strange atmospheric phenomenon. No luck. I flipped from one channel to the next. Not even the local station had any useful information. I searched for what felt like hours.

No strange occurrences.

No plane crash.

No meteorite.

No one had seen anything.

What if Peter was right? Could I have imagined it all? My mom always said that sooner or later all those stories I read would muddle my perception of the world, upsetting my mental equilibrium and blurring the line between reality and illusion. She wasn't all wrong; I'd always been a thousand miles from reality, but this was so, so strange.

Maybe Peter wasn't completely off-base. I probably just needed some rest. I turned off the television and opened my math book, forcing myself not to think about it. I had to put the whole thing behind me.

In a daze, I stared at the untouched tray of food in front of me, distractedly rolling a pickle around with my fork. The pit in my stomach I felt whenever I tried to wipe away the memory of that boy had completely destroyed my appetite.

Against my will, I kept searching for his face in my mind. I struggled to drive him out of my thoughts, but it was no use. It was like he'd planted a seed in me and its roots were growing. The memory of him kept resurfacing more and more clearly, eclipsing everything else. That face, so disturbing and yet so sweet. His warrior's gaze, fierce and troubled. And his body . . .

Thinking of him took my breath away.

I could barely make out Peter's blurry outline, though he was sitting beside me. He and the four others around our table were chatting away as if the world hadn't stopped spinning yesterday afternoon.

At first glance, our group might have looked like a clique in which everyone had found their other half. Jeneane Whitney and Faith Nichols often flirted with Brandon Rice, a blond guy with brown eyes, and Jake Wallace, dark-haired with piercing eyes. They were both jocks and had athletic physiques. The four of them weren't really *couples*, actually, but saying they were just friends would be the understatement of the century. For years now the two boys had hung on the two girls' every last word—not that that kept them from looking around.

Jeneane had a devastating effect on every male who looked her way. She was well aware of her attractiveness and had an incomparable power that she wielded as if it were an extra sense. Fair-skinned, with blond hair, a penetrating gaze, and a gorgeous body, she was very self-confident. Faith, who in my opinion had a more sensible and less cynical nature, tried hard to be the mirror image of

Jeneane, imitating her every gesture and idolizing her like a celebrity.

Faith had an entirely different kind of beauty: a head of fiery red hair, which she almost always wore up in a ponytail, pale skin, and stunning green eyes. She was a horsewoman, both in life and in spirit, although the shyness she tried hard to conceal sometimes tamed the fire that burned within her. Her parents owned a farm and horses were her greatest passion.

Faith and Jeneane even painted their nails the same color. That's how strong the bond between them was. They were like inseparable siblings. Pretty much the same thing went for Peter and me—minus the nail polish.

I'd never cared for the way Faith and Jeneane treated boys, but we'd been friends since we were in our cribs, so hanging out with them came naturally to me.

"Anybody know what's up with her? She's even weirder than usual." The whisper barely filtered through the wall I'd put up between me and the others.

"Hello? Gemma? You with us?" I became vaguely aware that Jeneane was trying to catch my attention from across the table. "Earth. Calling. Gemma." Her theatrical voice penetrated my comforting shell. I hadn't noticed that Faith was waving her hand in front of my nose to snap me out of it.

"Welcome back!" she exclaimed once I managed to focus my eyes on hers. I shook my head slightly, re-entering my body, and looked at their puzzled faces one by one. They stared at me as if they'd just witnessed me being reincarnated.

"Sorry," I said, biting my lip. "I was distracted," I added, hoping that would put an end to the discussion.

"Distracted?" Jeneane said, rolling her eyes. "Lost in space is more like it. On another planet! Ever heard of catalepsy? Anyway, you guys hear what happened in the woods yesterday?" I started, visibly shaken, and gave Jeneane my full attention as their expressions suddenly darkened.

"How could we not have?" Brandon said, pulling his cap down over his eyes. "Nobody's been talking about anything else."

"That's the best thing about small towns," she said, raising his visor and looking him in the eye.

"I hate this place, it's like living in an aquarium!"

"The best thing or the worst thing, depending on your point of view," Jeneane conceded.

"An aquarium?" Peter perked up. "What kind of fish would you be? Oh, I know: ever hear of a species called the donkey fish?"

"You learn that in one of your comic books?" Brandon jeered. Peter *lived* on comic books.

"There's nothing funny about it. Stop kidding around, guys," Faith said, a scared look on her face. "I saw the man's photograph in this morning's *Lake Placid News*. My God, I can't get the picture out of my head!"

"You're right, they shouldn't have published it," Jake said, as thoughtful as always when it came to Faith. "It really is gory."

I blinked, not following the conversation. "What are you talking about? What happened in the woods, Pet?" I whispered to him while the others delved into the lurid details.

"They found a man there last night. Dead."

My heart instantly beat faster at the thought of who it might be, but before I could ask, Peter said, to my relief, "It was Mr. Lussi, that bald guy who ran the tackle shop."

I was struck by the memory of the kind man in the woods. I heard his voice echo through my head: *I could give you a ride home-ome-ome . . .*

"He's dead," I whispered, my blood running ice-cold. My heart was pounding, betraying my suspicion, but I wasn't about to say it out loud.

"He was murdered." Jeneane's voice was distant and cold, almost as if to confirm my suspicions. I'd seen the boy just minutes after running into Mr. Lussi. Could *he* have killed the man? No one else had been out there in the woods except me and Peter.

"Nobody knows that, they're not sure of anything yet."

I forced myself to pay attention to Peter's comforting voice despite the confusion clouding my brain.

"What they do know is his neck was broken." Jeneane seemed to be having fun needling me. Or more likely she just wanted to poke her nose into everything, like always. "Jake, your dad's the chief of police. What do the cops say? Think they'll figure out the cause of death?"

"Do they have any idea who might have done it?" I asked cautiously.

"Right now they're clueless. It was probably just an accident."

"Maybe something scared him, made him trip and hit his head, like a bear—or something scarier," Peter suggested.

"What's scarier than a bear?" Faith asked, shuddering.

"Who knows, maybe there are werewolves in the forest," Brandon said, trying to frighten her. Jake stared at him hard and then smiled at Faith to calm her.

"It's unlikely, Pete," Jake said. "The position the body was found in was too unnatural for him to have just tripped. It's like he fell from a tree, but his wife says that's crazy because he was totally afraid of heights and would never have climbed so high up."

"Maybe someone forced him to," Jeneane said.

"That can't be ruled out. They suspect he was killed but they don't have any evidence to prove it. I overheard my dad talking on the phone last night and the weirdest thing is they didn't find any tracks on the ground. Mr. Lussi's footprints led up to his body, but aside from that there weren't any others. Not a single one."

I gulped, a tingling filling my head.

"Everything okay?" Peter's concerned voice reached me right after I felt the gentle touch of his hand on my back. For once I wished he didn't know me so well that he noticed whenever I was the least bit upset.

"Why shouldn't it be?" I said.

"Gemma, you've been acting so *strange* since yesterday. I'm starting to worry. What's up with you?" Peter insisted.

"Hey! Maybe *she* killed Mr. Lussi!" Brandon exclaimed.

Peter scowled at him. "Shut up, you moron!" He moved his lips to my ear. "If something's bothering you, you can tell me about it, you know that," he whispered, looking into my eyes.

I noticed that the conversation at the table had suddenly stopped. The others were stealing glances in our direction while pretending not to be interested. Embarrassment washing over me, I pulled back. "Why are you guys so nervous all of a sudden? Don't worry, really, it's nothing." The truth was I couldn't help but shudder at the thought that I'd been in the very spot where in all likelihood a murder had been committed. I'd seen that man and right afterwards, maybe just minutes later, he was dead.

Was I actually upset about the man's murder, or was it more that I was scared of finding out *who* might have killed him? I shook my head. The thought was insane. I had no reason to worry about someone who didn't even exist outside my imagination. There were no footprints other than mine in the spot where I'd met him. That was more than enough proof. I just had to convince myself.

My heart skipped a beat, reproaching me when I remembered those eyes. They couldn't not be real. His face haunted me, his eyes stalked me.

I *had* to know or I felt I'd lose my mind. As if it were a matter of life and death, the longing to find out who the boy was pushed me relentlessly to look for him. I felt that seeing him again would be enough to confirm to me he was real and, at the same time, prove his innocence. I was certain I'd be able to read the answer in his eyes. I was also convinced that something sinister was stirring inside me. An ill omen. A fear that seeing him again would mark a point of no return.

No matter who he was, I had to go back to the woods. No matter what it cost, I had to see him again.

The days flew by like the rapidly skimmed pages of a book, and as they passed, his memory faded more and more. But even when I'd begun to forget the details of his face, his gaze was branded on my memory. Against all reason, I clung to that glimmer of reminiscence that had hidden itself away in my heart. I didn't want it to vanish . . .

All day long, the school had been filled with a buzz of excitement about the spring musical that was opening that night. It was a really important event at Lake Placid High. Every April, the students put on a major production complete with costumes, music, dancing, and singing, and people from the whole community came to see it.

A few years ago they'd put on *Anne of Green Gables*, in which I'd played a minor role. Faith had begged me to audition with her, and I'd agreed. My mom had been so excited she'd insisted they close the diner so they could come watch the show, but in the end it was just proof that acting definitely wasn't for me. I didn't like being the center of attention. Faith was given the leading role, but it turned out the stage wasn't for her either; she felt more comfortable back on the farm with her horses than up on stage in front of an audience.

I walked into the auditorium and scanned the room, searching for Peter. It was a large, two-level space with lots of seats and a big blue stage. I recognized Faith by her red hair. She was sitting in one of the very back rows with the others. I went over to them and took a seat beside Peter, who was all alone in the row behind hers, earbuds in. In front of him, wearing navy Blue Bombers sweatshirts, were Jake and Brandon, with Faith between them. It was just before seven, and the murmur in the room grew louder as the seats quickly filled up.

"Jeneane! What are you doing? You should be backstage getting ready!" Faith said as Jeneane came over to us in full costume. "If Mrs. Hathaway sees you out here, she might just turn *you* into a beast!"

I knew Jeneane's only aim was to draw the attention of the entire audience to herself. Little did she care if straying from the rest of the cast made the drama teacher furious. Every year she landed one of the main roles. She was in the school chorus and the women's ensemble too. Unlike me, she loved being in the spotlight and took every opportunity she could to show off. Although I had to admit her voice was even more seductive than her gaze.

"I couldn't go on stage without getting a little dose of good luck," she purred. Moving dangerously close to Brandon, she kissed him on the lips, leaving him temporarily dazed.

"And to think you didn't even want to come, dude!" Jake said, laughing. She elbowed him.

"Pretty sexy, this hair color." Brandon wound one of her dark locks around his finger. Jeneane had agreed to wear a wig in order to get the lead role in *Beauty and the Beast*, but nothing under the sun would convince her to wear dark contact lenses.

"I look good in everything. Why, did you ever doubt it?" she asked provocatively. Jeneane was radiant in her powder-blue gown. It brought out the color of her eyes, a weapon she was an expert at using to her advantage. The long skirt reached her feet and the bodice hugged the curve of her bosom.

"No doubt at all, princess." Brandon stared at her lips, knowing the comment might be rewarded with another kiss. He'd always been full of swagger, but when Jeneane turned on the charm his arrogance gave way to adoration.

Once in a while I glanced over at Peter, who'd been quiet the whole time, picking out songs on his iPhone while the others laughed it up. I noticed a copy of *X-Men*, a Marvel comic he loved, in his backpack, which was lying open on his crossed legs. Sometimes it seemed a part of those characters lived inside him. Peter wasn't your classic knight in shining armor; he was a complex hero full of doubts and conflicting emotions who suffered from unrequited love. I realized that now.

When I'd said hello to him he'd replied with a little wave. I tried to casually brush my elbow against his arm but was sad to see that either he hadn't really registered my presence or—more likely—he was deliberately ignoring me.

But then again, hadn't I basically been treating him the same way lately? The house lights suddenly went out and the auditorium was plunged into darkness. I pondered my recent behavior as the murmur in the auditorium fell silent.

"Hey, Peter," I whispered, trying to get his attention, "want to come to my place afterwards?" I was surprised at how shy and insecure my voice sounded. Right then, all I wanted was for him to say yes.

Peter didn't even look up from his iPhone. "Sorry, I've got stuff to do," he said in a detached voice.

I felt like I'd taken a well-planted punch to the stomach. Desperate for his attention, my body reacted and, without even realizing it, I found myself grabbing an apple peeking out of Peter's backpack.

He turned to look at me, then at the fruit and back at me, confused, almost annoyed. My lips were curved into a little smile as I tilted my head in an unspoken challenge. Peter raised his eyebrows, not sure whether to grab the apple out of my hand or keep on ignoring me. He ate nutritious snacks on a regular basis throughout the day and I knew him well enough to realize that what I was doing would get a rise out of him. I smiled, anticipating the victory of my improvised plan. Childish yet effective.

Peter lunged toward me and I instantly pulled back, putting my hand behind me so he couldn't grab the apple, making our friends snicker. "Looks good," I said, kicking out in my seat to keep him away.

"Shh!" someone in the audience said.

"You wouldn't dare, you—" Peter lowered his voice to avoid disturbing the people watching the show.

"Oh-ho! No more Mr. Nice Guy, hmm?" Keeping him at arm's length, I turned my head, pressed the apple to my mouth and sank my teeth into it, tearing a chunk from the shiny red surface while the others threw their heads back with silent laughter and I savored my little victory.

"Hey Pete, catch!" Peter reached out and grabbed what Jake tossed over his shoulder. "Don't worry, it's low-cal."

"Keep it, I wasn't hungry anyway." Peter tossed back the Clif bar, tilted his head, and looked me straight in the eye.

"Mm, delicious. Want some?" I teased, chewing with a silly grin on my face.

"Of course not, now that you've slobbered all over it."

"Hey!" I complained, not sure if I should be offended. "I never slobber!"

The corners of his mouth rose, barely showing his dimples, although he was trying to keep his lips pressed together in a straight line. I decided he hadn't really been trying to insult me.

All at once, an electric charge like a bolt of lightning hit me square in the chest as my eyes locked with *his*, with *his* wild eyes. *He was there*, behind Peter.

I looked down, stunned, the earth disappearing beneath my feet, my head spinning. He stood there at the back of the auditorium, a confident look on his face, one foot planted against the wall. Was it really him or just a trick of the darkness? The pounding of my heart had already given me the answer. I gasped, almost sending the chunk of apple down the wrong tube. I was unable to move a muscle, my heart full of joy. The yearning to see him again, which I'd secretly been nurturing deep inside me, resurfaced, and with it the hope that he was real.

I trembled, my breathing agitated, hoping the others wouldn't notice. I secretly studied their faces in the darkness but soon turned back toward him, afraid he would vanish again. Shyly, I peered over and saw him in his spot, focusing on the play, the stage lights flickering on his face. My heart struggled between the longing to experience again the spark triggered by his powerful gaze and the timid yet just as overwhelming desire to stare at him undisturbed.

He suddenly turned toward me and my heart skipped a beat as our eyes found each other in a visual connection that canceled out all the rest. Even the voices in the background were reduced to a hush, covered by the frenzied thumping of my heart. A sensation so powerful it took my breath away.

He wasn't that far from our row but far enough to reassure me he hadn't heard a word of my stupid, embarrassing attempt to win back Peter's friendship. My body surrendered to a wave of heat that washed over me and my blood came alive, boiling in my veins.

"Gemma, did you see a ghost or something?" Faith's whispered question barely reached me as she tried to grab my attention by waving. "What are you staring at?" she murmured, looking over her shoulder to follow the trajectory of my gaze.

My anxiety about how she would react pulled me out of my waking dream. Deep in my chest lurked the fear that Faith, or someone else, might not see anyone leaning against the wall. For a while now, the idea that I might be seeing things had been growing in my brain, convincing me that Wild Thing—as I secretly called him because of the fierce, hard, powerful gaze that lay beneath those dark, unruly curls—was only a projection of my longing to see him again.

"Wow!" she said, instantly excited. "Where'd he come from?"

I looked at her, my eyelids fluttering nervously. "W-what? You see him? *You can see him?*" I blurted.

Their whispering suddenly stopped and they all turned to stare at me. "Of course I see him," Faith said, puzzled, like she was talking to a lunatic. "You sure you're feeling okay?"

"Who could help but notice a hottie like that?" Jeneane exclaimed a little too loudly when she saw who we were talking about.

"Shh!" The performance had just started and our whispering was ticking off the people around us.

"Who on earth is he?" Jeneane asked, lowering her voice and leaning over, a wild look in her eyes.

"He must have fallen from heaven." Faith, in front of me, stared at him, a dreamy look on her face.

I smiled to myself, triumphant, because he *existed*. That afternoon I really had seen him in the woods. I didn't turn to Peter and tell him this; it wasn't important to me any more to prove to him I'd been right. Just knowing I had been was enough for me.

But what was he doing here anyway? They all seemed surprised. He must be a new student. Still, that was strange because in Lake Placid everyone knew everyone else—especially people your own age—and, except for a few tourists passing through, it was impossible for anyone to move to our small town without everyone immediately finding out.

"Hey, Gemma, look." Jeneane had leaned over so close to me that her lips touched my ear. "He's totally checking you out."

A shiver ran down my spine. I instantly turned red and couldn't help but look down, embarrassed. My head started spinning and an uncontrollable emotion flooded my heart. Despite my embarrassment, I looked up again and found his gaze waiting for mine. The connection was as immediate as it was devastating. When light flooded the stage for a moment, I saw he was wearing a dark red T-shirt over faded jeans and gym shoes.

"Why's he staring at you like that?" The note of irritation in Peter's voice surprised me, distracting my attention from *him*. Dazed, I studied the expression on my friend's face, which was twisted into a grimace. He almost seemed angry.

"Well, well, well! Somebody's jealous," Jeneane jeered beside me. Peter didn't respond. He just glanced at me, waiting for my reaction, but I ignored him.

"Must be a new student," Brandon said, turning around for a second. "Never seen him before. Funny none of us have heard anything about him."

"I was just thinking the same thing," Jake added. "Wonder if he'll try out for the team."

"Maybe he's just passing through," said Faith.

But Jeneane quickly disagreed. "It's not like tourists come to see our school musicals, do they?" she said. She had a point.

"I wonder what he wants with you," Peter said in a low voice, more to himself than to me.

"He must think I was acting stupid, that's all." The fear of it actually crossed my mind.

"Doesn't seem to be laughing at you," Faith said, a mischievous look flashing across her face.

Kinda creepy, huh? Jeneane mouthed silently.

In the dimly lit auditorium, I had to admit that seeing his piercing eyes locked on me was a little scary. Light and shadow battled it out on his face. He looked like an angel, yes, but one of darkness.

"Maybe he's the killer who lurks in the woods," Brandon joked, and a shiver ran through me.

"Shut up, moron!" Jeneane bopped him on the head. "He's just a kid. Besides, Faith's right. Gemma, you sure you've never seen him before? He's looking at you like he knows you *intimately*," she said, choosing her words carefully. "Like there's something between you."

"He wishes!" Brandon raised an eyebrow in an unequivocal expression. Faith glared at him before looking at Peter to make sure he wasn't hurt.

"You're wrong, guys. I've never seen him before," I objected. "In any case, Jeneane, shouldn't you be backstage now? The introduction's almost over."

A huge burst of light coming from the stage helped me put an end to the conversation. The set filled with smoke while background music accompanied the prince, now transformed into the Beast, as he made his entrance and leaned over the glass dome containing the red rose.

"I'm up!" Jeneane shot to her feet and hurried away through the blue seats.

"Knock 'em dead!" Faith chimed as she disappeared.

I turned back to look for the boy and my heart skipped a beat as, in that new intimacy, we stared at each other from afar.

The first notes of Jeneane's sweet voice filled the auditorium as she walked through the marketplace on stage. It was soon accompanied by Gaston's more powerful one. I smiled, turning to look at the boy again. For a moment he seemed to be smiling back at me. I blushed and nervously faced the stage, my ears burning.

The play lasted a couple of hours. Jeneane changed costumes several times and was radiant in Belle's golden-yellow gown as she sat at an elegantly laid table with the Beast, but I couldn't follow a single one of their lines. My heart was trembling in my chest at the thought that he was right there, just steps away from me. I wished I could follow my instinct to run to him, but instead I sat there in the darkness of the auditorium, casting shy glances in his direction, longing for the warmth of his gaze.

The house lights went up to a burst of applause.

I felt a pang. Time was running out.

My friends stood up as the auditorium slowly emptied. Accustomed to the comfort of darkness, I felt more exposed with the lights on and was almost scared to turn and look at him again. I knew that if my eyes met his I would disappear into him. It was a wild feeling, as wild as the fierceness painted on his face. My mind insisted on using that adjective to describe him, because his gaze was wild. Wild was the power with which he drew me to him, into him. Wild was the emotion that had crept into me and was now growing uncontrollably. *Wild.*

I wished I could shout out for all to hear the incredible joy that filled my heart, but I was determined not to tell anyone about having seen him in the woods—as though he and I were somehow sharing a secret. The memory brought to mind another, more disturbing one. The investigation into Mr. Lussi's death had led nowhere, and admitting how we'd met might raise questions that had already been forgotten. Then again, there was nothing compromising about it, I'd just run into him somewhere in the woods. Nothing connected the death to him, otherwise the police would have found out already. They weren't even sure it had been a homicide in the first place.

I had no idea why I was protecting him. As far as I knew, Brandon might be right: the boy could be a murderer. There was no saying he hadn't committed the crime, but for some reason my instinct made me keep quiet. No one could find out how wrapped up in him I actually was, especially Peter. I couldn't risk hurting him.

I began to wonder if it was the last time I'd ever see him. I yearned to feel—if only for one more moment—the heat that filled me when his eyes burned into mine. Overpowered by the instinct, I looked around and was disappointed to see he was about to walk out the door.

For a moment I couldn't breathe and a terrible sensation choked me like a noose around my neck. What if he disappeared again? Could I stand losing him again now that I was sure he existed, or would it be even harder? Clenching my fists, I picked up my things and got ready to leave, a resigned look on my face.

"He's still staring at you," Faith whispered in my ear.

My eyes darted up and met his: hypnotic, piercing, intense. *Wild.* His expression wasn't hostile or angry, but it held a trace of dissatisfaction, almost like he was sad that his time with me there had run out.

Suddenly, Peter wrapped his arm around my waist and pulled me toward him as though I were his. Forcing myself not to react, I stared at him with a puzzled expression, but he ignored my tacit reproach, his eyes narrowed to slits, challenging those of Wild Thing.

"Let's go," Peter ordered me firmly, his eyes glued to the stranger. "I'll take you home."

Just then I realized that in order to leave the auditorium I'd have to pass right by him. My heart raced at the thought. I looked down, unable to hold his intense gaze. I was sure that once I got that close to him, I would be overcome with emotion. I already felt my legs trembling, my heart throbbing harder with every step, making me unsteady on my feet. Was I really so weak? *Emotional,* my mom would have said, but in his presence that's what I felt: weak.

Driven by desire, I found the strength to raise my eyes and look toward the doors again. I was devastated not to find him among the crowd leaving the hall. A wave of anger rose from my stomach; Peter's gesture might have driven him off. I forced myself to hold it down and went backstage with Faith to get Jeneane.

I needed to take pictures of the cast for the yearbook, a perfect excuse to turn down Peter's offer to walk me home. I made sure to hide my resentment, but he might have picked up on my mood swing anyway.

Anguish kept me from opening my mouth the whole trip home. In the back seat of Jeneane's mom's car, I sat in silence, staring blankly out the window, annoyed by Jeneane and Faith's nonstop chatter. They wouldn't stop talking about how awesome the new boy was and arguing over who'd seen him first. I rolled my eyes and shook my head, disgusted by how shameless they were being.

"God, did you see that body?!" Faith exclaimed.

"I don't think God wastes time looking at people's bodies," I muttered. I couldn't disagree with her, but I was trying nonetheless to mask my feelings with sarcasm.

"Hey, Gemma." Faith lowered her voice just for me. "Did you see the way he was smiling at you?"

I blushed. "What? Nah." But it was true. In the darkness, with the performance humming in the background, we'd exchanged smiles. Lots and lots of smiles. The sweet memory made me sigh.

"Why do you think he moved here to Dullsville?" Jeneane asked, intrigued.

"I don't know, but we're definitely going to find out!" Faith said excitedly.

I felt sorry for him. Those two would stop at nothing to learn everything there was to know about him. Jeneane and Faith were among Lake Placid's biggest gossips, unlike me, who couldn't be bothered with rumors. They had to know everything about everybody. And that boy would be no exception.

However, for the first time, I was actually interested in what they would find out. Not even Mrs. Whitney could keep from joining in the speculation the whole ride home, wondering who he was, where he came from, and how old he was. He couldn't have been much older than us, but something about his stern, inscrutable features suggested otherwise.

I was sure by the next day they'd have found out even his blood type. And my impatience to learn about him made me their accomplice.

Outside, the sky had thickened into a dark patch of clouds, and the mist on the streets had turned into a drizzle that dampened my hair as I went up our front walk. But I didn't care. I had sunshine inside me because he existed. Nothing could have made me happier just then. I went inside, walking on air, electrified, buoyant. The lights were on, which meant my parents were already home, but I didn't feel like letting anything distract me from reminiscing about the amazing night I'd had, so I ignored my mom, who called to me as I climbed the stairs to come have dinner. A tangle of emotions had left butterflies fluttering in my stomach, leaving room for nothing else.

"We grabbed some burgers on our way back. I'm going to my room to study!" I lied, shutting the door behind me. I threw myself onto the bed, lost in a hundred thoughts.

I wondered whether Wild Thing had left because of Peter or if something else had bothered him. He'd stared back at me during the entire show, so why had he slipped away without some kind of goodbye? Had he misunderstood my relationship with Peter? What a mess.

Now, free from his spell, I felt a strange sensation when I thought back on his eyes. There was something sinister in them that I couldn't explain. He seemed to have been studying me intently. Jeneane was right; it was as if something about me made him both curious and confused.

A ticking noise coming from somewhere in the room snapped me out of my total immersion in my thoughts. I looked around, listening, trying to figure out what it was, then realized it was coming from the window. Someone outside was tossing pebbles against the glass to get my attention.

My heart skipped a beat as it filled with hope. I leapt out of bed, eager to see him again. But it was Peter I found there waiting for me. Only Peter. Then again, who else could I have expected?

"Hey! What on earth are you doing here?" I asked, opening the window. Only after I'd said it did I realize how rude I'd sounded. Still, part of me held him responsible for what had happened back at the school.

"You invited me over, remember? I sent you a text," he said, being careful not to talk too loud.

I checked my phone and read his message.

I'M OUTSIDE. COME DOWN.

"Sorry, I didn't see it," I whispered. "My parents are still awake. You know I can't go out this late! What are you thinking?"

"I just wanted to see you." He seemed embarrassed, but only for a second. "Well, make way! I'm coming up!"

When we were little, Peter used to climb the ivy-covered trellis all the time to sneak into my room. He hadn't done it for years, and for a moment, seeing the top of his head from my window took me back to the past. My parents had never allowed Pet to be up in my room with me after curfew, not even when we were little. We'd solved that problem with the trellis, and he'd often snuck into my room through the window to talk and watch movies or reruns of *Dawson's Creek*. Sometimes, just for fun, he told me I was his Joey, but up until then I'd never actually realized that maybe he would never be my Dawson.

"Careful," I whispered, trying not to let my parents hear me. "It might not support your weight any more!" His stubbornness made me smile, though just barely.

"What are you trying to say? I don't weigh that m—" Before he could react, gravity pulled him down to the ground mid-sentence. I couldn't hold back a laugh. A sound from downstairs put us on guard and Peter pressed his back against the wall to avoid being discovered. I stifled another laugh and he looked up at me. "Think it's funny, do you? Well, I'm not giving up," he whispered.

"Are you trying to hurt yourself? You're too big, it'll never hold!" I whispered. My words didn't dissuade him. I didn't know anyone more stubborn than him. Except myself, of course. "Hang on a second." I went back to find my camera and slung it around my neck. "Okay, get out of the way. I'm coming down." I crawled over the windowsill, grabbed onto the trellis, and slowly climbed down. Peter came over and held me by the hips to make sure I wouldn't fall. "There we go. That wasn't so hard, was it?"

"Says the squirrel."

"Hey!" I punched his shoulder and he laughed. I'd always been a good climber. Peter got onto his bike and waited for me to get mine. "Where are we going?" I asked.

"The field. The guys are waiting for me. We're going to practice for the game day after tomorrow." I got on my bike and pedaled after him down the dark, silent streets.

When we reached the field, Peter threw his bike to the ground with a clatter that rang through the night. Jake, Brandon, and the other teammates were already there. "Root for me!" he shouted as he walked over to join them.

"I'll bet on the other team like I always do," I joked.

The bleachers were empty; there was no sign of Jeneane or Faith. Climbing to the top where there was a better view, I snapped a few shots of the guys. I zoomed in on Peter and was trying to get him in focus when a shadow passed over my lens. Lowering the camera as a shiver slowly ran through me, I looked around. Someone was there with me. I could feel it.

Suddenly I couldn't hear the guys' voices any more. All my senses were trained on a single sensation: someone was watching me. On my guard, I went down the steps. No one was there—only a gloomy aura that shrouded the night. Yet I had the feeling the darkness was deceptive . . . A noise made me freeze. I whirled around toward the back of the stands, but there wasn't enough light to see and I moved closer. Something on the ground stirred. I held my breath and crept nearer. A scream escaped my throat when I saw them: the feet of a corpse.

All at once someone grabbed me by the shoulder. I spun around, terror gripping me, but a shaft of light pointed at my face paralyzed me. "Hey, haven't I told you kids you're not allowed to go crawling around here at night?" The man lowered his flashlight and I finally exhaled. It was Jake's dad, the chief of police.

"What's with all the ruckus this late at night?!" another voice nearby grumbled. We both turned. An old homeless man muttered something and went back to sleep. It wasn't a corpse, I realized with relief.

"Well? What are you doing out here so late?" the policeman asked, turning back to me.

"Mr. Wallace, we weren't doing anything wrong."

"Maybe *you* weren't, but the streets haven't been so safe lately. Go home. That stubborn son of mine is going to hear me loud and clear this time," he said to himself. The police siren rang out just once, as a warning. "Jake! Move your ass and get in the car now!"

"Sir, yes sir," he answered, annoyed, as Brandon hurried off in the opposite direction.

I got onto my bike and waited for Peter.

"Let's get out of here before he changes his mind and escorts us back," he said.

I began to follow him toward home, but a sudden gust of wind penetrated my bones, forcing me to stop. As I looked around, still shaken, a headlight blinked on nearby, the bike hidden somewhere in the darkness. The sound of its engine coming to life broke the silence of the night.

"Gemma, are you coming or aren't you?" Peter called out.

I watched the motorcycle as it drove off. "Yeah, let's get out of here," I murmured as another shiver ran through me. Maybe the police chief was right: it was no longer safe to be out on the streets.

4

DREAMING

It isn't written . . . I can't fight it . . . I can't prevent it. I'm sorry . . .

The words were still echoing through my head as I opened my eyes, feeling groggy and lightheaded. I lay in bed for a few minutes, staring at the ceiling as day broke, letting myself remember his features before they completely vanished. Under my skin I had the strange conviction I'd just been with him again. But it had only been a dream.

What had made my heart begin to pound so hard it woke me up was knowing that he existed and I'd see him again.

Outside, thick fog filled the streets with a gloomy light, but I was too ecstatic to even notice. As I walked to school, the atmosphere took me back into last night's dream. I'd been in the woods, surrounded by trees, just like I had been that day. I was alone, but I sensed a hostile presence around me, as if someone was watching me. As if *he* was watching me. I felt his eyes on me, like a hunter's on his prey. The thought both excited and frightened me. Because this time I was the prey.

I tilted my head back and peered around, squinting as I searched the branches, driven by the strange awareness that I'd find him, but no one was there. The sun suddenly blinded me. I was mesmerized by the way the light touched the leaves, its delicate rays filtering through the interwoven branches.

Something moved. Right there, in the middle of the light. I tried to focus on the strange shape surrounded by golden reflections. Was it an animal? I moved closer.

It was certainly bigger than me. Maybe I should run. It might kill me, and yet that likelihood didn't frighten me. It was perfectly still, watching me from atop the lowest, largest branch. Whatever it was, it must have been more frightened than I was, because it seemed to be holding its breath and waiting for me to leave, like a chameleon trying to make itself invisible to the eyes of a predator.

I moved closer still and recognized him from the beating of my heart. Like a wave crashing onto a rocky shore, a wild emotion washed over me, drowning me.
The nameless boy had entered my mind, never to leave it again.

My eyes found his amid the pearly light reflected around him. His expression continued to darken, half fascinated, half amazed. I couldn't understand what was upsetting him, but once again I had the impression he was studying me. It wasn't that he was interested in me, exactly. Instead, he seemed confused by my interest in him. The closer I got, the more he backed up, alarmed.

There was something about his features that bewitched me. I felt lightheaded. All he had to do was meet my gaze to transfix my deepest essence. The blue shirt he wore brought out the icy shade of his eyes. Its long sleeves were rolled up to his elbows, the tattoo branching out on his arm, his facial features perfect, his skin firm and supple. I imagined his soft touch on me. I reached out, but then pulled back my hand, frightened by the powerful emotion that I knew would devastate me if I dared touch him. And his eyes . . . It was as if I held the memory of them within my deepest self.

I was disoriented by his confusion. He was studying my every movement as though he'd never seen another human being in his whole life. I ignored it and kept drawing nearer.

For a second I couldn't breathe. As he stared at me from under his dark, unruly hair, I saw thin, imperceptible streaks of amber sparkle in his eyes like diamonds, like liquid silver glinting in the light. The color was so unnatural and yet so perfect . . . Eyes of ice.

Our gazes locked, entwined like they had been the first time we'd seen each other. I stepped forward, resting my hand on the tree trunk for support as I leaned toward him, unable to control myself. In response, he set aside his hesitation, crouched, and leapt down to the ground. His eyes continued to study me. Slowly, he reached out to touch me and paused warily, inches from my face. I trembled because I yearned for his touch, if only for a moment. I held out my hand, seeking his, my palm facing him. My breath caught as the emotion that contact with him would trigger overwhelmed me. I'd never touched him before. He studied my hand for a second and, finally resolved, gently rested his palm against mine.

It was like a star bursting inside me. His eyes locked onto mine and an electric shock ran from him to me, connecting us. Eye to eye. Palm to palm. He looked astonished at the power of our contact, and closed his hand, interlacing his fingers with mine as though he never wanted to let me go. His eyes pierced deep, deep into my own. A shiver caressed my back at the extraordinary warmth of his skin. I half closed my eyes and at that instant heard the sound of his voice for the first time.

I won't hurt you. His sweet whisper crept into my mind, penetrated my soul, reaching places hidden and unknown even to me. It was so deep and intense it left me dazed and trembling. I felt he'd whispered directly into my heart. The world around us disappeared as I, at the mercy of some enchantment, saw nothing but him. A dark spell that enveloped my heart. Only when a puff of wind caressed my face did I re-emerge, realizing the forest around us had vanished.

I gasped. Now I was standing at the very edge of a cliff overlooking the sea. Frightened by the sudden height, I instinctively clung to him. Embarrassed by the stolen contact, I tried to pull back, but before I could he drew me to him with endless tenderness. For a moment I forgot how to breathe. His deep, hypnotic gaze was like a lasso around my heart. Powerful and dark.

Don't be afraid, a whisper replied to my thoughts. *Trust me, just this once.*

I looked at him, spellbound. His sensual voice enveloped me like black velvet, but his lips hadn't moved. The sweet sound had filled me from within, making its way to my heart. How could it be?

Incredibly, every qualm instantly disappeared, banished by a strange, unexpected feeling of trust. Suddenly I knew I could trust him completely. His voice seemed to have instilled the thought directly in my mind. I peered down at the empty space below us and held back a shudder. The endless sea crashed against the rock as though it were trying to seize us. Although the wind lashed at my skin, taking my breath away, I wasn't cold because he was with me. Or was I breathless because his face was so close to mine? A comforting, tingling sensation spread through my whole body.

I closed my eyes and let the emotion fill me. "I'll never forget this moment," I murmured. I felt a longing in my heart to gaze into his eyes, but when I looked up his expression had turned grim. Was he already regretting this?

"Did I say something wrong?" I asked shyly.

He seemed lost in a world all his own, but a second later his lips parted. "*All of this* is wrong. What am I doing? I shouldn't even be here." He said this as though trying to convince himself, but something was stopping him. I didn't dare hope it was me. "I, I *need* to understand. I need to," he whispered in a dull voice as he stared down at the waves crashing against the rocky cliff.

For a second I thought he might be on the verge of leaving me and I felt a pang in my stomach. "What's so wrong about this? Why do you think you shouldn't be here?"

His face darkened. "Bewitched are the eyes of those who are not allowed to understand. My eyes, my soul, prisoners of a fire that consumes my essence."

"What do you mean? I don't understand." Was he bewitched by me? Was that what he meant? No, he was talking to himself.

"It doesn't matter," he murmured, lost in thought.

"It matters to me. Tell me what's going on."

"You wouldn't understand."

"I could try."

"I can't," he said through clenched teeth. "I'm not permitted to."

I stood stock still, mystified. I had the impression that inside him a battle raged. He seemed angry with himself. What could be making him so upset?

Suddenly, his expression grew serious and every last hint of indecision vanished. Impetuously, he cupped my face in both hands. His piercing gaze, so intense, so close to mine, hit me like a wave of pure emotion. For a second I found that glimmer of authority disorienting. "Listen to me," he said. "I made a mistake by coming here. You must never think about me again. It's wrong—for you, for me, for everyone. Forget my face. Forget you met me. You never saw me in the woods, it was just your mind playing tricks on you. You must erase me completely from your memory," he ordered, as if he expected me to do exactly what he'd just said.

I was staggered. The coldness of his words went through me like a sword of ice and I shook my head, my face still cupped in his hands. "Wha—why? What you're saying doesn't make any sense. Why should I forget we met? Everything about you is unforgettable," I said all in one breath, staring into his eyes.

My objections produced absolute confusion on his face, as if he'd expected total acquiescence on my part. "What the hell? Damn it, I've ruined everything! It's all my fault! I keep coming back. I keep coming to see you, to touch your mind in the hopes of finding the key."

"The key to what?" I asked, exasperated.

"The key to you," he whispered.

I stared at him, dazed.

He focused again, his voice determined. "I have to stop coming to see you. I must pull back. I, I have to let you go. I've already broken too many rules. Things should never have gone this far. I lost control. Forgive me. I've only made things harder for you. What the hell's gotten into me? You *have* to forget about me!"

"Sorry, but it's too late. I don't want to forget you," I said, my heart trembling from this unexpected confession.

"You don't understand, damn it!" he snapped, making me start. But then his gaze became tender. "Gemma." For a second my heart lost its steady rhythm. Hearing my name on his lips sent a wave of heat from my belly to my chest. "We . . ." He stopped, weighing his words. I couldn't take my eyes off the curve of his lips. "We're bound by destiny, but not in the way you think. You've got the wrong idea about me. You don't know who I really am. Why I came here. You don't know what I'm being forced to . . ." His voice trailed off and he let his arms drop to his sides, trying to compose himself. "Everything would be a lot easier if you had no recollection of me."

"Why?" I asked, gripped by desperation. Suddenly I wanted him, I wanted nothing but him. I wasn't ready to lose him so soon.

His eyes narrowed to slits. "There are things we can't control. We can't fight them," he declared firmly, closing his eyes, clearly overcome by a feeling not even he understood. Resignation, maybe. "*I* can't fight it. I have my duty. I can't prevent it. I'm sorry," he whispered brokenly. I wasn't entirely sure whether he was talking to me or trying to convince himself.

I frowned. Why was he insisting I forget him? What had I done wrong? I didn't want to accept it, and the look of defeat on his face pained me. "What are you talking about? I still don't understand. What is it you can't control? What duty are you talking about, and what does it have to do with me?"

His eyes lingered on mine, his expression tormented, as if he was looking for the answers as well. "I only wish I could have more time." He gazed at me for a long, long while, seeming devastated. "It's my mission. I can't help it. It's all I know."

"More time for what? Here we are, just us. Right now. We've got all the time we need."

"You're wrong. There's no time, not for us. It isn't written. I can't fight it. I can't prevent it. I'm sorry." His voice whispered in my head until it faded away, cradling me in the stillness between sleep and wakefulness.

I was so lost in the memory of that dream that I realized I'd reached school only when Peter's familiar voice snapped me back to reality, the dream vanishing into the mist of the gray morning.

"Gemma!" he shouted, running up to me. "Hey, I saved you a seat on the bus. Why didn't you take it? Your mom drop you off?"

"I walked," I explained, a little evasive, a little irritated.

"In this fog?"

I pressed my lips together in confirmation. Had he always been this thoughtful or had I just never noticed before? His attention didn't bother me per se, but I still wasn't used to how awkward I kept feeling when I was with him. It was strange to feel that way around Peter.

I walked along, staring down at the sidewalk, still damp from the morning dew. For a while neither of us opened our mouths.

Two beeps broke the tension. We'd received texts at the same moment. We pulled our phones out to check.

"It's Jake."

"It's Faith."

Peter and I grinned at each other because we'd spoken at the same time. Our friends had met up at what we called Grassy Knoll and were waiting for us there. We had a little time before first period. Peter casually took my hand and we rushed off. We'd always held hands, ever since we were kids. And yet, after everything that had changed between us, I suddenly had a funny feeling. *Everything that had changed inside me.*

We found them there at the lakeside. I heard Taylor Swift's voice blasting from Jeneane's headphones. Her head was resting on Brandon's knees and his visor was lowered over his eyes. Was he sleeping? Probably. Faith was lying face down on the grass, engrossed in a magazine article about One Direction. In her locker she even had a poster of Louis Tomlinson, her idol. All three of them wore Blue Bomber lacrosse sweatshirts.

"Hey!" I said, sitting down beside Jake. He held up his hand in reply and went back to focusing on his math book. I pulled out my notes and handed them to him. "Here, use these."

"You rock!" he cheered.

"Don't mention it."

I pulled my old iPod out of my backpack. My friends made fun of me because I refused to change with the times and listen to music on my phone the way everyone else did. My iPod might have been a prehistoric artifact, but it was special to me, because my grandma had given it to me before she died.

I chose the Lana Del Rey folder and turned the volume all the way up. Her voice could carry me far away, delving into my soul and revealing things I didn't know about myself.

Music was my life, along with books. It was almost surreal how whenever I walked into Bookstore Plus it seemed to be the book that chose me. A perception, almost a mutual desire.

Peter sank down beside me and stole one of my earbuds. Together, we listened to *Born to Die*, one of my favorites by Lana. Maybe I'd never even noticed him doing that before. Peter was my best friend. We'd grown up together and he would always be a part of me. The thought that our relationship had changed made me sad. I smiled at him and pretended for a moment that everything was still the way it used to be.

I abandoned myself to Lana's melodious voice, thinking of *him*. The whole world, *my* whole world, seemed to revolve around those eyes.

Faith pulled the earbud out of my ear as I sang beneath my breath. "Hey, you guys already figured out where you're going to college?" she asked.

"It's not like we have to make up our minds now. There's still time to think it over," Peter said.

The others nodded. But I'd made clear plans all the way back in grade school: I wanted to be a journalist or a reporter that worked on documentaries. I liked being in contact with nature and animals. "You guys haven't thought about what you want to do after high school? Seriously?" I asked. How could they not care?

Faith thought it over a moment. "I'd like to be a veterinarian . . . I think."

"Good idea, you'd be great with animals," I assured her.

"You'll probably end up being a writer, Gemma," she said, making me smile to myself. I read lots of books, but it had never crossed my mind to write one, although I didn't dislike the idea.

"I want to work in fashion," Jeneane chimed in, sitting down on the grass between Faith and me. I would have guessed she'd want to be a singer or maybe an actress, given her passion for putting on a show. "Wait, guys, let's capture the moment." Jeneane pulled out her phone and adjusted her hat. Faith and I crowded into the shot. I kept my knees pressed up against my chest while Faith was practically lying on top of us. "We'll call this one *What Will Become of Us?*"

"Or how about *Happy Times Before Getting Our Math Test Results?*" Jake said, smiling.

"Ha ha." Jeneane shot him a not-so-amused look. "I'll post it on my Facebook page."

"Jake, what are you going to do after graduating?" Faith asked, clearly more interested in Jake than she wanted to let on.

"Enlist," he said, as if his mind was already made up. Faith went silent, stunned by his decision. Jake was the son of the chief of police, so it wasn't really a surprise that he would follow in his father's footsteps and choose a military career, but the very thought of it saddened Faith.

"I don't need to think about what I'm going to do after graduation," Brandon said with his usual arrogance. "I'm already what I want to be."

"What, a poser? I didn't know that was a paying job," Peter said, making us all laugh.

"I mean a *sports legend*, if you know what that is."

"You'll see for yourself when I outscore you during the game," his friend shot back.

Brandon, Peter, and Jake had played lacrosse together since they were little. They were very close, a team within the team, but they liked to compete and poke fun at each other too.

"What about you, Pete?" Faith asked. "What are your plans for the future?"

Peter thought it over a moment, although there was no need. I knew what his plans were. "I want to draw comics for Marvel. After college, of course." He shrugged in reply to the others' skeptical glances. I believed in him and he was so good that if he committed himself he would definitely reach his goal. "Doesn't cost anything to dream. Meanwhile, I'm going to work at my dad's smithy. That is, if he decides not to drag us all to Europe."

Even though we'd been a bit distant over the last few weeks, that possibility kept coming back to scare me. With a twinge of melancholy, I got up and walked over to the shore. I peered down into the water. Despite the fog, the surface was as clear as a mirror.

A strange flashback filled my mind as I stared at my reflection. It had happened a year ago, at Split Rock Falls.

I'd strayed away from my friends, drawn by some obscure force into the thick of the forest, to the bank of a small pond. I'd gone up to the water's edge and seen something beneath the surface. Against my instinct, I dipped my fingers into the water, curious to find out what it was. That was when I'd seen it. My own dead body, staring back at me with its eyes open wide. The reflection of a nightmare. I'd almost died of fright. Hearing my screams, Peter had run to help me, but when he got there, there was nothing in the pond any more. He was the only person I'd told about what I'd seen, but he thought it had all been in my mind.

I shuddered now, because despite everything it was still vivid to me. I'd had nightmares for days, tormented by the fear of seeing the reflection of my fate. The strange occurrences of the last few weeks had made the blood-chilling memory resurface. Even now I felt like I was being watched.

I thought back to the mysterious boy and the dream I'd had the night before. His presence was so strong in my mind that I thought he was everywhere, as if he were constantly lurking somewhere nearby, watching me.

I crossed my legs and rummaged through my backpack, looking for a book. I always brought at least two with me. I'd sought the company of books ever since I was a little girl. I pulled out *Divergent* by Veronica Roth in an attempt to distract myself from those unsettling thoughts. I had a not-so-secret crush on Four, the main male character. Resting the open book on my lap, I took a picture with my phone, including the book, the tops of my shoes and the lake in the background. The water was enchanting at that time of morning. I chose a rosy filter and posted the picture on my Instagram account with a few of the hashtags I always used: #homesweethome #books #bookstagram #booknerd.

Lying down on the cool grass, I thought back on the dream again and those incredible eyes of ice. It had split my heart in two, making it tremble with an emotion I'd never felt before.

Jeneane's shout shook me out of my thoughts. "You stupid moron! That's freezing!" Brandon must have splashed water on her.

"Gemma, c'mon!" Faith said, waving me over.

I laughed to myself and slid my things into my backpack. Peter and Jake were up ahead, probably talking over their attack strategies for the lacrosse game.

Just as I ran into the street to catch up with them, a huge black motorcycle appeared out of nowhere and came to a halt inches from me.

Breathless with fright, I looked at its rider. His eyes were directed straight at me. I saw them through the dark visor of his helmet. He continued to gun the engine, waiting, but the girl sitting behind him squeezed him tighter and he zoomed off, leaving me standing in the middle of the street.

I'd never seen that motorcycle before. Was is the same I'd seen last night? Could it be . . . I shook my head to drive off the thought of Wild Thing and ran after my friends so I wouldn't be late for class.

Peter and I were crossing the schoolyard when his face suddenly darkened. "He's still here." He clenched his fists at his sides.

My head shot up and my eyes darted everywhere, searching for Wild Thing like water in the desert. A second later I swallowed, my throat parched with disappointment. "W-who do you mean?" I asked.

Peter glared at me. "Don't pretend you don't know, Gemma!" The bitterness in his voice left me astonished. Peter was always so sunny, I'd never seen him this furious. "You know who I mean," he said through gritted teeth. "I saw how you were looking at him—and, more importantly, how he was looking at you." He lowered his voice, almost hissing. "I don't like him. There's something strange about him, something *sinister.*"

I already knew why he was saying it: he was jealous. "You're overreacting, Peter! He's just some guy. I don't even know his name! No reason for you to be jealous." I blinked rapidly, embarrassed by what I'd just let slip out of my mouth.

"I'm not jealous. I just don't like the way he looks at you. Last night after the show, before you left, I followed him to see where he was going."

"But why would—" I started to say, but Peter cut me off.

"He hid behind a tree, thinking no one saw him, but I did! And I don't like what I found out, not one bit. He kept staring in the same direction and when I looked, it was you, Gemma! He was totally spying on you!"

"That's enough, you've crossed the line, Pet," I warned him, losing my patience.

"Why won't you believe me?! Anyway, I don't want him getting near you. Haven't you heard what people are saying?"

"Since when do you care about gossip?" I snapped accusingly.

"Rumor has it he's a strange guy. He never talks to anyone, and I don't trust him. For all we know he could even be a murderer! And again, why was he spying on you like that? Besides, I haven't told you the strangest part yet: I looked away from him for a second and he vanished.

Vanished, you hear me?! It was like he vaporized or something. It was so weird, for a second I thought I'd imagined it. One minute he's there and the next he's gone, like a ghost. Look, I got goosebumps just thinking about it!"

"You read too many comic books," I said, trying to laugh it off. Inside I was turning pale, thinking of the first time I'd met him in the woods and the harrowing pictures of the man with the broken neck that Jake had taken a picture of in his dad's office. Worse than the ones published in the paper. "You're being paranoid!"

Peter was right. There was something dark and mysterious about that boy, I could sense it. It was my heart that was refusing to consider it seriously. Even the way he'd silently slipped into Lake Placid made me question him. No one knew anything about him—in our small town, of all places, where it was impossible to keep anything a secret.

And then there was that bizarre sensation that paralyzed me every time our eyes met. I didn't even know his name, so why was I so overwhelmed with emotion? It was like some obscure, disturbing, inescapable force had bound me to him. I realized I didn't care whether or not I knew his name or where he came from. The longing to be near him was too strong. And even if a part of me thought it was crazy, the intensity of those eyes whenever they met mine was enough to ignite a flame of hope in my heart.

DISAPPOINTMENT

I walked into the school, my pulse accelerated at the thought of seeing him again after my dream. We'd been together last night, he just didn't know it. The same emotion that pounded in my ears with every step kept my eyes glued to the floor, depriving me of the courage to face him.

I turned down the hallway, my head lowered, as the sound of students passing me mixed with the thumping of my heart. Everything around me suddenly seemed to slow down. I looked up to avoid losing my balance and instantly saw his face.

Some dark spell was summoning me to him. He was at the end of the corridor, looking cocky, leaning against the wall with one hand, his black sleeves pushed up to his flexed forearms, facing me.

Though the throng of students heading into the classrooms formed a wall separating us, the connection that bound me to him grew stronger and stronger as I made my way toward him, trembling with every step. My heart seemed to know him, my body seemed to be waiting for me to reach him and take his hand, letting him hold me tight, like in my dream. But this was the real world and I didn't even know his name. When a group of students moved aside, giving me a clear view of him, something pierced my heart, stopping it.

He wasn't alone.

There was a girl with him. No, not a girl, a goddess. The mere sight of them smiling and looking at each other was enough to paralyze me. I felt as though someone had ripped my heart out of its warm home only to toss it into an icy puddle. She was looking at him with a self-confident air, her shoulder pressed against the doorframe, while he leaned toward her. Their bodies were almost touching.

The image erased everything else. Students, teachers, the talking, the muffled laughter. The hallway was empty and silent like my heart, deprived of its beating, my lungs deprived of air. I saw every last hope drift away like a ghost, disappearing before my eyes.

The low murmur in the hallway returned and only then did I notice the whispering of all the boys, floored by the goddess's extraordinary beauty. She paid no attention; she must have been used to it. Or more likely, *he* was the only thing she wanted to focus on.

Even I could barely believe that so much grace and beauty could be concentrated in just one girl. Naturally Wild Thing would surround himself with girls like her. I reluctantly forced myself to admit it was crazy to have thought anything different. Her long blond hair caressed her back, curling at the ends. It looked so soft. Though it wasn't very warm inside, she wore a silky, sleeveless, white top, opened in the front. A pair of close-fitting jeans clung to her breathtakingly long legs. On her feet she wore open shoes that matched her shirt.

My heart started pounding in my chest again as the distance between us gradually shortened. The scent of delicate floral perfume wafted over me as I was about to pass them. Hers, no doubt. My legs struggled to keep moving. I stared at my feet, trying to pass unnoticed. While discomfort battled with disappointment inside me, from the corner of my eye I noticed her turn to look at me. I couldn't keep myself from pausing to look back at her—as if an ancient instinct were forcing me to establish that connection.

Intimidated, I turned to face the girl and unexpectedly looked deep into her fierce, sensual eyes, which stared back at me intensely. It made me feel naked, like she was reading what was inside me. Her piercing jade-green irises looked like they were being lit up from the inside. Sunlight shone through them, giving them a hint of aquamarine. An incredible color.

My breath caught in my chest as an uncontrollable instinct induced me to shift my gaze to Wild Thing. My heart skipped a beat when I found his eyes waiting for mine. I *had* to look at him, even if only for a second, no matter how wrong it might be. But now that girl was beside him, watching me, so I looked back down at the floor as the chatter in the hallway returned to its normal volume. Approximately three seconds had gone by.

I caught sight of Peter's triumphant expression. I knew he'd come to the same conclusion I had, and I was surprised to find myself horrified by the smug satisfaction I saw on his face.

For the first time, Peter had disappointed me.

I dragged myself to class, numb with disappointment. The boys' excitement about the new girl was almost tangible. They were all in a buzz about her, like bees around their queen. Even the girls, gathered together in a huddle, were talking about the news, although it was the boy that absorbed most of their attention.

Not being the least bit interested in joining their little group, I opened my notebook and started doodling as I waited for class to begin. I just wanted the day to be over.

"Hey, Gemma, seen the new girl yet?" Faith's voice distracted me, forcing me to look up at her. "Looks like they're a couple. Her and the new boy, I mean."

"You still haven't found out his name," I deduced. I had to admit I was curious despite myself.

"Can you believe it?"

"Exciting, don't you think?" Jeneane said, appearing behind her, drawn by our whispering. "He looks so *dark* . . . and nobody knows anything about him. And on top of that, today he shows up with the goddess of the nymphs! This is crazy. I never thought I'd say it, but the guy's a total mystery, even to me."

Mr. Butler walked in and everyone sat down at their desks, dropping their conversations. I looked down at my page of doodles, knowing that not even the most interesting class would inspire me to pay attention.

A sudden murmur made me look up. Every muscle in my body froze, leaving me breathless. Just like me, the whole class sat there spellbound by the mysterious allure emanating from the two new students standing beside the teacher. My heart was beating out of control.

"We have two new students," the teacher said. "As you know, the school year is almost over, so it would be considerate on your part if you helped them orient themselves." Mr. Butler paused. Even he seemed bewildered by their presence. "Very well, kids, introduce yourselves to the class."

"Thank you, Mr. Butler. My name is Evan James." His voice, velvety and sensual, mesmerized the entire class. His eyes darted to mine as a sudden shiver ran down my arms.

Evan James. Enchanted, I found myself whispering his name in my mind. His voice had an overwhelming impact on every girl in class, almost as if he had the power to control our minds. I tried to resist the fascinating effect of his half-closed eyes with their dangerous mix of aloofness and sweetness, but I couldn't keep my body from trembling.

There was something familiar about the timbre of his voice. *Trust me, just this once . . .* No. It couldn't be. It was ridiculous. That voice was *the same one I'd dreamed. Impossible!* I shook my head. I couldn't have heard his voice. And yet—

"And this is Ginevra—" he managed to add before the teacher cut him off.

"Very well, find a seat. I have a rather important topic to explain."

Ginevra. Her name whirled in my head. It had such a majestic ring to it. Suddenly my brain stopped. I lowered my head, panicking, pretending to study the mustard-colored paint of my desk. They were heading toward the two empty desks immediately to my right.

My heart in my throat, I waited to see if he would sit down in the one farther away, leaving her with the desk next to mine, but he sat down to the girl's left, leaving only the narrow aisle between us. A tingling sensation ran up my arms. My body was betraying me.

Mr. Butler's voice was reduced to a low murmur in my ears, completely buried under my thoughts and the frantic beating of my heart. He was too close for me to concentrate on anything else. I could even perceive his scent. Wild Thing almost smelled like the woods. *Evan,* I corrected myself.

From time to time, I would imperceptibly tilt my head in his direction, hoping he wouldn't notice. And every time I did, he would gaze straight at me, as if expecting my look. From that distance, I clearly saw the color of his eyes. They were *dark*. A warm, reassuring color, nothing at all like those icy colors my mind had changed them into during my dream. They perfectly matched the color of his hair, which was pure dark chocolate. And yet, I thought I could still make out those golden flecks in his irises, like fine strands of caramel. But then again, mine had only been a dream, inspired by my memory of what he looked like, which I'd probably confused because of the sunlight in the woods.

It bothered me to think how rude the teacher had been to cut his introduction short. If it had been up to me, I'd have let him talk nonstop for hours. I was sure I would never have tired of the sensual sound of his voice. A little embarrassed from feeling his deep, deep eyes on me, I reached up and, trying to act naturally, swept all my hair to one side, to feel less exposed.

I glanced at the other end of the classroom, where the kids continued to turn and squirm in their seats, trying to get a better look at the newcomers. Jeneane's conceited voice rose up over all the others, saying snidely, "You can all take a number. I saw him first."

My jaw dropped. Had she seriously not seen the queen of the goddesses sitting right there next to him? It was hard to believe anyone could have not noticed her. I smiled instinctively, because that accomplishment, though small, was actually mine: I'd been the first to see him. Still, it didn't matter which of us had looked into his eyes first. He had *Ginevra*. That was all that mattered.

"C'mon, he hasn't even noticed you exist! Just once, would you give the rest of us a chance?" one of the girls grumbled.

"You'd like that, wouldn't you? Well, I don't feel like being so generous! He'll notice me, wait and see."

If Jeneane wanted someone she went out and got him, no apologies. And now she wanted *him*. For the first time since I'd known her, I wished I had even one ounce of her self-confidence. This time, though, I doubted her strategies would get her anywhere. No boy could resist the disarming blue of Jeneane's eyes, but not even she could compete with Ginevra. No one could.

In reality, I knew it was just a game to Jeneane. Lots of times I'd heard her talking about her escapades. I could never figure out how she could always be so cold, how she never ended up in a real relationship with anyone. In her twisted mind, she probably saw it as a challenge, a sick sort of diversion no boy could resist. Sooner or later they all fell into her trap. Like a skilled, graceful spider, Jeneane wove a web no one could escape from. But once she'd caught them, she would cast them aside as though she were afraid to establish a deeper bond with them.

Not him, I growled in my mind, as though he somehow belonged to me. *Not him*, I thought, with a tremble of fear deep in my heart, hoping that just this once someone wouldn't succumb to her charms.

The hours flew by despite my desperate longing for time to stand still at school, since *he* was there. "You're wasting your time, guys." I set down my tray full of food, feigning disinterest while actually using the lunch hour as an excuse to pry into the other girls' conversation. My comment made them all turn their heads toward me.

"Why? Did you dig up some news?" Faith asked, looking as disappointed as she was curious.

"Isn't *Ginevra* news enough for you?" I reminded her.

"You give up so easily," Jeneane was quick to say.

"What do you mean?" I was anxious to hear her answer, hoping it might rekindle my hopes even the slightest bit.

"For all we know she could totally be his sister!" she said matter-of-factly.

My heart lit up again. Because of my insecurity, I hadn't considered the possibility that Evan and Ginevra weren't a couple. Thinking about it, I realized he'd introduced her as Ginevra, and the teacher had interrupted him before he could say her last name. Maybe Jeneane's idea wasn't so crazy after all. They both had the same hypnotic charm. That tiny hope, nourished by my heart, began to unfurl through my doubts as I looked over at the two of them, eager to spot some kind of resemblance in their features.

Evan was staring down at the table, which meant I could steal glances at him without his noticing. From the tilt of his head, it looked like he didn't want to be listening to Ginevra. Maybe she was accusing him of something. She talked and talked, but he didn't open his mouth once.

Like déjà-vu, Evan unexpectedly looked up at me, closing the distance between us, and my heart leapt to my throat. I saw a hint of curiosity against a backdrop of disconsolate bitterness that hardened the features of his face. I was certain it was the same bitterness I'd sensed the night before, as though it hadn't been just a dream, but an actual memory. Our eyes remained locked for a long moment as I tried to understand why he was so troubled. Had Ginevra noticed him constantly staring at me?

The bell rang shrilly, once again severing that invisible cord connecting us.

The repressed ardor in his gaze had struck me with such devastating emotion that I couldn't focus on my classes. My brain had shut down as it tried to grasp what lay behind his agony.

Peter was practically begging for my company when the bell rang, finally freeing me from what had become a prison. The crowd of students leaving the school headed off in two different directions: a small, elite group, to which I didn't belong, walked down the hill to get their cars from the parking lot behind the school; those who didn't have that privilege, like Peter and me, trudged over to wait for the school bus.

I watched Evan and Ginevra as they left the school, curious to see which way they would go. Evan headed straight toward the parking lot and I let out a self-deprecating sigh for having foolishly hoped to have his company on the way home. I expected to see them pass by in their car, but a high-pitched roar in the distance filled the street, making the hairs on my arms stand up. I'd heard the noise before, that morning. It was the same sound made by the engine of the motorcycle that had almost hit me. We all gaped when we saw Wild Thing riding the aggressive-looking black motorcycle. It had to be really expensive, judging from the reaction of all the boys around me. The sound was high-pitched but subtle, making me think of an angry feline's growl.

"Hey, Kyle," a boy behind me whispered, "you see that bike?! So awesome! I think it's an MV Agusta. Frame's totally carbon fiber. I've never seen such a *monster* before!"

"You definitely haven't. That's an F4 CC. Not even I've seen one so close up before. Check out those racing exhausts! Nothing but sweet music coming out of those four titanium organ pipes. I hear it can go up to 195 miles an hour. Shh, quiet! Listen to that. I've heard it on YouTube before, but hearing it live, it's sick! Look, I've got goosebumps," Kyle said, his voice breaking, almost beside himself.

"A CC?" the first boy asked his friend, who seemed to be an expert on the topic. I perked up my ears to overhear all the information I could.

"Don't you know anything? A Claudio Castiglioni! Two hundred horsepower of pure adrenaline! See the double C's on its fairing? There are only a hundred of those bikes in the whole world. That's all they made."

"Only a hundred?" his friend said. "Man, when I saw him with the hottie I thought there was no way I could be more jealous, but now? That guy's one lucky dude to have gotten his hands on one of those babies." His voice was tinged with envy.

"Lucky?! You mean loaded! Those few 'lucky dudes,' as you call them, shelled out a hundred thirty grand each. You can't find them anywhere any more. And if one of them ever happened to fall into your hands, man, I can't even imagine how much you'd have to cough up now," he said reverently.

Evan revved his bike as he impatiently waited for Ginevra to climb on behind him. They had their helmets tucked under their arms. I couldn't help but stare at them, feeling a pang in my gut. Still, despite the distance, I saw that his eyes were like headlights pointed straight at me.

He slid his foot onto the pedal, putting the bike in gear as Ginevra wrapped her arms around his chest and my heart started to tremble again. A sharp pain made my stomach burn. I wasn't very familiar with the feeling, but I managed to give it a name anyway.

Jealousy. Seeing them together made my whole chest burn. Unlike most other girls, I didn't envy Ginevra her beauty, grace, or elegance, but I would have given anything to be where she was just then.

They headed in our direction, both of them looking at me steadily. I couldn't figure out if it was just a coincidence or if they were actually staring back at me, but I couldn't bring myself to find out by looking away. That would mean giving up the ecstatic sensation of having Wild Thing's eyes on me. It was strange how such a strong, proud expression could seem both authoritative and puzzled at the same time. Pushing down my discomfort, I forced myself to hold Evan's gaze the whole time, even as the distance between us continued to lessen. My heart was pounding in my chest.

I watched him disappear around the corner, his scent lingering in the air behind him, the scent of a waterfall hidden in the depths of some mysterious forest.

DREAD

Captivated by the memory of his gaze, I distractedly watched the bus pull away without me. A moment later there were no more students in the schoolyard and everything was silent. A gloomy layer of fog covered the streets. I was perfectly accustomed to the grim, gray mist, but the feeling lurking at the bottom of my chest made it feel less familiar. I found myself unconsciously picking up my pace.

Suddenly the creepy feeling that someone was watching me from close by left me short of breath. I stopped and looked around, but there was no one on the streets. I stole glances over my shoulder, not brave enough to stop again and check, but as soon as I focused on the street again, the bone-chilling sensation came back to torment me.

I mentally calculated the distance between me and the comfort of home and put one foot in front of the other faster and faster, in unison with my heartbeat. Turning the corner nervously, I at last spotted our front gate in the distance, and sped up until I found myself running the last exasperating yards. I jammed my hand into my pocket and grabbed my keys in a desperate attempt to save time before I reached home.

Grabbing the bars of the gate, I tried to put the key into the lock, but my hands were shaking so hard I barely managed to keep it from slipping out of my fingers. Finally, it unlocked with a click. I anxiously threw the gate open wide and shut it behind me, whirling around, short of breath, to see who'd been following me.

I was astonished when I saw no one on the other side of the gate. Studying the street warily, I hurried to lock myself indoors, but not even within the walls of my own home did the feeling that a ghost was walking right through me over and over again completely disappear.

I walked down the hall, turning on all the lights, confused by the unusual silence that hung in the air. Only when I spotted a slip of paper on the table did I understand why. Casting a quick glance behind me, I leaned over the table to read what it said.

Squirrelicue,
Unexpectedly busy. I whipped up a little something in case you got hungry. It's in the fridge.

I'll make it up to you.

Love you,
Mom

I let out the air I'd been holding in my lungs and forced myself to stop trembling. They'd just ended up working longer than expected—nothing unusual. And yet, the feeling I was being watched continued to torture me. The house being empty did nothing but increase my panic. I rushed to my room, hoping to find some comfort in Iron Dog's company. But when I walked through the door, I went deathly pale.

Iron Dog was awake, on his feet, his image reflected in the mirror behind him. He turned and moved toward it cautiously, his ears low, in guard position, flicking his tail, not even noticing me there. Was it possible I wasn't crazy, that the ghost really existed and Irony could sense its presence? I felt a pit in my stomach as I watched him move his tongue in empty space, slowly, like he was licking the air. No, like someone was in front of him, someone invisible to me. I stood there in the doorway, petrified.

I tried calling him, hesitantly at first, finally getting his attention. As though I'd woken him from a dream, he trotted over to me.

I'd had a big lunch at school, but my stomach twisted with hunger. I went down to the kitchen, but despite Irony's reassuring company, not even entering that comfortable, familiar room gave me the solace I was hoping for. Disturbing things kept happening.

I'd once read that animals have an extra sense that can detect the presence of spirits. But if that were true, I wouldn't have perceived it as well. Or maybe humans also had some kind of sensory perception, just a less developed one? A sixth sense that made you shudder when a ghost was near. Given all the paranormal novels I devoured, I couldn't even be sure whether the source of the information was fictitious.

And yet, Irony's uneasiness made my stomach churn. I tried to calm him down, but he kept scampering all around the kitchen. I'd never seen him so on edge before.

Then I remembered. It had happened once before, just before he'd disappeared into the misty forest. I grabbed the phone, almost yanking it off the wall, and dialed automatically, hoping Peter would hurry over to keep me company. I was sure he'd find my fear laughable, but I didn't care. I needed him there. My knees were shaking at the thought of spending all afternoon alone.

Every ring reverberated in my spine, but there was no answer. Under my skin I still had the creepy feeling I was being watched.

In the silence of the nerve-racking wait, Iron Dog's low growl made me flinch. My heart in my throat, I turned toward the guttural sound. Trembling attacked my knees and then every other part of my body.

There was no one in front of him. Irony was growling at the empty wall. Scared out of my wits, I lunged for him, leaving the receiver dangling on its cord, and took the stairs three at a time. Inside my room, I locked the door and stood with my forehead pressed against it. I wasn't sure why I was so convinced I was safe in my room, but for some reason, my agitation began to lessen.

Sitting at the window, I started to reread my tattered copy of *Jane Eyre*, but the words eluded me as I watched the sun make its way across the sky, hiding behind occasional gray clouds, until my eyelids grew heavy and I gave in to the comfort of the darkness behind them.

Torn from sleep by a noise, I jolted awake. The old Charlotte Brontë novel lay on the linoleum floor, but I doubted its worn leather binding could have made a noise loud enough to wake me up. Looking out the window, I saw that the moon had already found its place in the sky, though it felt like I'd only dozed off for a few minutes.

There was a strange metallic clang. I walked cautiously to the door and opened it, straining my ears, trying not to make a sound. The hall was darker than night, but I forced myself to grope along it, following the dim shaft of light coming from the living room. At the stairs I paled. The noise was coming from the front door.

Someone was trying to break in. The phone rang, shattering the silence and sending my heart racing into my throat as I held my breath. The sound echoed through the darkness of the hall. Now a completely different concern turned my blood to ice: how could the phone be ringing if I hadn't hung it up? Could someone have come inside while I was asleep? And what about the lights? Who'd turned off the lights? I was sure I'd left them all on.

The lock groaned as if it were being forced. The knob began to rattle convulsively. Suddenly, there was another click and the knob froze, as did my heart. Breathless, I grabbed something off a shelf and drew closer. I couldn't see clearly what I was holding, but it felt heavy enough to hurt someone if I used it right. I watched the door open slowly. In the darkness I could make out a hand reaching inside and feeling around on the wall for the light switch.

"Gemma, what are you doing there with that doughnut?"

Light flooded the room, revealing my dad's reassuring face. I dropped my arms. "It's you!" I said, heaving a sigh of relief.

"Who did you think it was?" Mom asked, surprised.

"You almost gave me a heart attack!" I said bitterly. "What were you thinking, breaking into your own home?" My voice was still full of fear.

"You're a real scaredy-cat, you know?" my dad chuckled. "Did you mean to hit us with that?" A laugh escaped him as he pointed at the doughnut-shaped paperweight I was still holding.

"Sorry, Squirrelicue, your dad left the house keys at the diner and we had to force the lock. I tried calling but you didn't answer."

Just then, my stomach growled, reminding me that I'd skipped more than one meal today. Deciding to reheat my second lunch in the microwave, I followed them into the kitchen, pausing in the doorway to look at the phone receiver. It was in its place on the hook.

And yet I was perfectly sure I'd left it dangling. In any case, with my parents at home, everything seemed so unreal. Looking back, I realized I'd spent all afternoon terrified for no reason at all and that I'd conjured up creatures that existed only in my head. I really had to stop reading all those paranormal novels.

But later, when I was lying in bed, part of me was afraid to fall asleep. After the day's strange events, I was sure the night would bring nightmares that were even worse. I closed my eyes and, to my amazement, finally dozed off.

I turned to stare at the deserted street behind me. The fog seemed to want to hide it. I had the funny feeling I'd already lived through this experience before. My heart accelerated with every passing moment, hoping I would understand the warning it was sending me.

My footsteps pounded on the pavement like a hammer banging on an anvil and my senses were strangely alert, but my instinct to stay on guard took precedence over everything else. Someone was there with me. I couldn't see him, but I was sure he was there. I could sense him, like water running across my skin or a sound caressing my ears.

Someone was following me.

I picked up my pace, terrified, hurrying to reach our front gate as a battle raged in my body. My instinct was telling me to run while something else was forcing me to stay. I felt a pain in my heart but didn't give in until I found myself inside the gate, panting.

I whirled around. My heart stopped beating.

Evan.

His icy gray eyes were fixed on me with fiery intensity, narrowly assessing me. How was it possible for ice to melt as if it were fire?

Our surroundings suddenly changed and the metal bars between us faded away. My front walk disappeared, leaving behind it a place that was just as familiar to me: the woods. My mind continued to take me back there, as if it wanted to reveal something to me.

The fog drifted though the trees and floated past us like ghosts as our eyes locked. We were so close I felt the warmth of his body on my skin. My eyes were lost in his and his in mine, exploring unknown places, and I feared I wouldn't be able to contain the emotion that flooded through me. My heart was pounding so hard I could distinguish every upbeat and downbeat. It was like a concert of emotion—the most beautiful melody I'd ever heard.

An uncontrollable instinct—the deep, unstoppable desire to put my hand on him to see if he was real—made me reach out, but before I could touch him, Evan vanished into thin air as though he'd guessed my intentions and wanted to elude me, though I couldn't imagine why.

He silently reappeared behind me. An indecipherable shiver ran through me and I sighed, waiting for my breathing to slow. I whirled around, but he vanished again, reappearing among the trees, leaving a conspicuous distance between us. I stepped forward, trying to lessen that distance while keeping my eye on him so he wouldn't vanish again.

His gaze was fixed on me, intense and fiery. His clenched fists and jaw reminded me of the first time I'd seen him. Was he studying me? A chill seeped through my skin, going so deep it brushed my bones, and Evan's shadowy, handsome face was right in front of me, so close to mine.

I hesitated a second, holding my breath. The intensity of his gaze almost hurt. He smiled, his lips bewitching me, his wild eyes fixed on me as I melted, surrendering to him. As if he'd finally won the battle that had been forcing him to keep his distance, Evan raised his hand to my face, pausing only for an instant. I half closed my eyes, longing for contact with his skin.

Savoring every second, I shuddered at the warmth of his ardent hand as it set the skin of my neck on fire and slid down my arm. I watched it descend until it slowly reached my hand. His fingers moved lightly, searching for mine. He stroked my palm with his thumb, gently. I did the same and Evan passionately grabbed my hand.

With that warm, reassuring touch, every fear vanished, replaced by a deep feeling of peace that filled every particle of my being. Part of me was still mystified by his presence, his coming to Lake Placid, everything about him, but time and time again, all he had to do was reach out to me, even if only with his gaze, for every concern to be banished like fog dispersed by the sun.

"What is this power of yours?" His voice rose into the silence like a melody. "I try to fight it, but every time I can't help but surrender."

"Why do you want to resist?" My instinct tried to stop the words, but my heart wouldn't let them be silenced. Why was he struggling to fight that inexplicable connection that bound us? It was clear he felt it too.

"I didn't say I *wanted* to," he said firmly. His eyes on mine made my heart tremble.

"What power? Surrender to what?"

"Surrender to you," he blurted. He went back to studying my hand in his, as if I were a creature from another planet. "I shouldn't be here. I shouldn't interfere. It's just that . . . I don't know what's happening to me. I can't help it, I . . ."

He paused. "I can't do without something inside you, something it triggers *inside of me*." He pronounced the words clearly, one by one, seemingly realizing the truth of what he was saying as he said it.

But what could be so different about me? Why did he seem so fascinated by me? Every time our hands touched, his gray eyes flickered with surprise. Surprise mixed with something else. Something that mystified him.

Evan's face was a mask of uncertainty and confusion, but I sensed the euphoria he was trying to hide. It was as if he wasn't allowed to feel what he was feeling. He was mad at himself because he couldn't help it. I would have driven those feelings away if only I could. Instead, knowing there was nothing I could do, I watched him silently struggle with his ordeal.

"You don't understand." His face darkened for a moment and then cleared. "How could you—" He half smiled, his gaze growing misty. "It's always come so easily and instinctively to me. Why should it be any different with you?" He turned back to study me again, as if he could find the answer to his question there. He stared at our hands, still joined, and his eyes shot up to mine. "I can't control myself when you're around. Nothing works like it should. Why?" He was troubled. "Why don't I know who I am any more?"

Did he really hope to find the answer in my eyes? I could tell he didn't actually want me to understand what he was saying, but I didn't care. All I needed was to be there with him. I laced my fingers with his and squeezed them. "You don't need to control yourself around me," I reassured him. "Let yourself go."

"I can't. I'm . . . afraid I'll lose myself," he said, his voice suddenly resolute, his face growing sterner. "I need to abort the mission. I can't do it. I . . . I'm not the right one. Not this time," he sighed, letting go of my hand and clenching his fists. I looked him in the eyes and the bitterness I saw there told me he'd just made a decision. "I'll have someone else do it in my place," he whispered, turning his back on me to leave.

It sounded like gibberish, but I realized it was something important. "Abort the mission? Why are you talking like a soldier?"

Evan stopped in his tracks, his back still to me. I stared at his tattoo as the muscles in his arm flexed. "Orders come first."

What did he mean? My questions—and even the doubts arising in my mind—seemed to be pushing him away from me. I decided it wasn't important. Whatever it meant, no matter what it cost, I didn't want to lose him.

"It doesn't matter if you can't explain what's going on. I won't ask you any more questions." He stood up straighter, as though what I'd said had struck him. "I promise."

I needed to do something because I had the feeling I was about to lose him forever, and it made my heart ache. I walked up behind him and took his hand, just as he'd done to me. He hung his head, studying our fingers as they interlaced, then turned to look into my eyes. For a second the burden seemed to lift from his shoulders, as though the touch of my hand had regenerated him. But in his struggle against whatever was tormenting him, the relief was short-lived.

"I can't." His words drifted in the wind as he disappeared. Powerless and terrified, I watched him dissolve with the fog.

"Wait!" My shout echoed through my bedroom. I rolled over and sat up in bed, shaking my head when I realized it had only been a dream.

It was all so crazy . . . The dream had felt so *real*, I couldn't believe it hadn't been. All the mystery surrounding Evan had doubtless fed my imagination. I couldn't think of any other reason for my strange dreams, which by now were recurring, with Evan in the leading role.

I crawled out of bed, still dazed, and got ready for school. If nothing else, I knew what to expect from the day ahead.

ALCHEMY

The strange occurrences didn't disappear with the night. School was relatively deserted and silent when I showed up. The first bell hadn't rung yet and students were just starting to unenthusiastically fill the halls.

I used the time to organize my locker. The blue paint on its door was as shiny as ever, but a tornado seemed to have passed through the inside.

How can I resist you?

Evan. My heart skipped a beat and I closed my eyes. The lingering traces of his voice, as light as words whispered softly in my ear, drifted away, to my regret. I savored the last sweet echo, surrendering to the sound before it vanished entirely.

I turned around slowly, expecting to see Evan right there behind me, and gave a start when I saw him standing at the far end of the hall. But I was so sure I'd heard his voice . . .

"Hey, Gemma!" Brandon hurried over to me. "You seen Pete around? The game's tomorrow and we need to work on our attack strategy."

"Sorry, I haven't seen him yet today," I mumbled, still dazed.

"Hey, you feeling all right?" Brandon stared at me, worried. "Well, if you see him, tell him not to be late to practice. Speaking of which, why don't you come watch us?"

A shiver ran down my spine as my eyes lost themselves in the sight of Evan's face. Something was worrying him.

"Gemma, did you hear me?" Brandon asked.

"Huh? Yeah, sure, I'll tell him you're looking for him," I said.

I couldn't explain what was happening. I was starting to worry something might actually be wrong with me. I'd heard Evan's voice inside my head.

I was obsessed with him.

Embarrassed, I turned back and tried to watch him without his noticing. He was leaning against his locker, looking worried. As Ginevra continued to chatter to him, his expression grew more and more serious, almost shocked. What I would have given to know what she was saying to him! I forced myself to look away and walked into the classroom, disoriented by the paranormal experience.

In class I felt Evan's eyes on me even more than yesterday. Part of me kept telling myself it was wrong to feel the way I did. I wasn't even sure if he and Ginevra *were* related, after all. What if Jeneane was wrong? Evan's boldness did nothing but embarrass me, especially with her sitting right there next to him. But then again, Ginevra hadn't even bothered to notice that he kept looking at me. Confused by my conflicting feelings, I ignored the lesson. If I kept this up, my GPA would suffer, but for the first time in my life I didn't care.

What is it about you?

The sound of Evan's voice snapped me out of my trance and my eyes shot to him, my skin tingling. It had happened again: I'd heard his voice in my mind, like the sweetest of melodies.

I looked away, worried about what was happening to me. Evan was leaning over his notebook, drawing incomprehensible symbols like the ones in his tattoo. And yet I could swear I'd heard a trace of frustration in his voice, an equal mix of curiosity and irritation. I looked over at him again. He was fully focused on the crumpled paper which he continued to cover with ink.

His rolled-up sleeves revealed the veins in his firm arms every time he moved his pen. From time to time I caught a glimpse of the tattoo on his left forearm. It consisted of small, black, stylized symbols. Maybe it was a message written in some ancient language. I wished I could decipher the strange writing. The ink seemed to encircle his arm like poisonous roots branching out, trying to penetrate his flesh. A shiver ran through me as I stared at their ends: they almost looked like claws trapping him in their grip. At one point, he caught me with my eyes glued to his tattoo and his expression darkened. He looked down at it and then back up at me, a flicker of surprise in his eyes.

Now he wore an intense expression, as though he were concentrating on something more than just the page. A mix of desire and hesitation. I read the apprehension in those deep brown eyes that were as dark as chocolate. What was tormenting him?

It was impossible that I'd actually heard his voice. It was probably just another of my fantasies rooted in my uncontrollable desire for him.

The most frustrating thing was that I couldn't tell anyone about it.

Peter never cut class, but today I hadn't seen him at school.

After my last class of the day, photography, I felt too shaken to go home so I figured I'd take Brandon up on his invitation and watch the lacrosse team. They practiced every day from three to four, and I was sure Peter wouldn't miss it for anything in the world. At Lake Placid High they took sports very seriously.

The whole team wasn't there yet, but a few players were doing knee bends and jogging around the track, the yellow logo standing out on their Blue Bombers jerseys. I sat down on the lowest bench of the bleachers. It was still a good half hour until practice, so I decided to spend the time eating something and reading a bit of *Jane Eyre*.

I sat down cross-legged, opened my book, hung my head over it, and distractedly nibbled on a sandwich. It wasn't nearly enough, given how empty my stomach still felt once I'd finished it. I'd always been like that when I was stressed—I could never eat enough to feel full. Luckily, knowing I'd still be hungry, I'd stocked up in the cafeteria. My parents wouldn't be going home for a late lunch today so I'd gotten two helpings of everything.

I bit into a snack-size pizza without looking up from the page I was on, pulled out two chocolate bars from my backpack, and set them down close to me.

You're eating all that by yourself? Evan's voice came back to haunt me. I froze in confusion, then shook my head, deciding to ignore it. I distractedly cracked open a can of soda and took a sip, but it almost fell out of my hands when I heard his voice echo in my mind again. *I mean it, I think it's a bit much for just one person.*

I sighed, exasperated. I had to be on the verge of a nervous breakdown. I focused on my book but couldn't stop thinking about Evan.

Aren't you leaving some for your friends, at least? he said, laughing. Keeping my head bowed over my book, I continued to ignore the voice. By now it was clear something was wrong with my head. Years of lack of interest in boys were mutating into an insane longing for Evan that was overwhelming me to the point of obsession.

I'm bothering you. Sorry. There was a hint of sadness in his voice. *I didn't mean to be rude. We haven't even been introduced. I'm Evan James.*

My heart skipped a beat, sending a desperate signal to my brain. He was there. And he was talking to *me*. I tilted my head and raised my eyes.

Evan smiled. He was sitting just behind me, amused by the shock and embarrassment my face must have revealed. He stared at me in silence, waiting for me to say something.

I smiled meekly and for a second all I could think of was how relaxed his face was. I'd never seen it without a dark veil of confusion. "I'm really hungry," I stammered, still dazed.

"So do you always refuse to talk to strangers, or does that rule apply only to me?" he asked, teasing.

I blinked. I'd been so absorbed in Jane's mad reasoning as she rejected her beloved Rochester in my book that I hadn't noticed the bleachers weren't completely empty any more. The players on the field, on the other hand, had noticed the two of us talking and were looking our way, grinning. I must have been the only girl Evan had said a word to since he'd shown up in Lake Placid. Except for Ginevra, of course.

"I was just wondering where you put all that food. There's no way you should be in such good shape if you eat like that," he added, smiling.

"I only do it when I'm nervous," I said, my cheeks flushing from the hidden compliment.

"And are you nervous *now*?" he asked sweetly, leaning his face in toward mine. His voice was sensual, persuasive. My heart skipped a beat, crushed by the weight of those dark eyes so close to mine.

Of course I was, but I certainly couldn't tell him why. He'd think I was crazy if I admitted to being obsessed with him. I myself could barely believe what was happening to me. Dreaming about a total stranger every night and then hearing his voice in my head? It was insane. I forced myself to look away, afraid my body would betray me.

"I'm just . . . stressed out," was all I said, turning one of the chocolate bars over in my fingers. "I guess studying too hard really isn't good for you." I broke off a square and put it in my mouth. "Anyway, my name's Gemma Bloom," I mumbled, as the chocolate slowly melted on my tongue.

"I know your name," he replied in a self-assured tone, a seductive smile on his lips. I looked at him in surprise. *That* was certainly nice to hear. Or was he just teasing me?

Evan smiled, looking directly into my eyes, as if on the verge of revealing a mystical truth for my ears only. "It's written on your necklace." He reached out his hand to examine my pendant and an electric tingle ran up my spine the instant his fingers touched my skin.

Evan pulled his hand back, hiding his uneasiness behind a look of embarrassment. *No*, it wasn't simple embarrassment. Worry was more like it. It seemed I wasn't the only one who'd felt that energy flow through our bodies, and it had left him baffled.

"Sorry," he whispered shyly. His expression grew more confused.

I reached up and grasped the butterfly-shaped pendant that hung from its chain, bracing myself for the pang of nostalgia I always felt when I thought about it.

"It must be important to you." His hypnotic gaze searched mine, his curiosity probably roused by the sudden look of sadness on my face. His comment left me so astonished I couldn't speak. No one had ever asked me about it before. Not even Peter—but on the other hand Pet knew the whole story behind the heirloom.

"In a way. I've had it since I was a little girl. I never go anywhere without it."

Evan didn't respond. Sliding onto the bench beside me, he looked down at the pendant and back up at my face, encouraging me to go on. My heart did a somersault, having him so close for the first time.

I doubted he was actually interested in my past, but even though we were strangers, I felt a deep sense of intimacy with him. "It belonged to my grandmother," I stated simply.

"You were really close," he said intuitively.

For some strange reason, the words started to pour out of me like a swollen river before my brain could even approve them. For an even stranger reason, I didn't *want* to stop the flow of emotions. It was as if I'd known Evan forever. Not like Peter, but like a part of myself.

I told him how Grandma had been like a second mother to me. An example, a role model. I barely noticed how much time went by as I sat there in the stands talking to him. Part of me still believed it was just another dream. It was so easy to talk to Evan, so *natural*. He listened, fascinated, eager to know everything about me.

"When I was little, I couldn't understand why my parents kept leaving me with her. Inside, I resented them for neglecting me because of their work. But Grandma was happy to help raise me and for years she was my mentor. We were really close," I admitted, filled with sweet nostalgia. "The name engraved on my pendant is hers, actually. I was named after her. In Latin, Gemma means—"

"'A flower ready to blossom,'" Evan said, staring at me intensely as he finished my sentence. For a moment I was lost in his eyes. "But it also means 'precious gem.'"

I gulped, spellbound by his voice. I'd never known anyone so mysterious and fascinating. "This is so weird, *I'm* usually the know-it-all of the group," I joked, making him laugh. "Anyway, this pendant belonged to my grandmother. She died suddenly, unexpectedly." I struggled to hold back the sadness that the thought of her always caused me.

"She never really left you," he said, surprising me with his strange, solemn comment.

"Yeah, right, and now you're going to say she'll be here with me as long as I keep her in my heart." I was trying to be sarcastic but my listless tone betrayed me.

"Actually, I was about to say as long as you wear her necklace, but your version sounds a lot better." He looked into my eyes with exasperating sweetness and I couldn't help smiling back at him. His fingers moved slightly across the bench and touched mine. I found myself copying his gesture, resting my own against his. This light, light touch triggered a storm of emotions inside me: suddenly my chest felt heavier, my breathing slowed, and my lips parted as I watched our fingers barely brush against each other on the wooden surface, my mind in a fever. I raised my eyes and looked into his, swallowing hard because my throat was suddenly parched.

"I . . . I'm not so sure any more."

Evan cast me a reassuring glance and my eyes began to water. "You're tearing up," he said. A furrow of regret formed on his forehead. "I'm sorry, it's my fault. I shouldn't have opened old wounds. It's just . . ." He paused, meeting my gaze. "This is going to sound crazy, but I feel like I've always known you. I feel so *close* to you," he admitted, his eyes searching mine. "If I didn't know it was impossible, I would swear I've met you before."

I blinked several times, floored by his revelation. How was it we both felt the same thing? As though a powerful connection united us. As though our souls had known each other in past lives. A mystical, supernatural bond. "Hey! Are you reading my mind?" I asked, keeping my tone light.

"Now *that* would be interesting," he said, making me blush.

"What is it you want to know, exactly?" I asked, confused and embarrassed.

His expression grew deeper and more intense. He seemed quite serious. "I'd like to find the answers. Have more time. Understand what happens to me when I'm with you." The confession left me speechless. *When I'm with you?* It was the first time we'd ever been alone, so why did I also have the feeling it wasn't?

Ginevra's face popped into my mind. For a moment I'd almost forgotten she might be his girlfriend. Jeneane seemed pretty convinced she wasn't, but the possibility was still out there. At the thought of her, I quickly withdrew my hand from his touch, instantly missing it.

"I don't see Ginevra anywhere," I said, hoping he'd take the hint.

Evan answered without taking his eyes off mine. "She's . . . somewhere, I don't know where. I wanted some time to myself."

I'd never been so confused in my life. "Why are you here?" I whispered loudly, almost insolently. Evan didn't say a thing. His expression spoke for him: not even he knew the answer to that. He smiled at me, taking my breath away, and stood up without a word.

How rude, I thought. He wasn't even going to bother to say goodbye? After I'd opened up to him? I was puzzled by his ambiguous behavior.

Then his hand clasped mine. The warmth ran up my arm and spread all the way to my heart as his grip, at first impetuous and full of yearning, gave way to an endless tenderness. It was as if he knew what I'd dreamed last night and was giving in to the urge to relive it. He brushed his thumb against my palm, making my stomach flutter, and put his face next to mine, his voice caressing my ear: "You're forgetting your promise."

I closed my eyes as I felt his lips moving slowly, whispering against my skin. Swallowing as warm shivers ran down my body, I opened my eyes in a dazed, feverish state only to realize Evan had disappeared, leaving me to decipher his enigmatic message.

Lost in my fantasies, I heard someone call my name. One of the players was running toward me, taking out his mouthguard. I looked out at the field for the first time. Practice must already be over.

"Hey, Gemma!" Jake was holding his lacrosse stick and wore the required protective gear, along with a helmet, which was what had kept me from recognizing him.

"Hey, Jake! Faith's not here, if it's her you're looking for. She had a riding lesson. I heard Raul say he was taking her."

I bit my lip as Jake clenched his jaw. Raul was a dark-skinned boy with blue eyes who'd had a crush on Faith ever since grade school. His family lived on a ranch where his dad gave riding lessons and organized excursions on horseback for tourists. The summer before they'd dated a little and although they'd broken up, he was nuts about her.

Jake muttered something and swore through his teeth. Faith and Raul's closeness infuriated him. You could see from a mile away that he was crazy about her. "Actually, I came to make sure you were all right." He nodded over my shoulder, in a clear attempt to indicate my encounter with Evan. He was always such a protective guy, even toward me.

"Oh, you saw us . . ." My agitation grew. He must have noticed the intimacy of Evan's gesture when he took my hand and whispered in my ear. What if he told Peter?

"What was James doing, sitting here? You looked so shocked when he got up and left like that. Did he insult you or something? I can take care of him if you want."

"No, Jake, everything's fine. After he got up I thought he'd left without saying goodbye, that's why I was upset. I didn't realize he was right behind me, and when he took my hand I—"

"Took your hand?" The look on Jake's face made me freeze. "No one was behind you. I saw it clear as day, he stood up and walked off without even looking back."

I paled as doubt struck me: Had I only imagined it?

A FLEETING HOPE

All that afternoon I tried to decipher the last thing Evan had said to me, but it was no use. I didn't remember ever promising him anything. In fact, that was the first time I'd ever spoken to him, apart from the conversations we'd had every night in my dreams. Not that those counted, of course. And then there was the strange thing Jake had said. A mystery, an unsolvable riddle I couldn't make heads or tails of no matter how hard I tried.

My desk chair squeaked against the linoleum floor of my room as I got up to go out for some fresh air. Outside our front door, I glanced over at Peter's house. I was sure he would have been happy to keep me company, but not so sure I could give him the attention he deserved. And so, setting aside the idea of seeking refuge in the forest, I ran down my alternatives and realized it would be best to go to my parents' diner for a while. Leaving my sweatshirt hood down, I let the light rain caress my hair. As I walked, I read the names, one by one, of the high peaks in the Adirondacks that were carved into forty-six gray stones dotting the red brick sidewalk that skirted the two-plus-mile-long shore of Mirror Lake.

Main Street ran alongside the lake, surrounded by neighborhoods full of shops and restaurants on both sides. In the center, right on the shore, Bandshell Park was used as the venue for lakeside weddings and concerts, while across from it, on a rise, stood the beautiful Adirondack Community Church.

The houses downtown were smaller than the ones in the residential areas but they were charming and colorful. Some were painted white, others brown, blue, or green. Just outside the village, the shore was lined with beautiful wooden houses, farms, and even log cabins. The main attraction was the antique Victorian movie theater.

My mom was surprised to see me walk in. During the winter I usually spent my afternoons reading novels or my textbooks, so my parents were used to seeing me at work only over summer vacation.

"Hey, Alex!" I said to a young woman with dark blond hair who was waiting tables.

"Gemma!" A warm, engaging smile lit up her face. Alexandra McFaddin worked at our diner three times a week so she could set aside some money to go to Nazareth College in Rochester. When we were little, she, Peter, and I used to play together a lot, even though she was a few years older than us. But then her family moved into a bigger house in another part of town. Although we rarely saw each other any more, time hadn't changed our friendship and my affection for her was still the same. "Sick of studying, huh?"

I took the dark red apron out of Alex's hands and she offered to tie it behind my back. "Something like that." I smoothed down the front of the apron and smiled at her. She went to wait tables while I served the clients sitting at the counter, although I doubted I'd be able to concentrate.

I hadn't heard voices in my head at all that afternoon, which was reassuring. It took my mind off the idea of turning to a shrink for help.

Until that moment.

Hmm . . . muffins, doughnuts, or peanut-butter fritters? But then again, the blueberry crumble looks awfully good.

My heart skipped a beat. "Stupid voice," I hissed, hanging my head low over the counter and carefully arranging the fritters more neatly on their trays.

"So you don't like my voice?"

I looked up and froze, mortally embarrassed when I realized who was right there in front of me. "N-no," I stammered, unsure how to cover for myself.

"Ah," Evan said, surprised.

"No! It's just . . . I didn't see you there," I said, a burst of heat rushing to my face. I wondered what color my cheeks had turned. "I thought it was—"

"You thought it was . . . ?" Evan said, a grin on his face.

I couldn't string my words together in any sensible order. I bit my tongue and glanced over his shoulder at Alex, who was gesticulating at me to cheer me on, a surprised smile on her face. "I thought you were someone else, that's all," I lied, using the first excuse that my stunned brain managed to come up with. "Sorry about that."

Confusion spread over his face, as if my words had somehow put him on guard. I had the nagging suspicion he knew exactly what was happening to me, but I pushed the thought out of my mind.

"Anyway, I, I like your bike." What a stupid thing had just come out of my mouth, bypassing my brain!

"So, you like my bike," he repeated, cocking his head as a flash of satisfaction appeared on his face and his half smile turned into a grin.

"Yeah, I mean, I like the sound . . . I mean, it's nice, the sound, it . . . you know," I stammered, so embarrassed I wanted to run and hide. "It sounds like a lion growling," I went on, wrapping it up all in one breath. My eyes had grown wide from the shame. My God! What was happening to me? Was I possessed? Could I rewind the scene and take every word back?!

Evan smiled, half amused, half flattered, but before I could sink into the pit of awkwardness I'd dug, he leaned his face toward mine, his voice deep and caressing. "You should hear her when she's angry," he joked, his shadowed gaze fixed on mine.

"What brings you to this part of town?" I asked in an attempt to guide the conversation to safer ground.

He raised his eyebrows and looked from one end of the room to the other. "Well, this a diner, isn't it?"

Right. Was it my imagination or was he teasing me again? But then again, making a fool of myself in his presence came so naturally to me. I frowned and Evan let out a gorgeous laugh. I was starting to think there was nothing about him that wasn't attractive, but, like a moth drawn to a flame, I was sure that following my instincts would inevitably mean my own death sentence. When he sensed my embarrassed silence, he cleared his throat. "Sorry, I didn't mean to be rude. Let me start over." He squared his shoulders and put one hand to his chest, making a slight bow. His gaze was so powerful, so penetrating, so wonderful, all at the same time. "Would you be so kind, milady, as to permit me to indulge in your blueberry crumble? I'm certain it will be delectable and . . . sweet." He weighed each word as my body wobbled, lost in his gaze. "And my lips are anxious to receive it from your hands, to relish its flavor." I struggled to keep my heart from stopping.

"Gemma!" my dad shouted from the back, breaking the magic spell that bound us while Alex, pretending to be busy wiping off the tables, let out a little laugh that she immediately hid behind a coughing fit.

"Coming!" I called over my shoulder after a moment of hesitation as I tried to summon up my self-control from wherever it was hiding inside of me. I cut Evan a wedge of crumble, slid it onto a napkin and held it out over the counter. Suddenly I teetered, realizing I might touch him again. Why on earth hadn't I grabbed a plate like I always did? Evan reached out and my heart trembled.

I kept holding on to the napkin as he took it in his hand, sweetly brushing his fingers against mine as his eyes locked on mine. The contact with his skin inebriated my senses and electric tingles spread out all over me.

"Gemma, are you coming or aren't you?!" my dad insisted testily.

I pulled back my hand, noticing in Evan's eyes that the emotion had shaken him too. It was as though what happened when we made physical contact was a mystery for him as well and he wanted to touch me again to try to re-experience it.

Against my will I looked away, and with butterflies in my stomach, went through the doorway behind the counter. As I did, out of the corner of my eye I saw Evan sit down at a table by the window.

"What's all the fuss, Dad?" I asked, annoyed that he'd interrupted us.

"You need to . . . There are trays to be washed," he replied, choosing his answer carefully. He grumbled something I couldn't make out, though I think I heard the words "lips" and "relish."

"Why don't you run them through the dishwasher?" I asked, confused and exasperated.

"Joshua! Leave her alone," my mom said, coming to my rescue. She shot me a sidelong glance and lowered her voice. "*Who* is that boy?" Pleased, she opened her eyes wide and nodded toward the dining room. It was starting to dawn on me why Dad had called me into the back.

"Nobody," I said, hoping she wouldn't notice my cheeks flushing. "He's just a guy from my class."

My mom studied me carefully. "Nobody? You didn't look so indifferent a minute ago."

"Huh? Were you guys spying on me?" I said in a low voice, still embarrassed at the thought that my dad had heard me flirting with Evan.

"I'm just curious," she said with a shrug, looking almost hurt. "Aren't I allowed to be? You've never seemed interested in anyone before. I was starting to think something was wrong with you."

"Oh, thanks, Mom!" I groaned, not even trying to conceal my sarcasm.

"Well, what?! This is the first boy you've liked in *seventeen years*! You're so beautiful, sweetie, but you never notice the way they look at you."

"But you do?" I tilted my head, surprised.

"Oh please, you're the only one who never notices! Last summer the diner was full of boys, and I don't think it was because of your dad's strawberry malts. Not to mention Peter. Are you still convinced you're just a friend in his eyes?"

I blushed, embarrassed by how confidently my mom always told me what I could never figure out on my own.

"All I'm saying is, it was about time you finally took your eyes off your books and looked around. So, tell me everything! I want all the details!" she said enthusiastically. She'd clearly been waiting a long time for this moment.

"Shh! Not so loud. I told you, there's nothing going on between us," I insisted. But then, saddened by her obvious disappointment, I forced myself to give her some glimmer of hope. I was sorry to make her think I didn't want to share things with her. "Not that I haven't thought about it."

Her face lit up again like a little girl who's just been given candy. "Well? Tell me about him!" she insisted, touching my heart with those big, bright eyes of hers that sometimes reminded me of my own.

I shrugged, not knowing which details to expand on. "He moved here not long ago and I don't even know if he's available."

"What do you mean? How could you not know?" She took me by the arm, leading me away from the vigilant ears of my dad, who was pretending to work.

In a way, I was relieved to finally be able to talk about it with someone. Of course, I never would have imagined Mom as a confidante. On the other hand, she was probably the only one who wouldn't have ulterior motives. Before talking, I switched on the coffee grinder so the deafening noise of the beans would help cover our voices. "There's a new girl at school too. She's *gorgeous*," I admitted, grimacing. "And the two of them seem inseparable." I felt a pit in my stomach.

"Have you ever seen them acting intimate?"

"No, but they're always together."

"So what? That doesn't mean anything. You and Peter are always together too. What makes you think she isn't his sister, for instance?"

"Jeneane said the same thing," I replied, my tone lighting up again.

"I never thought I'd say this, but for the first time I agree with her," she said. In Mom's opinion, Jeneane had never exactly been "good company." "Why don't you go ask him?"

"What?! Mom, no!" I exclaimed, shocked. What made her think I'd be brave enough to ask Evan about Ginevra? Didn't she know her own daughter?

"Why not? He's right here, just yards away! What's holding you back!?"

"I'd be too embarrassed."

"You need to learn to seize the day. Shyness is a lasso that binds the wings each of us has. Only if you untie it can you fly. Don't give up on something if you might regret it later. Sometimes all you need to do is reach out and take what's in front of you. Someone else might beat you to it and you'll miss your chance. Spread your wings, Squirrelicue, and go talk to him."

I couldn't say she was wrong, but I just couldn't follow her advice.

"Does he look at her the same way he looks at you?" she whispered in my ear, then quietly stepped back and disappeared.

The instant my eyes darted to Evan's, so deep and warm, I found them waiting for me. Like two perfectly fitting halves of some mechanism, our gazes remained enmeshed for a seemingly endless moment, exchanging information words couldn't express.

My emotions left me dazed every time. I doubted the same thing happened to everybody. Such a devastating sensation couldn't be common. Every moment was leading me into a comforting, embracing abyss. A mysterious one. A dangerous one. But one from which I would choose never to return if only I could stay there forever.

Part of me sensed that path would lead me to my end, but I didn't care as long as he walked down it with me. It was too late for me to turn back now.

I'd begun to lose myself in him.

With each moment that passed, unconsciously and uncontrollably, I was beginning to fall in love with Evan.

9

FIRE

Although he'd long since finished his crumble, Evan lingered at the table, staring out the diner window at the rain. From time to time, I gave in to the temptation to steal glances at him, and I was reassured when I caught him doing the same with me. It made me happy. Finding comfort in my mom's advice for the first time, I pushed the image of Evan and Ginevra as a couple completely out of my mind.

I looked out the window and finally glimpsed the sun peeking timidly through the blanket of clouds. On another occasion it would have cheered me up, but now I was sure—no, I was *afraid*—Evan was about to leave.

Soon, the screech of his chair against the floor told me I was right. My heart in my throat, I watched him stride over to the cash register where my mom was waiting, eager to get a closer look. I tried hard to ignore the embarrassing looks of approval she kept sending my way. I was afraid Evan might notice.

Worried that after he paid he might leave without saying goodbye, I gestured to her from behind the counter, hoping she'd understand and get lost. To my surprise, she understood instantly and walked away, leaving us alone.

Evan shyly made his way over to me and my knees started to tremble again. "I hadn't tasted anything so delicious in centuries," he said, breaking the silence.

"Yeah, well, um, it's all thanks to Dad," I blathered. *All thanks to Dad?* What the heck kind of a reply was that?

"He's quite an overachiever then," he said softly. I didn't understand what he meant by that. "Pastries aren't the only sweet thing he's good at making," he whispered boldly, flashing the most seductive of smiles.

Trembling, my heart grasped the allusion, but I nervously talked around it. "Yeah, actually, his fritters aren't bad either. I think they're great. You should try one next time."

Next time. I so hoped there would be a next time.

My answer got a laugh out of him. Even his smile was perfect, like every other thing about him. His white teeth gleamed behind his full lips. I imagined the sensation of feeling them on mine and instantly shook my head, realizing I was standing there staring at them.

"Right, his fritters." He stifled a smile as he walked to the door. "Well, see you at school . . . sweet thing," he added, winking at me. His attitude was so disarming I couldn't even reply. My heart was beating like crazy as I watched Evan walk through the glass vestibule and out the diner door.

Was it just my imagination or was he getting bolder?

The sun was ready to retire after its long journey through the sky and darkness prepared to descend on the little town of Lake Placid. "I'm going to get going," I told my mom. I walked over to the table where Evan had been sitting and ran my hand over its surface. The wood beneath my fingers was rough, covered with graffiti left by tourists. Dedications, initials, engravings. But one stood out; it was carved deeper than all the others. I leaned over and looked at it.

Rise up
and gather
the brightest stars

My heart started pounding and I began to tremble.

"Why don't you wait for us? We can all go home together for a change." I looked toward the doorway leading to the back. Mom was standing there, her eyes on me.

"I'd rather go now," I said, walking off before she'd finished talking. "See you at home." I was riddled with doubt: could he have carved those words for me? I had a lot to think about, a whole afternoon to re-examine in my mind, word by word. My stomach was aflutter and I was walking three feet above the ground. My feet knew the way home all on their own, so I was able to take my mind off that.

Someone yanked me backwards, almost making me fall. From the force used I could tell a man had done it, but only after a moment did I catch sight of his uniform.

"You can't go down there, miss," the policeman said firmly.

"What do you mean? I have to go home."

"I'll repeat that: You can't go that way!"

The idea of taking another street bothered me. I didn't want to have to pay attention to where I was going. "Why not?" I asked.

"There's a fire. Now step aside and let me do my job. I need to clear the street."

"Moron," I grumbled. Only when I saw what was happening not far in the distance did I understand how serious the situation was. How could I not have noticed the chaos?

All of Lake Placid had gathered there. I nervously hurried past the policeman, ignoring his protests, and dove into the crowd, trying to make my way through.

They were all staring in the same direction. Trying to get a better view, I took a few more steps forward, the heat of the flames beginning to scorch my face. I glimpsed an apartment building, its walls engulfed in flames. People's cries of dismay grew louder and more intense with every step I took. Then sirens drowned them out, announcing the arrival of the firefighters. There was little they would be able to salvage from the inferno by now, though.

The flames rose from the blackened windows, blazing overhead and whipping back and forth like red and yellow ribbons. I was close enough to see the firefighters outside the building assisting men, women, and children, their faces covered with soot, their clothing torn. The less fortunate— those who'd lost consciousness from smoke inhalation or had more serious cuts and burns—were being taken to the hospital in ambulances. It was a terrifying sight.

A woman's shrieks rose up over all the other troubled shouts. A shiver ran down my spine when I heard her and instinctively I pushed my way through the crowd. I discovered it was a woman of around thirty, her face aged by pain as the flames burned in her eyes. She was sobbing and screaming desperately to the rescuers, who were trying to calm her down without effect.

"Amy!!! My baaaby! Please! Save my baaaby! You have to save her! She's only four!" she continued to shriek, overcome with desperation. A murmur of compassion mixed with dismay spread through the entire crowd.

"AMYYY!!!"

The deafening, agonizing scream wrenched the hearts of the people in the crowd, silencing them. From where I stood, I could barely overhear the firefighters, but by the serious looks on their faces I guessed the authorities were trying to inform the woman that it was too late: the flames had completely engulfed the building and nothing more could be done for the little girl.

"We didn't find anyone else alive. I'm sorry, ma'am." The unlucky policeman who had been given the painful task spoke with cold detachment, forcing himself to hide his grief from the young woman. It made no difference. No matter how he said it, nothing could change it: her daughter was dead. No words could relieve her suffering.

"No. No. No. Nooo!!! Saaave her! Please! You've got to save her! She's still alive!" the woman shrieked through her tears, making me shiver with every desperate sob. "Why? Why didn't it take me instead?!"

I longed to run to her and hold her close. But no comfort would ever be enough. She kicked and thrashed while the authorities tried to hold her down.

I was on the verge of bursting into tears but forced myself to gulp them down, looking up at one of the windows of the building in flames. Something inside caught my eye. I frowned, trying to make out the confused images, and jumped when I saw a shadow partly hidden behind the blanket of smoke.

I focused on the vague shape and for a moment everything around me suddenly fell silent as if someone had switched off the volume. I peered at the strange figure, trying to make it out. It was definitely a man, probably a firefighter. But all the smoke kept blurring and distorting the image. I wanted to shout out to everyone but was afraid it was just another one of my visions. I focused more intensely and was relieved to see he wasn't alone.

Another smaller form was next to him, holding his hand.

I gaped. *The little girl!* My heart trembled and I stumbled over myself trying to get a fireman's attention. "Quick! He found her! Get them out!" I shouted with a mix of elation and dismay.

"Calm down, young lady, what are you talking about?" The man tried to catch my eye, but I continued to stare up at the shadow in the building, afraid I'd lose sight of them.

"The little girl! He's got the little girl!" The fireman stared at the building blackened by flames, a puzzled look on his face. "There's a man up there with her, can't you see him?!" I insisted, seeing his skepticism. "You've got to hurry!"

He took me by the arm and said in a low voice, "If this is a joke, it's not one bit funny. That woman is devastated, for Christ's sake! Have a heart!"

Bewildered, I looked back and forth between him and the window. Was he blind? "But he's *right there* on the third floor!" I said desperately, fighting back tears. "How can you not see him?! It might be one of your men!"

The fireman swore beneath his breath and glared at me. "The third floor completely collapsed. There's nobody left in the building, damn it! Do I have to draw you a picture?" He composed himself and studied me carefully. "You didn't happen to inhale any smoke, did you? You feel okay?" I blinked, dazed, his voice fading away in my mind. "Miss, do you need a doctor? Why don't you go have them check you out? You look pale," the fireman was saying, but the sound seemed to be coming from far away.

Couldn't he see them too? How could he not? "I'm fine," I finally managed to say, hoping he wouldn't try to force me onto a stretcher. "I just want to go home." I raised my eyes one last time. The shadows twisted with the flames and became clear again: it was a man and a little girl. Or was it? I couldn't trust my own eyes any more. The shadows disappeared in a cloud of smoke.

I nervously scanned the building's front doors in the hopes the man would walk out, carrying the girl to safety, but no one else came out of the building. The flames died down, the smoke blackened the sky, and the crowd dispersed.

Was I having hallucinations too now? Wasn't hearing voices in my head enough already? If I'd had to bet on how reliable my perceptions were lately, I'd definitely bet against myself.

A thought crossed my mind. There was something about the man's form that . . . No. If my obsession with Evan could make me this irrational, I was going to have to admit there was something seriously wrong with me. But the more I thought about it, the clearer the image became in my mind. It was suddenly joined by a second one: the man found dead in the woods. Two incidents. Two deaths. And Evan was there on both occasions. Could he possibly be involved somehow? It couldn't be a coincidence. How could my feelings for him be enough to exonerate him from the cold, impartial eyes of logic? No matter how hard my heart struggled against it, there was something sinister about Evan.

But this time I couldn't be so sure I'd actually seen him . . . could I? I shook my head, exasperated by my own paranoia. I wasn't sure I could take any more of the pain that my suspicions had instilled in my heart. I forced back the urge to cry and headed home.

The woman's anguish continued to haunt me as I hurried down the sidewalk. Losing a daughter after having raised and loved her for four years was a pain someone could never learn to live with. Ever. Because losing someone you love is always unbearably painful.

I walked along, my head down, tormented by the screams that continued to echo in my mind. I'd never witnessed such desperation before. The only thing I could compare it to was scenes from books or movies, but in those a superhero always brought the little girl back to her mom's arms. This was real life. There would be no happy ending for the devastated mother.

Disoriented by the crowds filling the sidewalks, I'd been walking distractedly, paying no attention to where I was going. Only when it was too late did I realize I'd turned down the wrong street. The houses grew smaller and smaller behind me as I made my way toward the forest. I knew it wasn't the right direction, but something I couldn't put my finger on was driving me on. Not even my instinct. Quite the opposite, in fact: my instinct was urging me to get away from there, and fast. It was some kind of ancestral, mystical attraction, a beckoning I could neither ignore nor resist. It felt *dangerous*. But I didn't care. I sensed the path before me would lead me through my own inner labyrinth.

I came to a sudden halt, baffled. Thick stone walls towered overhead at the end of the path, an inaccessible fortress. What was hiding behind those mighty, majestic walls? Was it abandoned, maybe? The white rock was so ancient, it looked like it had been there forever.

I looked around, trying to figure out where I was. The path had led me out of Lake Placid and into an area I'd been to on occasion. Still, I was sure I'd never seen any piece of property like this before. Cautiously, I ran my palm over the wall and energy suddenly raced through my body. I flinched and jumped back. It was the same energy that had led me there.

I touched it again, but this time I didn't feel anything. Hoping to find a gate, a door, or some other way inside, I walked along the wall, running my hand along a huge crack in its surface. Curiosity consumed me. I had to discover what was hiding inside the fortress walls. Just as I began to think they were impenetrable, I saw the crack widen into a gap a few yards ahead of me, big enough for a slim person to squeeze through.

I hesitated, frightened by the foreboding appearance of the walls. The gap looked like it might lead directly to hell. But before I could heed my instinct to turn and flee, the impulse that had led me there forced me on. I squeezed through the gap and was almost overcome with emotion. I had no idea what heaven looked like, but if there was one on earth it had to be the place I'd discovered behind those walls. It seemed as if all the world's flora might have originated from that enchanting setting, a breathtaking sight to behold. Towering trees, guardians of the earthly paradise, lined curved paths.

As if coming to life in my presence, the green mantle covering the ground swayed, dancing in the gentle breeze. Springtime ruled supreme, painting everything with a thousand colors. Vines crept up the trees, spreading over the boughs, and flowers blossomed everywhere, filling the air with their delicate fragrance. Infinite droplets of water beaded the needles on the pine trees like little diamonds, sparkling in the last rays of sunlight.

I looked more carefully. Farther back, hidden behind lush hedges, I saw a roof. Although I couldn't be sure from where I was standing, I guessed it was the back of a house. If this was just somebody's back yard, I didn't dare imagine what wonders lay indoors.

Not far from where I was standing, something moved. I froze.

Someone was there, in the garden.

FATAL KISS

I felt as if someone had stabbed me in the heart. The foolish hope I'd been nurturing winked out like a candle in the wind. Entranced by the garden, I hadn't noticed the little wooden bench partially concealed behind some shrubs. Not until someone sitting there moved. Facing her, his back to me, Evan leaned in closer toward Ginevra, and my heart raged inside my chest.

What up until then had been only a suspicion was finally confirmed, shattering all my illusions. Although Evan was facing the other way, it was impossible not to recognize those soft curls that caressed the back of his neck, tinged with red by the warm rays of sunset.

He was wearing the same dark shirt he'd worn that day at school, and Ginevra was sensually running her hand up his back beneath it. Even the enchanted garden paled before Ginevra's beauty, fading as it willingly offered all its colors to her. Her long golden hair flowed over one shoulder and her skin had no need to be kissed by the sun; it glowed with its own light.

Their faces drew nearer until they were almost touching. A lump formed in my throat. Seeing them kiss would make my heart wither. I'd waited so long to find out what there was between them, I thought I'd be prepared for the worst. Instead, I felt like I'd fallen into a deep, dark pit.

There was no way they were brother and sister. My chest felt empty, as if an ice-cold hand had torn everything out of it as I stood there watching.

Anger. Disappointment. Frustration. Conflicting feelings battled it out. Above them all was a jealousy I hadn't realized I was capable of that suddenly rose up inside me like lava in an erupting volcano. I felt as if Ginevra was trespassing on some part of me, because for some utterly incomprehensible reason, deep in my heart I felt that Evan already belonged to me and me alone.

Seeing his hands on her, their mouths so close together, filled me with devastating rage. I felt like grabbing Ginevra by the hair, but then the thought of the afternoon with Evan came back, making my heart ache. Only a few hours before, he'd caressed my hand. I remembered the powerful jolt of electricity I'd felt when he touched me.

Now I was standing there watching those same hands cup another girl's face and draw it closer to his own. I wished I could know what it felt like to have his lips on mine. I felt betrayed. Fooled. Empty.

Could I really have misunderstood everything? His boldness, all his attention, had put a glimmer of hope into my heart that had grown stronger every time we met, but now it was being violently uprooted. Could I really mean nothing at all to him? My heart refused to accept the possibility.

"We have company." Still looking into his eyes, Ginevra informed Evan of my presence, not even glancing my way. I looked at her just in time to see her lock her razor-sharp eyes on me. Her opalescent irises were as intense as the sea where it touches the horizon. They didn't seem hostile, only curious.

For an instant we stared at each other. I tried to resist the hypnotic power that kept me glued to my spot, but even the air seemed to be working against me. And while all I could do was think about how I wished I could hit her with all the hatred I felt, her expression continued to reveal not a trace of hostility or even jealousy. There was just . . . frustration. The same shadow that often haunted Evan's eyes.

I desperately hoped it wasn't pity too. I'd rather she hated me.

Ginevra rose to her feet, snapping me out of my trance and making me step back cautiously, not taking my eyes off her face. She seemed to want to stop me, but now, freed from the invisible grip that had kept me standing there, I turned and ran.

"Hey! Wait!" Her voice reached me in a faded echo, but since it lacked the power of her gaze, it couldn't hold me back. I wanted to run as far away as possible. More than anything else, I had to avoid letting Evan see me. Being spotted by Ginevra was already humiliating enough. Having to hold back my tears in front of him, showing him my feelings, would have been too much to bear.

I stopped running to catch my breath and make sure no one was following me. My throat was dry and my eyes were brimming with tears. The path was deserted, and since it was far from the city, I was sure no one could see me. The knot in my throat dissolved, releasing an endless stream of tears that left pale streaks on my skin, ashen with misery.

I'd never cried over a boy before. I had no idea disappointment could cause such a reaction. I breathed in deeply, painfully filling my lungs with air, and started running again, hoping the wind would extinguish the fire burning in my chest. I wanted to go home and hide in the comfort in my room. That afternoon, so full of conflicting emotions, had been too much for me.

It was so strange how fast you could go from walking on a cloud to sinking into the deepest despair. But life doesn't always ask you what you think is fair. Moods change, like the seasons; the only difference is how quickly everything transforms.

Just a few hours ago I'd felt I was living a dream, but then it had turned into a nightmare. I'd been so stupid. Were a few moments of happiness really worth experiencing such excruciating pain? Was it better to be ignorant, to nurture false hope? Or to face the hard, painful truth?

I wasn't sure I knew the answer.

Even now, who could say I'd be able to turn the page and forget Evan just like that? Some irreversible mechanism had been triggered. Evan had gotten under my skin. But I'd discovered that it was truly agonizing to mean nothing to someone who meant everything to you. I could only rely on the healing power of time, hoping it would help me forget him.

Meanwhile, I kept seeing that petrifying, heart-rending image in my mind. Part of me had already considered the possibility that Evan and Ginevra were a couple, but actually seeing them together, so close, had changed everything. Nothing would ever be the same again.

The streetlights flickered on as I splashed nonstop across the wet asphalt. There were still lots of people on the streets, their anonymous features blurred to my eyes. The sky had cleared, revealing its stars. No clouds darkened the horizon. They'd all come together to darken my heart.

I didn't care what people might think, seeing me in that state. The only reaction I was worried about was my family's. Once I got home, I'd have to make sure my parents didn't see me this way.

A breeze blew gently on my face, drying my tears and tousling my hair like a comforting caress. I breathed in the fresh spring air avidly, then flinched when I suddenly banged into something solid. The impact threw me completely off balance and I fell, my nostrils filled with a scent that made my heart beat faster.

A scent as fresh as a waterfall in the depths of the forest. *Evan.*

"Ow! That hurts! Hey! Where are you running off to?" How was it that his voice could wipe away all my pain, physical and emotional? Or was it simply his presence that did it?

I pressed my lips together, fearful they would betray me by pouring out my anger at him. Like a vile traitor, my brain projected before my eyes the image of his lips on Ginevra's, but my heart, more loyal, erased it instantly, rebelling at its attempt to overpower me. It was strange, but I wanted to bask in the illusion that his kindness to me actually meant something. Just for a little while longer.

"Well? Care to tell me where you're off to in such a hurry, sweet thing?" A grin formed on his lips and my heart surrendered to him. I couldn't believe everything had changed since just a couple hours before, when we'd soared together between heaven and earth. But how had Evan managed to change clothes so quickly? He was wearing the red shirt he'd been wearing in the diner, not the dark one I'd seen him in back in the garden. And why was he acting like nothing had happened? Was it possible that Ginevra hadn't told him she'd seen me? If so, why? To spare me the embarrassment? Just the idea seemed ridiculous. Why should she cover for me when all I could do was think of the soft curve of Evan's lips? After all, he was her boyfriend.

The cold, damp surface beneath me reminded me that I was still on the sidewalk, unable to raise my eyes, which were puffy from crying. I must have looked like an idiot, but all my conflicting emotions were overwhelming me. I didn't know how to act naturally.

I wished Evan would go away and leave me alone, but instead he knelt down on the pavement, not worrying about getting his jeans wet. From that distance, there was no way I could hide my tears from him. His fingers tenderly lifted my chin. Like every other time, the physical contact generated an electric current, a light, comforting tingle that spread through my body and down to my stomach.

"You're crying."

I looked away. I didn't want him to feel sorry for me. But he gently grasped my chin, forcing me to look at him. I stared into his eyes that were misted with concern. They were too close for me not to yield to their spell. Almost in a daze, I felt his hand brush the hair away from my forehead and a sense of peace filled my head. It must be his gaze that had that healing effect on me.

His lips curved into the most seductive of smiles, taking away my newly regained breath. Evan was so handsome it almost hurt. I knew he was expecting an answer, but I also knew I wasn't about to give him one. He ran his thumb gently down my cheek, as if to wipe away the streaks left by my tears, and my heart quivered. "Well? Want to tell me what happened?" When I didn't answer, he offered me his hand to help me up. "You look so upset."

The thought of taking his hand made me tremble with desire. Even just brushing my fingers against his that afternoon had triggered such intense emotions. I shivered when my skin touched his and for a moment, erased the name Ginevra from my vocabulary. All that existed now were Evan and me and his hand in mine.

I noticed a mark on his skin I hadn't seen before, a scar on the back of his hand that looked a lot like a burn. Was it possible he really had been inside that building? I stood up, my eyes lingering on his hand before I let it go. "You're hurt."

Evan quickly pulled back his hand and hid it in his jeans pocket. "It's nothing." His face had suddenly darkened.

"Thanks for the help," I murmured, quickly changing the subject.

"So you didn't lose it, then." He stared at me, smiling again.

I frowned, confused.

"The power of speech. I was starting to think you bit your tongue off when you bumped into me."

I raised an eyebrow at his childish joke and he tapped the tip of my nose with his finger. Why did he keep touching me? Couldn't he see how confused it made me?

It wasn't my fault his attitude disoriented me. Part of me still felt betrayed and blinded by jealousy. Why was he being so nice? Was toying with my emotions really so much fun?

"I had a long afternoon, that's all," I said as my wounded pride tried to wrestle free of his deep, intense gaze. But my heart got the better of me and I stood there, longing to lose myself in the depths of his eyes.

For one single instant, I had the impression the same was true for him. Reason kept telling me to run, but every heartbeat was crying out his name. Was I mistaking his kindness for something else? Had I really been misreading the way he looked at me? I still sensed that invisible cord that connected me to him so strongly it made my heart ache.

"I'll take you home." The firmness with which he said it made it clear he wasn't going to take no for an answer. "I don't live far from here. Let's go get my motorcycle and—"

"No!" I blurted.

Evan stared at me, surprised by my vehemence. "I'm not letting you wander the streets in this condition. Follow me," he ordered, grabbing my hand.

No matter how much I longed for his company, going back there was out of the question. I didn't want to see Ginevra again. Now that I stopped to think about it, how could he have been coming from the opposite direction when we ran into each other?

More calmly, I said, "That's really nice of you." I reluctantly slid my hand out of his firm grip. "I'm almost there," I lied.

Evan leaned forward, forcing me to back up until I was pressed against the wall, and rested his hands on either side of my head, his eyes locked onto mine. My heart broke into a gallop.

"Don't be silly." His voice was persuasive, but it wasn't enough to change my mind. "I'm taking you home." There was something dark in his eyes, some kind of energy I couldn't fathom. Both sensual and wild.

"I told you I'm okay. Really," I insisted.

Evan seemed astonished by my stubbornness and dropped one arm to his side. "But your house is on the other side of town!" he added with exasperation, narrowing his eyes.

"How—" I stammered, confused. Why would he know that? "Never mind." Evan made no reply, skillfully letting the conversation drop. "Seriously," I reassured him, trying to act natural, "it's really nice of you to offer me a ride, but it won't take me long to get home. I walk really fast. Besides, the fresh air will do me good."

Evan frowned, uncertain, and then gave in, flashing a big grin at me. He leaned in to speak in my ear. "That means I'll miss out on the chance to have you with me on my bike," he whispered with a mix of sensuality and tenderness. A shot straight to the heart.

Wasn't he worried Ginevra might see us together? My head had caught fire again, ignited by his ambiguous behavior. "Yeah, um, some other time, maybe," I said, deciding he was just teasing me. A pang of reproach gripped my chest; my heart was screaming at me to accept. I forced myself to ignore it and pulled my hood up over my head. "See you at school," I mumbled, making sure not to look him in the eye, and started running again.

VISIONS

It was strange to have to deal with all these new, conflicting emotions. Usually logic guided me, but I'd heard that when it came to affairs of the heart, the voice of reason faded away and disappeared. I, too, had discovered that my instincts took charge when it came to Evan.

More than anything, I wanted to throw myself on the bed, bury my head under the pillow, and leave the long, grueling day behind me. But I knew that despite myself I would go back over that nerve-racking afternoon a thousand times.

No one had ever taught me to handle certain emotions, and I had the scars to prove it. When it came to others, giving advice had always been easy. Following it, not at all. And now that I was the one who needed help, I felt terribly alone. When I was little, my parents and teachers had encouraged me to socialize, but I'd spent more and more time in my shell, cut off from everyone. I'd always preferred the peace and quiet of a good story to the noisy company of other kids. Only now did I realize why they had tried for years to encourage me to let my friends in. But I never followed their advice, and now I was paying the consequences.

Still, I wasn't entirely sure it was due only to my loner personality. The truth was, I felt different from the other girls. And I couldn't even figure out if solitude was pursuing me or if I was the one seeking it out.

The only person I'd ever established a strong connection with was Peter. A boy. I'd never seriously imagined not being able to turn to him for help one day. For the first time I regretted not having a close girlfriend in my life.

I started to wish I'd accepted that ride from Evan. I was exhausted, drained not only emotionally but also physically, having run so hard, and my throat was parched.

Steps away from my front walk, I noticed the gate was ajar. I grumbled at myself for forgetting to close it, entered the yard, and clicked it shut behind me. The lights were off. My parents hadn't come home yet.

I hurried to the front door. I didn't like the idea of being in the dark, and the disturbing things I'd seen that afternoon still haunted me, along with older yet just as disturbing memories. The fire. The woods. The screams. The broken neck. I tensely searched my pockets for my keys. Right. Left.

Empty. I shrugged my backpack off, looking around nervously. I flipped through my two novels, checked the zipper flaps, and even looked in my camera case, but I couldn't find my keys anywhere, and it was so dark I could barely see. The longer I looked, the more panic overtook me. It was getting darker by the minute, the sky lit only by a pale quarter moon.

I had no intention of sitting outside and waiting for my parents to get home. I'd always had a problem with the dark. My mind went back to Evan over and over again, nagging at me for not accepting a ride from him. If only I had his number, I could call him and beg him to come get me.

I looked around nervously, trying to make out details of the yard, which in the dim light looked eerie. I could tell that Peter's family wasn't at home either because their shutters were all closed and their yard was pitch dark. High in the sky, the quarter moon mocked me, grinning, while an ominous half-light shrouded everything, reawakening my biggest fears.

Something moved behind me. My heart lurched and started racing. I whirled around, panting, but the yard was cloaked in silence.

Squinting from the corner of my eye, I glimpsed a shadow dart behind me. Fear paralyzed me. "Who's there?" I shouted into the night. My trembling voice faded into the darkness.

Hadn't I already had enough for one day? To the list of disturbing emotions, did I really have to add terror? Without moving a muscle, I peered in fright at the area around our front walk. Even the wind was still, holding the air hostage. The silence was so oppressive I couldn't tell if the thumping noise I heard was echoing through the darkness or coming from inside my chest.

"Looking for these?"

Evan's hushed, sensual voice sounded near the back of my neck. I froze without turning around and gulped, overwhelmed by unexpected emotion. Instead of startling me, his presence was like a soothing balm, triggering an immediate sense of relief. Recovering control of my body, I slowly turned to look at him. I couldn't be sure, but his eyes almost looked lighter, like I remembered them in my dreams. They seemed to reflect the moonlight. He held out the bunch of keys I thought I'd lost.

"Evan . . ." When I finally managed to speak, my voice was unsteady from surprise. "How, how did you . . . ?" I wasn't really sure what I was asking.

"I took my bike." Evan skillfully dodged the question.

"Okay, but how did you get in? I locked the gate." Suddenly I wasn't sure I wanted to hear the answer any more.

He smiled at me, his gaze captivating. "So what? I climbed over it. A damsel in distress needed me," he teased, shrugging.

"But I didn't see you climb over it. In fact, I didn't see you at all. I didn't even hear your motorcycle."

"Are you saying I'm a ghost rider?" Evan laughed at his own joke and I felt my cheeks burn. What was I insinuating, that he'd slipped into my yard like a phantom?

He noticed my embarrassment. "What can I say, sweet thing? I'm the silent type and you seem like a girl who's easily distracted." He hid a grin. "Besides, it's so dark out, you'd have to have eyes like a falcon to see me coming over the gate at the end of your walk, wouldn't you?" He moved his face closer to mine and pulled the hood of my red sweatshirt up over my head, lowering his voice. "But then again, what big eyes you have . . ."

I was caught off guard by how close he was. "Careful," I said, "I might mistake you for the big, bad wolf." *If you weren't so damn sexy,* I thought.

But it wasn't true. With him I didn't feel I was in danger. I felt safe. Irresistibly, dangerously safe.

Evan laughed. "You like fairy tales, Little Red Riding Hood?"

"Only the ones with happy endings," I shot back.

His face grew sad and he retreated a pace. "Not all fairy tales have happy endings."

I studied him silently. "Anyway, it's illegal to ride a motorcycle without a helmet."

"Huh?"

"Your helmet. Where is it?"

"I like to feel the wind in my hair," he replied, grinning, "and the thrill of speed." He raised an eyebrow, a mischievous glimmer in his eyes. I shut my mouth. I had the impression that arguing with him would be a waste of time. He always found a way to brush things off.

"For the record, you could have used the keys to let yourself in," I said, resigned, and he shrugged as if it hadn't even occurred to him. "Besides, how did you know where I live? Have you been spying on me by chance?" I asked, half annoyed and half worried. I was totally attracted, but I still wasn't sure who Evan was or how involved he was in the mysterious incidents that had begun to happen in Lake Placid.

A deep, melodious laugh rose up from his chest. "I had no choice but to follow you, sweet thing." Why on earth did he keep calling me that silly, childish . . . *adorable* nickname? "I ended up with your keys, Gemma," he explained, focusing the full force of his seductive gaze on me, despite the skeptical look on my face. He almost seemed to be trying to control my mind. "You dropped them when we bumped into each other. I thought I'd bring them back to you, but if you don't need them—" He pulled back the hand in which he'd been holding out my keys and turned to leave. "Well, I'll be off."

"Wait!"

Evan promptly froze. I couldn't be sure, since his back was to me, but I guessed he had a little smile on his face.

"Please," I forced myself to add, hoping to make up for the harsh tone I'd just used. I couldn't help it; hostility kept unexpectedly rising up in me. I didn't know if my rejection of Evan's attentions was because I knew he belonged to someone else or if my instinct distrusted him. It looked like I'd found out for myself why people say love is blind, because no matter how much my instinct insisted, my heart remained untarnished by doubt. "That was rude of me. You just wanted to help and I keep pushing you away."

My apology didn't have the effect I'd expected. My words seemed to awaken within him a slumbering agony. His expression darkened. He slumped his shoulders and hung his head so low I couldn't see his face. His silence almost convinced me he was on the verge of leaving, but then he unexpectedly turned.

The look on his face went straight to my heart. Evan stepped slowly toward me. From his grin, I could tell he was aware of the effect he had on me whenever he looked my way.

I let myself blush, comforted by the reassurance that the complicit night would hide the heat that rose to my cheeks. Moving with studied slowness, Evan reached out and took my hand as I watched him, mesmerized. He rested the keys on my palm and closed my fingers with his, cautiously moving his lips to my ear. The warmth of his breath left me in a daze.

What was he doing? And how was he depriving me of all control over my own body? My eyes half closed, lulled by the barely perceptible sound of his lips parting beside my ear.

"You have *nothing* to apologize for."

I swallowed, trembling at the hypnotic sound of his whisper. The meaning of his message eluded me. The heat of his breath penetrated my skin, spreading from my ear through my entire body until it softened into a tender warmth that filled my heart.

When I opened my eyes, Evan was disappearing around the corner.

Trying to shake off the emotion still gripping my stomach, I slid the key into the lock. Once inside, I leaned back against the front door as another shiver ran up my arms. I forced myself to walk down the hall and dumped my backpack on the floor. From the stairs, I could hear Iron Dog snoring noisily. I shook my head, smiling. The world had been filled with colors and I couldn't stop thinking about Evan's voice, the magnetic attraction his skin had on me when he came near, the power of his gaze. I headed distractedly to the bathroom, butterflies in my stomach. Could my brain be selecting which bits of information it retained? My face was still streaked with tears, but all I could think of was my hand clasped in his.

I turned on the tap and water flowed into the sink. While it was getting warm, I brushed my hair and put it up in a bun so it wouldn't get wet. I had the habit of wearing a black scrunchie around my upper arm. In winter, the long sleeves of my sweatshirts would push it down to my forearm. I couldn't even remember when I'd started doing it, but I never took it off, not even at night.

After brushing my teeth carefully, I leaned down, filled my cupped hands with water and splashed it on my face. The warmth on my skin was instant relief, rinsing away every last remaining trace of the day. Lingering there a few seconds, enjoying the sensation, I stuck my face under the tap. When my eyes had also been refreshed, I reached out my right hand, groped for a towel, and patted my face dry, especially around my eyes, which were still puffy and numb from the tears. I didn't want my parents to notice my mood when they came home. Wanting to check how red my eyes were, I looked into the mirror and saw Evan's piercing gaze fixed on me. Trembling with pure terror, I spun around, but the doorway to the hall was empty. A shudder ran over me.

Seized by panic, I slammed the door shut. With clenched fists, I wrapped my arms around my body, leaned against the wall and slid down to the floor. Even at that moment I sensed a dark presence hovering in the air, making me shiver. It was like someone was there watching me from close up, like they were *touching* me. I felt I was losing my mind. I was alone in the room, there was no such thing as ghosts, and people didn't come back from the dead . . . right? So why did it feel possible? Could my obsession with Evan be driving me insane? How could my head be coming up with the dark fantasies you only read about in novels?

I sighed. That afternoon had probably been a lot harder on me than I'd wanted to admit, that was all. Still, the idea of opening the door and going out into the hallway made me shudder. How I wished I had gleaned a little courage from my books instead of absorbing only the creepiest, scariest parts. But I wasn't a heroine in a book. When it came to real life, I couldn't help being scared about hearing voices in my head, sensing presences, and seeing shadows no one else could see. But why did it all lead back to Evan?

The light flickered and went out. I jumped up and threw open the door. There was something wrong in the air. I had to get out of there and fast. I ran into my room and slammed the door shut with all my weight, almost knocking it down. Trying to catch my breath, I locked it and scanned the room. Pulling my iPod out of a drawer in my walnut desk, I fell onto the bed, exhausted and drained. The music penetrated the barrier of tension that had built up inside me and slowly melted it as I stared at my light-green walls and my breathing returned to normal. I turned the volume up full blast, hoping to pull the plug on the world and let myself drift away with the mesmerizing voice of James Blunt. *Tears and Rain* lulled me until I nodded off.

WARNING

I was lost in the pitch dark. The cold had penetrated my bones. At least, I hoped the shivers running through my body were caused by the temperature.

It seemed the worst sensations I'd experienced by day had come back to torment me by night. I couldn't see where I was, but the idea of standing still terrified me, so I inched my way forward, feeling around on the floor with my foot before shifting my weight onto it. The wood creaked with each step, making a sinister sound that echoed through the room.

A window swung open with a groan. I jumped, but then was grateful for the beam of moonglow it let in, even though it drenched everything in a spectral half-light. The unmistakable smell of old wood and damp earth reached my nostrils, taking me back to when I was a little girl.

All the other children had avoided going near the big old house that was said to be haunted. Peter and I, on the other hand, made it our secret hideaway. To get there, we'd sneak through the woods to make sure some superstitious adult wouldn't try to stop us. From the eastern side of the house you could see Lake Placid partially hidden behind a tangle of branches and gnarled tree trunks. We would close the doors on the world and hide inside, letting our imaginations take us places no one else could go, where stories came to life and ghosts danced in the parlor, played the mahogany grand piano, took us by the hand. The house was full of secret places, as though specifically designed for people to hide in. It had lots of passageways that connected the various rooms or led down to the cellar. Still others led outdoors, to spots among the trees in the woods. Peter would spend ages searching for me until I got tired of waiting and would devise some way to let him find me.

The dusty, worn furniture, which was as old as it was majestic, reminded me of the huge manors I'd read about in nineteenth-century novels. Back when I was little I'd believed the portraits hanging on the walls were constantly staring at us.

I walked toward the window, guided only by the pale shaft of light, but something moved before I could reach it. A whimper escaped me. Someone was there, hidden in the darkness, in the farthest corner of the room. With unusual courage, I cautiously moved toward it as the floorboards creaked beneath my feet.

"Is someone there?" My voice came out tinged with fear that I tried to stifle. In reply, I heard a low groan as my eyes grew accustomed to the darkness. I made out the shape of a figure huddled on the floor, hidden in the shadows. The eerie rocking motion it was making, its body racked with sobs, made the blood in my veins run ice-cold. Was it the murderer, who'd come to hide in the house? I froze, terrified.

Suddenly, the window shutter flew open, banging against the outside wall. The noise made me jump as another shaft of moonglow poured in, illuminating the person's face. She stared at me fiercely, her eyes brimming with pain, bloodshot. I leaned closer, dismayed to see it was the mother of the little girl who'd perished in the fire. She continued to stare at me, her knees clasped to her chest, as if imagining she was cradling her daughter. Her dull, blank, exhausted eyes lingered on mine for a few seconds before she stared down at the floor again, rocking back and forth.

I was full of anguish, like I had been during that terrible fire. Her screams came back, echoing through my head. All at once they stopped. I reached out and rested my hand on the woman's shoulder. When she felt my touch, she slowly raised her eyes and stared into mine, but only for a moment—she was distracted by something behind me. "Amy . . ." she whispered in a frail voice.

I went deathly pale and slowly followed her gaze over my shoulder, my eyes open wide in a horrible presentiment. Terror trapped the air in my lungs. A little girl with golden hair stared at me from a few steps away.

Every muscle in my body was trembling. A strange perception made me absolutely certain that life had abandoned her little body. Her face was ashen and there were rings around her eyes, yet she wore an unusual look of serenity that prevented the shadows of death from showing through her skin. There was no hint of pain, suffering, or terror in the girl's eyes. Quite the opposite. She looked pleased, satisfied. Fulfilled. As if death had completed her, made her happy, even.

Her lips were upturned in a graceful smile. She raised her hand and slowly waved it from side to side, saying goodbye. I watched the scene, stunned. Amy reached out into the darkness, as if searching for the hand of someone hidden there.

I squinted and spotted a shadowy form. I wasn't sure if it had been there the whole time or appeared only later, like a ghost. Whoever it was seemed reluctant to come out into the open. Amy looked up at the person holding her hand as I stared at them, petrified and bewildered.

A scream pierced the silence. The mother's shrieks grew stronger, shriller, as she shouted her daughter's name through her sobs, afraid the person would take her little girl away. I turned back to the woman to comfort her, but she was gone. She'd disappeared, leaving behind only the echo of her grief-stricken voice and a bare, damp wall covered with mildew. Suddenly, a burst of heat lashed at my face, blinding me with its intense light. I whirled around and discovered the whole room had caught fire. The flames were consuming the wood.

No. Taking a closer look, I found I wasn't in the lake house any more. I was inside that building where little Amy's life had been cut short. Her fiery prison. I made my way through the flames; maybe if I got to her in time I could carry her to safety. The fire continued to throw up sheets of flame, separating us. Amy stared at me, not even blinking, surrounded by the flames.

"Run!" I shouted to her, but no sound came from my lips. I felt that the smoke was crushing my lungs. The shifting flames revealed what I hadn't been able to see before: the person hidden in the darkness.

"Evan," I whispered, my eyes going wide. My gaze locked onto his. He stared back at me, distraught, guilty. Breaking the spell, he turned his back to me, his hand clasping little Amy's as he led her away. I wanted to stop them, but Evan came to a halt, as though he'd guessed my intentions.

"There's nothing you can do," he warned me without turning around, sorrow in his voice. "There's nothing anyone can do." He sounded resigned.

Why was he so upset? The little girl was with him now. He could save her.

"I can't," he whispered through clenched teeth, replying to my thoughts. "I can't deny who I am." He raised his eyes to mine and his expression grew serious. "Time's almost up."

My body reacted to his words with a shudder. My instinct seemed to have grasped the meaning behind them.

Something ominous that my heart refused to understand. The look Evan was giving me seemed more like a *warning*. He closed his eyes and when he opened them again something glimmered. It looked like a tear, but it vanished in the heat of the fire before I could be sure. His gaze suddenly pierced mine. "I won't be able to avoid it. I'm sorry," he said.

Something was tormenting him. From this close up, it looked unbearable. I felt it coming straight from him to me, through my skin. I wished I could wipe it from his face, it was so hard for me to bear. Why was he suffering? And why was his sadness having such a contagious effect on me?

"What? What won't you be able to avoid?" I asked, unsteadily finding my voice again.

Evan looked torn, as though struggling to decide whether or not to answer me. "You'll be next." His words sliced through me like a sword of ice. Helpless, my eyes wide, I watched him begin to fade away into the flames, taking the little girl with him. His voice echoed through the depths of my mind, repeating the words endlessly, like a boomerang coming back over and over again. I watched in astonishment as they vanished, hand in hand.

13

SUSPICION

I opened my eyes, panting, my forehead beaded with sweat, and realized I was in my bed. The light was peeking through the crack between the curtains. The alarm clock on my nightstand read six a.m. School started at seven-thirty. At least I wouldn't be late, for a change.

Lying in bed, I stretched, noticing I was still wearing the same clothes I'd worn the day before. A cold shiver ran over me as my mind recalled the long day I'd left behind. It was no surprise I'd had another of those strange dreams. I was getting used to them, in fact.

I still had my shoes on and in my hand was the cord to my iPod, which I'd fallen asleep listening to. I found it lying upside down on the linoleum floor. Sitting up, I was surprised to discover it still had some power left. A somber melody was coming through the earbuds. I raised them to my ears and a shiver ran through me as Amy Lee's hypnotic voice sang *Before the Dawn*.

Not a sound was coming from the rest of the house except for my dad's snoring. Barefoot, I tiptoed to the bathroom, trying not to wake my parents. I carefully closed the door, turned around and started at the sight of my own reflection; the eerie memory of what I'd seen in the mirror the night before still made me tremble.

As the water in the shower was heating up, I let my sweaty clothes slide to the floor: worn jeans, a green military top and a dark red sweatshirt. I waited for steam to fill the room, tested the temperature of the water and stepped inside. Pointing the jet of water onto my neck, I slowly pushed my hair to one side, letting the boiling hot water run down my body. The comfortable sensation of the water on my skin melted the tension in my muscles and relaxed me, body and soul.

I didn't know what to expect today. I just hoped it would be less intense than yesterday. Despite myself, I couldn't banish the confused images that haunted me like malicious ghosts. Reality mingled with my dreams, blurring the line between the two. I attempted to assemble the memories connected to Evan into a logical pattern, but no matter how hard I tried, my heart kept me from putting the insane puzzle together.

For a second, I was tempted to crawl back under the covers and skip school to avoid seeing Evan. I wasn't sure I could face the confused emotions he was triggering in me. Even less did I want to see him with Ginevra, now that I knew they were a couple. She'd had all the time she needed to tell Evan about the embarrassing episode of the previous afternoon. It was too humiliating.

Then again, I couldn't hide forever, and I knew for a fact that unless you faced problems head-on, you risked failing. It was better to keep moving forward and overcoming obstacles than to just stand there doubting myself. That was what my grandmother always used to say.

Deep down in my heart, I had the feeling my sudden boldness stemmed from something completely different. The truth was, I was dying to see him again. I stepped out of the shower, steam rising from my skin and filling the room. I opened the window a crack to let it out, rubbed my wet hair with a hand towel, and wrapped my body in a large white bath towel. I went to the mirror but couldn't see my reflection, so I raised a corner of the towel to wipe it clean, then stopped, baffled.

There was something written on the mirror. I squinted, trying to make out what it said before the steam vanished and it disappeared. Stunned and shocked, I read:

Gemma
∞

Who could have left my name on the mirror in that graceful writing? And why interlace it with the infinity symbol?

Only when the steam had completely vanished did I realize I'd been standing there stock-still. I peered into my own eyes with the strange sensation that they didn't belong to me, watching as my pupils dilated at the memory of the face reflected there the day before. Could Evan actually have been there? My whole body trembled, but I drove away the thought as quickly as it had appeared. The very idea was ridiculous.

"Gemma, is that you?" My mom's groggy voice came from the hall. "Who are you talking to?"

Worried, my eyes darted back to my reflection. Had I been speaking out loud? What was happening to me? I felt more and more like my body was slipping out of my control. Or was my mind disconnecting from my body?

"Are you on the phone? Who is it, this early?" she insisted, raising her voice so I'd hear her.

"Nobody, Mom, I was just singing, that's all." The moment I said it, I felt a burden being lifted: no doubt the writing on the mirror was a message from my mom. She'd just been moved when she saw I'd fallen asleep still wearing my clothes. An unusual way to remind me that she loved me.

I shook my head and ran my fingers through my hair. Had I really thought Evan had come into my bathroom to leave me a coded message on the mirror? I felt like an idiot for even considering it.

I bounded down the steps three at a time and grabbed a chocolate doughnut from the kitchen table.

"Take your umbrella!" my mom shouted from upstairs. "The forecast says rain."

I opened the door, stopping on the threshold before leaving. "I love you too, Mom!" I shouted up the stairwell.

Cold drizzle fell on my head and ran down my hair as I hurried to the bus stop. Watching the rain through the bus window relaxed me. I leaned my head against the glass and closed my eyes, listening to the comforting sound of the raindrops splashing onto the leaves.

A loud noise made me open them again. My eyes darted to the road. I had no doubt it was Evan's motorcycle. I sat up straighter so my breath wouldn't condense on the cold windowpane, blurring my view. The motorcycle pulled up alongside the bus and slowly began to pass it.

Ginevra's eyes shot to mine without a trace of hesitation. Like she'd known exactly where I was sitting. Evan stared at the road ahead of him as locks of his wet hair, darkened from the rain, flopped over his forehead. Ginevra's golden hair streamed out behind her, carried by the wind. They both had their helmets tucked under their arms.

I felt a pang of uneasiness in the pit of my stomach. There was no denying they were perfect for each other. I was nothing in comparison with Evan, let alone Ginevra. Next to them, I was a puny, flickering candle beside a gigantic lighthouse.

Ginevra watched me until Evan sped up and they disappeared from sight. Had she told him? My heart was pounding in my throat at the thought that once I got off the bus I'd have to face the situation.

I glanced around the school parking lot, hiding behind my umbrella, sadly discovering that Evan's motorcycle wasn't there. In the English classroom, I sat down at my desk and looked out at the stream of students rushing inside to get out of the rain.

The room slowly filled up. I shifted my chair to make room for Jeneane, who showed up last, right before the teacher. My eyes darted back and forth distractedly. Evan's desk was empty. As though washed away by the rain, every last trace of anxiety about seeing Evan disappeared, eclipsed by the fear that I wouldn't see him again. Slumped dejectedly in my chair, I started to wonder what could have kept him from coming. Ginevra hadn't come either. If they hadn't been heading to school, where had they gone? I was consumed with curiosity. The thought of the two of them together, who knows where, made my stomach burn.

Now that I had to go without it, I realized Evan's presence had a soothing effect on my mind. Like a drug, it could make the outside world and all its problems disappear. The lesson felt endless, stifling. I couldn't stop glancing at his empty desk. Trig went by more quickly, probably because he wasn't in that class with me. During lunch I chewed slowly, staring silently at my tray, resigned to Evan's absence. The only thing people at school were talking about was the fire and the little girl who'd died in it. Hearing that the rain had stopped pounding on the roof, I turned to check the sky and my heart skipped a beat when I saw Ginevra sitting at the table by the window.

I held my breath and looked for Evan, but he wasn't there with her. She was looking blankly out the window. From time to time she squinted slightly, as though trying to follow a conversation. A crazy thought, since no one was sitting near her. She was so distracted that I stared at her for a little longer than I should have. Just then, she raised her eyes and looked straight at me like she had that morning. Unable to hold her gaze, I immediately looked down at my tray and felt the blood rush to my cheeks. Part of me felt guilty about the pang of desire that struck me whenever I thought of Evan, even though I knew he was with someone else.

The fact that Ginevra didn't glare at me with anger or jealousy like she should have just made me feel worse. Overcome with guilt, I shyly got up from my chair, said goodbye to the others, and left the cafeteria, feeling her cold gaze on me the whole time.

The newfound hope of seeing him during Spanish class wiped away the guilt the moment I escaped the weight of Ginevra's eyes. My instinct seemed to be behind it, not my heart. Or more likely, it was just a selfish side of myself I'd never known I had. Breathing in Evan's presence was becoming more and more of a necessity. It was strange how my desire had completely eclipsed the embarrassment that had made me want to avoid him. My blood longed for the emotions he aroused in me, like a junkie desperate for his next fix, well aware of how harmful it was. Who knew why?

I knew.

He can't live without it. Just like I couldn't go without Evan any more. When he wasn't there, I felt I couldn't breathe, even though I realized how crazy the feeling was. *Supernatural.* Could some dark magic have indissolubly connected me to him?

"*Encantado de tenerla entre nosotros,*" Mr. Wilson welcomed me to class with a hint of sarcasm as I walked to my desk, hanging my head.

"*Siento llegar tarde,*" I apologized sheepishly.

I considered Mr. Wilson an excellent teacher. He had the rare ability to keep us constantly interested, one way or another, and gladly interrupted his lesson to laugh with us students and speak openly, often touching on topics that weren't strictly scholastic.

Today, though, not even Mr. Wilson's Spanish class would be enough to take my mind off Evan. His absence filled the whole classroom. There was no reason for me to keep hoping he'd show up. Evan simply wasn't coming today. I forced my brain not to think about him any more, but my heart was screaming its dissent.

My last class of the day was photography, and the darkroom was located right off the school lobby. It was one of my favorite courses because it relaxed me. I'd always loved it, and in the half-light of the darkroom I could focus on my thoughts.

Before the teacher turned off the lights, I smiled and said hello to my friend Rhiannon Patterson, a sweet girl I'd known for a few years whose passion for the subject I shared. She was very pretty, blond, and had a captivating smile. Rhiannon had a knack for photography and was one of the most promising students in our class, even if my pictures weren't bad. The first time we'd seen each other was through the lenses of our cameras when we were thirteen. I'd been at the lake with Peter and he asked why I'd started laughing for no clear reason and, on top of that, why the girl with braided hair walking over to us was laughing too. She took us to her house and showed us her collection of shots in the darkroom in her basement. My parents had promised we would set up our own darkroom, but I was starting to suspect it would never happen. It was too expensive, and at home there were always more important things we needed to buy.

In the pitch dark, I handed Faith her camera. For the course, the school lent us film cameras. Once I'd sealed my film reel inside the lightproof canister in front of me, the teacher switched on the red light, making my classmates look like anonymous, sinister shadows. One by one, I added and removed the developer, stop bath and fixer. Each of us had taken pictures of animals. Mr. Madison was going to award extra credit to the most evocative one. My photo was of a squirrel on a tree branch that hung over the lake. Faith, instead, had shot a close-up of her beautiful horse, Hope. I'd always liked how their names sounded together. Faith and Hope.

The smell of the chemicals was so strong it was going to my head. I gave my canister to Mr. Madison, who was rinsing them for us in the sink, took a strip of negatives I'd developed the week before, and began to enlarge one of the shots on a sheet of photo paper.

I kept thinking about Evan, wondering when I'd see him again. I shivered, my skin tickled by a puff of cool air, though the door was closed. I went back to focusing on my project. *To focusing on Evan.* Why did I keep thinking about him so incessantly? Like a poison, he'd gotten into my mind and I couldn't think straight any more. Just then, I felt him right there beside me. Instinctively, I turned to check, even though the very thought was ridicu—.

I froze. My senses hadn't been fooling me. Evan really *was* there beside me. My heart raced. Why was he there? Was he taking photography too now? Even more, how had he gotten in? I was sure he hadn't been there when the teacher switched off the lights. I stared at him, incredulous, and he stared back at me insistently. With unexpected boldness, he stroked my arm, making me tremble. My heart was pounding in my chest. He took my hand in his and studied our entwined fingers. He moved so close to me it left me dazed.

Overcome with emotion, I tried to control my breathing. As I bathed the paper in the chemicals and hung it to dry, he followed my movements, accompanying my hands. I looked at the negatives but couldn't concentrate. His fingers continued to caress my arm and then slid down to clasp mine. He was slow, as if studying every tremble caused by the touch of our hands. He brushed the tip of his nose against my neck and I felt him draw a deep breath, right behind me, sending a shiver down my spine.

I closed my eyes and surrendered to emotion. "What are you doing here?" I murmured softly.

He was silent for a moment but finally answered, "I can't resist you."

I trembled at the sound of his whisper in my ear.

"Did you say something?" Faith's voice snapped me out of my spell.

"Huh?" I said, embarrassed. "No, I—" I spun around, shocked. Evan was gone. *How was it possible?*

"Hand me the photo paper, would you? Hey, what's wrong? You see a ghost?" she joked, but I didn't hear her.

My heart beat wildly. I took a breath, but the smell of the chemicals made me dizzy, as did the red light and my classmates' shadows. On the verge of fainting, I ran out into the hallway, into the light. The other students' protests about my having opened the darkroom door followed me, but I didn't care. I ran into the bathroom and leaned against a sink, gripping the gray plastic, my head down.

It was like I'd experienced a waking dream. But I couldn't tell if the genre was horror or romance. Evan's presence was everywhere. He was like a ghost who'd come to haunt me, to hound me.

I turned on the faucet and splashed water on my face. It was all so crazy. Evan hadn't even come to school today. Was my desire for him actually so strong it was causing hallucinations? My mind refused to accept that he'd really been there, but my body was my witness. He'd touched me. His touch had been real. Every part of me had sensed it.

I can't resist you.

And his voice? Had it all been in my head again? Ever since Evan had come into my life, everything had become bizarre and irrational . . . but full of amazing emotions.

I stared at my reflection, the blue doors of the stalls in the background. I'd just lived through that scene with a perfect stranger from the movie *Ghost*. And it had been so beautiful and magical. I was going crazy. It was official. And yet, why should it matter if an event was real or dreamed, if you really experienced it? No matter what you called it, it existed. It was an emotion you felt. A memory you kept.

No matter what had happened, I'd *felt* those sensations.

"Gemma!" Jeneane called out, catching up to me in the rain.

"Hey," I replied, raising a hand, totally lacking in enthusiasm.

"So what's up with you anyway?" The bitterness in her voice took me completely by surprise. "You're getting weirder and weirder," she scoffed, looking at me almost like she didn't recognize me any more. I hadn't thought about how the change in my behavior might come across to the others. "I'm not the only one who thinks so, you know. Pete and the others have noticed too. You come to school, but it's like your mind's a million miles away. Just make sure the teachers don't notice or your GPA is going to nosedive," she warned me, not troubling to hide the hint of sarcasm in her voice.

"I'm a little tired, that's all," I said.

"Faith told me you ran out of photography class. What happened?"

"Nothing. Nothing happened. I'm just a little stressed. I haven't been sleeping very well lately." Deep down, it wasn't a total lie.

Unlike Jeneane, I'd never been very talkative. My replies bothered people because they were too monosyllabic. Her vocal cords, on the other hand, were like an electronic device that worked nonstop. One word activated her voice, and it just kept going until you were desperate to figure out how to switch it off. And most of the time her brain didn't seem to be connected to it. Sometimes it was so hard for me to follow what she was saying that I'd just nod my head without even trying to understand the gist of the conversation. If there was one, that was. Instead, I'd often focus on her breathing, wondering when she would stop to take a breath. It was fascinating, her extraordinary ability to fill her lungs with such an incredible amount of air.

"So are you coming or not? Hello?!" Still blathering, Jeneane was waving her hand in front of my face. I realized I'd done it again.

"Where?" I asked, re-entering my body.

"There! This is exactly what I'm talking about. I bet you didn't hear one word of what I just said," she complained, exasperated. I looked at her guiltily. "We're going to the lacrosse game tonight," she explained. "Everybody's going to be there. Are you coming or not?" she asked, probably for the hundredth time. "It means a lot to Pete," she added. Where was Peter, anyway? "I bet you didn't even notice he's picked up the habit of cutting class." Jeneane said it almost reproachfully.

Pet. I was suddenly overcome with guilt. I hadn't been thinking about him at all lately. Evan had gotten into my head, driving out everything else. Regretfully, I realized Pet had begun to keep his distance from me too. Now that I thought about it, he hadn't called me for days. I tried hard to remember our last conversation, but my mind drew a blank. Was Jeneane right? Did I really seem so distant on the outside? Peter meant too much to me to risk losing his friendship. I had to call him and clear things up as soon as I could.

"Thanks for the invitation," I told Jeneane, "but I don't feel very well. I think I'm going to stay home." I said goodbye with a little wave and hurried off. I was certain the rain would be much more comforting than Jeneane if she was set on nagging me all the way home.

"Whatever!" Her exasperated voice reached me as she lined up with the other students to board the bus.

"What happened at school today, Squirrelicue? Your photography teacher, Mr. Madison, called right before you got home."

I rested my fork on my plate. "Nothing. I just got dizzy, that's all. The chemicals we use in the darkroom must have gone to my head. What did he tell you?" Did he know I'd had an imaginary love story right there in his darkroom?

"He just said you ran out of his class and didn't come back."

"Oh. Okay." That was a little reassuring. I'd hate to have to drop his course out of embarrassment.

"Now that I think about it, he didn't just call because of that. He said you'd forgotten to hand something in to him. His number's on the fridge if you want to call him back."

Shit. I was supposed to turn in the photographs I'd taken of the students during the school year. Rhiannon and I were in the Yearbook Club. In addition to the professional portraits of the students, the yearbook included shots we'd taken. The club was far from popular, since it meant a lot of work, which I didn't mind at all. I found it relaxing snapping pictures, choosing them, grouping them ... So many emotions captured forever on paper. I'd secretly immortalized moments of my classmates' lives. Candid shots were the best kind, because they showed the subjects' souls. Today had been the deadline for turning in our pictures to the teacher and I'd completely forgotten. I had to remember to call him. And I still had to think of a quote to include beneath my portrait.

After late lunch with my parents, I grabbed my backpack in search of my phone and holed up in my room. Sitting on the bed, I hugged my knees to my chest as I dialed Peter's number. The line began to ring as I drummed my fingers on my shoe, waiting for him to pick up. I'd been treating Pet so appallingly. How could I not have noticed his absence? I couldn't forgive myself.

My impatience grew with every ring. Peter had never taken so long to answer before. Was he mad at me? I couldn't blame him. I dialed the number again to make sure I hadn't gotten it wrong. The phone continued to emit its bleak tone but no one on the other end decided to take the call. That wasn't like him. On my third try, the sound of his voice calmed my anxiety. I realized how much I'd missed him, even though I'd seen him at school only the day before. Or had it been longer than that? "Hey, Pet!" I cheered, letting my excitement show.

"Oh, it's you." His voice, on the other hand, went dull when he heard mine. It hit me right in the heart. I knew it was entirely my fault. I shouldn't be giving Evan all that attention if it was going to cost me my friendship with Peter. To Evan I didn't exist. He had Ginevra. And I risked losing Peter too unless I managed to sort things out with him.

"You're not very happy to hear from me," I said sadly, hoping it wasn't too late to fix things.

"No . . . Gemma, sorry, it's not you," he replied vaguely. "I'm just wrapped up in something I've been working on." He clearly didn't want to tell me what he was talking about.

"You didn't come to school."

"Is that why you called?" He seemed to be in a hurry to hang up. "Everything's fine, thanks for asking," he said indifferently. Hearing the coldness in his voice tortured me. He'd put up a wall between us. Or maybe I'd been the one who'd done it.

"Come on, tell me about whatever it is you've been doing," I said, begging for his attention.

"Um . . . I'm not sure I should talk about it. It'd be better if I didn't get anyone else involved. Sorry, Gemma."

Anyone. The word echoed in my head. I'd become *anyone* to him. "Not even me? We've never kept secrets from each other." My tone had become almost imploring, but the words actually sounded fake to my ears. I'd been the first one to keep a secret from him. I wasn't sure now exactly what the secret was or why I'd kept it from him. Suddenly, I couldn't remember any of the stupid reasons I'd stopped confiding in Peter to such a point that I'd actually pushed him out of my life.

"You know you can trust me," I said, judging from his silence that he only needed a little coaxing.

"Okay! Okay, I'll tell you." His enthusiasm rose suddenly. "But don't think I'm crazy—and don't get angry. After all, you asked."

Get angry? Why would I get angry? "I'll remember," I reassured him. Still he hesitated. It was starting to get on my nerves. "Well? Don't keep me in suspense, Pet. What's it all about?"

"That James guy."

I almost dropped the phone. I was torn between curiosity about what Peter would tell me and anger at his contemptuous tone. "What's Evan got to do with anything?" I snapped, almost growling. It sounded more like a retort than a question.

Peter let out a groan of disgust because of the protective tone I'd taken. "Whose side are you on, anyway? Gemma, there's something about him and the others. I don't trust them. I know they're hiding something."

"What do you mean, they're hiding something? That's ridiculous!"

"I tried to look into his past, to find out what school he transferred from, but I couldn't find anything at all. It's like he doesn't even exist! The same thing goes for his girlfriend. Who are they? What are they hiding?"

I flinched. Of everything he'd just said, what bothered me most was the word "girlfriend." But there was something I was missing. "Wait, back up a second. You said 'the others.' What others? Are you talking about Ginevra?"

"There are four of them," he told me, sounding like a proud, satisfied detective who'd discovered an important lead.

"Peter, what are you talking about?"

"Evan and Ginevra aren't the only ones! There are two other guys. They're not much older than we are, I think," he explained, getting more and more excited.

"How do you know that?"

"I saw them! Gemma, I know where they live and—"

"What? You went to their house?" I said, appalled. Actually, I had no right to yell at him for something I'd done myself.

"This morning I went to school early to go running and I saw him ride by with the blond chick. I noticed they didn't stop, so I followed them in my dad's car and saw where they live. Man, you should see the place! It's this massive ancient manor. I'd never seen it there before."

I'd seen for myself how vast the estate was. "So what? What's so strange about that? I don't get it." I was trying hard to seem nonchalant, but a strange instinct was compelling me to defend Evan and his friends despite the fact that I didn't even know them.

"What's so strange about it? Gemma! Did you hear what I just said? I've definitely never seen a house there before. And you can't build such a huge place overnight."

"How can you be so sure? Maybe you'd just never noticed it. After all, you never go that far outside Lake Placid. You don't even like the forest."

"How did you know it's outside of town?" he asked quickly, catching me off guard.

I bit my lower lip so hard it almost started to bleed. "You . . . said so a minute ago," I lied.

"Gemma, I'm sure I'm right. There's something strange about them. I don't trust them. We don't know them. Who's to say it wasn't one of them who killed Mr. Lussi? Who else would have done it?"

The thought made my blood run cold. I should be trusting my best friend—I mean, this was Peter. But I couldn't ignore how upset I was that he'd accused Evan. I felt the need to flat out defend him, but I didn't dare. That would jeopardize everything. "Are you actually accusing them of murder? Don't you think you're overreacting? They're kids, like us. We don't know them, true, but that's not reason enough."

"Yeah it is, if somebody's dead. I saw something. I'm not sure of it, but—" Peter seemed to be on the verge of letting me in on something, but changed his mind. "I'm not going to pretend like it's nothing. I still haven't told you that this morning Evan went into the house with Ginevra. After a few hours, she rode out on his motorcycle. I watched the place all day long and nobody else left the house."

"So what? Ginevra turned up at school today. What's so strange about it?"

"Nothing, except that Evan just came home a moment ago."

From the silence that fell, I knew he was waiting for me to put two and two together, but I just couldn't follow him. "I don't get it," I admitted, exasperated.

"I told you nobody left the house! How'd he end up *coming back* later on?"

"Didn't it cross your mind that there might be some kind of back entrance?" As I was saying it, I realized how wrong that sounded. I'd seen the fortress wall for myself and there were no secondary exits. I hadn't even seen a main entrance. And if Peter had gotten in through that opening in the wall, there weren't many alternatives.

"I've never been more serious in my life. I'm going to find out what they're hiding. Nothing's going to stop me." Hearing how solemnly he spoke, I rolled my eyes, relieved that he couldn't see me. "And don't roll your eyes at me!" he snapped, making my jaw drop.

Thinking about it, I liked this supernatural-detective version of Peter more than his quiet, shy version. Maybe this was his way of avoiding the monotony of his peaceful little hometown life. Or, even more likely, he read way too many comic books.

"Did anyone see you?"

"Not only did they see me, one of them threatened me. Take my word for it, they're dangerous. Especially the girl. There's something creepy about her."

"Someone threatened you?"

"One of them was in the middle of an actual fistfight with Blondie when I noticed there was this other one crouching on the roof watching them. I hear a thud and I see that Ginevra's hurled the first kid against a tree trunk. The earth literally shook under my feet. Seconds later, the guy from the roof? He's right there next to me. Saw me spying on them. Asks if I'm looking for something. I'm so spooked by his reappearing act I can't say a thing, and then he mutters something that sounds like a threat."

"Well, don't forget, you were spying on them at their own home. He had every right," I retorted.

Peter ignored me. "I pretended to leave but I just hid nearby. That's how I saw Evan coming back."

"You're so stubborn!"

"I'm not afraid of them. And you might not believe me, Gemma, but I wouldn't trust them if I were you. Listen, I didn't want to say this and make the police suspicious, but the last time we were down by the lake, when you got lost, I saw Mr. Lussi in the woods. Right before I found you."

"Are you saying *I* killed him?" I asked sarcastically. I knew where he was going with this. "Peter, you shouldn't have kept it a secret!"

"Neither should you, then. He told me he'd talked to you." My heart leapt to my throat. "I kept quiet to protect you." I felt like a total hypocrite. Peter knew I'd lied to him, but he was still taking care of me, while I was stubbornly protecting some guy I barely even knew. "At first I didn't believe you'd seen someone in that spot in the woods where I finally found you, but then James showed up at school. I saw the look on your face. You recognized him! *He* was the guy you saw. A little while later, we heard Mr. Lussi had died. You don't have to be Sherlock Holmes to figure out what happened. Don't act like it didn't cross your mind. And after what I saw today, I'm even more sure they aren't who they say. Stay away from James," he said sternly. His voice softened. "At least do it for me."

I gulped. What if Peter was right? *No. What he's saying is ridiculous,* I told myself. Something in his voice as he said those last words told me I was wrong to think it was all because of his comic-book imagination. His suspicion of Evan was simply the result of his jealousy. He was just trying to prove that Evan was wrong for me. Like I didn't know that already.

"Peter, you don't have to prove anything to anyone. Just drop it, please," I begged him.

"Do you really not feel it? There's something evil about him. How can you not realize it?"

Yeah, I thought, *her name's Ginevra.* "You don't even know him," I sighed, my patience used up.

"I don't need to know him. It's something I can sense."

"And I sense you're getting paranoid. Come on, Pet, you can't be serious!"

"Goddamn it, Gemma, open your eyes! Have you seriously not noticed anything strange about those two? At school Ginevra does nothing but talk, and he never even answers her. It's like she's reading his mind. I've watched them. Even their showing up all of a sudden made me suspicious, but strangely, nobody except me seems to care."

I didn't want to admit it, but he wasn't all wrong. Lots of things had happened since I first saw Evan in the woods. Strange things that Peter didn't know about. Unlike Pet, though, I'd never really seriously considered they might have to do with him. "You're being paranoid. There's nothing strange about them!" I snapped, exasperated. And yet I couldn't completely shake the apprehension that had wormed its way into my mind.

"You're wrong, Gemma, and I'm going to prove it," he promised, not a trace of doubt in his voice.

"If you say so," I said, shrugging. There was no point in contradicting him any more.

"Gotta go. See you at the game?"

I would rather have stayed home, like I'd told Jeneane that afternoon, but I knew how much me being there meant to Peter. I owed it to him. "Of course, I wouldn't miss it for the world."

"Should I swing by to get you after practice?"

"I'll bike. See you there," I said, although it was nice of him to offer to walk me there right in the middle of his pregame concentration.

"See you later, then."

"Don't forg—" I began, but Peter had already hung up.

The conversation with Peter had taken a completely unexpected turn. A new wave of concerns had joined the ones already lapping at the shores of my mind. I began to suspect Evan really was hiding some dark secret. After all, from the very start I'd sensed something sinister about him. I'd followed some kind of primordial call all the way to his house. And then the voices, the visions. The nightmares. And Evan was connected to all of it.

Could Peter actually be right? I fell back onto my bed, my eyelids growing heavy. Could Evan really have something to hide?

EVAN

14

UNEASINESS

"Evan, finally you're back! It took you ages!" Ginevra came up to me as I forced myself to walk through the door. "Well? Don't keep me waiting, how did it go?" she asked apprehensively.

"They said no," I replied, furious. My jaw muscles ached from gritting my teeth for so long.

"I'm so sorry," she whispered, moving closer.

I looked at her, clenching my fists, overcome by frustration. I still didn't know how I'd ever manage to finish what I'd come here to do. They'd refused to pass my assignment on to someone else like I'd hoped.

"Don't worry," Ginevra reassured me, resting her hands on my shoulders. "I'll help you see this through. It'll be over soon."

"I hope so, but meanwhile we've got another problem to worry about. That guy Peter, he's suspicious."

Ginevra held back a laugh and went on, her voice filled with serious sweetness. "Yeah, I sensed that. Everyone except him stopped wondering about us. He must be immune to your thought control. In any case, he's harmless, Evan. I'm keeping an eye on him. Just remember to move your lips more at school, okay?"

"He's getting too curious. If he keeps it up I'll have to do something about it. This morning I saw him spying on the house through that hole Simon and Drake made in the perimeter wall," I told her, shooting a reproachful glance at my brothers.

"Hey, what? Can I help it if I'm a force of nature?" Drake said, flashing me a sardonic smile.

"I'll show you who's a force of nature! Bring it, you ape! I can take you anytime, anywhere!" Simon said, taking Drake's remark as a challenge and rushing at him.

"Stop it!" I yelled. I'd never been so on edge before.

"Whoa, at *ease*, soldier! Calm down! We're just having a little fun. What's up with you? Not long ago you used to have fun too. Don't you like boxing any more?" Drake said, trying to provoke me with a feint.

"At least try to be more careful. You knocked a hole in the wall, damn it! Somebody might have seen you!" I snarled, grabbing Drake's fist mid-swing and glaring at him.

"I'll seal it up personally if it'll make you feel better," he said, hearing how serious I was.

"You've wasted enough time already. Don't forget," I warned him sternly, "we can't attract attention. Things are already complicated enough as they are."

"You should tell Ginevra that. She almost uprooted a tree right in front of the kid."

"You what?!" I fumed.

"Since you're in the mood for confessions, why don't you tell him about your little chat with him?" she shot back.

Drake shrugged. "I just told the kid that if he kept holding his breath like that he might croak."

I clenched my fists. I was beside myself, but my brother seemed to think the whole thing was funny.

"You're forgetting the part where you said you could help him do it. Scared him half to death," Ginevra admonished him.

"I was really nice about it! I added 'if you want me to'!"

Simon, the wisest among us, sensed how on edge I was and shot a look at Drake to shut him up.

"Evan, relax. We noticed he was spying on us and had some fun putting on a little show for him. Who's he going to tell? Nobody would believe him. The whole town is under our influence. They barely notice us at all."

"That's not what I'm worried about," I admitted, filled with a strange anger. I fell silent for a moment, unsure whether to admit to them what I was feeling. "More than once I've had the urge to kill him."

"Be serious," said Simon reproachfully. "He's just a kid."

"Why, Evan? Because he's nosy? Or is it something else?" Drake raised an eyebrow and I shot him an icy glare. I wasn't in the mood to let him provoke me. "You know what your problem is?" he asked. "You do your duty, but deep down you've never realized how much fun it can be!" He grinned.

"There's *nothing* fun about what we do, Drake."

"There, exactly. This is where you mess up. Why can't you see? It's not a question of what we do, it's *who we are*. You refuse to look at things from the right perspective."

"And what's the right perspective? Why don't you illuminate us, Drake?" I growled, totally dejected.

"There is no Redemption. We are what we are and nobody can do anything about it. Their life flowing through you, the death you leave in its place—don't you find our power exhilarating? You're the one complicating your own existence, bro. Once you accept that, you'll start enjoying it!"

"Drop it, Drake," Ginevra warned.

"No, Drake's right," Simon interjected, "except for what he said about Redemption, of course." He panted as he dodged the occasional punches Drake continued to throw at him. "Evan, there's nothing different about the girl, and in any case it shouldn't matter to you. You've always seen our situation more clearly than the rest of us. Don't start doubting it now. You've always said one day all this will make sense. Hell, what happened to your Spartan nature, soldier? What's keeping you from seeing things objectively? Follow orders and don't think about it. Nothing simpler than that."

Having a serious conversation with my brothers when they felt like kidding around was far from easy. Their behavior usually didn't annoy me, but today I couldn't take it. I was nervous, irritable. I felt the weight of the world on my shoulders.

Honestly, I didn't have an answer to Simon's questions, and handling the situation had never seemed harder. "Not this time," I sighed, exhausted, staring at the floor. "Not with her."

Ginevra cleared her throat. "Speaking of which, Evan, there's something you should know." Her tone captured my attention. It even made Simon and Drake stop fooling around. "Peter isn't the only one who showed up here," she admitted, looking guilty. "I was in the garden," she said with unusual slowness, "on the bench out in back . . ."

"Get to the point, Gin," snapped Drake, not known for his patience.

"I was with Simon. I mean . . . we were *together*. And Gemma saw us." She lowered her eyes, feeling the weight of mine on her. "Simon had his back to her and she thought—she thought it was you, Evan. She mistook Simon for you. She's convinced you and I are a couple," she concluded, her voice full of remorse.

"Why didn't you tell me before?" I shouted.

"Why should I have? Her feelings aren't important, Evan. They shouldn't matter to you at all!"

I knew Ginevra was right. So why did it upset me to know Gemma was suffering? Her soul was so sensitive and incredibly deep. Was it the innocence in her eyes that made me worry about her, or was it something else?

"But that's not all," Ginevra continued. "For her it was only confirmation of a suspicion she'd had for a while. But don't be angry at me for not telling you before, Evan. I did it for your own good."

I held back the urge to punch a hole in the wall, then buried my face in my hands and cursed under my breath, unable to stop the flow of thoughts rushing through my brain. I didn't say anything, knowing I'd regret whatever came out of my mouth. All I could come up with were curses.

"I'm sorry," she said, sensing the anger I was bottling up. "I didn't want to make things even more complicated than they already are. You think I can't tell what mood you're in? I just wanted to protect you."

"It's my right to decide what's best for me, don't you think?" I growled, unable to hold back my resentment.

"I tried to stop her, but she ran off," she said regretfully.

"Now I get why . . ." My voice trailed off as I finally understood. "That must have been right before we ran into each other yesterday. She was so upset." I glared at Ginevra.

"Well, since we're on the subject, what were *you* thinking, Evan? What did you want to do, take her for a little spin on your bike?"

"I offered her a ride, that's all," I said, frustrated. *She'd been crying over me.* "If only I'd known it then. Fuck! Doesn't she already have enough pain in store for her?"

I felt a pang of sadness for her. I didn't want her to suffer any more than she already had to. Not because of me. If only I could prevent it, just this once. She'd given me so much. But the tears I'd seen in her eyes had been for me. I was the cause of her suffering. Yet again.

For some strange reason, I couldn't stand it. Her delicate face sprang to my mind, streaked with bitter tears. I thought she was still beautiful, even like that.

I felt the instinct to protect her, although I couldn't explain why. There was no denying I was actually here for a completely different purpose.

"Evan, by tomorrow it won't matter any more. Stop torturing yourself," Ginevra insisted, her eyes full of concern.

Tomorrow.

Was that all the time there was left? Just one more day and it would all be over. Everything would go back to normal and I'd go back to that semblance of an existence I insisted on calling "life."

"How could I not have noticed anything last night? I don't know what the hell's happening to me! I don't recognize myself any more." I buried my face in my hands wearily.

"Evan, this whole thing is insane. You can see that for yourself! You're going too far. You enroll in school, you act like you're one of them—you're living a life that doesn't belong to you! We shouldn't even have stayed in this place for so long."

"There wasn't time!" I retorted, my emotions leaving me helpless. "The most convenient solution was for all of us to stay in the same area since our assignments were all concentrated here," I said, trying to convince her. Or more likely, myself.

"No, Evan. Lie to me if you want, but don't lie to yourself. We all know why you wanted to stay here. It was because of Gemma."

Hearing her name made me flinch.

"It's hopeless, get it through your head. Snap out of it, Evan! We're what we are, each of us has responsibilities to bear. You've got to finish what you came here to do. It's not up to you to decide."

"You think I don't realize that?" I snapped, furious. I couldn't help it. Still, I wasn't mad at Ginevra, not any more. I was mad at myself, at my own nature.

"There's nothing you can do for her. We've already talked about it," she reminded me. Nothing she could say was going to get me out of the mood I was in. "It won't be much longer, time's almost up. *It's her time.* You can't change that. It's her destiny."

It was true, and we'd already talked about it over and over, but all our talk hadn't done anything to make me feel better. Less than a month had gone by since our arrival in Lake Placid. Meeting Gemma had made it the most difficult, most painful period of my entire existence. I couldn't understand why having to carry out this particular mission was so hard for me. For the first time in my life, I felt sorry. More than anything else, I couldn't figure out why I felt the need to protect her from the fate in store for her.

I sank down onto the sofa, planting my elbows on my knees, and buried my head in my hands, hiding my face, tormented.

A moment later, Ginevra came up behind me and gripped my shoulders gently. "Evan," she whispered, sounding concerned, "I'm sorry for you, honestly, but I've never seen you like this. This whole thing is destroying you."

I couldn't agree more. I was in pieces. The past month had been an interminable countdown that would soon reach its end. Just one more day, and then it would all be over. When we left Lake Placid, no one would have any memory of us. Simon would make sure of that.

And for us, everything would go back to normal.

But was that really what I wanted? Would the pain that was tearing me apart, the pain none of us could understand, would it vanish along with her in the space of a day's time?

It seemed impossible. I would never forget her face. Or her heart.

I'd never listened to my instincts, to my desires. Or maybe I'd never had any before. I'd never allowed myself to act entirely in my own self-interest.

Carrying out the missions assigned to me had always been what I'd done. Like a soldier, I followed orders. It was mechanical, nothing personal about it. But not this time, not if *she* was the target. I still couldn't figure out what was different about her.

"You're wasting your time. You'll never understand it. Stop torturing yourself," Ginevra said. Sometimes I forgot she could hear me even when no one else could.

My face still buried in my hands, I called to her in silence. *I don't know who I am any more. Please, help me,* I begged her in my thoughts. No one else in the room could hear it. *I don't know what to do*, I admitted in anguish.

I heard the guys' heavy footsteps as they left the room. Ginevra must have asked them to go with a gesture or a look, which sometimes accomplished even more than my powers could.

"Want the truth?" she asked cautiously.

Please. I looked up, miserable.

"I think you made a mistake in getting so close to her. You should have dropped it when you had the chance. Instead, you insisted on trying to find out why Gemma was different. You need to stop following her everywhere. Okay, she can see you and sense your presence, so what?"

It was unbelievable. I was leading my family to the brink of exasperation. But I couldn't help it. For the first time in a long, long time, I was finally *feeling* something, whatever it was. "I just wanted a little more time so I could figure it out. Gemma's different from anyone else I've ever met. No one else can see me when I'm in my ethereal form. There must be some explanation. I've always been good at controlling people's minds, but she won't do what I say, even when I straight out order her. And when I enter her mind to visit her in her dreams, she *sees* me even though she shouldn't be able to, and *she comes up to me*, wants to touch me. I try to resist her, to ward off the urge to experience it all, but I end up losing control every single time and giving in to the desire to feel her touch. I'm being driven by who knows what remote instinct I thought I'd buried over all these centuries. When I'm with her I just can't control myself. You wouldn't understand. I know I should stay away from her, but I can't. No one has ever touched me before." I grabbed my hair, frantic. "God, it feels amazing." I squeezed my eyes shut, overcome by foreign, totally incomprehensible emotions.

"I wonder if she would have the same effect on the others, too," Ginevra whispered to herself. "We could ask Drake to—"

"No!" A fire suddenly flared up in my chest. "No one goes near her."

I was surprised by my own tone. It had been a warning.

My mind was out of control, passing through the gates of time, moving backwards to the day we'd first met in the woods. The four of us had just arrived in Lake Placid. I'd been watching Gemma pet her dog, thinking I was invisible to her. But then she'd turned toward me like she could see me. The idea seemed ridiculous—there was no way she could possibly see me in my true nature—but she kept looking in my direction. She'd kept looking *right at me*, her eyes locked onto mine.

If Gemma had shown up only minutes later, she might have discovered my dark side. The predator. The Executioner.

The man's heart was supposed to give out—a natural death, like many—but I'd made a mistake. Gemma had left me so confused that I'd ended up taking it out on him. I'd broken his neck. It was brutal. And because of it, his death had seemed suspicious.

How was it that I'd become so desperate?

At first I was only confused; the mystery made me curious and awakened my most deeply buried instincts. I'd never felt so electrified over anything. *She could see me.* I was fascinated and scared at the same time. For four whole weeks I'd limited myself to watching her from afar, trying to figure out what made her different from anyone else I'd ever encountered.

Why was she able to see me? The question haunted me.

I'd followed her everywhere from a distance but learned nothing. Only in dreams had I let myself get close to her. Even then, she shouldn't have been able to sense my presence, but she did, and each time I'd felt something new, something different. Deep down, there was a part of her that was afraid of me, although she fought it. I'd realized it that night on the cliff, the first time I'd entered her dreams.

Ever since then, I'd been irremediably connected to her. She fascinated me—I couldn't stay away. I had to find out what was different about her. I had to get close, to try. Before it was too late. Over time, the feeling had changed until it slowly consumed me. Confusion, astonishment, and curiosity were soon replaced by guilt, suffering . . . and pain, when I realized I wasn't ready to be separated from her yet. Without realizing it, I'd removed the mask of the black knight I'd always worn, while allowing strange, soothing sensations to take me over. Like a lost child, I'd wandered into those big, dark eyes that looked at *me* like no one ever had before. It couldn't end like this.

"There's nothing you can do to prevent it. Don't you realize how crazy this all is? You even dragged me into it by forcing me to enroll at her school," Ginevra said, interrupting my train of thought.

Since Ginevra could read my mind, keeping secrets from her was virtually impossible. Though I'd practiced shutting off my thoughts to her a few times, I'd never worried about sharing them with her. No one could have asked for a more loyal, more reliable confidante. She was more than a sister to me. Blood bonds weren't always indestructible, whereas ours was. Ginevra was my whole family, along with Simon and Drake. I owed everything to them.

"I wanted to understand," I told her, "to figure out what's different about her. After the first day, I realized I couldn't do it without your help. You know that."

"During the day, maybe, but not at night. Thoughts can lie, they can hide the truth even from the person thinking them if they aren't fully aware of what's going on. The unconscious mind, on the other hand, doesn't lie—and only *you* have the power to interpret it. You can read *inside* her. When it comes to that, your power's stronger than mine."

I clenched my jaw, thinking about how spending a whole night with Gemma was never enough for me. I wanted more time so I could understand her—so I could understand myself. So I could discover the reason for my longing to be near her. I found myself spending all day long anxiously waiting for night so I could be with her without reservation, even if her dreams were so turbulent. And I was always disappointed when the first light of day caressed her face and I realized our time together was about to end.

"For the millionth time, what can it possibly matter?" Ginevra said, responding to my thoughts again.

I sighed, inconsolable. "It matters to me." During one of our nights together I had realized how wrong it was, but Gemma's promise that she wouldn't ask me anything as long as I stayed there with her had changed my mind. I would inevitably have to give her up; I might as well enjoy the emotions until the moment came. But the more time I spent with Gemma, the more I realized how hard it was going to be to let her go and give up all these new sensations.

"Plus, you've got to stop staring at her all the time. It confuses her."

"It's just that I can't understand her power."

"She hasn't got any powers! Can't you get that through your head?" Ginevra groaned, exasperated.

"She has power over me. You were the one who noticed she could hear my voice in her head. Even my thoughts are so drawn to her I have no power over them. Don't you see how weird that is? When I'm with her I lose all control. Yesterday I even followed her into her house," I admitted wearily.

"Evan!" Ginevra gasped in disapproval.

"There was nothing I could do. I couldn't help it. I tried to control myself, but it was no use. Then she saw me in the mirror and it scared her. I had to blow a fuse in her bathroom so it wouldn't happen again."

In the next room, Drake let out a snicker, which quickly turned into a stifled gasp. Simon must have punched him to shut him up.

"I did something even worse," I admitted. "This afternoon I visited her at school, but this time I let her see me. I lowered my guard, and on purpose."

"In front of everybody?" Ginevra snapped. "Have you completely lost your mind?"

"I couldn't resist. It was going to be the last time. I thought I would never see her again, after my request to the Màsala. But they wouldn't let me abort the mission." The game had already begun. Maybe that was what was driving me out of my mind. I couldn't bear it. All I'd had to make sure of was that she didn't turn in her photographs, but I'd chosen the self-centered way to do it. I'd wanted to have a little more of her before letting her go.

"For her own good, you should make her forget you. You've got to stay away from her, Evan."

"I *don't want* to stay away from her." I gulped, suddenly realizing what I'd said. What was happening to me?

"Do you know the consequences she's going to suffer if you keep this up? She's going to wait for you. Her soul's going to keep searching for you but it'll never find you. She'll have no peace, and for all eternity. Is that what you want for her?"

No, it wasn't, but even so, I couldn't control myself. Was I really so selfish? I ran my fingers through my hair as though it might wipe away the pain. "I need to understand why Gemma has this power over me. I know she's different, but it's not just that. Something's happening to both of us. It's been that way right from the start, like some sort of chemical reaction. It draws us together no matter how hard I try to resist. It's so intense it's almost unbearable sometimes. I thought I'd eventually manage to control it, but it's only gotten worse. My body, my powers, my mind . . . nothing belongs to me any more when I'm with her. It's like everything is shifting toward Gemma, like my spirit's surrendering to her, surrendering to this overwhelming power. It's like I'm not the one guiding it any more. Maybe my instinct is."

"Or your heart," Ginevra said in a barely audible whisper.

A shudder ran down my spine.

What was she trying to say? I didn't even remember having a heart. For centuries it had been crushed, buried beneath an empty existence. I'd forgotten myself, like ruins grayed with time, oblivious to the power of certain emotions. I didn't think I was still capable of experiencing them. Maybe I never had been, even before.

I'd seen countless eyes fill with desperation, pain, resignation, even love at times, but had always observed them as a detached spectator. They were distant feelings that never reached me. I'd always felt like a blade of steel that could reflect emotions but not absorb them, like metal does with light. Then along had come Gemma, throwing everything into confusion.

"I remember the first time she touched me," I murmured, losing myself in the memory of that dream. She'd been able to see me, but could she have physical contact with me too? The question had soon turned into a longing to know the answer, so I'd tried, and my world had changed the instant our palms touched. I never would have believed such intense emotions existed if the touch of her hand hadn't pierced my heart.

"She was sorry for me, can you believe it? She didn't even know who I was. She had no idea what I was capable of or what I might do to her. But she was worried about me anyway. She could read the confusion on my face, and I hadn't even said a word to her. How could she have known? The more I fought that connection, the harder I tried to escape it, the faster I went back to her. I followed the impulse against my will. I couldn't resist. For centuries, all that's mattered are orders. But now I'm taking orders only from her. It's like I *have* to be near her, to feel the warmth of her touch. I can't describe the feeling that runs through me when she's near. When she touches me. Why? What's happening to me? Is this my punishment? Or maybe it's some test that God is putting me through. Do you think this is my apple? Do you think Gemma is my forbidden fruit?"

I looked up at Ginevra in search of answers no one could give me.

"I don't know," she said without the slightest hesitation, her voice hard. "But you can't afford to give in to the temptation. Evan, you've got to come back to your senses. This whole thing has gone way too far. I'd be the first one to suggest a solution *if only there were one*. You're losing sight of who you really are and you can't afford to do that. You're an Executioner, remember? You need to focus on yourself and the mission you've been given."

I stared at the floor, overcome with frustration and the longing to live in another world. A world where I wouldn't have to hide my true nature. A world where I wouldn't be forced to carry out that damned execution order. Not my world. Not this one. But a place like that didn't exist. I felt trapped in a maze with no way out, where all paths led back to her.

"Face it, Evan: in a few hours Gemma's going to be just a memory. Accept the inevitable," she insisted, leaving no room for hope. "I want to make sure one thing's clear, Evan." Ginevra looked me in the eye. "It's not *you* that's going to kill her."

I shuddered when I heard her say it out loud. "Yes it is," I said. I was exhausted from the agony that hounded me. "I just wish it weren't true."

"You can't protect the person you have to kill. You can't deny who you are," she said, walking out of the room, her words echoing behind her.

The silence was short-lived. My brothers instantly strode in from the next room.

"The problem is that you're thinking about it too much." Drake plopped down onto the sofa beside me. "What do you care? She's just a mortal, and after tomorrow you'll never see her again. You just need to find a way to pass the time between now and then."

"You can't jeopardize everything because you feel guilty, no matter how unusual the situation is," Simon added.

"You know the name of the game: blood spilt, no guilt," Drake insisted, as though his words could change how I felt. "We can't afford to pity them, and up until now you've never had any problem with that. You've always been a perfectly emotionless Executioner."

"I don't need you to run through a list of my finer points, okay, Drake?" I snapped in frustration.

"All I'm saying is that even if the girl's making you feel something now, it doesn't mean anything. You always take things too seriously. You should learn to love it. Just enjoy the moment and get rid of her anyway!"

"*Enjoy the moment?* So I should act like you and go around seducing doomed souls right before taking their lives?"

"Can I help it if I'm irresistible?" he said, raising an arrogant eyebrow.

"Drake, we're more than that. We're their fate."

"That's not true! Their fates have already been written. In a sense, we're a gift. Is it so wrong to help them have some good clean fun before they die? Think of it as their last wish."

I forced a smile, masking my frustration. "And you'd be that wish?" I asked him.

Drake grinned, a cocky look on his face. "Most times I am."

"Would you cut it out already?" Ginevra groaned. "This conversation's going nowhere. I've already heard it a million times."

"She's right. Enough with the chitchat. I know what'll help. You need to remember who you are," Drake said, standing up and gesturing for me to follow him. His smile said more than his words.

I was feeling more and more nervous. I'd dragged my entire family into my own personal hell. I followed him without even thinking. Wherever he meant to take me, I decided it didn't matter. I just wanted to take my mind off the thoughts that had been gnawing at me for a month now.

"I'm coming with you," Ginevra said, having read his mind.

"Forget it. Guys' night out, so unless you know some magic spell to grow yourself a new toy between your legs . . . I mean, unless you've done that already."

"You're disgusting!"

"True, but that's what you like most about me." He winked at her and Simon glared at him. "What'd I say?!"

"Believe me, she's just fine without a toy," our brother shot back.

"No doubt about that. The two of you could wake the dead when you're at it."

"Careful," Ginevra said, slapping Drake on the shoulder. "I could always decide to make *your* toy disappear."

"You wouldn't dare," he said, but his laugh didn't completely mask the fear in his voice that she might actually be able to do it.

"I wouldn't provoke her if I were you," I told him.

Seconds later we were downstairs, our motorcycles roaring beneath us and our headlights shining on the garage door as it slowly opened.

GUYS' NIGHT OUT

The club was packed. The music we'd begun to hear five blocks away was nothing compared to what hit us when my brothers and I walked through the door. In his hopeless attempt to distract me, Drake had taken us to a nightclub in downtown Plattsburgh.

It wasn't the first time I'd seen Drake carry out his orders, but I was pretty sure he'd actually taken us out just so he could show off.

We pushed through the crowd, making our way to the bar. I had no idea who Drake's prey was, but judging from his watchful expression, they couldn't be far away.

I pushed my sleeves up to my elbows and waved the bartender over. "Something strong." I looked around the room: hundreds of bodies dancing frenetically under psychedelic lights.

"Hey, Evan," Drake said, pointing at the photographs on the wall behind the bar. "Didn't you take care of that guy?"

I took a closer look and recognized him. Jasper Mason. Most times we didn't talk about our assignments, but the soccer player's death had been big news all over the world, monopolizing the sports stations' newscasts.

"You could have taken that one a bit slower." Simon smiled. He'd been partly fascinated, partly amused by my encounter with the scumbag. I'd never liked rapists.

"He deserved it." I threw my head back and downed my shot, then gestured to the bartender, who refilled my glass.

I'd chosen a gruesome death for Mason, but he'd definitely asked for it.

We knew the exact place and time when our orders were to be carried out. As for the means, however, I sometimes gave myself some wiggle room. "Someone had to make him atone for his sins." His mind had been dark. Sometimes I wondered how filthy souls like Mason's could deserve redemption. If it had been up to me, I'd have let him suffer for his sins. Evil wouldn't have spared him for long. But then I told myself that, all things considered, it was for the best: a soul had been reclaimed rather than lost.

And at the end of the day, forgiveness had nothing to do with me.

"Your idea of a good time," said Simon.

"Definitely," I replied, smiling as I remembered the terrified look on Mason's face.

Drake had been quiet this whole time. I turned toward him and noticed his concentrated expression. He was listening. He turned to face me, looking determined.

Whoever his prey was, they must have arrived.

A shrewd smile on his lips, my brother nodded in his target's direction. It only took a second for me to spot her: a spirited blond who was going wild on the dance floor. She wore a gray see-through top with a plunging neckline and tight pants that showed off her toned legs. Her lipstick was a very bright shade of red, probably an attempt to draw attention to the rest of the package.

Despite the distance, I perked up my ears to hear her conversation, isolating her voice. All the other noises in the club went silent. The girl sounded anxious. "You got it? C'mon! Don't tell me you didn't bring it," she groaned. I'd seen a lot of girls like her. Most of the time it didn't end well for them.

"Would you chill, Selina? My buddy's not here yet. Which means you still have time to reconsider. You sure it won't be too much for you? There's always coke. What kind of friend would I be if I didn't warn you?"

"Since when did you ever worry about me?" she shot back, annoyed. "First you say it's like heaven on earth and then you refuse to show me the way there?"

Selina should have felt a shock run through her when she pronounced those words, but she had no idea her wish would soon come true, and in the most terrible of ways.

"All right, if you really want to. Just don't blame me when you're going through hell tomorrow morning." The boy was still reluctant. "If your brother finds out I was the one who got it for you, I'm dead," he grumbled.

"Don't be paranoid, he's not gonna find out! Axel, take the money and focus on having a good time!"

"Okay, Selina, but just this once. And don't forget: I warned you."

Axel walked away from his friend.

Simon, Drake, and I exchanged knowing glances. Having warned her wouldn't be enough to spare him the remorse. Guilt would consume him for the rest of his life.

Selina had started dancing again, sandwiched between two guys, probably total strangers, who were grinding against her to the music. Once in a while she'd look around for her friend, who was keeping a low profile, leaning against the wall in the darkest corner of the room.

I had Axel pegged in no time: he was the type who surrounds himself with beautiful girls just for the fun of entertaining them. He wasn't very tall or particularly good-looking, but his dark complexion and the scar running along his eyebrow made him look like a damned soul in search of atonement. Meanwhile, Selina's girlfriends had bought beers, which they drank straight from the bottle as they made their way through the crowd, their hips swaying.

Suddenly I froze, sensing a hostile presence. My eyes darted to my brothers and saw they'd sensed it too. We weren't the only ones out looking for fun tonight. I glanced back at the dark corner and a shudder ran through my body.

Evil was preparing to attack.

No one except my brothers and I could see it as it tried to corrupt the boy's soul. Would Axel resist Temptation?

"This is the second time this week." Another guy, taller and more muscular than Axel, had walked up to him. Despite all the noise, I heard them clearly, as though no one else were in the club.

"It's not for me, it's for a friend."

"Who, the hottie you were talking to? If you think you're going to tap that after giving her this, you're kidding yourself."

"I've already tapped that. Besides, it's none of your business, Chad. You gonna sell it to me or not?"

"I don't know, how old is she? At least tell me she's not a minor."

"What, you got a conscience all of a sudden? She's twenty-three. Or maybe you're just asking because you want to tap that yourself."

Chad looked like a bouncer. The two of them must have been pretty tight, because Axel didn't seem intimidated by his muscles.

"What would I want with a bitch like that? I'm just sorry for you, man, 'cause you're gonna have to take her home all messed up."

"Fuck! If her brother catches me he'll kill me."

Chad rested his hands on Axel's shoulders. "What are you doing, man?" he said, sounding almost fraternal.

"Don't get yourself into trouble for a bored little slut who just wants to party and screw. This is strong stuff and she's just a kid, for fuck's sake!"

The dealer had managed to get through to the boy's conscience; Axel seemed to be on the verge of changing his mind. But he didn't, because a stronger voice was whispering its dissent inside him. The voice of evil was laying claim to him. Though Axel was unaware of it, heaven and hell were contending for his soul at that very moment. Only his decision could save him.

"It *is* a lot of money," he said, reconsidering. Suddenly he seemed to lose all his qualms; evil had whispered its promises to him. "Sorry, man, she paid me up front."

I gritted my teeth. Axel had made his decision. The wrong one. He'd given in to his personal temptation.

The Màsala held people's lives in their hands, but not their souls. They decided how long humans would be on earth, but their destinations depended on the people's own decisions, a fact they were less and less aware of.

When Axel's time came, it was more than likely he wouldn't find one of us waiting for him.

"I'm up." Drake threw back another shot and strode toward Axel, who was hurrying back to Selina. Drake collided with him and the boy tumbled to the ground.

"Hey! Watch where you're going!" Axel shouted, groping around on the floor in search of the baggie containing the yellow tablet that had slipped out of his hand. He took one look at Drake's build and instantly fell silent, shooting to his feet and holding his hands up defensively. Drake flashed a cunning smile and looked him in the eye. His voice was low and persuasive, his words commanding: "I'm not really here. You never saw me. You gave Selina the ecstasy, but you're tired, you overdid it with the stuff, and you can barely stay on your feet. Take a taxi home and sleep until tomorrow. When you wake up, you'll have a lot to feel bad about."

Axel nodded, hypnotized by Drake's voice as he continued to look him in the eye. Controlling humans' minds was one of the things Drake enjoyed most. Axel turned and disappeared into the crowd.

Drake leaned down and picked up the pill from the floor. When he straightened up again, his appearance had changed. He pulled the hood up over his head and strode over to Selina in his new body.

"Axel, finally!" she shouted.

"Good things take time." It was Axel's voice that had spoken, but I knew it was my brother in the guise of the boy. An Executioner. Just like me. Drake's ability to change his appearance was useful for his missions, but he often used it just to have fun.

Axel held the tablet out to Selina.

"Can I trust it?" She looked confident, but I heard a slight tremor in her voice, almost like she'd recognized the shadow of death lurking beneath his hood.

"Quality stuff." He winked at her reassuringly.

She popped it into her mouth and swallowed. "Outta my way! I'm gonna take over the world!" She let out a yell and grabbed a bottle of beer from her girlfriend, who was shaking her thing on the dance floor.

Axel turned around and Drake's face reappeared as he walked back to me, grinning. "Kids today! They just don't know how to have fun." He leaned against the bar and drained the contents of my glass, the hood still over his shaved head.

"But it seems you do," I shot back. He grinned again, a familiar glimmer in his eyes. The predator inside him was preparing for the hunt. He'd laid his trap; the dirty work was yet to come.

"Feel free to take notes, bro," he said, grinning even more broadly.

I'd always considered my missions an unavoidable duty. They'd never caused any reaction in me other than indifference or a sense of obligation. For some strange reason, though, Drake found them fascinating. A dangerous game in which others always paid the price.

"My idea of fun is a little different from yours," I said.

"Give it up, Drake." Simon, who'd been elsewhere, walked up behind us. "You'll never convince him."

"You're telling me! You two are both hopeless. Still, I felt it was my responsibility to try."

I shook my head and Simon laughed. We saw things very differently from Drake, who would never understand our faith in Redemption.

"For the last time, there's nothing fun about bringing a human being's life to an end," I said.

"Wanna bet?" Drake smirked, knocking back another shot and slamming the glass down on the bar. He walked off, suddenly looking ravenous as headed toward his victim.

"He's still convinced there's no salvation for our kind."

"It's a lost cause." Simon shook his head, half amused, half worried, about how lightly our brother took his responsibilities as a Subterranean. "One day he's going to wind up in trouble."

"It's just his perverted tastes. Just because we're not crazy about killing people doesn't mean we don't know how to have a good time," I said.

Simon raised his glass in a toast. "*I* can't complain." He tried to conceal a smirk, but it was obvious he was referring to Ginevra and the overwhelming passion they shared.

"Low blow." I clinked the rim of my glass against his. "My idea of a good time can't compete with yours, but if you ask me, no execution order could be as thrilling as a late-night race." I'd had more fun on our ride there than I'd had since we'd set foot in the club.

"That a challenge?"

I shrugged, tempted by the idea. "Unless you're backing down—"

"I never back down, you should know that by now."

"No handicaps."

Simon thought it over: we wouldn't be able to use our powers during the race and he knew I was unbeatable on the road, but he couldn't refuse.

No rules. No limits. Only the road, the wind, and the roar of our engines. I couldn't have asked for anything more.

"I'm in. Let's wait for Drake and see if you can beat not one but two of us," he said. "That is, unless he gets carried away with something else." Simon nodded over my shoulder in our brother's direction.

I turned to look. Drake was in the middle of the dance floor, surrounded by Selina and her girlfriends. "He's going for it, for sure," I said, shaking my head.

Selina was sensually grinding her body against his, clearly trying to seduce Drake, who was holding her by the hips.

"If I didn't know how this was going to end, I'd leave him here to enjoy the evening," Simon remarked.

"Doesn't matter," I said, shrugging. "I'm sure he'd find a way to have fun even without Selina."

I watched them dancing in the crowd. Drake seemed so at ease among humans, almost like he was one of them. But then again, he was used to putting on whatever mask would work most to his advantage. It was just another disguise, even when his appearance didn't change.

Even so, Drake hadn't forgotten the role he was there to play in the girl's life. He'd just decided to take advantage of it. When the time came, the Soldier would carry out his mission without fail, because for our kind, no matter what your mood was when duty called, orders were all that mattered.

I smiled. For the first time I was fascinated by my brother's way of doing things. He was running his lips down her neck, his hands exploring her bottom.

Confusion was still churning inside me, but watching Drake took my mind off it for a while. I knew my respite wouldn't last long, though. Gemma's time was drawing nearer and nearer, and soon I'd have to reckon with the ghosts haunting me. The thought made my heart stop.

For centuries I hadn't felt the slightest emotion when obeying orders. Why did the only feeling I'd finally managed to experience have to be so grim? My emotions had reawakened, but in the worst possible way.

I drove the thought from my mind and focused on Drake again, hoping his upbeat spirit would be contagious. Selina was stroking his forearm. "You never told me your name. I don't think I've seen you around here before."

Drake lifted one corner of his mouth in a half smile, because she'd brushed her hand right over his tattoo, even though she couldn't see it. That was our curse, and soon it would be hers too. "You don't need to know my name." He began to kiss her again, this time more passionately, as she moved against him rhythmically.

Suddenly, his expression changed, and his face took on a look of determination, unnoticed by the girl.

"Why don't we go someplace quieter?" Selina asked, bolder than ever. It was the drug kicking in, lowering her inhibitions. "It's so hot in here." Her speech was slightly slurred from the mix of ecstasy and alcohol. Her body lurched in a desperate attempt to resist before surrendering, but she was too wrapped up in Drake to notice.

"Sorry, babe." Drake looked at her for the first time with his eyes of ice. His grin revealed his amusement. "Time's up."

He nodded over Selina's shoulder and she turned to look. The crowd, too, had stopped moving, frozen between confusion and terror. The girl's eyes bulged as she saw the empty shell of her body lying on the dance floor.

16

PRISONER

At the club exit, Drake slapped me on the shoulder, pleased with our night out. "Tell me you learned the lesson."

"If there's one thing I learned, it's that you've got even more cheek than I imagined. I didn't think that was even possible." We left the crowd gathered around Selina's body behind. All attempts to reanimate her would be useless; Drake had already completed his assignment and helped her transition. She hadn't even noticed when her body had begun to jerk harder and harder until, no longer able to withstand the lethal dose she'd taken, it had surrendered. Had Drake actually made her death more peaceful by fooling around with her? Maybe I was wrong after all and my brother's approach offered his victim one last moment of pleasure, just like he'd always said. I knew Drake, and his main goal had definitely been his own pleasure, but was it so wrong if, in the process, he ultimately made her transition less traumatic? I couldn't answer these questions, and in the end it didn't matter to me anyway. Now that the doors of the club had muffled the music, deafening confusion had filled my head once more.

My brothers and I walked toward our motorcycles, parked at the curb, but a whistle not far away caught my attention. I looked over and recognized him. It was Chad, the dealer who'd sold the drugs to Axel. He was leaning against a car with a girl smoking a cigarette who must have been Selina's age. Without thinking, I rushed at him, grabbed him by the shirt, and hurled him into the windshield. The girl screamed as the glass shattered beneath Chad's weight.

"Hey! Are you crazy?! You wanna kill him?!" she shrieked at me over the shrill squeal of the car alarm that filled the night.

"No." I smiled to myself and stepped toward her. "It's not his time yet."

The girl stared at me, unsure whether to be afraid or fascinated. Unnerved by what I'd done—or maybe just trying to seem older—she raised her cigarette to her lips and took a drag. Without taking my eyes off her, I snatched it away. The girl coughed, surprised.

"Open your purse and take out the powder," I ordered her, and she did exactly as I said. "Dump out every last speck." My voice was deep and persuasive. Again, she obeyed without hesitation. She opened the packet, her eyes locked onto mine, and the drug scattered on a gust of wind that I'd raised myself.

"You should take better care of your health." I threw the cigarette on the ground as she continued to stare at me, hypnotized by the darkness concealed in my voice.

I turned away and a moment later she snapped out of her trance, finally free from my spell. "Asshole!" she yelled after me, rushing to help her friend, who was sprawled on the hood, unconscious. What I'd said hadn't been a suggestion but an order, and she would have no choice but to follow it.

I had no idea why I'd acted like that. I usually didn't pay much attention to what humans did. Maybe I'd just wanted to take out my frustration on the guy . . . or maybe something inside me was changing. Whatever it was, I sensed that the new emotion was *human*. At least Chad would stop doing his dirty job for a little while.

We kicked our bikes into gear and the roar of the three engines filled the street. Adrenaline coursed through my veins. I turned to Simon, ready to race, but immediately recognized the focused look on his face: he'd just received an order. "You'll have to take a rain check, right?" I groaned.

Instead, Simon smiled at me. "*Au contraire*. It's just what we needed." He accelerated and powered away, tires squealing, challenging us to follow him.

The stakes would be different, but this time we'd be having my kind of fun.

We roared down the wet streets in a heart-stopping race.

Speed always made me feel alive. I was hoping the wind would wipe away the disorienting confusion I'd been feeling. I was a Subterranean. Following orders was all that mattered. That's how it had to be. I impulsively sped up, as though to underline the conviction inside me.

Simon passed me on the curve. His Desmosedici had instantly proved its horsepower and pulled him out into the lead. He and Drake had warmed their back tires by peeling out, leaving behind a huge cloud of white smoke, but that wouldn't help them shake me off their tails. I was determined to win—not only the race against my brothers but also the battle raging inside me. I overtook Drake and with a flick of my wrist popped a wheelie. I reveled in the determination I was pursuing, but it continued to elude me.

We tended to keep a low profile when we were around other people, but when we got on our bikes that good intention went straight to hell and we usually put on quite a show, competing to see who was the most daring rider on the back roads. I let my brothers pass me and lagged behind as they tried to put more distance between us, teaming up to block my way, a clear sign of how much I intimidated them.

Drake was pushing his bike to its very limits, on the verge of losing control. Instead of using his powers to avoid crashing into the guardrail, he leaned to the right, oversteered and accelerated to top speed. Realizing he wouldn't be able to avoid impact, he dragged his hand against the ground to slow down, then cranked the accelerator to the max and shot off, howling in victory when he righted his bike.

I planned to overtake them on the straight stretch.

Simon had taken the lead and Drake, in an attempt to pass him, sped up too quickly and found himself unintentionally rising up on his back wheel. He released the accelerator and the bike slammed back down, shearing off Simon's mirror, which shattered against the asphalt. I instinctively accelerated and veered to avoid it, my back tire skidding.

I smiled because it was my turn now. Approaching a curve to the right, I sped up and passed them, taking advantage of their deceleration as they headed into the turn. I hit the brakes so hard I popped a wheelie. The second the bike touched down again, I accelerated, and Simon and Drake lost any chance of catching up with me. At each curve, my bike sideslipped beneath me. It was incredible how exhilarated it made me feel.

The roar of the engine filled my head. Right then, on that stretch of road, there wasn't room in my mind for anything else. I concentrated on the sound, how it made me feel. I swerved sharply and the bike reared up, roaring through the night. My engine was so powerful that all it took was a slight flick of my wrist to make it rise up on its back wheel. I carved such a deep turn in the curve that my elbow brushed the asphalt.

Racing made me feel powerful. Invincible. Fulfilled.

I shifted my weight forward to lighten the rear and make it skid into the curve. Oversteering, I left a cloud of white smoke behind me for my brothers as a sign of victory.

Knowing I'd soon have to face reality, I tried to escape it a little longer: I shifted down a gear and, accelerating, popped my front wheel up, driven by the powerful engine. I continued like this for quite a while, playing my wrist to keep the front wheel raised. But the faster I went, the faster that grim, tortured reality pursued me. I couldn't outrun it; it was inside me. It had taken me prisoner. I was a Soldier, but just then I felt like a hostage.

Drake pulled up alongside me, also on one wheel, and we both lowered our bikes at the same time, as if in some mysterious choreographed dance.

We pulled up even with a minivan, one of the few vehicles we'd encountered over the last half hour. In the back seat, a little boy was watching our wild race, fascinated, his hands pressed up against the window. I wondered what he was thinking, at his innocent age of five at most, without the weight of the world on his shoulders.

Simon nodded to me and I understood instantly.

The minivan was his target.

Drake pulled up in front of the van while Simon and I positioned ourselves to each side. The man driving looked confused by our maneuvers, but probably thought we were a group of thugs.

He had no idea he was about to have a blowout and that because of the wet pavement he'd lose control of his vehicle . . . and his family.

The sound of our engines echoed through the silent night. It was Simon's assignment, but I needed to feel back in my place again. I needed to remember what my duty was. What it always had been. Heartless. Merciless.

I pulled in closer to the van and delivered a sharp kick to the back tire. The impact was so strong that the minivan skidded, screeching across the wet asphalt with a flat.

The man tried to regain control, but Simon jumped up onto the seat of his motorcycle and leapt onto the hood, crouching down to look the driver straight in the eye. The van crashed to a halt, marking the end of its wild ride—and the lives of its passengers.

A trail of smoke rose from under the hood, the back tire still spinning. Drake and I pulled over as Simon finished what we'd started. I should have stayed out of it, but I couldn't help it. Tonight, desperate to change my feelings, desperate not to feel that heavy weight on my chest, I wanted to bend the world to my will.

I knew taking it out on strangers would do nothing to relieve that burden or make me go back to being what I'd always been: a Soldier, the black shadow of destiny that takes away your last breath. Devoid of emotion. Just like I was right then. I didn't feel anything. So why should it be different with Gemma?

The little boy stared straight at me, pulling me out of my thoughts. When I looked back at him, he partially buried his face in his mom's lap, still peeking at me.

She held him tight. Though she realized what had just happened, her instinct to protect her child kept her from showing her shock at the sight of her mangled body lying in the wreckage. A body she no longer inhabited.

We could sense every one of their emotions. "Come here, Logan," said Simon, but the little boy shook his head, scared.

"Mommy, why does that man know my name?" he asked after a pause.

She stroked his head reassuringly.

"I'm afraid, Mommy. Don't leave me."

The mother held him even tighter. "I'm right here, honey. I'll never leave you again," she said softly.

Simon knelt down to look the little boy in the face and stroked his temple, washing away his fear.

"Where are you taking us?" the boy asked, instantly confident.

Simon smiled. The parents looked at him, holding each other close. "To a beautiful place."

Logan smiled back at him. They disappeared, leaving the minivan on the road. Inside the wreckage lay three bodies, but not a single soul.

VENTING

I punched the thick leather over and over. The bag filled with cement rocked under my pounding, jerking on its chain. The skin on my knuckles was cracking from my brutal blows.

After Simon's execution order I'd gone home, pushing my bike to its very limits, and when the engine had reached maximum performance I'd used my powers to make it go even faster, challenging the air itself. I was like a bolt of lightning escaping the storm. The only problem was that the storm was inside me.

Strangely, the race hadn't satisfied my need to vent. Once home, I'd shut myself up in the workout room, the only place where not even Ginevra's mind could follow me. I'd taken off my shirt, wound black gauze around my palms and begun to punch. And punch.

I could have vented my frustration in my ethereal form but I decided not to. I wanted to feel the violence of each blow on my flesh in the hope of smothering another kind of emotion—a stronger, more uncontrollable one. But, as I'd feared, not even physical wounds could take my mind off the pain deep in my chest. The cuts on my hands were bleeding, but they'd disappear in a minute or two. Would I be able to recover in the same way once Gemma was dead? The question haunted me.

The answer came to me from places unknown: those wounds would never heal.

I was about to deliver another right jab when a puff of air brushed my ear. I dodged the blow, raised my hand and blocked the fist that Simon had just swung from behind me. In a second, I had him pinned against the wall. He wrenched himself free and tried to hit me again. I blocked his punches, faster and faster, until it was my turn. The workout room had suddenly become our battlefield. It wasn't the first time. My brothers and Ginevra and I often sparred for fun, but today I was driven by a completely different emotion. I wasn't sure how to define it: aggravation, rage . . . powerlessness. It was a feeling that, no matter how fast I'd ridden earlier, I hadn't been able to shake. Even the punches I was throwing had a different energy because they were coming from some part of me that I couldn't identify. Simon was attacking me more ferociously than normal, sensing my need for it.

We moved through the massive room in a dark dance, a hand-to-hand battle in which our brutal blows would have killed the strongest of humans.

Even the walls became part of our battlefield. We used them to elude each other with backflips and a range of acrobatics. Using my powers, I sent the punching bags that hung from the ceiling hurtling around with lethal precision. Simon attacked me over and over with a long fighting stick, but I dodged his blows. It was a ferocious, grueling battle that I had no intention of losing. In the challenge against the Màsala I was powerless, but in the one against my brother nothing could stop me. I felt like a swollen river confined by a levee that was ready to burst. The walls were cracking open and I was prepared to destroy everything in my way. I tried to catch Simon in a series of different holds, but he skillfully broke free and counterattacked.

"You can always say uncle when you've had enough," I sneered.

Simon ran up the wall to avoid my attack. "What, now that I'm starting to enjoy myself?" He smiled and swiftly spun me around, managing to push me down to the floor. "You upstaged me in battle earlier," he told me, still smiling. True, back on the road I'd struck the minivan instead of leaving it to him.

I swung my legs around, freed myself from his grip, and trapped him under my body. "I couldn't help it. I'm doing it right now too, in case you hadn't noticed." I leapt to my feet and pinned him against the wall. "Besides, you should change. You're a mess." His shirt was torn to shreds. He hadn't taken it off before our fight.

The door burst open, distracting me, and Simon seized his chance to reverse our positions. "I'll add it to the list of things you owe me. Right below the new mirror for my motorcycle that Drake's going to be getting me," he said, looking at our brother standing in the doorway.

"I take you guys out for a night on the town and then you don't invite me to your little party down here?" Drake said sarcastically. "Well? Who won? I'll take him. Right here. Right now."

"I accept," I answered firmly. "But let's make it two against one. I haven't finished with Simon yet."

The two of them fist-bumped in a show of brotherhood.

"Haven't you had enough?" Simon slapped me on the shoulder.

"I'm just warming up."

Simon smiled at my persistence, or maybe it was because he'd actually believed I'd vented all my rage. "Unfortunately, it'll have to be for another time. I just got an assignment. Half an hour tops and I'll be back."

"Busy day," I said, smiling to myself.

Simon had been assigned two missions in a matter of hours, but it was a pace we knew well. We were all accustomed to giving Death a hand whenever it ordered us to deliver its icy breath to the life of a mortal. The frequency of the executions varied from day to day for each of us.

"Same as usual," he replied sardonically.

We were almost always summoned to duty several times a day, but none of us saw it as a sacrifice. To a Subterranean, following orders was a badge of honor. It was a way to atone. Even so, periods of intense activity might also be followed by days—at times even weeks—of total calm. None of us could know for sure when our next assignment would turn up, although we normally didn't have to wait very long.

We received some orders months in advance, others with just a few moments' notice. Natural deaths were easier. For accidents, on the other hand, we had to plan everything, checking every little detail that would help bring the victim to their end.

"That's better," Drake said. "It'll give you guys the chance to clean up. I mean, look at you two. Christ! Were you in an arena full of lions? Go change, Simon, or your victim will think you're a zombie straight out of hell."

Simon looked down at his clothes and laughed, because for once Drake was right. I joined him, and our laughter filled the workout room. "I didn't expect such a quick surrender, but in that case I'll go take a shower."

"Not a surrender," Drake said. "Once you're back in shape we can talk."

"More in shape than this`?" I spread my arms to show off my well-trained body and make it clear he wasn't intimidating me. I was sweaty, my jeans had been torn here and there during the fight, and the cuts on my chest were already healing, but I could have beaten him with both hands tied behind my back.

"Meanwhile, I'll go check on Blondie," Drake said, just to provoke our brother. Simon pulled off his shirt and threw it at him. With a sly smile on his lips, Drake vanished from the room.

In the ensuing silence, Simon slapped me on the shoulder. "Better?" he asked. It was clear now that by fighting me he'd been trying to help me battle my demons. He'd understood my need to vent.

"Yeah, thanks." I bumped my fist against his.

It was a lie, but he had no way of knowing that. I didn't want my brothers to see me so vulnerable. I'd never been weak, but these new emotions were wearing me out.

"Evan." Simon looked me straight in the eye. "I know this mission is going to be more difficult than usual for you, but don't forget what we're fighting for. *Na svargo narakam vina.*"

Without hell, there is no heaven.

I nodded, lost in thought, and he disappeared, summoned to duty. Redemption was our promised land. Why did I have to face such a difficult trial to prove I was worthy?

Tossing a white towel over my shoulder, I walked out of the room, reaching the bathroom in my human form. I didn't want to shed my physical body, even though I was sure that was where the sensations I was feeling were coming from. They were human, even though they'd put down roots within me. Or maybe I was afraid that in my angelic form, in which everything was amplified, I wouldn't be able to bear it.

I turned on the water in the shower and pulled off my jeans. In moments, the room was filled with steam. I leaned my palms against the wall and let the water run down my back.

The image of Gemma in the shower came into my mind. I thought about how she'd closed her eyes, the way she'd pushed her hair to one side as the water flowed down her skin . . . and the longing I'd felt.

Spying on her was wrong. I knew that, but I couldn't help it.

I closed my eyes and my vision seemed to become reality. Suddenly she was there in the shower with me. I ran my nose down her shoulder, breathing in the scent of her wet skin. It was so intoxicating. I slid my hand down her side and clasped her flesh, overcome by an unknown desire. Overcome by the longing to draw her to me. I was shaken by the madness of my own thoughts.

She lifted her chin and I looked into her big, dark eyes. A shiver washed over me. I was breathless.

A knock on the door snapped me back to reality. I clenched my fist and slammed my palm against the stone wall, cursing. The wall cracked under the blow.

I shook my head, my hair dripping wet, and ran my hands down my face. I felt like I was losing my mind. I had to stop torturing myself. That new part of me trying to emerge had to be held back.

I was a Soldier. And Gemma was my target.

TORMENT

I sank down onto the sofa and closed my eyes, overcome with frustration. The night out with my brothers had helped clear my head, and I'd realized the soldier in me was still strong, even if he was crushed by confusion. I just had to give him space so he could fight it off. Or maybe I was just kidding myself and the confusion was stronger than the soldier.

I was alone. On the verge of collapse.

Ginevra was right. I knew it. I knew I had no choice. Destiny had drawn Gemma's name and bound it to mine in death.

What was I questioning, then? It was just a waste of time. I would do what I had to, no matter what. It wasn't up to me to decide. No one cared what I wanted. Someone else had already decided for me, for her, *for us.*

No, I had to force myself to accept that there would never be an "us." Her destiny was already written, her path chosen, and I had nothing to do with it. Now that I'd finally found something worth living for, I had to give it up. Could fate be any more merciless?

There was only one day left. Gemma had to die.

I would lose her forever, and along with her I would lose the feelings I'd rediscovered. I would go back to living in an empty, unfeeling, lifeless shell.

I lay there on the sofa in the dark until my eyes closed and I forgot about the inexorable passing of time.

I had no idea how long I'd been lying there. It could have been minutes, hours maybe. It felt like days. And I would have stayed there if an unexpected mission hadn't called me to duty. Another execution order to carry out before dealing with Gemma's life. Before saying goodbye to the emotions that only she triggered in me.

Maybe it was better that way, being able to distract myself, force the soldier in me to re-emerge so I could face Gemma's mission with more conviction. *With more detachment*, like Drake said.

My new victim was a boy in Kentucky. I focused on his soul and a moment later materialized where he was: a large field right in the middle of a football game. The players were all running from one side to the other but I had no doubts about who my target was. His soul was summoning me, as though it recognized me. In those few moments that preceded the passing, a mortal's soul was inexorably linked to that of the Subterranean who'd come to take it, although the person couldn't see him yet.

Except for Gemma.

I clenched my fists to drive away the thought. I had to concentrate.

The boy passed me, rushing after the player with the ball. I focused my attention on him, taking away all the oxygen around him. A few steps later, he stopped, rested his hands on his knees and gasped for air. No one took any notice of him, thinking he was tired from running.

He ripped off his helmet and threw it to the ground. I stepped over to his side to study him more carefully.

There comes a moment during every execution when the victim's fear transforms into awareness. The very instant right before dying, when the target realizes his time is about to end, that I'm there beside him . . . that Death has come to take him. It had always been an exhilarating sensation because for that brief moment it felt like his soul could sense me. For a long time, that fleeting sensation of power had been enough for me. Until Gemma had looked deep into my eyes.

I focused on him again. There wasn't a trace of oxygen in his lungs. He seemed desperate.

Without hesitating, I rested a hand on his heart and felt it beat for the last time. His eyes opened wide. He clutched his chest, crumpled to his knees and fell to the ground.

Seconds later, chaos erupted all around him.

Drake was right, feeling a mortal's life flow through you was exciting, like an adrenaline rush.

I stepped back, making way for the paramedics who'd rushed out onto the field to try to revive him. The team had gathered around the boy's body, the crowd had fallen silent . . . but he was gone.

Something caught my attention.

I scanned the crowd and my eyes locked onto Gemma's. She was staring at me, perfectly still in the stands.

A shiver ran through me. *It was her.* I couldn't be wrong. What was she doing there? Had her power led her to me? Had she seen me as I took the boy's life?

The thought scared me. It was crazy. Pretty soon I'd be taking Gemma's life too, but I still didn't want her to see the darkness that lurked inside me, Death.

"Where am I? What happened?" The boy's voice distracted me from my thoughts. His soul had definitively left his body.

I glanced at him but then turned back to search for Gemma. She was gone. I stared at the empty stands, stunned. I felt crazy. My soul had never been in such agony before. Gemma wasn't dead yet, but my thoughts about her were already haunting me like she was a ghost. What would I do once she passed on?

"Ryan! Scott! I'm right here! Coach? Help me, please! Why isn't anyone helping me?"

The boy's desperation recalled me to my duty.

"They can't," I said softly, knowing his soul would hear me loud and clear.

"I'm dead?! What happened?"

He was kneeling beside his body, but moved aside when they loaded it onto a stretcher. The thoughts of Gemma had distracted me, and I'd let him see his own lifeless body in the worst possible way. *Damn it.* How many more mistakes would I make because of her? No, it wasn't Gemma's fault. I was the one who'd lost control of myself because of her.

"I'm here to help you," I reassured him, forcing myself to concentrate.

His face lit up. "You mean you can heal me? You can make me go back into my body?" he asked, full of hope. A hope I would have to deprive him of, just as I'd deprived him of air.

"No one can do that. Life on Earth is only borrowed time. We need to appreciate the time that's given to us, because ultimately we have to give it back. And your time is up, Jimmy."

"But it's too soon!" he cried. "I'm just a kid!"

"We're not the ones who choose how long our journey lasts. But we can choose our destination. I was sent for you, to take you to a place without time. Come with me."

"Do I have a choice?" He looked around, searching for a way out.

"Every mortal soul has the right to choose. But you wouldn't like the alternative. Trust me and you'll be fine."

Jimmy peered into my eyes, drawn by the comforting spell of my voice. In my angelic form, I sensed every emotion emanating from his soul.

I held out my hand. He took it, and I felt all his fear vanish instantly. A second later, he disappeared before my eyes. His soul was safe. Nothing counted more for a Subterranean. Like every other time, I was pleased that I'd completed my mission, but it only lasted a second. A darker sensation had gripped my heart.

It was Gemma's turn. Her time was up too and I was the one who'd been sent to do it.

Gemma ran, earbuds in her ears, almost like she was in a hurry to meet her fate. *To meet me*, Death. The grim reaper that would cut her life short.

I materialized on the street in front of her and she stopped, sensing I was near. It was strange, her managing to do that. She looked behind her hesitantly and took out her earbuds, from which came a melancholy song about death and destiny. Funny how she'd picked that particular song.

Time was up.

I had to act fast or I risked going insane. The nightmare had to end. It was the only way I could find myself.

Gemma started running again and I turned my back on her. I would have liked to take her hand and accompany her on that last stretch of road, to feel the power of her touch one last time. But I lacked the courage. I decided I wouldn't watch.

I clenched my fists as Gemma's foot landed on a circular wooden platform. On my command, the wood broke into pieces and Gemma tumbled into the darkness.

There was a scream, and then silence.

I gulped. I was almost afraid to move closer, but I had no choice. I had to see my orders through to the end and have her soul pass on.

I stopped on the edge of the hole that had swallowed her up and searched the darkness.

It was a stone well and she was at the bottom of it. She stirred and I held my breath, cursing myself for making everything so difficult. She was unconscious, her face streaked with blood. I couldn't turn away. I'd made a huge mistake. Gemma was supposed to have died on the spot. Bleeding to death would be much more painful for her.

But this way we can spend a little more time together.

I instantly banished the selfish thought.

Gemma opened her eyes and looked around, frightened. Totally oblivious to the fact that Death was looming over her—in my guise. She tried to get up, but the pain in her head had left her in a daze. The impact had been brutal.

She looked up. I was petrified. I felt like a vulture staring down at its prey, waiting for it to die.

"Help! Is anyone there?" she cried. "I'm down here! Somebody help me!"

I clenched my fists at my sides, confused. Why didn't she see me? Had she lost her power? She was injured, as frightened as a caged animal. Though she continued to call out, no one was going to pass by. I'd hidden her traces; she wouldn't be found in time.

"Peter! Pet! I'm down here!!"

Hearing that name turned my insides to ice and made my muscles tremble. Once again, I felt the senseless urge to take the boy's life. All it would take was one touch . . . Why was I thinking that? It was a question with no answer.

It was strange. Gemma couldn't see me in my ethereal form, just as should have been the case from the start. But this was the first time it had happened, and I couldn't resist the urge to look at her from closer up, now that she might not have her power any more.

I materialized at the bottom of the well, hiding in the darkness. I still wasn't sure she couldn't see me, even though I'd transformed.

I stopped, staggered by intense emotion. She was crying. I clenched my fists, forcing myself not to move closer. I knew being next to her would make things worse, but maybe I could touch her one last time, to commit to memory the power of the sensations she made me feel . . .

No, that would be crazy. Ginevra was right, I was self-centered. I had to stop now and get it over with. She was right there, just steps away from me. I'd waited too long.

"Who's there?"

Her voice was so confident I almost jumped. I stepped back, hiding in the shadows. But she huddled up and turned away. She couldn't see me.

I cautiously drew closer and sat down beside her, so close I could feel her fear resonate in the air. I studied her carefully: her big dark eyes, the pale freckles left by the sun. She raised her eyes and looked at me. Or more accurately, she looked *through* me. I'd fooled myself into thinking she could see me, that her deep eyes were searching mine . . . one last time.

Instead, she rested her head against the wall and began to talk as if she were delirious, her breath halting.

I closed my eyes. I couldn't wait any longer.

"Are you here to kill me?"

I flinched and turned to look at her. I wasn't sure if she was talking to me; she seemed to have lost contact with reality. I decided I could give her one last moment of comfort before taking her away. Or maybe it was just another self-serving gesture on my part.

I wrapped my arm around her shoulders and she rested her head on my chest.

"Am I going to be okay?" she murmured in a frail voice.

I took her hand and stroked it. "Yes. You'll be fine."

Gemma smiled, reassured. "And you? Are you going to be okay?" she asked, leaving me defenseless.

I didn't know the answer to that question. It might have been the one that agonized me the most. Maybe not, maybe I wouldn't be okay. But the time for being self-centered was over.

I laid a hand over Gemma's heart.

"Evan . . ." she whispered.

My eyes opened wide.

But I'd already followed the impulse to kill her.

I woke with a start and looked around, utterly confused. *I'd been dreaming?* How deeply rooted inside me was this agony? Deep enough to shake me to the core? I was a master of dreams, but I myself dreamed only on rare occasions. I ran my hands down my face. It had all seemed so real. I'd felt Gemma's life flow inside me, but this time I hadn't felt that shiver of exhilaration from the death I'd brought her. I'd felt devastated.

The answer to the question she'd asked me; I had to accept it. Meeting Gemma had changed me. Losing her would condemn me. That's what my subconscious was trying to tell me. I'd always been so focused on the subconscious of others that I'd never listened to my own.

Even so, there was nothing I could do to change her fate. Gemma would die by my hand. Despite everything.

It was so quiet I heard every tick of the clock on the wall in the next room. It marked the time, each second more oppressive than the last.

Tick-tock-tick—tock—tick——tock.

Even the sound was mocking me by seemingly slowing its pace.

I would gladly have gone unconscious if only I could have, and eluded time entirely. But even my dreams were tortured. Trapped in an ethereal form I no longer recognized, I would have to bear every minute between now and the end. An end that, I began to hope, would come to us quickly.

"Come to *us*," I whispered, surprised by how naturally I had included myself in that inevitable end which would cut Gemma's life short. Hers—not my own. So why did it feel like I would be dying too?

I couldn't stand the idea of losing her, but if I couldn't prevent it, I might as well spare myself the agony right away. I sat there, perfectly still, for what felt an eternity before footsteps snapped me out of my trance.

I didn't need to look up to know who it was. I was well acquainted with the sound of each of my family members' footsteps. From the soft, graceful touch with which the shoes caressed the marble floor, I recognized her instantly.

Gin, you're still here?

"Sorry, I can't stand seeing you like this. You're still thinking about her." There wasn't a shadow of doubt in her voice.

"Did you read that in my mind?"

"I read it in your eyes."

I looked up at her questioningly.

"Every woman would love to see that look on her man's face. It's so clear you're thinking of her there's no need to read your mind."

"I can't do without her. I've tried to stop thinking about her but I can't, not even for a minute."

"You guys just killed off an entire family and now you're grieving over one girl?"

Ginevra was right. I didn't feel the slightest bit guilty about those people, about that little boy. Why didn't I feel anything? I'd never wondered about that before. Gemma had made me question everything. Drake had fun with it, at least, and Simon had Ginevra. What did I have? I'd never felt anything, and now I was being forced to give up the one person who'd managed to reawaken my emotions.

Maybe I was just being selfish. After all, I knew her soul would be fine. But what would become of me? I couldn't bear the thought of giving up the euphoria Gemma made me feel.

"You dreamed," she said, searching my thoughts.

"Crazy, isn't it?"

"It's human."

That's exactly why it was crazy. "What sense is there in being able to control others' dreams when you have no power over your own desires?"

"Desires often lead to perdition, don't forget that."

"I already feel lost."

"No. You aren't. And I'll always be here with you to remind you of that. Did you receive your instructions?" Ginevra's voice was cold, icy, emotionless again. A clear attempt to declare the case closed.

There was nothing I could do for Gemma. They hadn't even relieved me of the assignment so I wouldn't have her blood on my hands. They'd left me with no choice. The Màsala had been adamant. No one dared speak their name out loud. The earth had even shaken in their presence when I met with them.

Reluctantly, I forced myself to nod. None of us ever knew what the others' instructions were, but Ginevra could read them directly in our thoughts.

"Good. Gemma will leave the house to go to the school, but South Main Street will be closed off, so she'll have to take Station Street until she reaches Mill Pond Drive from the other side tomor—um, in a while," she corrected herself, looking out the window at the veil of night. I followed her gaze to the garden, filled with a darkness as grim and relentless as the wild beast lurking inside me. The monster who would take Gemma's life.

I looked at the clock for the hundredth time. Anxiety gripped me. It was two in the morning. Just five hours until the end.

My chest grew tighter and tighter as the minutes passed.

"First, you make sure she turns down that road and then you make sure the truck loses control. You know what has to happen next: Gemma will never show up at the school," she said coldly, as if the whole thing had nothing to do with us.

I was unexpectedly struck by mental images of that imminent future. They burst into my mind, stunning me, flashing before my eyes as though I'd already experienced them. Instead of sleeping in, like she would do on a normal Saturday, Gemma would leave her house early to go to the school. Destiny had wanted her to forget to turn in a project the day before. And I'd made it happen. I'd had no choice. She would take her bike, as she often did, only to find that that whole area was blocked off, closed to traffic due to a problem with the gas pipes, which I would see to myself. By manipulating the air, I would make her lose control of her bike.

I'd gone over everything countless times, something I'd never done before. Gemma wouldn't miss her appointment with Death. Her appointment *with me*.

With a wave of my hand I would seal her fate.

I visualized the truck barreling out of control from her perspective. I could almost sense the terror she would feel the second before it hit her. At exactly seven o'clock.

I saw it, her green backpack lying on the pavement, her light-colored clothes splattered with blood, her bike reduced to a twisted tangle of metal . . . and her lifeless body crumpled on the pavement.

She was so beautiful, even like that, like a precious necklace cast into the sea, sparkling as it slowly descends amid the silvery reflections of the water streaked with rays of sunlight, growing fainter and fainter until, making way for darkness, the chain settles on the sea floor for all eternity. In my mental image, her eyes were closed like they were when I watched her sleep, but her heart had stopped beating.

I looked at Ginevra. In her eyes shone the same coldness that had always shone in mine.

We can't choose what we are. But when it came to Gemma, every last trace of that coldness disappeared.

So many lives cut short, one after the other. Men, women, children. I'd never hesitated to carry out orders before. I'd never questioned my duties. I knew I was just a pawn in the hands of the Brotherhood.

Why did it have to be so difficult with her? Why had I grown attached to someone I couldn't keep? What did Gemma have that I hadn't already seen thousands of times? It was so strong it made me feel a guilt I'd never known before. And then, that yearning for her, that uncontrollable urge to surrender to the emotions she and she alone conjured up in me.

The thought filled me with a sudden longing. I had to see her again.

I wanted to be with her one last time. Wasn't I allowed to say goodbye? Wasn't I permitted to spend one last night together with her? That was a decision—the only one—that I could make for myself.

I closed my eyes and concentrated on Gemma's face in my mind. When I opened them again, I was in her room. I stood there at the foot of her bed for a while, making sure I didn't wake her.

Her dog let out a low growl from his cushion. He could sense my presence, even though he was asleep, but my scent didn't alarm him any more, not enough to wake him. I smiled. It hadn't been easy, but in the end he and I had become friends.

Gemma stirred in bed. From the way her body was tangled up in the sheets, it seemed her sleep had been restless. Her reading glasses had fallen to the floor, along with her copy of *Jane Eyre*. That book must be special to her. Judging from how worn the cover was, she'd probably read it many times. I wished I could show her my original 1847 edition of it, just to see her eyes light up with amazement.

She was so adorable. She must have nodded off while reading. I was tempted to pick up her glasses, but then I remembered how I'd frightened her that night by turning off the lights and hanging up the phone. I had no idea what made me want to take care of her like that, even in those little things. The urge was almost uncontrollable.

The walls were covered with pictures. Curious, I stepped over to look at them. There were photographs of her as a little girl, and other, more recent ones. In almost all the snapshots, Gemma was with her friend, that guy. In a few close-ups she was alone, a smile lighting up her face tanned by the summer sun. *He must have taken those.* I grunted, thinking about how Peter was always hovering around her.

When I'd seen him climbing up to her window, a strange emotion had boiled up inside me. Not even thinking, I'd clenched my fists and made the wooden slats give under his weight. I had no idea what drove me to react that way, but suddenly I hadn't wanted him to go into her room. Gemma had smiled at him and he'd tried again. I'd had to force myself to leave. If I hadn't, I might have broken his neck.

Gemma continued to toss and turn under her powder-blue sheets. With every movement, the scent of her skin rose into the air, inundating my supernatural senses. A corner of the sheet was pulled back at her waist, as was the bottom of her shirt, revealing a glimpse of the sensual dimples of Venus on her back. My breathing went almost perfectly still, as though my lungs had a will of their own.

Thin lines creased her forehead. For a second, I hoped it was because I wasn't in her dream. In any case, I decided to wait a little longer before joining her there, wanting to savor that special moment when she couldn't see me.

I took another step toward her so I could watch her from closer up. Once I was beside her, I reached out to caress her face, unable to control myself, longing for the sensation that only her skin could make me feel. It was as though it were imbued with a stimulating substance, some sweet, intoxicating poison. But her skin beneath my fingertips was so soft . . . Supple and warm.

I slowly leaned down until my lips almost brushed her ear.

"I'm here," I whispered, closing my eyes, to soothe whatever was upsetting her in her dream. I knew she could hear me, only she was capable of that.

Gemma reacted instantly, relaxing at the sound of my voice. The crease on her forehead disappeared and she began to breathe evenly, comforted by my presence.

I couldn't take my eyes off her. Despite how long I'd lived, I'd never seen such a wonderful creature before. Her dark hair was spread out on the pillow in disarray, flowing down to her shoulder. From time to time a soft lock caressed her face and I found myself gazing at it ravenously, as captivated as a thief staring at treasure. A shaft of silvery light illuminated her skin from nape to cheek. Her skin glowed like a diamond.

It took all my self-control to resist the urge to touch my lips to hers, run them along the curve of her face and taste her skin, my warm breath on her, moving down to her chin, her throat, then her shoulder, her breast that rose shyly beneath the shirt that was too insubstantial to curb my need. For a moment I was lost in that desire, that delirium, that prelude to madness.

I found it adorable, that stubborn, intense look that would fill her big eyes, as dark as black diamonds, when she searched my face, struggling to understand what was causing me such agony.

It felt like some mysterious power stirred within her when I was near. A power not even she could hold back, one that struck both of us, carrying us away to some distant place inhabited by only the two of us, our gazes forever locked. A power that deprived me of the strength to escape her.

Deep eyes full of life, as bright as stars, twinkling like fireflies in the night. Was it too much to ask that this light not be taken from them?

Gemma . . .

Whatever it was that had been troubling her faded away, leaving behind peaceful, rejuvenating sleep. For a second, I felt a pang of disappointment that I'd wiped away the uneasiness she'd felt because of my absence. Her longing for me probably wasn't as deeply rooted as mine for her.

Gemma parted her lips, shaking her head as if she'd perceived my thought, and a wave of emotion washed over my body.

God, my heart is pounding.

I winced at my own thought; I didn't have a heart, not any more. Then why did I feel the way I did? It felt like it was still there in its place, beating to the rhythm of Gemma's breathing. Like it wanted to burst out of my chest and scream with rage.

It was as though I were chin-deep in water, consumed by the knowledge that I wouldn't be able to breathe much longer. Overwhelmed by this feeling, I gasped a deep breath as though it would be my last before sinking into the abyss and losing my senses. There were still a few hours left before I would drown in pain, forever extinguishing the spark that had brought me back to life.

All my self-control was gone. My thoughts wandered aimlessly as I stared at her face, at the pure innocence of the creature before me. The creature I had to kill. Confused, incoherent thoughts dominated by savage emotions I couldn't comprehend, that I couldn't stop.

No matter how difficult it was to face the harsh reality of the unlucky star under which I'd been born, I couldn't put my emotions before fate.

After all, who was I to challenge destiny? No one.

Who was Gemma to cause me such pain?

Everything.

The answer came to me from places unknown. No matter how darkened I was by my emotions, I *had* to find the strength to battle the hidden enemy haunting me like some spiteful ghost, dissuading me from my duty. A duty I couldn't question. A duty I couldn't disregard.

Who, then, did I need to fight to drive away the pain? Myself? Unlikely. It must be coming from a stronger entity, and I no longer felt strong. I couldn't even control my own thoughts. It was definitely a powerful energy, an uncontrollable one. But if I didn't know its nature, how could I fight it and keep it from clouding my mind?

I felt like I'd gone insane.

It was getting harder and harder to resist that uncontrollable force I couldn't name. It continued to grow. Torment, desire, yearning for her. An enemy as powerful as it was obscure. It made my chest ache.

God, she takes my breath away. I felt like a madman, consumed by incomprehensible emotion. *Why do I feel this way? Where is this power, this pain coming from? I don't understand it, I can't control it. Yet I feel that it's part of me. It's inside me, silently devouring me. It put down roots without my noticing it, and there's nothing I can do to stop it. I can feel it growing every day.* My mind was reeling, overwhelmed by the growing wave of desperation, as I brushed the back of my hand over Gemma's fingers, barely touching her so I wouldn't wake her.

I can't name it, but it hurts. Could it be regret? No. It's stronger than that. Is it pain, then? No, it's deeper, fiercer. Is it the other side of pain, as wild and ardent as fire? Could this be the love *everyone talks about? Would I be able to recognize it if it pierced my heart with its arrows?*

There was no way I could be sure; I'd never felt it for myself. Not during my mortal life, let alone during the empty shell of the existence in which I'd been trapped for hundreds of years since.

Could love strike so suddenly, like a train barreling down the tracks, unable to stop? Could an emotion be so devastating that it burns like lava, clouding your thoughts, leaving you utterly unable to choose? Like a stealthy, greedy thief who steals your heart and every part of you while you stand there and watch it happen, a helpless spectator, with no way out?

A wave of pure emotion washed over me, and all at once, everything became clearer.

That heartbeat I felt was her, growing in the deepest corner of my heart like a flower pushing its way up through the ice and snow.

My apprehension cleared away like mist as I realized I loved her. I loved this sweet creature. And I would love her forever.

It was a brutal twist of fate: now that I had finally managed to give a name to my torment, now that I knew I loved Gemma more than myself, I was about to lose her forever.

Could destiny be any crueler?

And could a man, having seen the light, return to the darkness? Maybe a man could, but I wasn't a man. She would never leave my mind.

I would be hers forever.

How could I go on without her? Forgetting her would be impossible—it would be like forgetting myself. Gemma was a part of me now, an essential piece of my own spirit. Torn away from me, she would leave behind a wound that would never heal.

What sense did living forever make if I couldn't see her, touch her . . . love her. I would give up eternity to live as a mortal with her if only they would let me. But my wishes didn't matter. I was a predator sent out by Death, and I wasn't allowed to choose my prey. I just had to carry out orders.

Anguished by that awareness, I understood that everything I'd always fought for, everything I'd always believed in and defended, didn't matter any more. The new emotion was like a volcano that after centuries of lying dormant suddenly erupts, destroying everything in its path, everything I'd once been.

Nothing was worth anything any more if I couldn't have her. The only thing that mattered was contained in the little body lying there in front of me. Gemma.

Looking at her, for the first time I felt I wasn't alone. But that fleeting sensation wasn't destined to last. I drew a deep breath and filled my senses with her scent. I held that breath inside me until my soul was satiated.

I felt like I'd known her forever, but only a few weeks had gone by since we'd first met. Like a bolt of lightning, her gaze had pierced my heart, opening a permanent laceration there.

I let the memories flood in. Thinking back on the anger in her voice made me smile, now that I knew the reason behind it. She thought I was involved with Ginevra when instead I only wanted her. I hadn't known it then, but I was already hers and would be forever. I'd thought I'd been suffering because I had to give up all the emotions I was finally experiencing, but I was wrong. It was *her* I didn't want to give up. The memory of the brief moments we'd shared warmed my heart. Those nights, in her dreams, they were all ours, although she would never know it. Those were the moments when I'd felt for the first time that I could be myself, fully and without reserve.

I took another deep breath.Would I ever feel like that again, as only she could make me feel? Free. Satisfied. Complete.

Impossible. How could I feel complete if half of me had been torn away? Because that's what Gemma was to me:

my other half, my Eve. Without her, part of me would die forever.

All at once a ray of hope appeared in my thoughts, lighting them up like a comet and driving away the darkness into which I'd been slipping.

It was then that, for the first time, I glimpsed another path. I would come up with an alternative plan.

There was no way I'd be able to bear the empty existence that awaited me once Gemma's light had been extinguished. There would no longer be any existence left to live. Death, cruel witness, was mocking us. Fate had allowed me to fall in love with her. Maybe this had been written too. It was inevitable, and Death would be doubly satisfied. If I couldn't prevent her death, I would seek my own. After carrying out my orders and sealing Gemma's fate, I would bring my own existence to an end. My mind was made up.

I looked at the clock on her nightstand. Only two more hours and a tragedy would take place. Two lives would be cut short: that of a human and that of an Angel who was desperately in love with her.

I didn't have much time. It would have been easier to leave the room rather than force myself to suffer through a farewell, but the longing to look into her eyes again, to feel her gaze burning into mine, overpowered me.

I would have one final memory of her to treasure, to bury in some inaccessible corner of my heart where I would take refuge before disappearing forever.

I stroked the back of her hand. At my caress, her lips parted. The almost imperceptible words she whispered would have been incomprehensible to a human ear, but they weren't to mine; I grasped their true essence, what her unconscious was trying to tell me.

My eyes opened wide as I deciphered her soft, tormented murmur.

Where are you? Where are you and why can't I see you? I can feel you're here, but I can't see you.

My heart trembled. She was waiting for me. Knowing that Gemma felt the same yearning I did filled my spirit. But why should that matter now? Soon it would all be over. So why was my heart brimming with happiness?

Too late, I'd discovered in love a humble emotion that could thrive on fleeting moments of joy despite the awareness that they couldn't last.

"*Evan . . .*"

Gemma's anxious whisper made me even more impatient.

I wanted to be with her one last time. I wanted to say farewell.

Farewell forever.

FAREWELL

Once inside Gemma's mind, I found myself in the darkness—pitch-dark even to my eyes—in which Gemma often hid. In it, I sensed the uneasiness her soul harbored. Something was troubling her, but she wasn't afraid, which meant she suspected nothing of her imminent death. She hadn't read my mind like I'd feared.

I groped along, seeking her in the gloom. The sound of water led me to her. She was kneeling on a rocky shore, the waves flowing toward her gently as if to comfort her, lapping against the very edge of her black gown's organza frills. I wanted to embrace her, I wanted to protect her, but my embrace would be nothing but a deception, because I was there to take her away.

"Evan."

Her voice rang gently through the cool night air. The sweetness with which she uttered my name made me burn with guilt. She should hate me but instead she was happy to see me. She had no idea who she was dealing with, no idea that the person who loved her more than any other was the same person who would soon take her life. How would I find the courage to kill her? I clenched my fists, forcing myself to repress those thoughts, to lock them up in a remote corner of my mind that Gemma could never explore. Tonight would be our last chance ever to be together.

The instant she turned to look at me, I understood why darkness had fallen: her glowing beauty had lit up the night and the jealous stars had run to hide.

She smiled, motioning me over. Like a ghost mingling with the air, I vanished like mist and reappeared next to her. Without asking permission, I sat down next to her and took her hand. Lacing my fingers with hers, I lifted them to brush them against my lips, still holding her gaze. Like a dark spell, the emotion that swept over me made me forget, if only for an instant, the cruel destiny we were heading toward, lurking behind the first light of day.

In that endless moment, it was only her and me, Evan and Gemma. No one could ever take tonight away from us.

"I was afraid you wouldn't come." Gemma moistened her lips, watching mine as they slowly slid down her hand, brushing her palm, her wrist and her fingers again.

I forced myself to look away from her as the ocean beneath us transformed into a chasm that grew ever deeper. "Nothing in the world could have kept me away," I reassured her.

"Tell me what's worrying you."

I flinched, gripped by a sense of foreboding as the ocean sank lower and lower. Was I reading inside of her, or vice versa?

At times Gemma's insight amazed me. She could interpret emotions in me that were inaccessible even to me, but since I wanted tonight to be magical for both of us I had to struggle to conceal them, to seem calm, to hide the anguish consuming me.

I didn't want Gemma to share my agony. I wanted to give her a part of me tonight so she could remember me forever, even after her soul had left her body.

I stroked her cheek, trying to reassure her, and brushed my thumb along that little line of concern on her forehead, hoping it would disappear.

"I'm better now that you're here with me," I whispered. I was lying, naturally. Having her there in front of me and being able to read her soul through her eyes was making me suffer all the more.

We moved closer together, so close our bodies risked touching with each breath. A magnetic energy pulsed all around us at the mere possibility of physical contact. It exploded when her elbow brushed mine, sending a quiver through my ethereal body as it spread out, a dark, irresistible energy that overwhelmed me.

The air grew cooler as the plain on which we were now sitting continued to levitate imperceptibly, carrying us higher and higher.

I suddenly realized our height was reflecting Gemma's mood. Her elation was making her walk on clouds, but in the meantime, the emptiness below was growing deeper and gloomier. There was an abyss beneath us, the ocean no longer visible. I couldn't make sense of that gaping chasm. What was worrying her? No matter how hard I tried, reading Gemma proved to be more difficult than it had ever been before.

There was no way she could have sensed the truth in my mind; I'd been careful not to reveal my emotions. Then I understood: the abyss was reflecting *my* worries, not hers. Gemma could read me, no matter how hard I tried to keep my anguish hidden from her. She could sense my uneasiness and it was sounding alarm bells inside her.

She wasn't worried about herself. She was concerned for me, for the assassin who was going to take her life.

Touched by her incredible selflessness, for a second I was tempted to tell her everything, to explain what was torturing me. I barely resisted the urge, realizing what a mistake it would be to give her the key to her own death.

I looked away and scanned our surroundings in search of something that might take Gemma's mind off my mood. There was little I could do for her, but I wanted to at least offer her a memory of us that she could cherish deep in her heart. As she did in all her dreams, Gemma had conjured up a place of extraordinary beauty and I let it inspire me.

I stroked the back of her hand until her fingers returned the caress and let myself slowly sink back onto the carpet of grass, inviting her with my eyes to join me. Overhead, the sky was dark, black.

"Think a storm's coming?" I asked, folding my arms under my head.

Gemma bit her lip, thinking. "I hope not. It really is a shame it's cloudy tonight."

I smiled. She didn't realize she was an artist. In that little world of ours she could paint the night with sparkling diamonds, using the sky as her canvas.

"Are you so sure it is?" I asked, seeking her eyes. Gemma looked at me for a moment and stared back up at the sky, puzzled, as my eyes studied her features.

"I don't see a single star," she replied after careful examination.

"Look," I whispered, pointing my finger at the sky above us.

"There's nothing there," she insisted, shaking her head.

"It just seems that way. Sometimes you need to dig deeper to see what you're looking for. Just because you can't see something doesn't mean it's not there. *Look closer*," I whispered, my head brushing hers.

"I think I've heard that somewhere before." She smiled slightly, her voice hushed, but the shiver that ran over her spoke louder than her words.

I caressed the air, stroking the mantle of black above us as if to erase the darkness. As my hand swept across it, the darkness slid from the sky, pulled away like a cloth, revealing the infinite stars behind it. Gemma gasped and the smile disappeared from her face, leaving only astonishment. A silver glimmer sparkled in her eye, reflecting the starlight. "Evan, what— Did you do that?" she stammered.

Actually, she could have done it herself, she just didn't realize it. I hid a smile. "It's a beautiful night, isn't it?" *Our last one*, I thought, but forced myself to push it from my mind.

"It's *amazing*! I've never seen anything so wonderful in my whole life."

"That's only because you've never seen yourself through my eyes," I whispered.

Gemma stared at me for a moment and looked away, embarrassed by my boldness. I could read her every emotion, her every heartbeat, so I knew it was making her uneasy, but I couldn't help it. I couldn't be next to her without constantly wanting to touch her. At times I tried to sublimate my desire through compliments, to subdue it through words.

Despite the darkness of the night, the starlight illuminated her face enough to reveal the soft blush on her cheeks. I couldn't get enough of the breathtaking sight. While Gemma was admiring the firmament, I was contemplating her, utterly spellbound. Like two endless mirrors, her deep eyes reflected her soul, showing me its inner splendor.

A myriad of stars covered the night like the vault of a diamond-studded cave. A myriad of emotions passed through my ethereal body like an incandescent meteor shower.

She sighed. "I feel so small in the presence of all this immensity."

"You shouldn't," I said, the words coming out on their own. "All this is nothing compared to what's inside of you, Gemma. There's something in you, something I can't do without any more. I don't know why, but your light shines brighter than any other. Don't feel small, because there's no star more precious in all the firmament," I whispered, holding her gaze. "This night belongs to you. Rise up and gather the brightest stars." I'd carved those words into the table at the diner, hoping it would encourage her to follow her mother's advice. Gemma had tried to avoid being overheard, but I'd heard them all the same.

I was aware that the things I was saying were throwing her emotions into turmoil, but no matter how hard I tried I couldn't hold back. Like every other time I'd been with her, I'd lost control. How could I master myself now that I knew I loved her?

"Ever wonder what might be up there?" she asked. "The universe is so immense, so full of secrets." Embarrassed, Gemma avoided my eyes and instead stared intensely at the sky, a fascinated expression on her face as she waited for her discomfort to pass. "Isn't that Ursa Major?" she asked, pointing to a spot among the stars.

"You know the constellations?" I said, surprised. It meant I'd chosen the right topic.

"Not really. But I think they're fascinating, *mysterious*, even." She stole a glance at me and went back to staring at the night.

"Don't mysterious things scare you?" I asked despite myself.

Gemma looked down, grasping my allusion.

"You should hear some of the myths behind the constellations," I said, returning to the topic to make her feel more at ease. "I'm sure you'd like them. I like learning about mythology."

"Oh, so there's something you don't know already?" She grinned.

A smile escaped me. "I know a few stories, if you'd like to hear them."

"Why not?" she said, trying to sound casual. She didn't realize I sensed the curiosity building up inside her, and the excitement she was trying to hide made me smile. Was she trying to seem more mature in my eyes? Didn't she realize I found it adorable?

"The one you just pointed to is Ursa Major. Callisto," I added.

"Callisto?" she asked, shaking her head.

I nodded and smiled at her. To my surprise it was enough to make her blush again. "She was one of Zeus's countless lovers," I continued, as more and more interest appeared on her face. "Legend has it that when Zeus's wife Hera found out about his betrayal, she took revenge on Callisto, first by turning her into a bear and then by having her almost killed by Arcas, Callisto's son by Zeus and an expert hunter. But Zeus intervened just in time and placed the bear in the sky along with her son, who became Ursa Minor, keeping both of them safe from harm."

Lying at my side, Gemma stared at the sky, engrossed in my story, while every breath she took intensified my attraction to her. I longed to touch her, even just for a second. I desired her with my whole being, with every fragment of my tortured self.

"It's fascinating. I'd never heard it before," she said.

"That's just one of the hundreds of stories I know. Greek mythology has always interested me. Look," I whispered, pointing over our heads. "See that V-shaped line? That's Perseus, son of Zeus. To prove his valor,

Perseus was sent out to slay Medusa the Gorgon, a monster who could turn anyone who looked her in the eye into stone. The night before his departure, Athena appeared to him in a dream and gave him a magic sword to cut off Medusa's head and a shield to use as a mirror. Hermes, on the other hand, gave him winged sandals to reach the island where Medusa dwelled.

"During his journey, Perseus encountered the three Nymphs of the North who gave him a magic helmet that would make him invisible and a magic sack to hide the monster's head in. Armed with these gifts, Perseus easily accomplished his mission. Pegasus, the winged horse that he rode on his journey back, was created from the blood that dripped out of the sack, mixed with seawater. See, he's the four-sided shape over there," I said, pointing out its stars.

"The boxy one?" Gemma asked.

I lowered my head in a nod.

"That's called Pegasus's Great Square. One of its four stars is also part of the constellation Andromeda."

"Andromeda. I think I've heard that name before."

My gaze lingered on hers a moment before I continued the story, happy it was having the effect I'd hoped for; there was no trace of worry on her face. "During the journey, Perseus saw a beautiful princess off the Greek coast—"

"Andromeda," Gemma said.

"She was chained to some rocks on the shore of a tiny island, terrified by the horrible monster that was creeping toward her, about to devour her. Perseus swooped in, pulled Medusa's head out of the sack and faced it toward the monster, instantly turning it to stone. As a reward for saving Andromeda, he was offered her hand in marriage.

So, what else do you want to know? Ask away," I said, seeing her eyes full of questions.

"What was Andromeda doing on the shore? I mean, who chained her up there?"

I looked at the sky in the direction opposite Ursa Major. "See that W-shaped constellation?" I asked, indicating its exact spot. Gemma moved closer to me to have a clearer view of where I was pointing. I held my breath. As soon as she noticed, she sat up, embarrassed, and hugged her knees to her chest. I sat up too, and leaned in toward her, unable to resist my longing another second. A longing I felt under my skin that was growing wilder and wilder.

I moved my face near hers, almost brushing against her cheek. She didn't move. We'd never been so close before. I could even hear her heartbeat accelerating.

Slowly, I turned to look into her eyes. Our lips were just inches apart, yearning to be closer. Her warm breath came faster and faster against my skin.

I couldn't resist any longer. My body escaped my control as my gaze lost itself in her parted lips. I tilted my head and drew closer. One kiss . . . What could possibly happen with just one kiss? With my lips I barely brushed the corner of her mouth, delicately, almost imperceptibly. An overwhelming emotion took my breath away.

I'd never felt so elated before.

I was anticipating the taste of a stolen kiss, and I could feel Gemma's warm lips trembling in expectation, but she suddenly pulled back, breaking the magic of the moment. It wasn't a refusal, though; I could read her emotions and knew she longed for that contact too.

"Um, yeah . . . I see it," she stammered as I stole a glance at her, a half smile on my face.

Breathless from the emotion of that brief, forbidden contact, I made myself pick up my story where I'd left off.

"That's Cassiopeia," I said, peering up at the sky. "She's Andromeda's mother."

"Her mother?" she asked, frowning. I knew exactly what she wanted to ask.

"Cassiopeia was proud of her daughter's beauty and her own. She was so vain she boasted that they were even more beautiful than the sea nymphs. That enraged Poseidon, the god of the sea, who sent the terrible monster Cetus to destroy their city."

"The monster Perseus killed," Gemma said, following the story closely. "But I still don't understand. Why was Andromeda chained to the rocks?"

"The only way to appease Poseidon and save the kingdom was to sacrifice her daughter to the monster," I explained, smiling.

In contrast, her face instantly grew darker. "What a horrifying story!"

I was surprised to see how suddenly her mood changed. I still wasn't used to it. "But Perseus saves her in the end," I reminded her.

"It doesn't matter! It's so sad. She was her mother. I can't imagine how anyone could sacrifice someone they love."

Her words ran me through like a blade of ice, leaving a chill inside me, a chill that crept into my soul.

Isn't that exactly what I was about to do myself? My heart sank. I was overwhelmed.

"Sometimes a person has no choice," I said through clenched teeth. "Sometimes we're forced to do something against our will," I said, staring at the ground, filled with self-loathing.

"There's always a choice," she said sternly, looking into my eyes. "*Always.*"

I would have given anything to be able to believe her. But I knew it just wasn't so.

Devastating silence filled the night, a witness to our sadness, until Gemma looked up at the stars again. "Is that Orion?" she asked, breaking the silence.

I nodded, still unable to pull myself out of it. "It might be the most beautiful of all the constellations," I whispered from the void into which I had sunk, my voice stifled with pain. "It's the easiest one to spot. He's shaped like a hunter holding a club and a shield. At waist height, you can clearly make out the sword in his belt."

"Orion's Belt." Gemma was surprised to recognize the name. "What's his story?" she asked, fascinated.

She'd shaken her sadness again and for a moment I forced myself to forget my own. "Orion was the greatest hunter of his time and he would often go hunting with Diana, the goddess of the hunt. But one day Diana's brother Apollo noticed that she was neglecting her duties because of Orion, so he decided he had to die. And so, while Orion was swimming in the open sea, far from shore, Apollo, the sun god, shone a bright sunbeam on him and challenged his sister to hit the shiny speck with one of her arrows." I shuddered, realizing how much the story resembled my own. Suddenly, I felt incredibly sorry for Diana, forced to kill the person she loved most in the world. "Oblivious to the trick, Diana accepted the challenge and shot her beloved, slaying him."

Images of the imminent tragedy burst back into my mind, silencing me. For a moment I was lost in those visions, as vivid as photographs: my own love lying on the ground, lifeless, as blood seeped from her body, drenching her sweatshirt, which had once been as candid and pure as her fragile human heart. The sight of the blood sickened me, as did my contempt for myself and my nature. I could almost feel the hot liquid on my fingers, see it on my hands that would be guilty of committing the involuntary crime. I could have ripped open my own chest from the excruciating pain I felt inside.

Suddenly her delicate hand touched mine, bringing me back to the present, to my spot beside her, the only place I wanted to be. She lay back on the grass, the better to see the sky, and I followed her example.

I noticed her expression had saddened and quickly tried to repair the damage. Hoping to avoid giving her worries the chance to return, I continued my story.

"When Diana found Orion's body, she put it in her celestial chariot and took him up into the sky, attaching him there with brilliant stars. She placed his most trusted dogs at his feet to stand guard, but that's another story."

"Where did you learn all these myths? At the school you went to before moving here?"

I smiled. "Not really. Let's just say I've had a lot of time to cultivate my interests."

"You could write a book," she said with admiration.

After a moment of excruciating silence, I found my smiling mask in my mind and put it on. Deep in my heart I was racked with pain. I'd always known those stories but strangely enough it was like I was hearing them for the first time. Only now did I seem to grasp their meaning. After all, they weren't so different from my predicament. I'd never thought much about the tragic theme common to all the stories: the main characters finding themselves killing their beloved. It had happened with Diana and Orion, with Callisto and Arcas, and even Cassiopeia and her daughter.

Now it was our turn. Evan and Gemma.

I was going to end her life forever and it was eating away at my conscience. If only I could place her among the stars to protect her. Her light would outshine all the others and the whole world would fall in love with her. Fate would realize what a mistake her death would be and revoke its cruel sentence.

Gemma was about to die. I felt like I already had. When you know you have to give up the person you love, you die inside. How could I even think of spending eternity without her?

Mine was a fate worse than death. I could never accept the empty existence that awaited me without Gemma. I'd made up my mind, and it was an irrevocable decision: this night would be the last one for both of us.

The silence was deafening. I didn't speak, Gemma didn't speak, but inside we were both screaming, though for different reasons.

I shifted my weight onto one arm, leaning on my elbow, my torso turned toward her. Gemma continued to lie there on her back on the grass. The longing to remove the distance between us came back to overwhelm me. I struggled to overcome the almost irrepressible urge to touch her. Her skin must be so hot compared to the cool night air . . . For a moment I let it control me, I let myself be driven by the emotion.

I delicately brushed back a wisp of hair that had fallen over Gemma's face, the back of my finger lingering on her skin as it followed the soft curve of her cheek, her skin silver in the diamond starlight. For the first time, she didn't move away from my touch. In fact, she seemed to enjoy the contact.

She studied me with a focused yet calm look. The immensity of the night paled before the infinite reflection in her eyes.

I gazed at her steadily as she peered up at the sky, her mind wandering among the stars, following the heroes I'd told her about. She turned on the grass, rolling onto her side to face me. Our bodies were so close, lying one in front of the other. Gemma clearly hadn't come so near intentionally; she wanted to move away a little but at the same time she didn't want to show me how embarrassed she was, so in the end she didn't move.

In the silence of the night, our desires rose and intertwined in gazes full of promises. Our souls spoke voicelessly, harmoniously, as we listened to their silence, holding back the desire to touch each other. Like an unstoppable energy, my repressed desire caused a tremor that spread through my entire body.

I looked down at the narrow space that separated us and, in a bare patch between the blades of grass, I smoothed down the sandy earth and slowly moved my finger, writing on that makeshift page what my soul was crying out.

$$\theta\alpha\tilde{\upsilon}\mu\alpha, \text{ -}\alpha\tau o\varsigma, \tau\acute{o}$$

I looked up into her eyes, which brimmed with curiosity. "What did you write?" she asked.

"*Thauma*," I whispered, gazing at her. "It means 'thing of wonder.' The ancient Greeks used it to describe something unique. Like you are to me."

Gemma looked down, probably to hide the blush on her cheeks that was returning at regular intervals. She stretched her hand out toward mine and began to draw imaginary lines on my palm. Unable to hold back my desire any longer, overcome by a passion more intense than I'd ever known, I grasped her fingers in mine, wanting never to let her go. I forced myself to breathe deeply, hoping to drive away the emotion that had clouded my mind.

"I haven't finished telling you about the stars," I said, trying to regain control.

She shook her head slightly and looked at me with curiosity .

"See that star up there?" I asked, pointing.

"Which one?"

I leaned in toward her, my cheek almost touching hers. "The brightest one," I said, pausing to look at her as she scanned the sky. I brushed back the locks of hair that cascaded over her shoulder, revealing her delicate skin. She continued to stare upward as my breath drew invisible symbols on her neck.

"I see it now. That's the morning star," she whispered uncertainly.

I shook my head slowly.

"Oh, I thought it was. What's it called?"

"Its name is Gemma," I whispered in her ear, "because it lights up the night all on its own. Just like you. Can't you see? It's shining brighter than all the others, Jamie." I ran the tip of my nose along her skin and she trembled. "It's your star now," I said in a hushed voice.

The star must have heard my whisper; it began to shine more brightly in the sky.

"Nobody can own a star."

"But you can connect it indissolubly to the memory of someone. That way, deep down in your heart, a part of the star becomes yours forever. Every time you feel alone, no matter where you are, every time you miss me, look for it in the sky. It will help you remember me," I whispered, holding back the emotions that threatened to overwhelm me. In the place where she would go, there was a spot where she'd be able to see it whenever she wanted to think of me.

"Memories are for people who aren't together any more. What are you trying to tell me, Evan? I don't want memories. I want you."

For a moment I almost suspected she'd guessed the destiny that would soon separate us. "All things considered, I'm happy," I said, dodging her question. I didn't want to lie to her.

"You don't look the least bit happy." She was repressing the anguish she'd felt when I said that, but I sensed it all the same.

"Gemma, I can't regret the destiny in store for me. Can anyone blame the spark that lights a candle, even though it means condemning it to slowly burn up? For a little while, the candle sees the light. In the same way, I've been blessed to have had you in my life."

"What do you mean 'for a little while'?" she asked, her voice filled with tormented anger.

I looked down, holding back a curse for letting that slip, for venturing into a conversation I wasn't sure I could handle.

"Stop talking as if all this were about to end. What are you planning? I can't lose you now that we've found each other. I need you. *My soul* needs you, and yours needs mine, I can feel it. We have to stay together, Evan," she whispered, imploring me with the sweetest eyes I'd ever seen. Like I had a choice. Hearing my name on her lips was salt rubbed into an open wound.

I'd have done anything for her. Everything. But despite myself, that was the one wish it was impossible to grant her.

Stroking her cheek with my fingertips, I gazed directly into her eyes, trying to reassure her, although it was no easy task given how distracted I was by her full lips drawing me nearer .

Our bodies were very close: two fires that burned with the desire to fuse together and blaze. Every single cell within us yearned for that contact.

I moved my face toward hers, slowly, to give her the chance to pull away if she wanted to. She didn't, and my desire flared even higher, setting me on fire as my mouth lingered a fraction of an inch from hers, our foreheads touching with each breath. I lifted my chin and felt her lips brush against mine, soft and warm like I'd imagined them. I closed my eyes, surrendering to the emotion, and touched her lips again at their very corners as Gemma stayed perfectly still, almost without breathing.

Her lips parted to match mine, making my heart leap. Their consent made my chest burn. I raised my eyes imperceptibly and looked into hers, eager and full of desire. Our lips remained perfectly still, suspended against each other for what seemed like an eternity. As if we both wanted to capture the moment forever.

I touched her mouth lightly, caressing it. Savoring that anticipation was like chasing the stars yet never reaching them. I burned with desire, a desire I knew was reciprocated, a desire I had no intention of denying. I pressed my lips against hers, tenderly coaxing them apart as the emotion grew with each breath.

Gemma parted her lips and her warmth merged with mine as my tongue gently brushed hers, guided by the movement of our lips. Emotion swept me, exploding in a tumult of passion. My hands moved with a will all their own, my fingers sinking into her hair as I tried to control my breathing. I was a slave to my desire. All my resistance vanished like fog in the sunlight. My body pressed against hers, longing for contact, and pinned it under my own as our lips moved and locked at the mercy of some unknown delirium. I could no longer subdue the whirlwind of passion that had overwhelmed me, the heat that throbbed in my chest. Feeling her body beneath mine made me shudder. I separated my mouth from hers for just a second and rested my forehead against hers, glimpsing her desire for me in her eyes.

Holding her gaze, I let my hand slip down her body, barely touching her, until it reached her back. Her formal black gown had disappeared and she now wore everyday clothes. I slid my fingertips under her top. Gemma ran her hand up my arm to my neck. I leaned down and kissed her palm, closing my eyes, trapped in a whirl of heat. When my lips parted, her finger slid slowly down my face, pulling my lower lip down.

She caressed my neck, running her fingers along the contours of my muscles. I couldn't take my eyes off her as her fingers continued down my shoulder and arm. She slowly stroked my chest, utterly thrilling me. Never before had I felt such powerful emotions. My eyes closed at the shudder her sensual touch caused in me.

When I opened them again, Gemma was clasping the military dog tag I wore around my neck. She turned it over in her fingers, puzzled, and pulled me back toward her, inviting me to press my lips against hers again.

Her gaze was so sensual, my reaction utterly indescribable. There was something in her eyes that roused a part of me I couldn't control, making me feel like a wild man at the mercy of his desire.

She was so tiny beneath my body, so defenseless. I felt the need to protect her, wrap my arms around her and hold her tight against my chest where she'd be safe.

Her delicate touch enthralled me as our eyes exchanged silent vows only our hearts could hear. Until my lips slowly pressed hers yet again.

I wished I could stop time and make this moment infinite. Eternal. Indelible. I would stay with her forever in our little world. Nothing would separate us ever again.

Suddenly, the sky took on a faint golden hue, drawing my attention. There was a change in the air. A glimmer.

I took my eyes off Gemma's and my heart stopped. A pale, soft light glowed on the horizon over the sea. Lighting up the sky, darkening every part of me. Bringing me back to reality, wretched and cruel.

Dawn.

The sun was about to rise. Inside, I felt it setting forever as an emptiness deep in my heart reminded me of the cruelty of our imminent fate.

Time had run out.

I stood up, avoiding her gaze. I didn't have the courage to look her in the eye. I was afraid the lump in my throat that was keeping me from breathing might dissolve into tears.

I held out my hand. Gemma took it and when she was standing in front of me she took the other. Only then did I finally look into her eyes and see how worried she was.

I squeezed her hands and drew her toward me, almost pulling her. "Hold me tight," I begged her. I wanted to keep her close to me, hide her in my arms until our bodies melted into one so no one would come looking for her.

I locked her in my strong, desperate embrace. There was no reason for me to control my reactions. Nothing mattered to me any more. Gemma was my whole life and cruel destiny was about to take her from me.

I cupped her face in my hands, sinking my fingers into her soft hair, breathing in her intoxicating scent so I'd be able to remember it when I took the poison. That way, when I closed my eyes, I could imagine her still there with me. I was drunk on her and our impossible love.

I gazed at her intently, still amazed at how beautiful she was in the warm colors of the first light of day. I rested my forehead against hers so she wouldn't see the torment in my eyes, unable to shed those forbidden tears, and kissed her fiercely.

Gemma returned my kiss with the same intensity. An intensity that cried out in desperation. Mine . . . hers . . . By now I couldn't tell where I ended and Gemma began. Like two halves, our hearts had become one.

It was pure anguish to know that our first kiss would also be our last. And that Gemma would never realize it. I held her against me, moving my lips on hers, longing desperately to cling to her forever. I knew that once our lips parted, the light would take her from me.

In the distance, the sun rose insistently, mercilessly, growing stronger as it imperceptibly lit up the sky and Gemma's face. I tried to separate my lips from hers but instantly felt lost without her warmth and pulled her back to kiss her again . . . and again.

I wanted to rule that moment. I wanted time to stop. Right there, right then. By now I was desperate, on the brink of insanity, of inconsolable madness. I didn't want the light to take my Gemma away from me.

Night, wrap us in your starry mantle, hide us, please! I cried silently, hoping the night would grant me a few moments more, lingering before surrendering to the day. *Or at least hide my Gemma, my blossom, hide my precious gem within your dark folds. I offer you all of myself in exchange for her protection. I beg you, Night, silent accomplice of all lovers, don't let the cruel judge that is the light take her away from me, depriving you of all your stars.* But the sunlight was deaf to my final cry of desperation. It advanced quickly, threatening to steal my Gemma from me.

When the first sunbeam touched her skin, the heart I'd found again after all those centuries shattered.

In utter agony, I kissed her forehead. "Remember . . ." I whispered, my eyes searching hers. The tips of our noses touched. Desperation filled me. My hands gripped her face more tightly. I never wanted to let her go. "Don't forget me. Promise. Look up at the sky every chance you get and you'll know I'm there with you." I pressed my lips against hers, utterly resigned. "Don't forget us, Gemma." I felt defeated in a battle I hadn't even been allowed to fight.

"Evan . . ." Hot tears fell from her eyes, bathing my hands. I dried her cheeks with my fingers. "Don't leave me. Please," she begged, sobbing. "You can't leave me now that I love you."

I was awestruck by the effect of those three simple words. Simple, yet all-important. So painful I felt a tear run down my face and for the first time I discovered my body was capable of crying.

My elation from her unexpected confession dueled with the incredible desperation her words had also triggered within me. "*Samam*," I whispered. *So do I.* This time it wasn't Ancient Greek, but the world's oldest language, the one I knew best. I couldn't find a better way to say it to her.

I was sure she would understand. I tried to remember how to breathe, but the pain was suffocating. I held her tightly against my chest and moved my lips to her ear. "You've been the only one for me," I whispered tenderly. "Farewell."

I felt her body trembling, and vanished before her eyes.

I found myself back in her room. Infinite pain was wound tightly around my heart like barbed wire. Gemma was so *perfect* lying there in bed. Even with that little frown, her face was so beautiful. Unique, extraordinary. No one could have imagined that soon her body would stop breathing, her heart cease to beat. I would gladly die in her place if that would be enough to save her. The thought of taking her life revolted me, precipitating within me a savage loathing of the world, of the Màsala. Of myself.

I gazed at her one last time, stopping to stroke her hand before making way for those cruel rays of sunrise streaming in through the window uninvited, heralding the dawn. The morning. The end.

My heart had shattered into a thousand pieces. And with it, every fiber of my being disintegrated, like a vampire exposed to the light. Full of bitterness, I prepared to say goodbye.

GEMMA

20

REAWAKENING

I muttered incoherently, bothered by the light. Shooting pains ran through my head and I was dazed. As I tossed and turned, half conscious, I had a strange feeling of loss like a gaping hole in my stomach.

I wasn't sure where I was. Still groggy, I forced my eyes open and cut the cord connecting me to another world. I touched my pillow, overcome by sadness, my eyes brimming with stifled tears.

No. Not this time, I thought, desperate. I couldn't have dreamt it, not this time. I felt I was sinking into a bottomless pit, into the void, into darkness.

Alone.

What kind of trick was my mind playing on me?

I couldn't accept that it had only been a dream. I could still feel Evan's hand clasped in mine. I'd felt his skin against mine. I was sure I'd felt the warmth of his body. And his lips . . . I brushed my fingers against my own with a whimper. I could still taste him.

Was it possible none of it was true? The magic of last night together couldn't have been only a mirage, a product of my imagination, a secret desire hidden in my unconscious. It had all been so real!

Overwhelmed with grief, I sat up but couldn't drag myself out of bed, as though staying there would allow me to keep my memories, prevent them from fading away with the morning. I rested my elbows on my raised knees and buried my face in my palms.

Unwelcome light was coming in through the window, insolently robbing me of that night, that magic . . . robbing me of my Evan.

I had the terrible feeling nothing would be as it had been.

Unable to hold them in any longer, I let the tears stream down my face. They took me back to that memory, that desperate farewell. What was my unconscious trying to tell me with such a somber dream? Then I remembered: I'd seen Evan and Ginevra together. Was it because of that?

In a flash, my disappointment was replaced by the fear that the dream might vanish at any second. I wanted to keep the memory intact, not forgetting even one detail of last night, preserving it like a precious treasure. I clung to the pictures in my mind with all my might, but for some strange reason I found I didn't need to; they didn't seem to be fading. They were as vivid as if I'd actually experienced those moments and those emotions. They seemed more like a memory than a dream.

Relieved, I trudged to the bathroom to take a shower. I realized I was guilty of ingratitude. I should have been overjoyed at the gift the night had given me. So why did I feel so heartbroken? Why did I continue to despise the morning, the sunlight, which, like thieves, had taken him from me, coming between us and tearing me away from his embrace?

I couldn't remember ever having such powerful emotions before. Why should I be feeling them now?

Evan's farewell had been so intense. When he'd disappeared before my eyes, pain had washed over me, crushing me, and although the light continued to grow stronger, I felt darkness envelop my heart. I was alone. The cold had seeped into my bones, depriving me of Evan's protection that had warmed my heart.

How could those sensations not be real? I could swear they were.

If I hadn't woken up in my bed, I would have leapt into a fire just to prove I'd actually experienced those moments with Evan. And yet—no matter how ridiculous it might seem—I couldn't completely shake that nagging doubt, as if there were some remote chance I hadn't made it all up.

I distractedly went back to my room and rifled through my disorganized closet. I wanted to wear something dark today, to fit my mood, but instinct made me choose a white sweatshirt, probably hoping it might lift my spirits somehow. I slipped on the first pair of jeans I found plus a pair of dark boots, which in summer I replaced only with Nikes. I pulled open the curtains to let in a little more light and was about to open the windows so the room could air out while I was gone, but the minute I touched the handle I stopped, filled with a sense of foreboding. Although I'd grown accustomed to it, the feeling I was being watched had never been so strong before. The curtains stirred, as though from a puff of wind, but the windows were still closed.

I slowly searched the room, scrutinizing the air as if it would reveal something. The room was empty, and yet the sensation didn't fade. It felt like a dark presence lurking beneath a mantle of invisibility, studying me from close up. This morning, fear had given way to curiosity. I was beginning to be fascinated by all those strange sensations that had been bubbling up inside me for some time now. If I couldn't avoid them, I might as well learn to tame them.

Before leaving, I scratched Iron Dog's head, but today I felt the unusual need to stay and pet him, watching his muscles relax at my touch.

"Hey, lazybones," I whispered. "I'll take you for a walk when I get back," I promised, smiling. "I'd love to know how you manage to sleep all day." I shook my head as he opened his round, dark eyes in reply and closed them again after a moment.

I walked to the door, pausing as I grabbed the doorknob. Another sensation. Stronger. Harder to ignore.

I was suddenly struck by an uncontrollable need to turn around and engrave every detail of my room in my mind. I studied the shelves filled with mementos, looked at each of the objects that, like pieces in a jigsaw puzzle, formed my life.

Grandma's clock, the giant stuffed bear Peter had won at Great Escape in Lake George a few years ago, the stacks of books in the bookcase. Each volume a part of my life. One glance at the spine and I could remember exactly when I'd devoured the story. Every page brought back a different emotion.

The paint on the walls was flaking slightly in some patches, but I'd never felt ready to paint over it, as if the very color were a part of my life. Photos covered the walls, evidence of the slow work of time that had silently changed my appearance. Memories of my childhood spent with Peter. Fishing with Peter. Camping with Peter. Going to school with Peter. A carefree life that felt more and more distant.

How many times we'd played together in that room. The memories came to life for a moment, as though my mind had rewound a tape. While my body remained perfectly still, I watched two children chasing each other, jumping on the bed, trying to frighten each other with horror stories, and the girl, when she grew frightened, starting a pillow fight to make the boy stop.

Like a ghost in my mind's eye I watched Peter come in through the window and pull out a movie he'd tucked into his hood so he could use both hands to climb up the trellis to my room. I would never forget those memories. Peter was a part of me. That was clear from the pictures on the walls; he was in so many of them, always sunny and smiling, even when I was pouting.

My heart leapt as it made a wish. Evan. Maybe one day, on one of those walls, I could add a photo of the two of us together.

Maybe I was still just dreaming.

I took a deep breath and forced myself to open the door. Before leaving, I grabbed my iPod from the desk and put it in my pocket, casting one last look around the room. I had the funny feeling I'd never see it again, like I was about to set off on a journey.

From the comforting murmur of their voices, I knew my parents were already awake. I found them in the kitchen, lounging at the table over piping-hot cups of coffee.

"Morning, sleepyhead!" my dad chimed, half-closing one eye. He'd never been good at winking and his contorted face was amusing.

"For the record, I woke up at dawn with a terrible headache. What's for breakfast?"

My mom nodded toward the oven. "It's still hot—don't burn yourself."

I pulled out the blueberry crumble and cut a slice for each of us. With the first bite I thought of Evan sitting at the table in the diner. I couldn't believe that had been only yesterday. So many things had happened since then. Imaginary or real—my mind could no longer tell the difference between what was true and what wasn't. The thought of him and Ginevra together didn't upset me as much as it had the day before when I'd seen them. I couldn't be mad at either of them, because in the meantime something inside me had changed. The overwhelming emotions I'd felt last night, the pain in Evan's eyes, the warmth of his mouth had wiped away all the rest. It didn't matter if my brain said it wasn't real; my heart had *experienced* those sensations. And that was enough for me.

After breakfast, which lasted longer than usual, I got up to leave.

"Where you off to in such a rush? Today's not a school day," my dad asked, curious.

"I need to turn in my yearbook pictures. Mr. Madison gave me an extra day since he's going to be at the school for a couple hours this morning." Yesterday afternoon I'd called him to apologize and luckily he'd given me this second chance.

"Sick!" my dad exclaimed.

I glowered at him. Once in a while he tried to imitate teenagers' slang to sound younger, but it just made him sound ridiculous. Not that he was old. He was just, well, Dad. I got my backpack ready, making sure to remember my flash drive with the school photos.

"Stopping by the diner afterwards?"

"I don't think so. I'm meeting up with Peter and the guys at Mirror Lake later on."

"How'd the lacrosse game go last night?"

"It wasn't anything special. The Blue Bombers lost by a hair."

"What bad luck," my dad said.

It wasn't luck, I thought to myself. I'd known Peter my whole life and I'd never seen him so distracted before. And that's what had cost us the game. Before we went home, we'd agreed to meet out at the lake in the morning. No, I was the one with bad luck; because I'd been so scatterbrained I had to go to school on Saturday.

"Want a ride?" my mom asked.

I considered her offer for a split second. "Thanks, but I feel like taking my bike." I wanted to spend some time reliving the dream in my mind on my way there. I leaned over my dad's shoulder and grabbed a doughnut from the middle of the table.

"My little girl nervous about something?" Dad was familiar with my habit of turning to calories when something was upsetting me. Actually, I had a funny feeling in the pit of my stomach.

"Nothing in particular," I reassured him. "And don't call me your little girl, you know I can't stand it." I instantly regretted the bitter tone I'd let slip out of my mouth.

"You're still my little girl. Don't you forget it," he insisted, mischievously tousling my hair.

I forced myself not to reply and opened the door, my backpack slung over my shoulder. Acting on some strange impulse, I looked back and stared at my parents, still immersed in conversation at the kitchen table. I felt the urge to run and hug them like I used to when I was a child. Maybe it was because Evan's farewell had upset me, but suddenly I wanted to tell them how much I loved them. I held back the impulse and shut the door behind me.

21

THE END

In the front yard, I still had the strong feeling I was being watched. I looked around, an act that had recently become automatic. This morning, the feeling was stronger than ever.

I raised the garage door and pulled out my old mountain bike. My dad had wanted to get me a "girlie" bike but I'd asked for a more rugged model that would be better for going on trips with Peter in the Adirondacks.

I put in my earbuds and chose a Lana Del Rey album: a mix of melancholy and sweetness. Exactly what I felt in my heart. Leaving Cherry Street, I turned down Hurley Avenue, pedaling with my head bowed, totally lost in thought as the cars passed me by.

The memory of my dream was a sweet blanket totally enveloping me, protecting me from the cold. I barely noticed the cars racing past, swerving to avoid hitting me. I couldn't concentrate on where I was going. Realizing all my distraction was putting me at risk for not showing up at the school, I forced myself to slow down and pay more attention.

I turned right on Station Street and crossed the intersection of Sentinel and South Main like I did every morning, already forgetting to pay attention to where I was pedaling. I almost rode straight into a fireman. Was it starting to become a habit? The road was closed. I took out one of my earbuds and overheard a man complaining about a gas leak in the neighborhood pipes, and the fireman telling him to move away.

I sighed, grumbling over my distractedness. The whole neighborhood had been closed off but I hadn't noticed the barriers they'd put up. Since I couldn't go through there, I took a longer route so I'd have time to relish the memory of my dream. I turned back, passed the train station, and headed down Station Street to reach Mill Pond Drive from the other side. After a few yards I slowed down, almost frightened by how strongly I felt that invisible presence hovering around me.

It was intense. I felt like I could reach out and touch it. I inhaled deeply, my nostrils tickled by a fragrance I knew well. I stood there, perfectly still, as my eyes dilated from the scent.

Evan.

I sniffed my shirt to see whether it was coming from me and checked the road, almost as if I expected to find Evan hidden there behind one of the maple trees.

No one was following me, and yet the familiar scent lingered.

I shook my head to drive the ridiculous notion out of my twisted mind and pedaled faster. Meanwhile, *Bel Air* had begun. I loved that song. Melancholy and so magical. The soft touch of fingers on a piano carried me off, back into my dream. I remembered Evan's kiss, which sent electrifying tingles under my skin. I reached out my hand and brushed it against the leaves of the trees lining the road, letting them tickle my fingers. To my right, the lake shimmered as I sped past it. I'd never had such an intense feeling before. It wasn't like butterflies in my stomach—it was more like an Evan-shaped hole in my heart that burned whenever I thought of his absence. I closed my eyes and let the fresh morning air caress my skin, singing in a whisper.

Evan's eyes, shadowed and gray, hounded me. I couldn't get them out of my head. I distractedly slipped a hand into my sweatshirt pocket, took out my phone, and punched in the code. The screen lit up, showing the time: 6:55. I crossed the tracks and went straight on toward Mill Pond Drive. The street skirted the woods.

Lana Del Rey's voice was like a soothing balm.

As I passed, a flock of birds rose up from the trees, casting a broad shadow on the pavement. I looked up, following their flight, drifting away with the notes of the piano. Uplifted. To another world. Into Evan's arms. The moment had been magical, mesmerizing. Because it wasn't a dream, it was a *memory*. I didn't care if my brain opposed it. I'd never felt as good as I had last night.

I stretched out my arm again toward the leaves. They brushed against my fingers. This time I sat up straighter and let go of the handlebars, surrendering to the melody, the cool morning breeze caressing my skin.

I wished I could close my eyes and relive the thrill of his kisses. My lips remembered their taste, as though even my body could take part in that imaginary journey. Evan had worked his way under my skin.

The beating of my heart accelerated impulsively at the thought of his chest pressed against mine, pinning me to the grassy lawn, his lips brushing against mine, the flames growing stronger and stronger. The way he'd held me tightly in his arms had made me tremble.

The wind blew harder, distracting me from the memory. My skin shivered in response, almost as if it sensed a veiled threat as the aura of that invisible presence grew more and more powerful.

I regained control of the bike and pulled the phone out of my pocket to check the time again. 6:59. I lowered my hand to put it back but caught my iPod cord by mistake, pulling an earbud out of my ear. As I instinctively hunched my shoulder to try to hold it in place, a shrill blare turned the blood in my veins to ice. Without the music in my ears, I heard it loud and clear for the first time.

My heart froze, shrouded by a black cloud of terror, and the phone slipped from my fingers as I saw a looming shape as red as blood racing toward me. Time, the air, my breath, every single thing was trapped in that frozen instant.

A bone-chilling sound, shrill and insistent, reverberated throughout my body. The deafening blast of an air horn. Too loud. Too close.

Terror petrified me. I couldn't breathe and my muscles refused to move. I felt a pain in my chest. The screeching squeal of tires grated on my ears, drowning out the sound of the cell phone clattering to the street. Everything else turned dull and colorless as that single red flame whooshed straight at me. I couldn't get out of the way, I'd lost control of the bike. I was frozen, but the wheels continued to carry me toward my fate.

A horrifying realization shook me to my core: it was a semi, and it was too close to avoid me.

It was going to hit me. My journey would end here, on this street.

Like the last remaining bowling pin, unable to move as the ball comes barreling down the lane straight at it, I too was perfectly still, awaiting death, as my mind raced back to the faces of those I loved, the last gift given to me by time. Peter. Mom. Dad. *Evan.*

For a second, my heart stopped at the intensity of his silvery gaze. I couldn't tell whether it was just a memory, a mirage projected by my heart, of if he was really there, hidden behind a tree, his crystal eyes staring straight at me like they had in my dreams, now filled with more torment and anguish than ever before.

The last grain of sand was poised to slip through the hourglass of my life. I closed my eyes, imagined it falling inexorably. When it touched the bottom, it would all be over. The truck would hit me.

I sensed the exact instant when that last grain of sand fell into empty space, propelled by the powerful wall of air that washed over me an instant before impact, lashing at my face so fiercely it took my breath away. The whole world grew muffled, the blare of the horn reduced to a hum as I surrendered to panic, the beat of my heart pulsing deafeningly in my ears, pounding in slow motion as I took my last breath.

Another, stronger gust of air struck me and then, impact. In my heart, the memory of Evan's kiss.

Game over.

22

GHOST OF ICE

I had no idea what to expect from death, if I'd live on in another form or another body. My only certainty, so strong it was almost palpable, was the feeling of calm that enveloped me like a protective shell as I slid through an icy tunnel that caught at my body and face, hindering my breathing.

The last thing my eyes had seen before everything went dark was my bike, reduced to a tangled heap of metal. And yet the impact hadn't been so overwhelming. Maybe the darkness had eclipsed the pain.

A loud rustling noise like dry leaves stirring grated on my ears. I wanted to cover them but it was no use. I couldn't move. Something was pinning my limbs. Something hard.

Dazed, I tried to open my eyes. My eyelids were heavy, but I wanted to escape from the darkness pressing down on me before it was too late. A glimmer appeared in the darkness, then a blinding flash of light struck my pupils, forcing me to shut my eyes again. I kept trying, although I was so confused my brain wouldn't let me focus on my surroundings.

Walls of splintered colors raced past me dizzyingly. The speed blurred the colors, though I could occasionally make out patches of blue and splotches of green and brown.

My head was spinning. I felt as if I'd woken up on a runaway merry-go-round. The icy air took my breath away. I had the strange feeling my body wasn't moving, that everything else was speeding by, as if I were suspended in midair. Or was I drowning, at the mercy of the current maybe? No, I couldn't feel water on my skin. I felt like a ghost made of ice. If my surroundings hadn't been so confused, if that whirlwind of cold air weren't taking my breath away, I would have sworn I wasn't moving. Instead I was slicing through the air like a particle of wind, protected by a firm grip that enveloped me like a warm shell. Overcome by sensations too overwhelming for me to work through the confusion clouding my mind, I closed my eyes again, allowing myself to be gently rocked.

Wherever I was going.

Was this death? A frenzied journey through a tunnel?

The earth stopped spinning and the whirlwind died away. I felt myself falling backward but with a comforting feeling of security. My back touched a cold, damp surface, while something warm brushed my temple. A gentle, familiar touch.

I forced my eyes open. Like liquid silver, eyes of ice, caring and intense, shone through the darkness that had trapped me.

Evan.

"Shh . . . Everything's fine. You're safe now."

The protective sound of his voice lulled me in another world.

"Do you realize what you've done?"

"I couldn't help it. It all happened so fast . . . just a second before it hit her . . . I think it grazed her ankle."

The distant, hushed sound of voices infiltrated the fortress in which my mind had sought refuge.

My ankle. Only then did I sense the point from which the pain radiated up to my knee. A blaze raged in my head. I reached down and felt the surface beneath my back, finding it cold and damp. After a few seconds, I realized it was earth.

Disoriented and still dazed, I struggled to understand the low, agitated murmurs. A shaft of light struck my pupils, forcing me to squeeze my eyes shut, but slowly I managed to open them again. Emerging from the darkness, I recognized the silhouettes in front of me. Evan and Ginevra were arguing, unaware that I'd regained consciousness. I tried to shake off the grogginess that wouldn't allow me to focus on their faces. I still couldn't move any part of my body without excruciating pain.

Evan was speaking to her in a tone I'd never heard him use before. Powerful, authoritative, determined. I barely recognized him. I squinted, trying to focus, fascinated by the new tone in his voice. I studied his features, his clenched jaw and piercing gaze as he looked at Ginevra and, for the first time, I didn't detect a trace of the confusion that often afflicted him. It was as if he'd cast off one mask and was wearing a different one, illuminated by the new light that shone in his eyes. He was laying down the law for Ginevra, his face stern and determined, free from shadows. I stopped caring about whether or not I was still alive as long as Evan had that new light within him. I was probably dead, and they didn't notice my presence simply because they couldn't see me. I wasn't sure I wasn't a ghost, and I was too weak to find out. Everything seemed so strange and surreal.

"Relax, Ginevra." Evan's voice was calm now, with a hint of satisfaction. The exact opposite was true of Ginevra's. She was spouting a stream of curse words. "And don't swear, it doesn't become you." With effort, I managed to see a dimple form in Evan's cheek as he smiled, perfectly relaxed.

"Relax?!" Ginevra was absolutely hysterical, and though she was trying hard to keep her voice down, she sounded like an enraged tiger. "Oh, right, you tell me to relax! Do you have the faintest idea what's going to happen now?! To all of us?"

"You're not involved, Ginevra."

"Well, Simon is going to be, you know he is. What on earth were you thinking?" she hissed contemptuously, her voice filled with bitter reproach. "We're all in trouble now. *You're* in trouble, Evan," she corrected herself.

"Are you saying I can't count on you?"

Ginevra's pride kept her from answering right away. "I didn't say that," she said after a moment of silence, still frowning. "What you did is *extremely serious*. How are we going to fix it?"

Evan's relaxed expression turned into a threatening sneer. "*Fix it?*" he repeated, disgusted, and shot her a fiery glare that made her flinch. "I'd do it a thousand more times if I had to!" His expression suddenly softened, verging on sadness. "Don't you see? I'd given up. I thought I was ready. I did everything I had to, right up to the end. But then she turned toward me and *looked at me*. I saw the fear in her eyes and felt the most excruciating pain I'd ever experienced. Right at that moment, everything became clear. I knew what I had to do, without a shadow of doubt. I knew I couldn't let it happen."

"You threw away your only chance for Redemption. This is *not* going to end well. They'll come looking for her, you know that, and your sacrifice will have been pointless. You can't prevent it!"

"Yes I can. It's not going to happen. I'm going to protect her." Evan's voice was filled with pride.

"And how are you going to do that? The Brotherhood is going to find out about it soon enough."

"We have a little time before they do. I need to think." Evan rubbed his temples, agitated by Ginevra's warning.

"You can't be sure."

"Fuck it, I don't care about them! The Màsala could never—"

"No!" Ginevra cut him off and lowered her voice. "Are you crazy? Don't say the name out loud," she warned, looking around, as if worried someone might have heard. "Christ! Have you gone completely insane?" she snapped, pacing back and forth until a furrow formed on the ground. Suddenly, she stopped and glared at him. "Don't even think it, Evan. You can't be with her, not like that. It'll never happen!"

"I realize that." Evan's voice, filled with resignation, was lower now.

I had no idea what was going on between them. Was it a lover's quarrel? My ears were taking in the words, but my mind couldn't hold onto them. They were disappearing before I could process them. In any case, I was getting fed up with Ginevra's attitude. It was like she was trying to lead Evan back down the difficult path he'd been on when I met him.

I didn't care if he was hers. I wished I could shut her up, scream at her to stop yelling at him, but I didn't have the strength to open my lips. An involuntary groan escaped me, making them turn in my direction.

Evan shot Ginevra a reproachful look, as if it were her fault they hadn't noticed I'd woken up. I shook my head, trying to drive off the last trace of confusion. I didn't perceive any movement, but I instantly found them both leaning over me. I must have hit my head.

"How do you feel?" Evan's whisper reached me like a gentle caress as he ran his hand over my hair.

I managed to focus on his face, but there was something strange, something I couldn't put my finger on.

His eyes . . . Was I dreaming, maybe? Evan's eyes shone with a silvery light, shadowy and gray, almost as if they belonged to some supernatural creature. Like the day we'd first met. Like in the secret world where I saw him every night in my dreams. Evan stared at me intensely, allowing me to study him. I'd never seen his eyes from so close up before. Amber streaks ran through them like gilded lightning in an icy sky. From that distance, they emitted such power I wasn't sure I could keep looking into them without them piercing my heart and making me faint.

"I can't, I can't say, exactly," I made myself answer. "My head hurts."

Evan and Ginevra exchanged a look.

"What happened?" I asked, tripping over my words.

To my surprise, it was Ginevra who spoke up. "You should learn how to ride a bike. That truck was about to kill you. Evan pushed you out of the way a second before it ran you over." Her voice was so bitter cold it could have done the impossible and frozen fire. For a moment I almost felt guilty for still being alive. "You were lucky," she told me, crossing her arms and turning her back on me. "This time," she added in a low voice. It almost sounded like a threat.

Evan shot her a piercing glare. If looks could kill, Ginevra would have dropped dead on the spot.

Her contempt for me was clear from her voice. Why did she hate me so intensely? I couldn't believe it was because she was jealous. She couldn't actually want me dead because of that. In a moment of lucidity, her words echoed in my head: *We're all in trouble now*. Could it be my fault?

Even then, I sensed her hostility in the way she looked at me.

"Come on, I'll take you home." Despite the irritation in Evan's voice, there was no longer any trace of confusion, and he drew me back into his spell. "Can you walk?" he asked, helping me to my feet.

I would have liked to seem fearless to him, but the movement made me moan with pain. "My ankle hurts," I admitted, rotating my foot gently.

"We should take her to the hospital," Ginevra said, but Evan scowled.

"No need. I'll take care of her. It'll heal," he snapped. I watched them exchange challenging looks, as if they were communicating in secret.

"You wouldn't dare." Ginevra narrowed her eyes to slits. "Don't complicate things, Evan," she hissed.

"I know what I'm doing," he said, finishing the conversation. He turned to look at me. "Put your arm around my neck. I'll carry you."

It was incredible how tender his voice became when he spoke to me. I did as he said, feeling my heart warm at his offer. The blood rushed to my face and I found myself blushing at the thought of being close to him.

He and I had done far more than that in my imagination, but he didn't know that. A wave of images filled my head, melting me. Memories of Evan and me, his mouth on mine, his hot body on top of mine. No, not *memories*, I forced myself to admit. None of it had ever really happened. How could I act casual? How could I look him in the eye and forget his deep, passionate kiss as though I'd never experienced it? Because this was real life. None of what had happened in my dreams was real.

He lifted me from the damp ground with a single fluid movement, effortlessly, as my lucidity returned. Looking around for the first time at the trees towering overhead, blocking the sunlight, I understood where I was, although I didn't recognize that exact spot.

What were we doing in the woods?

"Hold on tight."

His voice was so close to my ear. I tried hard to hold back a shiver but it didn't work. I rested my head on his shoulder, studying the way his neck muscles flexed with every movement.

"Cold?"

My heart trembled when I saw a half smile appear on his lips, so close it almost left me breathless. He'd noticed the effect the sound of his voice had on me. "N-no, I'm fine," I stammered, blushing. Actually, I was burning up as I clung to his warm, muscular body.

Around Evan's neck was a dog tag, the same one he'd worn in my dream. I must have seen him wear it at some point but forgotten I had. It was resting against his sleeveless dark-green T-shirt, over which he wore a matching shirt that was completely unbuttoned. My hand brushed against the metal and I blushed again, remembering how shamelessly I'd pulled him to me, yearning for his lips. The memory was so vivid I was tempted to do it again, almost like it was a habit.

My fingers moved on their own, clasping the chain, and Evan smiled at me as though he recognized the gesture and knew my intentions.

I forced myself to drive off that insane thought, because nothing like that had ever happened between us in real life. Because there was no "us" and there never would be. There was just me, him . . . and Ginevra.

"Something the matter?" He'd clearly noticed the change in my mood.

"I'm just a little . . . shaken," I lied, hiding my face in the fabric of his shirt. His check was so close I had to fight the urge to surrender to the magnetic pull drawing me to him. In his arms I felt incredibly light. Taking a deep breath, I filled my nostrils with his scent, the smell of the dew-swept forest on an April morning, delicate, fresh, able to reach inaccessible places inside me, to pluck unknown strings and make them vibrate with warmth.

Now that I could breathe him in from so close up, I was more and more convinced I'd smelled his scent in the air that morning.

What a crazy thought. And yet, there was a small part of me, one completely devoid of reason, that continued to go against all logic by confirming my suspicion. Evan looked at me as though attracted by that reflection, and I lost myself in his eyes. I let his gaze explore mine as I realized that . . . *Impossible*. I started, confused, distrusting my own senses. There was no longer any trace of the silver that had been shining in his eyes a moment ago.

They were dark.

What kind of trick was my mind playing on me this time? I didn't say anything, afraid he'd think I was crazy. But I knew what I'd seen. I was sure I'd seen his eyes clearly in the forest. Or had I? But then again, it wouldn't be the first time my senses had betrayed me.

"What now?"

I couldn't see Ginevra's face behind Evan's shoulder, but her voice was unmistakable. I hadn't even noticed she'd been following us.

Evan leaned down and set me on the ground, looking around cautiously. "I'll secure the perimeter. Keep an eye on her," he ordered Ginevra in an authoritative tone before striding off.

Secure the perimeter? What on earth was he talking about? I'd probably hit my head harder than I thought. I'd learned to deal with ambiguity when it came to Evan, but right now I was too drained to think about it.

I wasn't sure if I was more baffled by the fact that I had to rely on Ginevra's support as she helped me reach my front door or the way Evan was scanning the street with concerned eyes, checking every corner as if expecting to catch a thief lurking somewhere. My instinct objected. Not a thief; an *assassin*.

"Your parents aren't home," Evan said. It clearly wasn't a question, so I just nodded. My parents would be working the breakfast shift, so there was no need for me to check. "Lock yourself inside, Gemma. I'll be back in a minute."

I was confused by Evan's serious tone. His eyes darted around the street, but instead of being scared by his behavior, I couldn't help but think how fascinating it was to see him acting like that first day I'd seen him in the woods, like a warrior. Fierce. Wild.

I followed Ginevra's suggestion to hide inside the house, but looked at both of them one last time before closing the door. They both seemed concerned, though for different reasons.

After I'd locked the door, I limped over to the couch. Without Evan's comforting presence to take my mind off my ankle, the throbbing pain returned to center stage. I dumped my backpack on the floor and collapsed onto the cushions, covering my eyes with the back of my hand.

As I thought about it in the silence, what had happened seemed even more insane. How could I still be alive? My mind rewound the tape and relived the entire sequence of those terrifying seconds. I had been sure the semi was about to hit me. What had Evan been doing there in the middle of the woods? In my mind's eye I clearly saw my final glimpse of him standing there in the trees, staring at me with a devastated look on his face. I'd thought it was just a mirage, a last wish hidden deep in my heart. And yet, he really had been there and he'd pushed me out of harm's way. But how had he managed to get to me in time and then end up unscathed? I'd seen what had happened to my bicycle. A fate for which I too had been destined. My aching head told me this was no time to think it all through.

I was still alive. Like the heroes in the novels I read, Evan had come to save me, rescuing me from a fate that had already been ordained.

Evan.

Knowing that was enough to push the whole experience from my mind, like a puff of breath on a dusty surface, in spite of how terrifying it had been. I remembered the feeling of being clasped in Evan's arms and my breathing spiraled out of control. I buried my head in the cushions and lost all sense of time, keeping my hand over my eyes to block the light as I steadied my breath and tried to relax. I let myself be lulled by the half-light, finding it comforting.

In the darkness and silence, fear began to creep over me. Evan's warning gradually returned to my mind, making me realize only then that up to that point I hadn't been afraid. As though my brain had stored it all up in a drawer to be opened later. The tension I'd heard in his voice began to sound alarm bells, making my anxiety flare up again.

Why had he seemed so worried? After all, he'd pushed me to safety, so why was he talking as if it weren't over? As if I weren't completely out of danger? Did he think it hadn't been just an accident? The thought that the truck driver might have tried to run me over on purpose was ridiculous. It had just been a terrible mishap, a brush with disaster. Evan had saved me from certain death, so why all the concern over my wellbeing now? What else could happen to me?

The air stirred, giving me goosebumps and making me wish I'd closed the windows. When I smelled Evan's scent I got up from the couch but was surprised to find the living room completely empty. The windows behind the couch were both closed. I took a deep breath, filling my nostrils with the aroma. I had no doubt it was his, not after I'd smelled him from so close up. It was so strong now I doubted my own senses. It was like Evan was there and my eyes were playing tricks on me, keeping me from seeing him. I instinctively grabbed the hem of my top and sniffed it, wondering if my clothes had absorbed his scent. But the smell wasn't coming from me. It filled the air, it was everywhere.

"Feeling better?"

I jumped at the sound of Evan's voice. Whirling around, I found him standing behind me.

"Evan . . ." The fear made me let out a groan and I sank down onto the couch. "You scared me half to death!"

"Sorry, I didn't mean to. You've already had a big enough scare for today." He walked over to the couch.

"H-how did you get in?" I asked, stunned.

"Through the door." His eyes wavered, as though he'd given himself away. "I told you I'd be back," he added.

I swallowed, panicking. "The door was locked, Evan," I said, my voice breaking as a new feeling arose inside me: the survival instinct, which had been hidden who knows where and for how long.

"Don't be silly," he said, trying to sound convincing. "I mean, I told you to lock it but you were pretty shaken up. You probably forgot." He stared at me, trying to get me to believe it, but I knew what had happened.

"I clearly remember locking it," I insisted, looking hard at him.

"Come on." Evan sat down beside me on the couch. "How else could I have gotten in? The windows are closed and you would have noticed if I'd knocked the door down, don't you think? Listen, you just came face to face with death. You were still shaking when I set you down. I know you *think* you locked it, but you can't be sure." His eyes stared steadily into mine and he was strangely concentrated, as if trying to brainwash me. He cracked a smile, but I sensed his hesitation. "Gemma . . ."

My heart began to beat irregularly. For a moment his black-velvet voice had gotten past my defenses.

"You've been through a traumatic experience," `he continued, stroking my forehead sweetly. An uncontrollable impulse made me pull back from his touch. I was surprised to discover that the shooting pain in my head was coming from that very spot. "Does it hurt?" His voice had grown tender.

"Only a little," I lied, tightening my lips. Actually, the pain was coming from my forehead and shooting out in a circle around my skull, leaving it aflame. Evan clearly wanted to drop the subject of how he'd gotten in, and not for the first time, but I didn't want to insist. It might make me come across as ungrateful. After all, he had saved my life.

"You need to rest. You've had a traumatic morning. It must have been rough, finding yourself facing death."

"Can I ask you something?"

Evan seemed surprised that I'd ignored his comment and had been so blunt, and he was probably nervous about my question. Or maybe about the answer he'd have to refuse to give me. There was clearly something about Evan

I wasn't allowed to know. And instinct told me I was better off not knowing it.

"Why is Ginevra so mad at me?"

The simplicity of the question took him by surprise.

"No one's mad at you, Gemma," he said, clearly relieved. What had he been afraid I might ask him?

"Then why was she so angry back in the woods?" I insisted. I was sure it was because of jealousy. Ginevra had doubtless caught me staring at her boyfriend now and then. Not to mention all the attention he gave me or the way his voice became so sweet just for me. Ginevra must have noticed, but did I actually intimidate her enough to trigger a homicidal instinct in her? The very idea made me smile. I was so insignificant compared to her.

"She's mad at *me*, not you," Evan reassured me, a touch of sadness crossing his face. "You haven't done anything wrong, Gemma."

My heart leapt every time he said my name, enveloping it in the spell that was his voice. "She wishes you'd left me to my fate," I said.

Evan hesitated, as if I'd hit the nail on the head, but I couldn't believe Ginevra could actually be so cruel. Could she really want me dead, literally? Did I really pose such a threat to her?

"It's not what you think." For a second, it seemed like Evan was replying to what I'd been thinking. "It's complicated. You can't understand. And I can't explain it to you."

"Try," I said encouragingly.

"Out of the question." His tone was peremptory. "I can't."

Discouraged by the authority in his voice, I closed my mouth and let the silence separate us.

23

CLOSENESS

More than ever now, I felt like I'd known Evan my whole life. The accident had brought us closer. We were alone in my house, sitting side by side on the couch, and yet I felt strangely comfortable. There was a level of harmony I'd never reached before, not even with Peter. Reluctantly, I forced myself to remember that what I felt was mine and mine alone. Evan was with Ginevra.

"Try to get some rest," he suggested, stroking my hair, his tone thoughtful. I wasn't sure whether the room was spinning because I'd hit my head or if his hand left me in a daze whenever he touched me. "I have to take care of some things. I'll come back to check on you later." He stood up.

"Evan—" My voice came out in a broken sob. I couldn't resist the urge to try and stop him. I didn't want him to go, but I had no idea how to make him stay. "Do you really have to leave?" I asked sincerely, surprising myself with my assertiveness.

"Yeah, I do." He stared at the floor as though something were upsetting him. When he raised his eyes again, he found mine waiting for them. "Don't be afraid. You won't be alone. Now you need to rest." As he said these last words his eyes bored into mine, almost as if in a last-ditch effort to control my mind. I suddenly felt so sleepy that when the door closed behind Evan my eyelids grew heavy and I found my way back to unconsciousness.

I felt a deep sense of peace, like I was swimming in a sea of languid serenity or cradled in a bed of harmony. And yet sleep hadn't entirely stolen me away from the real world. I was in a strange limbo halfway between the two. I was perfectly aware I was lying on the couch. I could feel the sunbeams growing brighter and more penetrating as they streamed through the window and warmed my skin. Though my whole body was bathed in warm sunlight that filled me with lassitude, I felt it especially on my head and aching ankle. It was probably just the pain that gave me that impression. I'd never felt such an incredible sensation of wellbeing in my whole life.

Unfortunately, the sound of a door slamming tore me out of that languor. I recognized my mother's hurried footsteps in the hallway. "Mom, you're back!" I raised my torso just in time to see her start at the sound of my voice.

"Honey, what are you doing home so early? Weren't you supposed to meet your friends at the lake?" she asked, looking concerned. "Did everything go okay with your teacher?"

"Um . . . It's a long story, Mom. I'm sure it would only bore you," I stammered, not sure what to say. I didn't know how presentable I was—there hadn't been time for me to look in a mirror. It suddenly dawned on me that I'd have to explain the gash on my forehead. I raised my hand to the spot to check how deep the cut was, but before my fingers touched it, I noticed the pain in my head was gone and I now felt an amazing sense of lightness.

There was no more ache, no more soreness. The burning sensation had vanished entirely. I ran my fingers over my forehead, puzzled to find the skin smooth. There was no cut. In any case, I wouldn't be able to hide the fact that I'd sprained my ankle because of my limp, and I certainly couldn't stay there on the couch all day long. I'd have to make up an excuse.

"What time is Peter coming to pick you up?" she asked from the kitchen.

Peter? I didn't remember making plans with Pet.

"I stopped by the dry cleaner and picked up your dress. You're going to look beautiful tonight, Squirrelicue."

My eyes grew wide with alarm. I grabbed my backpack and pulled out my assignment book to check what day it was.

April 20th. Prom.

My jaw dropped. I was shocked by how disconnected I was from the world.

Prom? How could I have forgotten?

At our school, prom was always in mid-May, but this year it was being held early. Was that why it had slipped my mind? Or was Jeneane right? Had I totally shut myself off from everything and everyone around me? Even worse, how could I go to the prom in my condition? I couldn't bail on Peter at the last minute and disappoint him, but then again I didn't want to make him spend the night sitting in a corner with me while everyone else was having fun. I certainly wouldn't be good company with a twisted ankle.

I searched my pockets and backpack for my phone and, with horror, remembered what had happened to it. My fingers snagged in my iPod cord. I stared at it, astonished. I didn't remember still having my earbuds in. The sensation of the earbud being pulled out of my ear filled my mind and I couldn't stop the flashback. The deafening squeal of brakes, the red blur rushing at me— I closed my eyes to shut out the terrible memory. Death had come to take me but for some unknown reason, I had escaped it. My heart skipped a beat, contradicting me. I knew the reason. Evan had saved me from my fate, risking his own life in the process. I could never repay him for the gift he'd given me.

I got up from the couch and strode over to the wall phone, then stopped, staring at the receiver, when I realized how quickly I'd reached it. I raised my foot and rotated it slowly, more and more confused.

The pain was gone.

"Everything okay?" My mom stared at me, puzzled.

"More than okay," I said, astonished. How had I healed so quickly? I bore no trace of the horrible accident. Not a single trace. Could it all have been a dream?

Great. I couldn't even trust my memory any more.

Still stunned, I dialed Peter's number to confirm our plans. Although going to the prom together had been a foregone conclusion, we hadn't talked about it recently.

The phone rang only twice before he picked up.

"Pet!" I said when I heard his voice.

"Hey, Gemma! Where the heck have you been? We were all supposed to hang out at the lake this morning. I tried calling you a million times. We need to make plans for tonight. Did you forget?"

"I, um . . . Right. Yeah." I stole a glance over my shoulder at my mom, who was fiddling around, pretending not to be interested in the conversation. "It's kind of a long story. I'll explain later. The invitation still stands, then, right?" I asked, suddenly unsure whether the recent events might have changed something.

"Of course it does. Why wouldn't it?" He sounded so calm, all my fears drifted away.

Peter and I always went to the school dances together. We'd decided it back when we were little kids and had always stuck to the agreement. By now, everyone at school was so sure they'd see us show up together that for years no one had even wasted their breath inviting one of us.

"I'll swing by your place at seven." It sounded like he was in a rush.

"Okay, see you then," I said, ending the conversation. I wondered if he still had his suspicions about Evan.

Evan.

For a minute I let myself wonder what it would be like if I'd made an exception, if for the first time I'd gotten an invitation from someone other than Peter. A *real* invitation. But deep down I knew it would never happen.

I wasn't even sure Evan was going to the prom, and in any case Ginevra would definitely be his date. I had to face the facts. She was his girlfriend. Not me. Why couldn't I get it through my head? Was I really still jealous of her?

As I helped my mom make lunch, I gradually realized how fit I felt, as if I were wearing a new skin. Like when I was a little girl, always scampering through the trees as spry as a squirrel, my long ponytail flying behind me. It was back then that I'd earned the nickname Squirrelicue. I couldn't remember the last time I'd felt so in shape physically, although mentally I was still a bit exhausted from the intense morning I'd had.

After all, I'd looked death straight in the eye. I pushed the bone-chilling thought out of my mind before my mom could notice how upset I was.

"Well? What time is Peter coming?" She was ecstatic.

"Seven," I said distractedly. "And when's Dad getting back? I can't eat too late, I have a lot to do before I get ready," I lied. Actually, I just wanted to go to my room and be alone for a while to reflect on the bizarre day.

"Well, put your bike in the garage first. You know your dad hates it when you leave it in the driveway."

I froze. What was she talking about? A vague suspicion spread over me. I rushed down the hall and opened the front door, my heart in my throat.

"Gemma, everything okay?" my mom called from the kitchen.

But I didn't answer. I was gaping at the sight of my bicycle. It was leaning against the garage door. It was really mine. And it didn't have a scratch on it.

The oven timer rang, announcing that the meatloaf and potatoes were ready just as my dad came through the front door.

"Perfect timing," I said. I looked at their faces and was struck by the sudden awareness of what I'd almost lost today.

"How come you're home? Weren't you going out with your friends? And did you turn in your—what was it again?" he asked.

"Yearbook photos. Actually, I didn't even end up going," I admitted. At least that part of the story was true. "My headache was so bad that halfway to the school I turned around and came home to bed." I hated lying—it was natural to feel an aversion to something you couldn't do well. I was rarely able to come up with believable stories and I normally ended up giving myself away one way or the other. I wasn't cut out for secrets. And yet, I had no choice.

"Have a seat, you two," Mom said. "Gemma, try to finish it all. There's no telling when you'll have the chance to eat something tonight," she added, knowing how much I disliked meatloaf.

"Don't worry, the school's serving refreshments. And if there's food anywhere within a ten-mile radius, rest assured

I'll track it down," I replied. After all, I was bound to be pretty nervous tonight.

Besides, the unusual energy flowing through my veins this afternoon was making me insatiably hungry. My mother was amazed to see me clean my plate even before my father had.

After a hot shower, I fell onto my bed, earbuds in, shutting off the outside world. I closed my eyes and surrendered to the notes of James Blunt. Suddenly I sensed a presence in the room. I opened my eyes and jumped, surprised to see Jeneane standing by the bed.

"Jeneane!"

"Hey! I knocked but you didn't answer, so I figured I'd come on in."

"What are you doing here?" I blurted, realizing only a second later how rude it sounded.

"Hello to you too!" she said, shrugging. "I hope you don't mind me stopping by. Where were you this morning? I wanted to talk to you down at the lake, but you never showed. Are you sick? Did you catch something contagious?" She backed up, looking me up and down to check the state of my health.

"No, I'm just . . . just a little tired, that's all. What did you want to talk to me about?"

My question made her eyes sparkle and her face light up in a breathtaking smile. "Listen, I've got an awesome idea! And you absolutely can't say no!" A makeup bag appeared in her hands. She'd clearly been hiding it behind her back.

I shot her a reluctant look, but Jeneane ignored it completely and sat down on the bed as I crossed my legs. "So here's the plan."

"I'm all ears," I said, letting a hint of sarcasm slip out.

"Tonight's prom, right?" She looked me straight in the eye to make sure I was following every word.

"Right," I said with a nod.

"Well, you've *got* to look gorgeous. I'm going to take care of that!"

"Jeneane," I began, hoping to dissuade her.

"Don't say anything. Just leave it to me."

"Wait—wait! What are you doing? What's the plan?" I asked, terrified by her expression.

Jeneane flashed one of her perfect smiles and sat me down at my desk, pulling back my hair even though I hadn't agreed to anything yet.

"No time for questions. First I have to put this on you. Don't move."

As she smoothed a creamy foundation onto my face I let out a groan. "Jeneane, what are you doing?" I tried to ask, but her hands on my cheeks made me smoosh the words together.

"Girl, I'm going to turn you into a princess!" For some strange reason, it sounded more like a threat than a promise.

"Aren't you going to the prom too?" I asked as she skillfully applied makeup to my face.

"Are you kidding?" My question was so ridiculous it made her stop and look me in the eye "You think I'd skip it? I wouldn't miss it for anything in the world!"

"Who's your date?"

I instantly regretted asking. I was sure Jeneane must have told me a hundred times and I simply hadn't been listening. I also knew I must be the only person in school who would let such an important piece of information slip. My mind had been only on Evan lately.

"I know what you're thinking, but don't worry, I never mentioned it to you," she said, smiling smugly for catching me red-handed. "I asked Brandon to go with me."

She asked Brandon. Yeah, I bet.

"And you . . . are going with Pete," she said matter-of-factly. "But you'd rather be going with somebody else." She looked at me out of the corner of her eye as I started, surprised she knew. I stared at her, as stunned as if I'd caught her reading my diary. I had to admit, Jeneane was pretty sharp. "Don't gape at me like that!" she said. "I'm an expert when it comes to that kind of thing. Besides, I just put two and two together, that's all." She shrugged, looking pleased.

"Is it really so obvious?" I asked, annoyed that I'd been so easy to read.

"Only to me, don't worry. So what's up with Pete?"

"I don't know how to handle things any more. He's never been so jealous before," I forced myself to admit.

"Only because you've never really been interested in anyone before. Why do you think I'm here? Gemma, I've known you literally since we were born and I've never seen you interested in *anybody*. I've been waiting years for this to happen and there's no way I'd let you mess it up. Tonight you're going to be beautiful. You'll turn every head, believe me." She looked me in the eye, one eyebrow raised.

"It's just a shame the only boy I've ever been interested in already has someone. You're forgetting *Ginevra*." I said her name with reverential contempt.

"I already told you you're wrong. Trust me. I've seen the way he looks at you. It's through our eyes that we decide what kind of connection we want to have with another person. If you let them look into your eyes for longer than a few seconds, you're letting them see inside you, bond with you. It's like you're opening your heart to them. I have to admit I'm a little jealous of you."

"You? Jealous? *Of me*?" I couldn't believe my ears. "But you're, like, the queen of the whole school! *I'm* the one who's jealous of *you*. I've always envied your self-confidence."

"You see? That's exactly what makes you irresistible. You're *beautiful*, Gemma. How can you not realize that?"

A sound escaped me, a mix of surprise and disapproval. "Yeah, sure! And to think I've never had a boyfriend. Well, except Derek McCullagan, but he doesn't really count."

"That's only because you never wanted one in the first place. Guys need to be encouraged, even with just a look, otherwise they'll never make a move. Do you honestly think no boy has ever been interested in you? How can you not notice them checking you out all the time? You're so pretty, I think it intimidates them."

"What?! Are you kidding? Listen, stop teasing me, it's not funny—"

"Pete's crazy about you! You must have at least noticed that, seeing how tight you guys are."

Okay, maybe I wouldn't have noticed what was going on with Peter if my mom hadn't pointed it out. Could she be right? I couldn't believe she was being serious. I felt like I'd been living on another planet this whole time.

"It's easy for you," I told her. "You're so self-confident. When you want someone all you have to do is reach out and grab them. Well, not literally, of course."

"That's exactly my point. The interest the boys at school take in me is totally superficial. You think I don't realize that? No one's ever honestly interested in *me*, in who I am on the inside. But if *you* decided to show a guy you liked him, you'd totally steal his heart. That's why I never let anyone get really close to me. I can't risk falling in love because I know what guys want from me. I know what they see when they look at my body. On the other hand, the way Evan looks at you . . ." Her happiness for me was tinged with sadness. It showed in her eyes, although she was clearly trying to hide it.

"Then why do you go out with them all?" I asked, shocked that she was aware of the situation.

"At least that way I can convince myself I'm the one using them. That's why I never really commit, so I can avoid being let down when I find out they weren't really interested in me after all. Which is inevitable."

"Jeneane, you can't say that! They're all crazy about you. Maybe one of them is right for you and you just don't realize it because you're too scared to get hurt. Don't ruin your own chances! I mean, Brandon's been crazy about you since grade school. And not for the reason you think. Okay, maybe a little," I admitted, biting my lip. "All I'm saying is you'll never know unless you give it a chance."

"Don't feel sorry for me, it's not that bad. It gives me a sense of satisfaction and I'm fine with it, at least for now. Maybe when the right guy comes around I'll realize it. Meanwhile, nobody else is going to have me."

"I thought you liked Evan too," I admitted, glancing at her, curious.

She pursed her lips, trying to hide a smile that was both sly and sweet. "I'll admit, he's *fascinating*, but I would never try to compete with you."

My jaw dropped. I was floored. "You can't be serious." I raised an eyebrow, unable to believe she really felt that way.

"Besides, to be honest, he kind of scares me. There's something different about him, something mysterious. He's got this allure to him, like there's a Prince of Darkness lurking behind his sexy smile. Sometimes it actually gives me the creeps. And you should see the way he glares at

Pete! A couple times I even got the impression he'd kill him, if looks could, but is just holding back."

I gulped. I'd sensed the same thing, but part of me stubbornly refused to acknowledge it.

Jeneane's voice softened and I realized she was staring at me. "But then I see how he looks at you and I confess I've never been so envious of anybody in my whole life." Warmth slowly spread over my cheeks. "I'm totally convinced nobody's ever looked at me like Evan looks at you. He wants you, Gemma. I'm sure of it. It's *you* he wants."

After everything she'd said, I discovered there was a little corner hidden deep down in my heart that still had hope. But I knew what I'd seen in Evan's garden. Jeneane didn't know about it, which is why she kept pushing me toward him. Strangely, I let her go on believing it. Maybe I wanted to leave room for that tiny hope that she continued to nurture in me.

"Well, I hope you're right," I added as she passed a blush brush over my cheeks.

"*Et voilà!*" Jeneane straightened up and stepped back to admire her work, looking satisfied. "Perfect! Even better than I imagined!"

"Let me see." I tried to get up from my chair, but she held me down by the shoulders.

"Slow down. I'm not done yet. You expect an artist to present her work before it's finished?" She grinned.

Hanging out with Jeneane wasn't so bad after all. It had been such a long time since we had.

"Here, take your dress," she said. "Put it on so we can start working on your hair." I felt like a doll being handled by an impertinent little girl. "And no peeking in the mirror!" she warned me.

I did what she said with resignation. I put on the purplish-red dress, making sure I didn't muss the makeup—I wasn't used to wearing stuff on my face—and went back to her. She stared at me in silence.

"Jen, is something wrong? Did I smudge my lipstick?" I raised a hand to my mouth, seeing her enigmatic expression.

"Oh my God. Your dress is . . . perfect. I'm speechless."

"Now *that's* hard to believe," I said, looking at her out of the corner of my eye with a smirk.

I loved that dress. I'd seen it in a shop window and instantly knew I wanted it. As it so happened, it perfectly fit the occasion, because later on they announced that the theme for that year's prom was *Red Carpet: A Night Out in Hollywood*.

The shade of red flattered my dark hair and fair complexion, although I tanned quickly in summertime. The neckline was woven into a sort of bow and the fabric flowed gently down my sides, flaring just above the knee.

"Ugh!" Jeneane groaned, "what is that, a nest on your head? You waiting for squirrels to move in or something?"

I laughed, although I wasn't so sure to what extent she was kidding. "My hair isn't so bad, it's just a little messy."

Her parents were hair stylists. They had a salon downtown and Jeneane's hair always looked perfect, unlike mine, which was a little wavy, curled at the ends, but nothing disastrous.

"Good thing I showed up. I don't know what you would have done without me."

"Yeah, it was a real stroke of luck," I said, a hint of sarcasm in my voice.

Jeneane helped me sit down, making sure the dress wouldn't get creased. For a minute, given the intimacy we'd suddenly rediscovered after all this time, I considered telling her what was going on with me. It felt like if I didn't get some of it off my chest I'd end up losing my mind.

As her hands sank into my hair, my lips parted against my will. "Listen, something . . . something strange happened to me today. It's got to do with the reason why I didn't meet you guys," I continued, still hesitant.

"Are you trying to drive me crazy? Don't keep me guessing. You know how impatient I get! Spit it out!" she said excitedly, not even trying to hold back her curiosity.

"I was biking to the school to drop off my yearbook photos and a semi almost ran me over."

Her hands stopped, still in my hair. I tilted my head a little to look at her and saw the blood drain from her face, leaving her incredibly pale. "Evan saved me," I told her, suddenly overcome with emotion. For some reason, an unknown instinct warned me not to continue.

"Shut up! You're joking, right?"

"How could anybody joke about something like that?" My skin went ice cold at the memory of the death that had passed me by.

"Wow! That is so *romantic*!"

"Romantic? I almost ended up under a truck!" I shot back, aghast. "Besides, Ginevra was there with him."

"Still getting in the way?" she grunted.

I repressed a laugh. "She's his girlfriend, Jen." Why was it Jeneane always seemed to forget that?

"Ooh, you're jealous! You're in love!" She'd probably noticed how red my cheeks had become.

"What? No! It's just that . . . well, I've felt this incredible *attraction* ever since I first saw him. I can't think about anything else, it's like an obsession. Something inside me has changed. I don't feel like the same person any more."

"It's called *love*." Jeneane was sure of herself, but I was talking about something completely different, and maybe I was realizing it for the first time. It was a new sensation, but at the same time, familiar. It was like Evan had reawakened some part of me that was buried deep, deep inside.

"Hey, have you seen that strange tattoo on his arm?" I asked. "I wonder what it means. I'm pretty sure it's some foreign language. Maybe it's Ginevra's name or something." I actually just wanted Jeneane to say it wasn't so. She'd ogled him so thoroughly that by now she must have deciphered whatever it was that was written on his arm.

"What tattoo? Evan doesn't have a tattoo on his arm. If he did I'd have noticed it. You mean you're even seeing things now? You really are messed up," she teased me.

I sat there, stunned. How could she be so convinced? I'd seen it clearly enough.

"Don't be so tense. Tonight Evan will only have eyes for you. Trust me, you're irresistible. Speaking of which, make sure you stay away from my Brandon," she warned with a hint of sarcasm. "One more curl and . . . done. That's it, you're ready!" She spun my chair around so I was facing her and fell silent.

"How do I look?"

Jeneane took me by the hand and pulled me over to the mirror. "See for yourself."

I looked at my reflection and gasped.

"My God, you really do look like a princess, Gemma."

I raised a hand and ran it over my cheekbone, surprised by what Jeneane had managed to do with my skin.

The makeup was so light it was barely noticeable, but it was enough to bring out my eyes like never before. My lips had just a hint of color while my hair fell down my back in soft curls, a few locks pinned up to frame my face.

"I'm speechless, Jeneane. You've worked a miracle," I admitted, still amazed at how different the reflection in the mirror was from how I normally looked.

"What miracle? I just enhanced what was already there. You'd already done the lion's share of the work. Don't be so modest," she said affectionately.

"I don't know how to thank you, really."

"I do—let me run, or I'll never be ready in time!" she called from the door after hurriedly collecting her things.

"Thanks!" I shouted as she left.

Jeneane popped back into the doorway and winked. "I've done my part, the rest is up to you. Good luck."

"Jeneane!" I impulsively grabbed her arm before she could shut the door behind her. "Please don't tell anyone what I just told you, okay?"

Jeneane smiled at me with a conspiratorial look. I had no idea why I felt the need to hide what had happened, but something was telling me that not even I knew all the answers.

24

INTIMIDATION

About an hour had gone by since Jeneane had left my room. The clock read 6:45, reminding me that Peter would be there any minute. For the Spring Dance they usually rented an outdoor venue somewhere in town like the Crown Plaza Resort, the Lake Placid Golf Club, or the Whiteface Lodge. But this time the teachers had decided to hold the event at school.

The doorbell rang sooner than I expected, so I slipped on my ballet flats and rushed downstairs. Peter was already standing there at the front door.

I saw how surprised he was by the sight of me. My mom watched his reaction out of the corner of her eye, pleased. Peter wasn't used to seeing me dressed up. Or, more likely, something had changed in him since the last time he had.

"Wow," he exclaimed, not trying to hide his surprise, "I'm speechless. What'd you do with my Gemma?"

My mom's eyes darted to me and a hint of embarrassment hung in the air. Peter's cheeks flushed the instant he realized he'd affectionately insinuated that I belonged to him.

I nudged his shoulder in an attempt to ease the tension while my mom snapped pictures of us. "It might seem crazy, but even I can be feminine once in a while. Let's go," I said, grabbing the lapel of his black tux and pulling him forward, "or we'll be late."

If I hadn't been obsessed with Evan, tonight I would have found Peter attractive. I wasn't used to seeing him dressed up for a black-tie event either, although he was wearing gym shoes and his shirt was a bit too untucked to actually consider him formally dressed. But despite everything, the bar was set too high now for me to be attracted to him.

"Bye, Mrs. Bloom!" Peter gripped the doorway with one hand before letting me drag him away.

"Have a good time!" my mom called across our front walk as Peter started the car he'd rented.

The ride to school felt endless. From time to time I glanced out the window to make sure Peter hadn't taken a longer route. It wasn't the first time I was going to a school dance with him, but it was definitely the first time I'd found myself worried about his expectations. I was terribly uncomfortable inside the cramped car, and my discomfort made it feel even smaller than it actually was—almost too small to contain all the tension our bodies were emanating.

I could clearly read Peter's hopes for that evening in his eyes and was almost overwhelmed by the awareness that I couldn't make it happen.

I felt like I'd lost my best friend.

"You didn't have to . . . I mean . . . you could have taken your dad's car," I said, trying to ease the tension, "like last year."

"Not tonight," he said. "You look really, really good."

I bit my lower lip but stopped the moment I noticed the strange taste of the lip gloss. "You too," I said, embarrassed. "But, what, no bow tie?"

Peter cast me a sidelong glance. "I refuse to wear ties!" he exclaimed, laughing at himself.

"I thought this year would be different. I mean, we're growing up."

Peter grinned at me and snapped the elastic band I wore on my arm as always. "Some things never change."

He was right. I hadn't given up my habits just to satisfy a social convention either. Being true to myself felt good, no matter what the circumstances were.

I silently thanked heaven when we pulled up in the school parking lot. I felt unable to handle this new relationship which, against my will, was starting to go beyond the limits of friendship.

Peter hurried to open the passenger-side door for me and offered me his hand to help me out. No matter how comforting and familiar his touch was, I could think only of Evan as we walked up to the gym, which had been turned into a ballroom for the occasion.

The doors were opened by brawny boys in tuxes who were in charge of checking the tickets. The warm light coming from inside made me look up from the red carpet that led from the entrance into the main part of the gym. Suddenly anxiety gripped me. I forced myself to hold my breath as my heartbeat wavered at the thought of seeing Evan again. He was the only thing on my mind and I was dying to be near him.

After a few deep breaths, I walked through the door. The space was so elegantly decorated I could barely believe it was actually the gym. Our very familiar school colors—blue and yellow, which covered the walls every day—were barely visible, as the whole gym was draped in velvet. From the ceiling hung a massive chandelier laden with crystal prism drops that sparkled, reflecting the light on the floor and walls. Regal and majestic, the long red carpet crossed the entire room, forming a perfect walkway to stroll down for professional photos.

Peter took my hand and held me back. As I turned to look at him, he pulled out the corsage he'd ordered.

"I asked your mom what color your dress was." He slipped it onto my wrist, looking into my eyes as he did so, while our picture was taken. I held his gaze. Peter was so sweet and I loved him so much. Not the way he wanted, though. There was nothing I could do about that. I wanted to be swept away, I wanted a love that consumed me.

I looked down at the corsage sheepishly.

"Thanks," I murmured. It really was beautiful: a small cluster of white carnations interwoven with a black lace bracelet. Only then did I notice that Peter had pinned a matching boutonnière onto his lapel. That particular flower symbolized eternal faithfulness. I wondered if he knew that.

I looked around in an effort to relax. It was still early, but the room was already pretty packed. My first instinct was to look for Evan's face among the crowd. I peered around, scanning the entire room.

"Looking for someone?" Peter didn't even try to hide the reproach in his voice.

"Don't start, Pet."

"I could tell you the same thing. You're here with me— try not to forget it. I'm going to go look for the others. I have the funny feeling I'm going to need something stronger than punch tonight. Maybe I'll get a little drunk before I come back. That way it'll be easier to pretend you care anything about me."

"Peter, please, don't ruin everything!"

"I don't have to, you're already taking care of that yourself."

Peter stormed off, leaving me stunned. I almost didn't recognize him any more. I watched him walk away and my eyes met Ginevra's. She was on the other side of the gym.

It was impossible not to notice her. She shone like a beacon in the dark of night. A star in full Hollywood style. Everyone's eyes were glued to her. Even the girls couldn't help but stare at her and her radiance. Who could blame them? Ginevra left everyone breathless. Her fringed pearl-white gown, so fine and elegant, made her look like an angel who'd descended from heaven. Among the crowd she sparkled, shining like a comet amid simple stars. The flounces of her gown draped her body softly, clinging to her until right above the knee, baring her long, sensual legs, while the back ended in a sheer train, like a phoenix rising from silver flames. Her golden hair hung over her shoulders in a myriad of shiny curls, while around her neck she wore a thin, eye-catching necklace in the shape of a dangerous-looking serpent that wound down to her neckline.

No matter how elegant I felt tonight, seeing Ginevra shattered any fantasies I'd had.

Unable to crawl back out of the deep pit of inadequacy into which I'd fallen, I walked over to the refreshments table to drown my disappointment—along with the hope that Evan would "only have eyes for me," as Jeneane had sworn—in punch.

Discouraged, I began to seriously consider whether I should reassess Peter's interest in me. He was more in my league. Evan was definitely too good for me. Actually, he was too good for any girl other than Ginevra.

When the cluster of students beside her moved away, I finally saw Evan and suddenly Ginevra's light faded, eclipsed by the powerful dark magnetism that drew me to him.

It would have been difficult not to notice Evan tonight. First of all, he was the only one not wearing the traditional tuxedo. Over casual slacks, which did nothing but make him even more attractive, he wore a dark gray top, the sleeves pulled back to the elbows. His black tattoo stood out on his arm. But it certainly wasn't his clothes that monopolized my attention.

I had to admit it: they were perfect together, he and Ginevra. The classic couple everyone envied.

Someone must have spiked the punch, because I suddenly felt dizzy. Or maybe the thought of the two of them together was addling my brain. I couldn't accept it, even though I felt ridiculous for thinking Evan might be interested in a run-of-the-mill girl like me. I was the naïve nerd that kids at school would borrow notes from, while Evan was as beautiful as an angel.

I hid among the crowd so I could stare at him undisturbed, confident that having all those people around would keep him from noticing me. Ginevra moved her lips nonstop while Evan listened to her, not even opening his mouth. Judging from his expression, somehow what she was saying both bothered and amused him. I couldn't take my eyes off the sensual curve of his lips as he smiled and his eyes as they narrowed, making him so irresistible and sexy.

All at once Evan whipped his head around and looked at me, catching me staring. My heart leapt. He'd moved so quickly I hadn't had time to look away.

His eyes locked onto mine instantly, as if he'd known exactly where to find me, but he hadn't noticed me standing there before, I was sure of it. Was Ginevra talking to him about me, maybe?

Involuntarily, my lips twisted into an awkward greeting. In reply, Evan cocked his head, staring at me intently, one corner of his mouth raised in the most seductive smile I'd ever seen.

His gaze was attentive, like I remembered it, but the sensuality in his smile was entirely new. My heart threatened to escape my control.

Despite the distance between us, our eyes were glued to each other. It felt like everyone around us had disappeared and that invisible cord had returned to connect my heart to his.

But Ginevra's presence was strong enough to distract me from Evan's gaze. Out of the corner of my eye I saw her looking back and forth between him and me, irritated, until her cold, razor-sharp eyes slashed the cord that united us, bringing Evan's attention back to her.

When he took his eyes off me, I returned to the punchbowl and filled the still-empty paper cup I'd been clutching. Or maybe I'd already filled it up and finished it all. I couldn't remember.

I didn't feel like being at the prom any more. My expectations for the evening had already gone up in smoke at the sight of Ginevra's intimidating glare. And I'd ruined Peter's hopes too. Speaking of Peter, I wondered where he'd gone. I'd completely lost sight of him. Neither one of us would be getting what we wanted tonight. Deep in my heart, I hoped he'd at least found company. The room was full of dolled-up girls who would have given anything to be his date tonight. Not that any of them deserved him. Maybe such a girl didn't even exist. Even I felt I didn't deserve his attention.

"Hey, hot stuff!"

A loud, arrogant, masculine voice distracted me from my thoughts. It was close. Too close, actually. It had come from right behind me but, slurred as it was from whatever they'd used to spike the punch, it didn't sound very familiar. Judging from his breath, which reeked of alcohol, he must have finished the rest of the bottle himself. I looked up from the table and cocked my head to listen without turning around, afraid of bumping into him.

From the corner of my eye I recognized him. A swimmer's shoulders, ash-blond hair, beady blue eyes. Daryl Donovan. King of the Winter Carnival that was held every February at our school, not to mention the hockey team champion.

And he was talking to me.

Anyone else would have been flattered by his attention, but I was torn between contempt for his arrogance and fear that Evan might see me with him and get the wrong idea.

I ignored him, looking down at the table, hoping my indifference would make him go away. Instead, his presence grew stronger. He was looming over me like a bear towering over its prey.

"You look sexy tonight," he whispered directly into my ear.

He'd tried to make his voice sound sensual, but it had the exact opposite effect, sending a disgusted shiver down my arms. When I caught a whiff of his breath, a wave of nausea rose up from my stomach.

To my horror, I discovered that my indifference was doing nothing but amusing and exciting him even more. It was very likely he wasn't accustomed to being turned down. "So where've you been hiding? Pretty lil' flower like you's just waiting to be plucked," he whispered, leaning forward until his chest touched my back.

Overcome with disgust from the brief contact, I turned around and tried to push him away, but he was too heavy and didn't budge an inch. Though he was having a hard time staying on his feet because of all the alcohol, he still completely overpowered me.

"Get away," I warned him, horrified.

"Aw, c'mon!" he insisted with a grin, continuing to edge closer. "I just wanna have a lil' fun, just for tonight."

I found him repugnant. He was getting more arrogant and insolent with every passing second. I began to worry I wouldn't be able to stop him.

I looked around for help, but no one seemed to notice us at all. Screaming would have been useless—the music was too loud for anyone to hear me. And he was way bigger than me. If he'd felt like it, he could have dragged me out of the room and no one would have tried to stop him. Nobody would dare stand up to Daryl. He was a big shot at school, as well as a troublemaker, and my rejection was only arousing him more. He'd taken it as a personal challenge, I could tell from the gleam in his eye.

Panic washed over me. I tried to hide my terror, but doubted it was working.

"You know how many girls would love to be in your shoes?" he said, irritated. He was seriously turned on, I could feel it. And he was starting to lose control.

"I told you, leave me alone!" I shouted, my fear growing and my eyes brimming with tears. Where was Peter? With his build, he wouldn't have any problem getting Daryl off my case.

"C'mon, chill, I know you want it too. I promise you won't regret it," he said breathlessly, his voice hoarse with excitement.

This was getting serious. Daryl was moving closer and closer, and my attempts to push him away were futile. I was already backed up against the table and he was blocking my way with his muscle-bound body.

"Don't be such a prude," he panted, his breath hitting my face.

Tired of waiting for my consent, he reached out, but his reflexes were slow and his hand wavered in midair, giving me the chance to realize that he intended to grab me by the neck and press his slobbery lips against mine.

Unable to push him away, I squeezed my eyes shut in disgust, bracing for the worst, but nothing happened.

I opened my eyes again and my heart skipped a beat when I recognized the tattoo wound around the arm that had gripped Daryl's hand a second before it made contact with my skin.

"Don't touch her," Evan growled, taking my breath away as he squeezed the boy's wrist. Daryl was confused by his presence. Judging from his fiery glare, Evan seemed ready to reduce the guy to ashes.

"So who are you, her boyfriend?" Daryl asked, irritated. The threatening tone in Evan's voice hadn't registered, probably because of how wasted he was.

For a moment, Daryl's question eased the tension in Evan's angry expression as his gaze went to my face. Our eyes met for a single moment in the acknowledgement of a deep, unspoken desire. For a second, the warmth it conveyed to me almost nourished my hope that he felt the same way I did.

And for one fleeting moment—maybe because of how he protected me whenever I needed him, maybe because I longed for him with my entire being—I felt like he was mine. I was already his forever, but he would never know it.

Evan's expression grew bloodthirsty again, as if he were fighting the urge to kill the guy. "Believe me." He flashed a captivating half smile, his eyes still burning into Daryl's. "I'm somebody you do not want to mess with. Stay away from her." Evan's authoritative growl rang out like a command, but Daryl would have been wise to take it as a warning.

Despite his own order, Evan continued to grip Daryl's wrist so tightly he couldn't move it. I was sure that if he didn't let go soon he'd snap it in two. I could almost hear bones creaking, though Daryl wasn't letting any pain show on his proud face. His expression was bewildered, as if he couldn't figure out where he was. He was probably stunned that someone had not only stood up to him, but had no intention of relaxing his grip. Evan continued to glare at him, ready to act at any second, like a puma staring at its prey before pouncing on it and slaughtering it.

I shot him a look, trying to tell him it was enough. His dark, narrowed eyes were still locked onto Daryl's, and I was overwhelmed by the feeling that I was sinking into a dark well, hypnotized, as a strange glint, golden and almost imperceptible, flashed across them.

Daryl's expression changed radically, as if awakening from a drunken slumber. Finally lucid, he grasped the threat in Evan's eyes. Suddenly he looked terrified, as though frightened by a private conversation between them, one I hadn't heard.

"Okay, dude, let go."

I couldn't believe how much fear edged Daryl's trembling voice as he begged Evan to leave him alone. I mean, this was *Daryl Donovan*.

Only then did Evan brusquely unclench his hand. Daryl backed away, gaping at him, only turning around when he was sure he was far enough away to have a head start if he needed one.

Seeing him disappear into the crowd, I heaved a sigh of relief. Evan's face relaxed into a reassuring smile. "Everything all right?" he asked, his voice incredibly caring.

"I think so," I said, still shaken by his presence.

Not even the terrifying experience I'd just been through had made my heart race like his smile did. I'd seen two different, totally opposite sides of Evan today. Tough and authoritative with others, sweet and caring only with me.

His expression completely changed when he was dealing with me. Not even with Ginevra was he so... *protective*. The thought warmed my heart.

Suddenly, the wild, booming music, which up until a moment ago had echoed against the walls, softened into a sweeter melody, one I'd never heard before.

"I don't see your date anywhere." Evan's seductive gaze locked onto mine, making me wobble as I stood there. "I got you away from that thug—don't I deserve at least one favor in return?"

His question left me baffled. I couldn't imagine what he might want from me, but before I could ask him, the answer came and my heart stopped.

"May I have this dance?" he said softly, offering me his hand without taking his eyes off me even for a second. A dark, seductive look in which I read the promise of forbidden places inaccessible to all others. A gaze in which I knew I risked losing myself.

My brain was still trying to come up with a reply when my hand moved, guided by a surge of pure emotion, and rested gently in his palm. A jolt spread through my body with the intensity of a flaming arrow the instant my skin touched his.

Still fixed on me, his eyes sparkled. He raised my hand to his lips and hesitated a second. My heart raced at the thought that he would press them against the back of my hand, but instead he turned it over and tenderly kissed my palm as my heart trembled from my intense emotions. Why had he done that? Shivers ran through my body. I was suddenly struck with déjà vu: he'd done that in one of my dreams. How was it possible?

Evan's charm was like moonglow in the forest. It drew me closer, yet frightened me at the same time. Even so, I couldn't do without it. We made our way to the dance floor, hand in hand.

Who knew how long and how intensely I'd longed for, dreamed of, this moment, but I was frozen stiff with embarrassment, and it kept me from moving closer to him.

The air was electrified, as if my body were being magnetically drawn to his, but every time I tried to move closer, a shock raced through me like a lightning bolt. The attraction between us was so strong it could have caused a city-wide blackout.

The lights were dim, a glowing amber color as soft as candlelight. Evan clasped my hand as our bodies swayed to the rhythm of the soft music. The notes of a violin trembled in the air, a sad, intense, desperate, yet incredibly sweet motif.

"I've never heard this song before," I said between the harmonious notes, breaking a silence in which I actually felt perfectly comfortable. It was as if the song were delving into me. As if he himself were the song. Fascinating, dark, and mysterious all at once. It was inside me, I could feel it.

"Do you really like it?" His narrowed eyes smiled at me enigmatically.

"I think it's beautiful. Do you know what it is?"

"It's ours," Evan replied softly. "This is our song," he repeated, wearing the sweetest look I'd ever seen. Shaken by his remark, I rested my other hand on his chest to steady myself. I had the impression he was staring at me more intently than usual. Unable to hold his gaze, I looked at his dog tag, which made me blush every time I found myself staring at it. It must be important to him if he never took it off.

Evan cradled my back gently, moving like a gentleman from a bygone age. I felt his eyes on me, but I couldn't find the courage to look directly into them. Not from that distance—he was so close. I felt I might lose myself forever in him, in his eyes as deep and dark as the universe.

Suddenly, the soft touch of his hand grew stronger, and smoothly yet firmly he drew me to him, making me gasp with emotion. The blood rushed to my head and I looked up into his eyes, dizzy. His whole body was touching mine and his eyes were making me melt like honey over a fire. It was as if he also felt the need to cancel every trace of distance between us, to allow our bodies to fuse together in a dance guided by our heartbeats. Evan squeezed my hand firmly. It seemed that he too had fallen prey to the same sensations.

I was intoxicated by my emotions, totally deprived of self-control, utterly at the mercy of the sweetness in his gaze, afflicted by a fever I didn't want to recover from. Every heartbeat drew me to him. Every cell in my body belonged to him. I felt his warmth through our clothes. *No.* It was me who was burning up.

I lowered my eyes, resting them on his full, enticing lips. The blood in my veins boiled with the longing to feel them on my own.

You've taken my breath away tonight.

His hushed voice filled my head, enveloping me like black velvet. Dazed, I looked into his smiling eyes, trying to understand how he'd spoken to me. I'd heard his whisper, but his lips hadn't moved. I was sure because I'd been looking right at them. Was my obsession with him really confusing me that much? Was it simply my longing to hear those words that had made them appear in my mind? In response to my troubled expression, a reassuring smile appeared on his face.

I felt the compelling need to say something, if for no other reason than to take my mind off the thought of biting his lips. I wasn't sure I could control myself any more.

"I still haven't thanked you for today. This is the second time you've saved my life."

"You're dancing with me. That's all the thanks I need," he said promptly, wielding a seductive smile. "Are you all right?" He stroked the spot on my forehead where I thought I'd been injured. His eyes were tinged with sadness. "Just the thought that you were about to die—"

"Evan, why didn't you take me to the hospital?"

He smiled at me sweetly. "Because there was no need to."

Had nothing happened to me? Really? That's not how it had seemed at first. I'd clearly seen my bicycle lying on the street in a mangled heap. But then later, I'd found it intact in our driveway. Then my wound had vanished after Evan had left. Everything had disappeared as though the accident had never happened. I was on the verge of pointing this out to Evan, but he squeezed my hand even harder and stared at me insistently, making me forget all about it.

"Please don't look at me that way," I begged, my heart in my throat because his warm gaze was constantly on me.

"Why?" he asked with a sly smile. The dimple in his cheek melted me even more than his voice had. What could I tell him, that it threatened to drive me crazy?

"Because I risk losing myself in you." The words escaped my control.

"*Samam*," he whispered, making my heart tremble. I had no idea how I knew, but I was certain the word meant *me too*.

Some self-destructive impulse made me look away. Not far off, Peter was watching us, looking both resigned and furious. He gulped down what was left in his paper cup without taking his eyes off me, then clenched his fist, crushing the cup in his hand. He stared at me for one last minute, as if saying goodbye, and disappeared into the crowd. I wanted to stop him, but my place was there with

Evan. Then I looked over and my eyes met Ginevra's. She was watching us from a distance, looking incensed.

Unfortunately, Evan's place wasn't with me.

I regretted allowing myself to be distracted by the two of them, leaving room for my feelings of guilt to re-emerge. From the magical little world in which we'd hidden away, we'd returned to reality, and it was all my fault. I was overcome with sadness. "Ginevra's waiting for you," I murmured dejectedly, nodding in her direction.

Evan's lips curved upwards, as if he were mocking me about something only he understood. It was the most sensual smile I'd ever seen and for a moment it mesmerized me. It had me nailed to my spot, keeping me from running off. He brushed his fingertips over my shoulder, following the movement with his eyes, and with unbearable sweetness swept my hair back from my neck. His mouth moved to my ear until his lips were brushing against it. "I don't care at all about Ginevra, haven't you figured that out yet?" he whispered sweetly.

I swallowed, trembling at the sensation of his hot breath on my skin, while a dreamy lassitude filled me until I melted. This time I was sure he'd actually said it. That gentle puff of air was proof. I couldn't remember how many times I'd longed to hear those words from his lips.

Our foreheads were so near they brushed together with every breath. Feeling our bodies touch made me tremble, pulling me back into the dream.

"I enrolled at this school just for you."

"But you didn't even know me," I murmured shyly.

"I know you. I know you like no other. Because I know your soul."

The confession pierced my heart. What did it mean? A shiver ran through me.

As though in answer to a summons, I stroked his forearm, mesmerized by the symbols covering it. It was the most mysterious thing I'd ever seen.

He watched me, letting me touch him, but his expression slowly darkened, as if my gesture had awakened something inside him. Melancholy glimmered in his eyes as he looked at me. "It's you I want to be with," he whispered in a barely audible voice. "If only it were up to me to choose . . ."

Like a beautiful spell transformed into a terrible curse, I felt my heart shatter deep in my chest. Searching for answers, I sought his gaze, but the sadness I found there took my breath away.

"You can't?" I asked, disillusioned. Following an impulse I couldn't hold back, I said, "Is it because of Ginevra?"

Evan rested his forehead against mine and squeezed his eyes shut, overcome by this new emotion. I couldn't understand: why the sudden change of mood? What was worrying him now?

"Ginevra has nothing to do with it. A world where you and I can be together doesn't exist, Gemma."

His rejection ran me through like a blade of ice. Coupled with the words I'd so longed for him to say were the only ones I would never have wanted to hear.

"But why?" I asked him, caught between confusion and misery. If Ginevra wasn't a problem, what was keeping him from being with me?

"I don't . . . I can't, I'm sorry," he said in a broken voice, suddenly unable to look me in the eye. "It's complicated." He leaned his forehead against mine again, his expression torn by the painful denial. "God only knows how much I wish I could be with you, but I can't."

His emotions were so powerful they brought back the memory of my dream. As Evan squeezed his eyes shut, not wanting to look at me, I felt like I'd already been through this whole thing. And I didn't like the way this was turning out at all.

"You can't tell me you want me and then leave me like this," I whispered desperately, my forehead still resting against his. I struggled to gulp down the knot in my throat, trying to keep the tears from coming. I'd yearned for that confession for too long to give him up right after discovering that he wanted me as much as I wanted him.

Suddenly his jaw clenched and something in his expression radically changed. His gaze petrified me like cement as his eyes, so intense just a second before, filled with dark poison. It was as if he was caught between two worlds. He stared into space, seeming to be concentrating on something completely different, heeding some kind of signal I couldn't perceive. He cocked his head as if listening for something.

Ginevra abruptly appeared at his side, looking worried. "He's here." She said it so gravely it made me start.

"I know," he replied firmly, looking down. His stony gaze revealed overwhelming concern. I'd never seen him so intense and grim, not even when I was about to be run over. For the first time, something entirely new tinged his expression. *Fear.*

"What do we do?" Ginevra asked nervously, staring at him.

Evan clenched his fists and set his jaw. "I'm not letting him near her," he said in a resolute tone.

"What's going on?" I spoke up anxiously, having been totally excluded from their conversation. Neither of them paid any attention to me, as if I'd become invisible.

"I'll be back in a minute," Evan said, his shadowed gaze scanning the room, worried. "I'll deal with him. You take care of her. *Don't lose sight of her*," he commanded. Ginevra nodded unquestioningly.

I was completely lost. I couldn't understand what all this meant. Why did everything always have to be so confusing and complicated when it came to Evan?

Suddenly he grabbed my face and looked straight into my eyes with matchless intensity, as though on the verge of kissing me. "You have to trust me," he whispered in response to all my fears.

My body turned to stone as I watched him stride off through the crowd.

25

THE RECKONING

Evan was gone, leaving me alone with Ginevra, which was enough to make me shudder. The tension between us was palpable. I'd never been alone with her before and the particular circumstances tonight made everything even more bizarre.

"There's no time to explain." Her cold warning left me speechless, as though she were reproaching my thoughts. "You need to come with me," she ordered, grabbing my hand before I could protest. When her fingers touched mine, a strange jolt ran through me. A powerful, *familiar* connection. As if with that touch my blood had mixed with hers. It was such a strong sensation that I impulsively jerked back my hand. Ginevra turned to stare at me as if she'd felt the same energy.

"*There's no time,*" she snapped.

I was in danger of being overcome by panic. What the hell was going on? Why was *Ginevra* dragging me across the ballroom? And why was I letting her? Deep down I knew the answer: Evan had asked me to trust him and in order to do that I had to follow her.

As we silently slipped through the crowd like fish swimming upstream, a loud, sharp noise that sounded like the crackling of electrical cables made my heart race. I whipped my head around, trying to spot the source of the noise, but Ginevra continued to tug on my arm to keep me from slowing down.

A shower of blue and red sparks burst from the enormous amps like fireworks. It must have been a short circuit. Everyone panicked. The lights flickered and went out, plunging the room into total darkness. There was a crescendo of alarmed voices.

Invisible in the gloom, Ginevra came to a halt, my hand clutched in hers. The students' shouts disoriented me.

"Look out!" she screamed.

Everything happened very fast. Before I could react, she let go of my hand and something rammed into me hard, as if a football player had suddenly tackled me. For a moment I couldn't feel the floor beneath my feet. There was a crash. A deafening one. The terrifying sound of thousands of glasses being shattered against the wall.

At first I thought the impact hadn't been so brutal, but acute pain shot through my arm as I realized the floor was too close. In fact, I was lying on it.

The blue emergency lights blinked on, dimly illuminating the room. A murmur spread through the crowd. Dazed by the confusion that had filled the gym, I looked around for Ginevra and was shocked to see she was on the opposite end of the room. How had she managed to push me so incredibly far? And why?

Frightened and confused, I looked around and my blood ran cold. An ocean of broken glass covered the gym floor. I was shocked to see some of my classmates stanching the blood that ran from their arms while others clutched wounds on their legs, their trousers and gowns torn by the shards. My heart skipped a beat when my eyes crossed the room and saw, at Ginevra's feet, the skeleton of the massive chandelier that, until a moment ago, had illuminated the room. It lay on the ground, shattered. My corsage had been crushed by its crystals, the white petals scattered everywhere. It must have fallen from my wrist when Ginevra pushed me away. I went deathly pale. Tremors ran down my arms at the realization that she'd just saved my life. Though I still couldn't figure out how she'd done it, she'd pushed me far enough out of the chandelier's way to prevent the shards of broken glass from hitting me.

In spite of the distance between us, my terrified gaze was locked onto hers, cancelling out everything else. Ginevra strode across the room and forced me to my feet, though my knees shook, threatening to give way beneath my weight. Her face was devoid of emotion—she looked like she was wearing a wax mask. "There's no time for thank yous," she said, paying no attention to how shaken I was. "We've got to go, Gemma!" She pulled me along again as I struggled not to fall into a catatonic state.

My dry mouth and parched throat felt like I'd swallowed some of the pieces of glass. I couldn't explain what was happening, but it seemed to be something far more frightening than a short circuit. It was something that had alarmed Evan and Ginevra—something that had to do with *me*. But I could tell I wouldn't be getting any answers out of Ginevra. I'd have to save my questions for Evan. He *had* to give me an explanation.

Instead of leaving through the main doors of the gym, Ginevra pulled me into the corridor, which looked more ominous and foreboding than it ever had. The flickering of the fluorescent lights overhead did nothing but increase my tension. I had the bone-chilling sensation I was in one of those horror movies Peter often made me watch. Evan and Ginevra's confusing behavior, the alarmed looks on their faces, and most importantly, my complete incomprehension of what was going on all increased my terror as we hurried down the corridor.

"Okay, you've got to tell me what's happening," I insisted, but my voice trembled, revealing how upset I was.

"No, we've got to get out of here. Evan won't be able to hold him off for long." The fact that Ginevra didn't bother to hide her concern increased the panic gripping my chest. The eerie moonlight crept in through the windows of the side doors, filling the hallway with a ghastly glow. I forced myself to hasten my steps, aware that those doors were our only means of escape, even though I had absolutely no idea who or *what* we were trying to escape from. As we neared the doors, panic hit me so hard that I broke free from Ginevra's iron grip, rushed to the exit, and threw myself against the door, pressing down with all my might on the push bar, my panic at stellar levels. As I raced through the door, I whirled back toward Ginevra, who'd almost caught up with me, but her face turned to a stony mask of terror.

"NO!!!" Her shriek sliced through the silence of the corridor, her eyes locked on something behind me.

I spun around, but the door slammed shut on its own, trapping Ginevra inside. I shook the handle violently, trying to open it, but it was jammed, leaving me abandoned outside. In the dark. Alone.

I stared at her through the window, terrified, as she uselessly banged on the push bar, trying to unjam it.

"Run!" Her dismayed shout came through the door. But what frightened me even more than her voice was her icy gaze, fixed on something behind me. I turned around, terrified, and saw nothing but ominous darkness awaiting me.

If this was a joke, I didn't find it the least bit funny. I would have believed I was actually in an episode of *Scare Tactics* if my instinct hadn't told me Ginevra's terror was definitely real.

"Go, Gemma! Run!"

Her voice bewildered me. Panic seized me. I forced myself to move away from the door, but my paralyzing fear had atrophied my legs, leaving my feet glued to the sidewalk. I couldn't figure out why there was so little light. The short circuit must have affected the whole block. I didn't know what to do, but an archaic instinct tingled beneath my skin, telling me to follow Ginevra's orders.

Something stirred in the trees. Something eerie and sinister.

I continued to tell myself it was all too crazy to be true as my eyes slowly grew more accustomed to the pitch dark of the night.

A blur shot from one side of the street to the other and claws of icy fear gripped my heart. Even my breath refused to make a sound, threatening to suffocate me.

With a sharp pang of terror, I forced my limbs to move and walked away from the building as Ginevra stared at me through the window. She looked more and more frightened, devastated that she couldn't help me.

I began to run aimlessly, my heavy breathing in my ears as the sound of my footsteps against the asphalt filled the street with a lugubrious, hair-raising echo. I just wanted to get far away, to escape from the nightmare.

Almost all my energy drained, I stopped to catch my breath, resting my hands on my trembling knees. Suddenly, just when I thought I was safely alone, headlights flashed on in the silence, blinding me. I instinctively shielded my eyes with my hand. Who on earth was in the car? And what did they want from me?

The engine roared to life, slicing through the deathly silence.

Whoever was in there seemed set on scaring me to death. As if I weren't already frightened enough as it was. The driver revved the engine over and over, each time more aggressively, and each time they did, the sound hit me straight in the heart. I hoped I would wake up from this nightmare any second now.

Only when I heard the squeal of tires did I understand the driver's true intentions.

Whoever it was didn't want to scare me. They wanted to kill me. Again, and on the same day? I was starting to think death was pursuing me.

The tires spun faster and faster. The smell of burnt rubber reached my nostrils. The car was on the verge of hurtling toward me, but just before the driver's foot left the clutch, the squeal of the tires was drowned out by a fiercer roar coming from another direction. I spun around as a black motorcycle thundered onto the street. My heart leapt in my chest when I recognized it. It skidded to a halt an inch away from me.

I looked up, breathless.

"Get on!" Evan ordered.

Without hesitating I grabbed his arm and leapt onto the seat behind him just as the car raced toward us like an arrow shot by a skilled archer.

Evan gunned the throttle. The bike reared and we shot off. I tightened my arms around him as we flew down the road at an inhuman speed in an attempt to lose the car. I should have been terrified, but every ounce of my fear had been eclipsed the moment Evan appeared, replaced by a deep feeling of safety and protection.

As we passed under a streetlight, I looked back at the car and recognized it: a bright-red Viper I'd often seen in the school parking lot. I'd heard kids mention it, but I'd never been interested enough to find out who it belonged to. I tried to see who was driving but couldn't make out their face through the windshield.

In seconds, Lake Placid disappeared behind us. The lights of the town cast our shadows on the pavement before us as we zoomed down Old Military Road in the direction of Saranac Lake, the berserk car close behind us. My heart leapt when it came close to ramming the back of the bike, but Evan noticed in time and twisted the accelerator. "Hold on!" he roared into the wind.

I squeezed my knees around him and clung to him with all my might. Evan sped up even more, raising the front wheel off the ground and leaving the car behind. My adrenaline shot to levels I'd never felt before, a mix of terror and thrill.

The sense of security Evan instilled in me curbed my fear enough for me to realize that the speed was going to my head, filling my veins with a rush of energy that ran throughout my body. I felt like an arrow slicing through the wind. The air lashed at my face, whipping my hair around wildly behind my shoulders. But even more exciting was feeling Evan's chest under my hands, flexing at every curve. I could feel every muscle through the light fabric of his shirt.

Driven by an irresistible urge, I stroked his chiseled abs, as hard as marble. Desire threatened to overwhelm me. For an instant, I forgot what was happening, as if nothing else existed. Evan wanted me and I was on his motorcycle, clinging to him, engulfed in the heat of his body.

He said something, and the vibration in his chest distracted me from the thought. I couldn't make out the words, but I knew he was cursing the relentless car. From my position, I could see his jaw was clenched and he seemed more and more furious. Something told me he was beside himself with anger.

The icy wind lashed at my fingers. As if he'd read my mind, Evan took his left hand off the handlebar and a second later I felt its heat on my own. His hands were more exposed to the wind than mine, but his skin was far warmer. I trembled at the contrast. He laced his fingers with mine and squeezed them, silently comforting me. The gesture made me giddy, a tremble running from my heart down to my stomach and back up again.

A second later, Evan tensed and gripped the handlebars firmly with both hands again.

We roared along through the lights of Saranac Lake. Before I knew it we'd left the town behind us. I leaned to the side slightly to look at the road in front of us, but the wind took my breath away. I wondered how Evan could breathe while going so fast without a helmet, but he didn't seem to be having trouble. As for me, I could barely keep my eyes open.

The road in front of us branched into two forks: the first continued in the same direction we were traveling, skirting the woods; the other led downhill and away from town. Evan sped along without giving any indication which way he meant to go.

Almost imperceptibly loosening his grip on the accelerator, he allowed the car to approach until it had almost caught up with us. I guessed from the determined look on his face that he was doing it intentionally, but instinct made me squeeze my eyes shut and brace myself when the fork in the road was dangerously close.

Only at the last second did Evan veer hard to the right, accelerating as he did so, the back wheel skidding. We managed to shake the car, which was caught off guard and ended up going the other way. My heart leapt when I turned and saw that the road behind us was empty.

Something was wrong, though, because Evan was still tense and didn't release his grip on the throttle. Why wouldn't he relax, now that the car was no longer behind us? The wind hindered my movements, but something made me look to our right.

The blood ran cold in my veins.

There was a black shadow racing through the trees beside us. A shudder ran through me. I had no idea what the thing was, but it definitely wasn't human.

The howl of Evan's motorcycle was joined by another deafening noise. I was shocked to discover it was the car again, racing through the trees on a dirt road to our left, heading toward us.

My entire body shuddered with terror. Who could want me dead so desperately? I quickly ran down a mental list of the people I'd dealt with recently, everyone who might have something against me, but nothing made me think any of them would be homicidal. None of them would be capable of that. Except...

My eyes opened wide. *Daryl Donovan.*

Was it possible his pride had been wounded so badly? To the point that he wanted to kill me? Evan's reaction must have enraged him, or maybe he was simply too drunk to realize what he was doing.

Evan accelerated again, making us fishtail. The car gave no sign of giving up. It raced through the trees on the rocky terrain. I ventured to glance at our speedometer and gasped when I saw how fast we were going, slicing through the wind like a fiery arrow—191 miles an hour.

How was I even managing to breathe at that speed? And how could the car actually be keeping up with us?

Just as I turned to look at the dirt road, the car, going at top speed, swerved brusquely in our direction. In front of it were two trees so close together they formed what looked like an impenetrable obstacle. Instead of slowing down, the car sped up. Its side mirrors smashed against the trees, the pieces flying into the air before crashing to the ground. Tires squealing, the car skidded onto our road without losing speed and resumed its wild pursuit.

I heard Evan curse again. I could feel his tension in his tight chest muscles. The bike fishtailed as he accelerated hard, skidding onto a hidden back road.

But not even that sudden maneuver was enough to shake the car behind us. I hoped Evan had a backup plan.

I leaned over his shoulder to see where the road led and uncontrollable panic left me breathless. I was so shocked I inadvertently relaxed my grip on Evan, but he quickly grabbed my hand before I could slide off the seat, clasping it to his chest to encourage me to hold on tighter. I obeyed and closed my eyes, wondering what he intended to do, given that the road in front of us ended in a heap of rubble that was drawing closer and closer—huge blocks of cement that we were zooming straight toward. I held my breath. At the very last moment the bike spun around, coming to a dead stop a handspan away from the wall of cement, so close that the gravel scattered in the process sprayed back onto me.

I tried to catch my breath, but the car was barreling toward us and I was horrified to realize we had our backs to the wall. We were completely trapped. He was going to crash right into us! What on earth was Evan thinking?

"Evan!" Panicking, I looked up at him in terror, but saw that he wasn't at all scared or even the least bit concerned. Quite the opposite. A strange fervor glimmered in his eyes, as though he was excited by the challenge.

He cursed and I finally managed to make out what he was saying.

"C'mon. Come and get her. Just a little closer." His gaze grew keener as his mouth spread into a crafty smile. "Hold on tight," he told me. The low whisper came directly from his chest, filling me with apprehension. It wasn't a suggestion. It was a *warning*.

What did he mean to do? My instinct told me I didn't want to know. In any case, he didn't give me the chance to ask, but jammed his foot onto the left pedal, putting the bike in gear. With a flick of his right wrist he gunned the accelerator and the bike shot forward, jerking me back.

The bike headed straight for the car, instantly gaining incredible speed as the distance between the two vehicles shortened inexorably.

No matter how much I trusted Evan, he was putting me through a test that was too grueling to ignore. Had he decided to kill us? I held on to him tightly, adrenaline preventing me from closing my eyes. The car came toward us like a missile. I held my breath and tensed every muscle in my body, bracing for the crash, but at the last second Evan squeezed the clutch hard and, before releasing it, accelerated to the max. The motorcycle rose up onto one wheel a moment before impact, leaping up onto the Viper's low hood with a deafening crash. The tire skidded over the windshield, leaving a dent all the way up to the car's roof.

I heard the hair-raising sound of shatterproof glass being crushed beneath the back wheel. An instant later, the bike landed on the road in perfect balance and skidded to a halt, raising a huge cloud of dust. I gasped for air as we watched the car continue its crazed course, too late to stop. It swerved to avoid the wall in front of it, but it was no use; it crashed into the thick cement barrier.

The driver's door burst open on impact, revealing the inside of the car.

My heart stopped. It was empty. The driver's-side airbag had deployed, but no one was behind the wheel.

"Evan." I tried to speak, but only a confused gasp came out. What on earth was going on? How had the car been driving all on its own? I had the impression Evan knew more than he was letting on. At that point I was absolutely certain he was hiding something from me.

Even though I didn't trust my senses any more, I couldn't deny what I'd just seen with my own two eyes: the car was empty. Ever since Evan had burst into my life, bizarre things had been happening. Things that were impossible to explain, at times things I wanted to believe didn't matter. There was one thing I could no longer deny, though: there was something about Evan, something disturbing and sinister, that my instinct had detected from the moment I first laid eyes on him. Something my heart had refused to accept.

A dark, ominous secret.

Part of me, the more instinctive part, recommended caution. As for the other part—the one blinded by love for Evan—all it took was one look from him to silence my instinct.

And yet, I could no longer ignore what was going on around me. I couldn't pretend I didn't see the sinister glimmer in his eyes. A shudder of terror ran through my bones.

Evan glanced at me as I stared at the empty driver's seat, struggling to steady my nerves that were threatening to go to pieces from all the tension I'd stored up inside me tonight.

Something dark had crept into my life. And I didn't intend to ignore it any longer. Evan owed me an explanation.

As though he'd heard my silent demand, he jammed his foot down onto the gear lever, putting the bike into first. We roared off, rearing up and leaving the crumpled wreckage behind us.

26

DISTURBING SUSPICIONS

On our way back to Lake Placid, Evan took it easy on the road for the first time since I'd climbed onto his motorcycle. I eased my grip on his chest, finally reassured, but he immediately twisted the gas, forcing me to cling to him again. I looked at the road, my heart in my throat, worried about his sudden acceleration, but there was a twinkle in his eye and a sly smile on his lips, showing it had been his silent protest. A smile warmed my heart and my fingers moved up his abdomen, sliding onto his chest.

The sensation of holding him so close made my head spin, and with the fear of being chased now gone, the physical contact made my blood boil, eclipsing everything else. I couldn't believe I was really there. I rested my temple on his back, overwhelmed by emotion, and Evan unexpectedly grabbed my hand, sending an electric charge racing up to my head and back down to our interlocked hands.

I realized I was probably being too stubborn about ignoring what I should be paying attention to: my instinct, which demanded I distrust him. I also knew I should feel something entirely different from that overwhelming emotion that blotted out everything else, like ocean waves washing away a message written in the sand. Just like those ocean waves, Evan's warmth could smooth the sharpest shards of glass, wipe away the confused tracks of passing footsteps, dispel my every concern. Pervaded by the comfort of his protection, my heart wasn't capable of containing the slightest trace of fear.

I had no idea where his bike was taking us—to the moon, the stars, or a universe all our own. But it didn't matter to me, as long as he was there by my side. The sky had cast off its dark mantle and was studded with stars.

The moon, almost full and curved like a shell, shone high above, illuminating the road. Its soft, silvery light reflected off the surface of the lake, casting moonbeams that streamed behind us like the train of a shimmering gown.

The night didn't seem so ominous to me now. The wind had softened, greeting us with a tender caress before gently flowing away. Even the trees that had looked so daunting in the darkness now seemed to offer us their protection, diffusing the night's scent through the air. I took a deep breath of the spring breeze, tasting the musk and pine that filled the air. I loved the smell of the woods.

Something caught my eye. It was a bright dot that shone more brilliantly than any other star in the infinite darkness above us. Filled with tender emotion, I found myself smiling. Only when he returned the gesture, sending another tingle through me, did I realize I'd squeezed Evan's hand tighter. I couldn't believe I was there with him, after all the times I'd longed with bitter envy to take Ginevra's place on that seat.

Instead he wanted me. Not her. Yet something was forcing him to deny himself what he longed for.

A world where you and I can be together doesn't exist.

His words had frozen my heart like icy water, leaving it brimming with piercing pain. Even so, learning his true feelings had given me the strength to hope, and nothing in the world could make me accept a conclusion different from the one my heart believed in.

Evan's expression revealed no emotion, but there was something about the way his eyes scanned the road that made him seem apprehensive. His body was tense, his back muscles stiff, his gaze watchful.

What was worrying him now?

The answer came to me in a spine-chilling recollection, destroying my sense of calm. I'd pushed it into a dark corner of my mind, far from my attention.

What was that thing that had chased us?

Evan definitely knew something about it and was keeping me in the dark—that was why he was so worried.

Like a million moths fluttering around in my head, his strange conversations with Ginevra clouded my brain. Incoherent memories began to take shape in my mind, fitting together like pieces in a jigsaw puzzle until they formed a picture, albeit an incomplete one.

There was something about Evan. Something dark. Peter had sensed it before I had. An avalanche of memories surfaced in my mind. Unintelligible, senseless pieces of information, but they all had a common denominator: Evan. I knew that to get to the bottom of everything I had to crack the code. Many strange things had happened since he'd moved to town, things that, up until then, I had to admit I hadn't really thought much about. The constant feeling I was being watched, the mysterious shadow I'd seen in the fire, Evan's voice echoing in my head, the way he'd rescued me from certain death, saving me from being hit by that semi—

The memory sent a wave of tiny shivers all over my skin.

What was the mysterious secret he was trying to hide from me?

The motorcycle's engine softened to a purr. I looked up to discover we weren't at my house. My heart skipped a beat, giving me a clue as to where we were. I'd already seen those majestic, impregnable walls. He'd taken me to his place.

Without giving me the chance to object, Evan sped up, passing through a massive wrought-iron gate. The bike slowly wound its way down a path lined with pines and cypresses that looked like they were centuries old.

The moonlight seemed to be shining more brightly here on his estate, lighting up the fortress hidden among the trees. He turned the engine off, but its roar continued to echo in my head.

"Did you enjoy that?" Evan climbed off, smirking. Irresistible. God, he was utterly devastating when he looked at me that way.

"Oh, sure! I can't wait to do it again," I forced myself to say, matching his sarcasm. I looked down at the motorcycle, finding I was stroking its black leather seat. "Actually, I have to admit it was really nice," I said softly. "A boy at school said they only made a hundred of these. I guess I should feel lucky to have had the chance to ride on one. Maybe I should go back and thank that guy!" I joked, trying hard to seem relaxed and laugh off all the tension weighing on my chest.

Evan smiled openly, clearly pleased by the interest people had shown in his precious toy. "Not a hundred. Not if you start counting from zero." He looked at me with satisfaction. "They made a hundred and one of them, to be exact." His smile made me imagine there was a memorable story behind this as his fingers stroked a little platinum plate attached to the steering column, on which his name was elegantly engraved alongside a small zero. "Let's just say it was a somewhat *special favor*," he admitted, his smile curving into a grin. "Anyway . . ." Unexpectedly, he leaned his face closer to mine, his look turning seductive. "You would have come for a ride with me sooner or later."

I began to tremble as he stared at me with the smile of a wolf hidden in the thick of the forest. I still felt a strange uneasiness, as if behind that smile lurked a threat.

Avoiding his seductive gaze so he wouldn't see the wave of emotion that had washed over me, I peered around the garden, a disoriented look on my face. "Where are we?" I stammered, my voice transparently fake as I pretended I'd never been there before.

Evan glanced at me, hiding another smile. "You sure you don't know?"

I couldn't help but look down, unable to meet his eyes. I wished the ground would swallow me up. It was obvious Ginevra had told him.

I looked up at the sky again and my star shone more brightly, catching my attention. I stopped to stare at it, lost in a world all my own, a world where Evan and I could be together.

I felt his gaze on me.

"What's so interesting up there?" His mouth was close to my ear again.

I made myself look away from the sky, suddenly embarrassed. "Nothing . . . nothing important," I stammered, uncomfortable now for a totally different reason as I examined the ends of my hair before pushing it all to one side, nervously smoothing it down with my hands. Looking down, I didn't realize how close he'd come until I felt the warmth of his breath on my bare neck.

"I bet you were looking at your star, Jamie," he whispered, wrapping my heart in a cozy shell.

My knees began to shake and I struggled to stay standing. "What did you call me?"

Jamie. He'd called me Jamie, I was sure of it. No one else had ever called me that, with the sole exception of Evan in the dream I'd had last night. The memory was still crystal clear in my mind. "Wait, how did—how did you . . ." I couldn't find the words. How did he know about the star?

Evan smiled, enjoying my reaction. "Everyone has a star, Gemma," he replied, as if he'd read my mind.

"Even you?" The question escaped my lips. "Which one is your star, Evan?"

He smiled to himself, as if amused by something I didn't know about. More and more frequently I had the impression he enjoyed teasing me. He leaned in closer to my cheek, never losing his impertinent smile. "I can't tell you." The warmth of his reply tickled my skin.

I shook my head, steeling myself against the charms he boldly continued to use on me. He was enjoying himself as he observed my reactions.

"You owe me an explanation," I stated firmly.

"For what?" He feigned confusion, his eyes darting to the side. Evan knew perfectly well what I was talking about.

"I want to know what happened tonight. I'm sure you and Ginevra know exactly what's going on. You've got to explain it to me, Evan."

"Gemma, there's nothing to explain." The hesitation in his voice betrayed his uneasiness. "That guy at the prom, the one who was all over you. I'm pretty sure it was him following us."

"Don't lie to me, Evan. I'm not stupid—you can't fool me. Daryl wasn't in that car. *No one* was in that car. It was empty! Cars don't drive themselves. How do you explain that there was no one behind the wheel?"

I tried hard to hold his gaze, but I had the impression he was trying to get inside my mind again, like he wanted to force me to give up. "And what was that thing that was following us? I saw it, Evan." I looked at him hard, almost accusingly. My lips were trembling again at the thought of that creature chasing us and how scared I'd been that it might have grabbed me from the moving motorcycle. Whatever it was, it certainly had an evil, hostile aura. A dark, malign presence I'd sensed under my skin.

"I don't know what you're talking about." No matter how hard he tried to act cool, Evan seemed more and more nervous.

"Yes you do, and you owe me an explanation." My voice grew harsher as I insisted yet again. "I'm not staying one minute longer unless you tell me what's going on!"

Evan looked down and clenched his fists, staring at the gravel path beneath his feet, but his lips didn't move. In that silent refusal he admitted he had the answers but wasn't willing to tell me what they were.

"Okay, whatever." I looked him in the eye and turned my back on him.

"Where do you think you're going?" His voice conveyed an equal mix of anger and concern.

"Home," I snapped. "It's late."

"You can't go!" More than a suggestion, his growl was an order.

"You can't stop me," I said stubbornly, setting out down the path.

"You don't understand!" His furious, frustrated hiss stopped me in my tracks. "You have to stay. It's dangerous."

Evan imbued those last words with such sweetness that I began to change my mind.

"Please," he went on, "you're only safe here. Stay with me."

My heart wavered as Evan wore down my defenses. I wasn't willing to give in, though. I wouldn't let the mysterious power concealed in his voice soften me up. I wanted the truth. "Safe from *what*?"

Although my back was turned to him, his sigh of exasperation overwhelmed me. "I can't, Gemma. I can't tell you anything. *Why won't you understand?* Fuck!" he shouted, enraged.

"Safe from *who*, Evan?" I wasn't about to drop it. He had to tell me everything. "Who's keeping you from telling me who you are?" I shouted. "Who's keeping you from being with me?"

I wanted to shout a thousand other questions, but of all the things tormenting me, this was the answer that meant the most to me. I stared at the bars in the gate, waiting, still amazed at how bold I'd just been.

Judging by Evan's sigh, the answer wasn't easy for him to say. "Gemma, we—I'm not like you."

A piece of my heart disintegrated. Of course we were different. *I* was too different from him. He deserved better and he'd realized it himself.

"I wasn't prepared to hear that," I replied stiffly.

For a brief moment a painful silence divided us like a cement wall.

"Damn it, it's not what you think! You wouldn't want me any more if I told you who I am." His voice, at first hesitant, became charged with disarming frustration.

The lump in my throat suddenly eased, taking with it all the bitterness that had gripped my heart. I'd misunderstood him. Evan didn't think I wasn't right for him; he thought he was wrong for me.

I couldn't imagine anything more absurd, more ridiculous. What did he have to confess that could possibly be so terrible? He'd already stolen my heart. The rest didn't matter, just as long as he stayed with me.

"It can't be that bad." I shook my head, a little smile on my face revealing the relief I felt in my heart.

"You don't know what you're talking about. You'd run away from me," he said, half frustrated, half regretful.

"Then why wait?" His hesitation made my voice harden again. "I'm leaving anyway."

"All right. Okay! Go, if you believe it's best for you. But think carefully," he warned, and from the nearness of his voice I knew he was right behind me. "Are you sure you want to go out this late at night? All alone? It's a long way back to your place." His voice took on a tinge of gloom that made my body go tense in spite of myself. "Aren't you afraid that shadow might catch you?"

The blood in my veins ran ice cold. I gulped before turning to face him. "So you admit something's out there!" I said accusingly, looking him in the eye. "Evan, on more than one occasion I've found myself just a step away from death. And all in one day. Do you want me to believe it's just a coincidence?"

Something in Evan's gaze made me think he was about to give in. His voice suddenly became gruff and hesitant. "There's no such thing as coincidence," he replied, articulating each word carefully. "I need you to trust me, Gemma."

"Then give me a reason to. Tell me who you are, Evan," I insisted.

He shot me a piercing look that was so fierce it made me wobble. "You sure you're strong enough to bear the burden?" he asked, his jaw clenched, trying to intimidate me. His question opened unknown doors inside me, reaching obscure places I'd never been allowed into before. Trapping me inside them. "Think it over carefully, Gemma. Some things are better left unknown," he continued, noting the glimmer of fear that appeared in my eyes. "There'll be no turning back."

I forced myself to nod, lowering my head slightly, unable to persuade my lips to open and utter the words, keeping my eyes locked onto his the whole time.

"Then it's decided. I'll explain everything." Although he'd given in, the tortured look on his face showed no sign of lessening. Evan looked around, suddenly on the alert. "But first let's go inside where it's safer."

The concern he was trying so hard to keep out of his voice was devastating. That thing must still be out there. And it was after me. I followed him up the path as my heart struggled between the satisfaction I felt over winning our argument and the fear his warning had reawakened in me.

Was I really sure I wanted to know? Maybe I wasn't ready, but it was too late to change my mind now.

27

CONFESSIONS

The path led to an ample courtyard with an imposing structure behind it. It wasn't a house, but a magnificent, ancient mansion, consisting of two floors topped with a massive yet graceful roof supported by majestic wooden beams that matched the dark window frames.

In the upper part of the façade, half of which was decorated with bas-reliefs in rough stone, were patches of light-colored plaster. Each carefully designed detail was in perfect harmony with the unspoiled natural beauty that ruled in the immense garden.

In the right-hand wing, the linear structure was interrupted by a giant, hexagonal picture window that disappeared around the back, above which ran a splendid terrace with an ornate wrought-iron railing.

I paused to admire it, forgetting for a brief moment the circumstances that had brought me there. Hesitating for a moment, I took a deep breath before beginning to climb the circular stone stairway that led up to the front door. Sensing my agitation, Evan took my hand, encouraging me with a warmhearted smile.

The large door of dark wood slowly opened. I stopped on the threshold, peering inside in search of Ginevra or whoever had opened it for us. My confusion grew when I discovered that the immense, marble-floored, grand salon was empty. Moving cautiously, I glanced at Evan, both curious and a little frightened by what I might discover.

"Please, come in," he said gallantly with a flourish of his hand as I continued to look back and forth between his face and the regal salon in front of us. "Welcome to my home. I mean, *our* home," he corrected himself after a brief hesitation.

"You mean . . . yours and Ginevra's?" I realized only after asking the question that I was afraid to hear the answer. I still wasn't sure what kind of relationship they had and the thought of the two of them living together felt like pins pressed into the palms of my hands.

"Actually there are four of us," Evan said, smiling, almost as if he sensed my jealousy.

Despite everything, I couldn't keep a bit of relief from appearing on my face. But then again, he hadn't shown any particular romantic interest in Ginevra, except for . . . I realized my emotions had completely erased the memory of their kiss from my mind. Evan definitely owed me more than one explanation in that regard. "Me and my family," he continued, weighing the last word before pausing to study my somewhat bewildered expression.

"You're *all* related?" I asked shyly, hoping he'd grasp my allusion.

"We're more like comrades, actually. War buddies, soldiers." He laughed, but I didn't see anything funny about it. Was he teasing me again? He noticed my confusion and winked at me. "We don't have a blood relationship. At least not in the way that you mean," he explained, looking me in the eye. "It's not just that. It's something even stronger." His expression had suddenly grown proud.

Knowing that Evan was beginning to trust me instilled a sense of security in me, making me feel closer to him— even though deep in my heart I felt I'd always known him. I couldn't see Evan as someone who'd come into my world to be a part of it. I saw him as a part of me.

"We watch each other's backs, at the cost of our lives," he continued while I stood there staring at him, fascinated by the fervor with which he described the sentiment that united them, jealous that Ginevra was also a part of it. "I used to think it was the strongest bond there could be between people."

"Used to?" I asked instinctively, surprised and embarrassed by my bouts of boldness, which were becoming more and more frequent.

"Before I met you," he stated simply. His dazzling smile and warm gaze searched my eyes. "Happy? I'm answering your questions." He grinned mockingly.

"Oh, you're not getting off the hook that easy!" I shot back, playing along, surprised to notice how easily I was growing accustomed to being so close to Evan. Just a few hours earlier I'd been talking to Jeneane about him when we were up in my room. I had to remember to thank her one day for that.

"Come with me," he whispered sweetly, taking my hand and gently pulling me to the center of the grand salon.

Once we were inside, the door closed behind us with a gentle click, making me spin around. I glanced at Evan, but his expression didn't betray any emotion at all.

It must have had a sophisticated sensor system. And yet a tiny voice in my head contradicted me, scoffing at me for the ease with which I tricked myself into driving away the apprehension that continued to creep up inside me like a worm inching its way through the soil.

Deep in my heart, I was afraid it was another one of the mysteries Evan would have to explain.

The white marble floor reflected the light of an immense chandelier whose fine steel branches alternated with tiny crystal spheres, forming a giant ball that hung over a low table, also of crystal, in front of a couch.

The rustic stone interior was combined with luxurious, elegant, modern decor. Narrow panels of purplish-red stone graced the walls, perfectly matching the giant couch in the same color in front of which a massive, ultrathin, plasma TV hung on a stone panel a shade darker than the walls. Soft, warm light issued from behind the panel.

To the left of the couch was a rectangular fireplace set into the wall in which a pile of cinders and ash could be seen. The upper part, which protruded slightly, was chocolate-colored, while the cherry-red plaster within was varied at intervals by small stone protrusions.

To the right, the massive hexagonal window reached almost to the entryway, offering a heavenly view of the garden, which was illuminated by small spotlights that sparkled on the ground like tiny stars.

On the opposite side of the room I glimpsed the kitchen, separated from the living room by a series of closely positioned chocolate-colored walls, set at a diagonal to each other and almost overlapping. It was huge, in light oak, raised a step higher than the room we were now in, with another giant picture window overlooking the garden.

My mouth was dry with astonishment. I'd never seen anything like it.

"This is all Ginevra's work," Evan explained, noticing how amazed I was. "She's more attached to material possessions than we are. She likes everything to be glamorous, elegant. Actually, it reflects her personality. I'd be just fine with a smaller house, but when she gets something into her head, who can stop her?" He laughed at something I didn't understand. "I wouldn't dare stand in her way!"

"Come on, let's go upstairs." He clasped my hand, looking pleased at my reaction to his home, and led me across the living room to a long, wooden, floating staircase. The steps zigzagged their way up a stone wall with a thin layer of water sliding down it like artificial rain. I couldn't help myself—I reached out to touch the silvery trickles in the miniature waterfall, giving a start when the water dampened my fingertips, almost as if I'd thought it wasn't real.

Everything was so incredibly luxurious it left me gaping. Evan grinned as he studied my expression.

"I guess you must be used to seeing the amazed expressions girls have when they first see this place," I said. *Who knows how many of them he's brought here?* I added in my mind.

He laughed, leaving me in suspense. "The girls who come here are usually too drunk to look around."

"Oh," I sighed, my heart sinking. The smile didn't leave his face. He must be used to this too, to breaking the hearts of foolish girls who fell for him, thinking they were special. After all, what did I expect? It was hard to imagine an Evan who didn't take girls up to his room, with that gorgeous smile and dark, penetrating gaze of his. Maybe it was his obvious aloofness towards others that made me think so. Even the attention he paid me at school had come as a surprise to everyone. I'd always had the impression there was some sort of mysterious relationship between us, a mystical, intense one, as if we had belonged to each other in another life. Or maybe I was just imagining it all.

"I wonder what time it is," I blurted out of embarrassment, instantly regretting the words. I'd gladly stay there with him forever.

"Must be pretty late," he said, grinning. It was as if time didn't matter to them. If Evan had said his family told the time by looking at the stars I could easily have believed him.

"My parents know I went to the prom, but they'll worry if I don't get home soon," I reflected aloud, growing nervous.

"Don't worry," Evan said softly. "I got in touch with Drake. He's already taking care of it."

"You did what? And when?" I asked, puzzled. "And who's Drake?" My agitation grew and my heartrate accelerated.

"Don't worry, Drake's one of my brothers. And you can relax, your parents won't even notice you're gone." Evan seemed to enjoy keeping me in suspense.

"How can you say that? Not long from now, my dad is going to check my room. Believe me, you have no idea how worried he gets. He'll stay up until I get home."

"Drake knows what he's doing. Your folks aren't going to notice the difference." He laughed. "You'll see for yourself soon enough."

I climbed the last step, trying to understand what he meant, but it was no use.

The upper floor was more dimly lit, with recessed lighting shining softly on a broad, unusually shaped corridor paneled in warm colors ranging from purple to brown to gold. The hallway wound its way past the different rooms, each of which had a door in dark wood that stood out against the light parquet. The hallway was so long I had the impression I was looking at an infinite reflection in a mirror. The wall opposite the stairway, in contrast, was a single pane of glass overlooking the garden.

"What's in there?" I asked, seeing a door that was far larger than all the others.

"Ginevra's room." He smiled to himself as I stared at it uneasily. "She loves to overdo it."

I was suddenly eager to go out and see how the amazing estate looked from above. Driven by that impulse, I caught up with Evan and followed him through a French door and out onto the terrace.

As he shut the door behind us, I admired the railing in wrought iron, twisted into exquisite interwoven motifs resembling a tangle of branches and flowers with snakes slithering through them here and there.

From that height we could see the entire front section of the estate and a good part of the side. A large oak tree had gracefully overgrown the terrace, its branches brushing the floor. Below, the stone path wound through the trees, illuminated by the small spotlights positioned on the ground. In the distance I glimpsed a little wooden footbridge by an enchanting pond partially hidden by the foliage.

Paradise.

The sky was intense. I'd often seen it at that hour but there was something different about it tonight. I closed my eyes, stopping to breathe in the cool, moist air.

Suddenly a gentle breeze ruffled my hair, bringing with it a scent that was even fresher and more delightful. I opened my eyes and Evan was there in front of me, though I hadn't heard his footsteps.

"Like it?" he asked.

"It's absolutely amazing," I said softly, looking for just the right words. "But where are the others? I haven't seen anyone." The thought of meeting them made me nervous.

"Simon and Ginevra must be down in the workout room. They'll turn up soon. For now, we're all alone." The sinister glimmer that flashed in his eyes made me start, but then I remembered it was Evan. I didn't know what had sent that shiver through me—the emotion of being alone with him, or *fear* caused by the very same thing. It was probably both. For some bizarre reason, I was torn between the two. I couldn't help but notice it, although my heart continued to rebel.

"I wish I had the keys to enter your world," I admitted in a small voice.

"You don't need keys. My world is your world. You just need to learn to see it through my eyes."

I wasn't sure what he meant by that. A part of me, albeit an insignificant one, was afraid of him and continued to shout that I should run away, challenging the voice of my heart that was overpowering it. Suddenly I wasn't sure I wanted to delve into conversations I might not understand, but by now I was too far in to turn back. I swallowed hard.

"My throat's a little dry," I said, my voice hoarse.

"Wait here, I'll get you some water."

Before I could say anything Evan was through the door. Two seconds later he appeared behind me, making me jump. Gaping, I stared at the crystal glass full of water he held in his hand. I hadn't even had time to step over to the railing.

"How did you do that?" I gasped, not sure whether to be amazed or terrified.

Evan didn't lower his gaze but held my eyes, moving closer cautiously. "That's what I am," he replied, his forced smile not quite masking his uneasiness.

Perplexed by his remark, I raised the glass to my lips and took a large gulp of water. I turned to look at the trees beyond the terrace, but actually stared into empty space as I tried to organize my thoughts and decide what questions to ask him. I wasn't sure I wanted to know the answers any more.

Evan had moved away, confused by my ambiguous reaction. I glanced at him as he leaned against the railing on the other side of the terrace, his fists clenching the wrought iron, his arm muscles tensed. For a moment, I was hypnotized by his tattoo. Something told me it played an important part in all this.

I forced myself to look away from him, turning back to stare at the shapes formed by the entwined tree branches. Something darted behind me at warp speed, stopping right behind my back, preceded only by a little gust of wind. I held my breath, a shiver of terror rushing over my skin.

"Sorry, I didn't mean to scare you."

His gentle whisper made the hairs on my arms stand on end. Out of the corner of my eye I looked at the spot where I'd just seen him a split second before. He wasn't there. The glass slipped from my hands and I flinched, expecting to hear the crystal shatter against the floor, but the sound never came. Evan grabbed it a second before it made impact, looking at me the whole time, as if studying my every reaction.

Confused emotion clouded my mind, preventing me from using my vocal cords. All I could do was mumble something incomprehensible as his focused gaze tried to decipher mine.

"T-thanks."

Evan handed me the glass, intact and still full. "Don't mention it." His gaze had never been so penetrating as it was just then.

"I suppose this is one of the things you need to explain to me," I managed to say.

"Yeah," he admitted.

The silence of the night covered us with its mantle as I stroked the glass with my fingers, waiting for the explanation. Evan's face sweetened, dimples appearing in his cheeks.

"It's you," he whispered tenderly.

"It's me what? What do you mean? I don't understand."

"I'm answering your question." He smiled and my expression darkened. "You asked me which star was mine. It's you."

His unexpected statement took my breath away but I made myself ignore it. "You know I'm not going to take that as an answer," I shot back in a vain attempt to cover up how self-conscious his remark made me.

Clearly discouraged, Evan grew serious again and stared blankly at the floor. "I don't know where to begin," he admitted, looking uneasy for the first time. "What do *you* think?" he asked with exasperating sweetness, but on his face I saw a look of fear as he waited for my answer.

Why was he asking me? No matter how hard I tried, I couldn't think of a logical explanation for anything that had to do with him—that was the whole point. Maybe I would have to set aside all logic. "Evan, there's *something* about you, something different. I can't explain what it is, but I can sense it beneath my skin and I have to admit it scares me sometimes. What I know for sure," I said, trying to keep my voice steady, "is that you have the strange habit of saving people." I was certain this would brighten his mood.

His reaction took me by surprise. "That's what you think? That I *save* people? Nothing could be further from the truth. You have no idea how wrong you are," he whispered bitterly.

"Wha—how can you say that? Look at me, I'm alive thanks to you! You've saved my life more than once. Plus . . ." I paused, debating whether it was really a good idea to give in to my ridiculous, relentless longing for answers. "Plus there was the girl in the fire," I blurted before I had the chance to regret it. I'd kept the suspicion bottled up for far too long.

"Amy," Evan whispered, looking regretful and visibly shaken by what I'd said.

"You were there," I whispered in a tiny voice, unsure if I should tremble or let the hope that he'd saved the girl light up my face. "You saved her."

"Only in part," he said, keeping his gaze low to avoid looking me in the eye.

"I was sure I recognized you in the flames! So it's true, you *did* manage to save her!"

"That's not what I said," he replied coldly. "This isn't what normally happens. You . . ." His voice broke with frustration and his face grew grim. "You shouldn't have been able to see that," he admitted all in one breath. "What else did you see?"

On the one hand Evan was plainly upset by the unexpected turn in our conversation, but on the other he seemed to need answers himself.

"I saw you there with her. She was alive. You were holding her hand, but the flames were getting higher and higher," I said, sorting through my jumbled memories. "A cloud of smoke covered you. I couldn't see past it and you both disappeared. I *tried* to get them to pull you out of there, but nobody would lis—" I had to stop. Evan's face had become a dark mask torn by remorse. If I'd reached out my hand I was sure I could have touched his suffering with my fingertips.

"It's not like you think," he said coldly, his gaze lost in a memory all his own.

I'd never seen Evan so serious. I was shocked to notice that the iron railing he had clasped was now twisted.

"You mean you didn't manage to save Amy?" I made myself look away from his hands, afraid the door that had opened between us would suddenly close.

He was consumed by the guilt and remorse that had appeared on his face the moment I reminded him of what he'd done. My glimmer of hope that the little girl was alive slipped away like a ghost.

"Don't blame yourself, Evan." My hand obeyed the impulse to rest on his arm. "You were brave enough to rush into the flames to try to rescue her. You risked your life for someone you didn't even know."

Evan raised his eyes and looked into mine. When they met, I knew something was wrong. Suddenly I remembered how quickly he'd moved a moment ago and my instinct reawakened, warning me not to go down this path.

"Weren't you afraid of dying?" I whispered.

Evan didn't move a muscle. The weight of the silence that fell threatened to crush me. It was so deep I could hear his lips part. "I couldn't have," he gulped, looking almost frightened.

"What do you mean, Evan? You have to be clearer; I'm still not getting what you're saying," I insisted. There was no turning back now.

Evan frowned as if holding back tears, in the grip of an uncontrollable emotion. I wondered what could be so traumatic and so important as to make him this frustrated. He looked away and narrowed his eyes before turning back to me, as though he needed a second to summon his courage.

"I could never be afraid of dying, Gemma," he admitted.

My heart trembled. "Why not?" I asked cautiously, filled with apprehension. Evan looked straight into my eyes, making my whole body shiver.

"Because I'm already dead."

I gave another shudder and my blood ran ice cold.

28

INSTINCT AND DESIRE

"Gemma, say something, please."

I couldn't. I couldn't feel a single muscle in my body. I was frozen. Trapped in a slab of ice. For some time I'd suspected Evan was hiding a dark side from me, but no matter how afraid of his secret a part of me had been, I could never have imagined anything like this. It was too much for me.

It would have been too much for anyone.

His words were still whirling in my head, trapping me inside a limbo from which I felt I would never return, my gaze lost in the distance over his shoulder as I tried to avoid looking into his eyes. I could see he was anxiously waiting for me to respond.

As soon as my brain had processed the information, the cloud of confusion fogging my mind dissolved, replaced by the rush of adrenaline that immediately followed. Without warning, the little part of me that had always been afraid of him came to the fore in my mind, taking control and yelling at me for not listening to its repeated warnings. As fear gripped me, I bolted for the door, guided by an irresistible instinct, but before I could reach it, it slammed shut. I stopped, petrified. Anxiety flooded me and I could feel my chest heaving spasmodically, but it was as if my body no longer belonged to me. Before I could look for another way out Evan appeared in front of me, barring the way. My legs threatened to give way under my weight. My heart was pounding so hard it throbbed in my ears as if it, too, were searching for a way out. My head began to spin, warning me it was about to surrender. Never before had I felt so powerfully the emotion that filled me at that moment: pure terror. Black. Ominous. Sinister.

Hands rested on my arms in a gentle embrace. I felt their warmth but my mind was somewhere else, lost in darkness, while my body was paralyzed, nothing more than an empty shell.

"Calm down. Everything's fine."

I looked at him but could barely see.

"Gemma."

Evan's voice was very close to my face, as if he were trying to come in through my gaze and join me in whatever place I'd lost myself in. My body trembled, warning me not to return.

"Look at me, Gemma. Look me in the eye. It's still me, it's Evan. Nothing's changed."

I couldn't snap out of it. Since my body wasn't able to escape from him, my mind had sought shelter somewhere far away. I was trapped in a dark cell with no way out.

"Don't be afraid of me. I would never hurt you. Please, stay with me."

My mind clearing for a fleeting moment, I understood what he was saying and fought with all my might to silence the voice in my head that continued to scream at me to run away.

The love I felt for him that had been buried by his confession was trying hard to crawl up out of the darkness into which it had descended, making its way past the almost uncontrollable urge to flee. And while that part of me wanted to escape him, the other part, which was larger but being suffocated by the former, was screaming that I should stay.

"Here, drink some water," he said, concerned, handing me the glass, which was still full.

My lips trembled as they parted and I took a swallow, trying hard not to let my teeth chatter against the glass. "I need to sit down," I admitted hesitantly, resting my hand on his arm to steady myself.

I'd barely perceived a break in our physical contact—as if he hadn't moved at all—when I was astonished to discover he was holding a giant cushion in his hands.

He'd done it again.

I cast him a sidelong glance.

"Sorry," he said in a soft, tender voice before looking at me. "I'd better take this more slowly, huh?"

"Sounds like a good idea," I admitted, embarrassed to realize he'd been right all along when he warned me I wouldn't be able to handle it. Still, he couldn't blame me; his terrible secret weighed more than I could bear. I wasn't sure yet whether or not I could deal with such a shocking confession.

"It's just that with you it's so easy to lose control." He smiled and helped me put the cushion, which was big enough for both of us, on the floor and sit down. "It's been like that from day one," he admitted, gently sweeping my hair back over my shoulder.

I forced myself to look him in the eye, trying to repress the little patch of fear nestled in the back of my brain that stubbornly refused to go away. By now the worst was over, and knowing it comforted me.

"Nothing like this has ever happened to me before," he said as I looked at him in silence. "It's like I go into tilt when you're around." He stifled a laugh. "Completely haywire." His face brightened, though cautiously. "It feels so good to be getting this off my chest."

I struggled to understand the logic behind what he was saying, adamantly refusing to acknowledge the fact that I was going to need to set aside all logic if I was to be on his wavelength.

"From day one?" I repeated, suddenly overcome with emotion. Did Evan also feel that strange connection between us?

"Ever since I came to Lake Placid. Since the first time I saw you, in the woods." Evan leaned closer, his face an inch from my lips as he studied my expression, clearly interested in something I didn't know was in me. "I have no idea how you do it. I've wondered a hundred times. My body reacts strangely to your presence. I can't control it when I'm with you. Maybe that's why you can see me when you shouldn't be able to. I shouldn't have gotten so close, but I couldn't help it. I was so fascinated by you. The urge to see you—to *touch* you—was so hard to resist that I gave in to the temptation each and every time. I lost myself. You led me to madness and then brought me back again.

"I can't resist you. I *don't want* to resist you. It's like I can breathe only when you're with me, only when you're near. The rest of the time is an eternity of suffocating breathlessness. I've battled myself, I've battled everyone, but I haven't been able to hold back what I feel. I've discovered I *need* you, Gemma." His intense gaze and black-velvet voice left me dazed. It felt like a powerful poison that dulled my senses and clouded my mind. His words intoxicated me, his whole self, his sensual voice. I was on the verge of passing out, with his scent so close and so strong it made my head spin.

"Wait," I said, having taken a moment to process what he'd said. "What do you mean I can see you when I shouldn't be able to?"

Evan looked down and smiled to himself, his voice as low and penetrating as a sinister shudder. "Have you ever found yourself, when you're all alone, detecting a *presence* in the silence? You can't see it, but you know it's there."

A wave of emotion washed over me and my eyes opened wide. I was petrified. "It was you," I said in a tiny voice, thinking back on the feeling I was being watched that had become so familiar to me. "It was you all along," I repeated, struggling not to fall into a state of shock.

Evan nodded cautiously and smiled, looking almost pleased.

"And was it you who wrote my name on the mirror?" The question came out all on its own as I tried to get a grip. Embarrassment colored my cheeks at the thought of Evan in my bathroom and me naked in the shower. "Why did you do that?"

Evan shrugged. Maybe he wasn't really sure himself. "I don't know what got into me. I thought it was crazy but I couldn't help it. My fingers moved all on their own. I felt insane. I wanted to understand, no matter what. I probably thought I'd find the key to understanding who you are." He looked at me out of the corner of his eye, his lips suddenly enchanting. "Or maybe it was only to distract myself." He winked and my face flushed instantly. I opened my mouth, unable to find anything to say, and Evan raised his hands defensively. "I only took one little peek!"

"You creep!"

"Okay, okay, I deserve that." He laughed, but this time I wasn't sure he was kidding. I punched his arm and his laughter instantly died down, his eyes locked tenderly onto mine. He'd felt the same sensation I had.

"Why do you think I feel energy running through me every time you touch me?" I'd tried to ignore it, but instead of fading away it continued to tingle under my skin, as though there was a part of me, deep down, that wanted to understand its message.

Meanwhile, Evan had lost himself in a world all his own. "I don't know. You're my demon and my angel on earth," he said, deep in thought. There was tenderness in his words, tenderness mixed with melancholy.

"It's so *bizarre!* Part of me is still waiting for you to tell me this is all a big joke."

"And the rest of you?" he asked, almost as if afraid to hear my answer.

"The rest of me," I confessed, looking into his eyes, "knew it all along." As the words came out, I realized along with Evan that it was true. "I didn't know how it was possible—I thought it was just an obsession—but I kept *sensing* you, even when you weren't there."

"An obsession, huh?" he said, a grin appearing on his face. "You thought you were obsessed with me." He raised an eyebrow, looking pleased.

"I couldn't help it, I didn't know what to think!" I stammered. I made myself change the subject. "So what else can you do, read people's minds?" I asked, holding my breath as I waited for the answer, suddenly afraid. His scrutinizing my most intimate thoughts would be more terrible than his seeing me naked.

Evan, on the other hand, seemed amused. "No, I can't do that. Although—" he laughed to himself—"I have to admit I wish I could. It's a pain having to turn to Ginevra every time I can't figure out what you're thinking."

"Hold on—Ginevra? What's she got to do with me?" I asked, both confused and annoyed because he'd brought her up. Then came a glimmer of clarity. "You mean . . ."

Evan continued to nod, his lips curved sensually upward. His expression was finally free of his past agony.

Ginevra could read people's minds. What on earth could possibly be worse than that? *My God . . .*

"Don't worry." Evan broke the thread that my brain was mechanically weaving into a tapestry of awareness as it worked backwards through my memories. "Some things stay between the two of you. She'd never tell me anything you wouldn't tell me yourself. She considers it a sort of woman's code of honor. We've even argued about it a few times."

I exhaled, unable to keep my heart from racing. I should remember to thank Ginevra if I got the chance.

"In any case, I'd never ask her for any information that's too personal. In compensation," he said, his smile growing crafty, "I have my own way of communicating with you. Let's just say it's like *you* can read *my* mind." He laughed out loud.

My eyes opened wide as I suddenly understood. "I've heard you! I've heard you in my mind!" I exclaimed, at the mercy of conflicting emotions. The pieces of this insane puzzle were starting to come together. There was nothing wrong with me after all. I should have just listened to my instinct. I wasn't crazy, I'd actually heard his thoughts. The relief of knowing this cleared the way for curiosity.

I looked into his eyes as his voice echoed gently inside my head. Deep inside, as though it were coming from my heart. *"It's called epis-numa. It's a tiny region of the brain that mortals don't even know they have. My mind can link to it, forming a unilateral connection. I can send my thoughts to you, even from miles away. It's the exact opposite of Ginevra's power, which works in the opposite direction by connecting to the epis-mantra."* He smiled, enjoying my astonished expression.

"Normally it only happens if I'm the one who decides to establish that connection, but with you it's different. You make me lose control," he said, frowning, still confused by the situation. "Once the connection's made, the mind of anyone I want is completely under my control," he said, and a part of me trembled at this confession.

"Have you ever forced me to do something?" I asked, disconcerted.

Evan smiled. "I've never been able to." I didn't have to read his mind to see how frustrated it made him. "Although I have to admit I've tried lots of times."

"Well, if it's any consolation, my dad always says I'm the most obstinate person on the planet," I joked.

Evan laughed, turning back to look at me. "I have the power to bend anyone to my will. *Any mortal soul*. But when I'm with you, I don't even have power over my own thoughts. I can't maintain my ethereal form very long and I materialize unexpectedly. My mind connects to yours without my permission. It's like you unmask every spell I'm capable of. My powers seem stronger in your presence, but I can't control them. They elude me. My body and mind respond to you and not to me any more. How do you explain that?" He seemed to find the mystery irritating and fascinating in equal parts. His eyes had lit up and were studying mine, as though he expected to find the answer there.

"If it hadn't been for Ginevra, I never would have found out about it. The first time it happened was at school, when you were sorting out your locker. She was listening to you and all of a sudden she heard my voice in your thoughts. Both of us were floored. We couldn't explain how it had happened. I already knew you could see me, but nothing like that had ever happened to me before."

I searched my mind for that hazy memory and blushed, remembering the emotion I'd experienced at the time. It felt like months had gone by since that day. So much had happened since then, culminating in his confession that finally explained the mystery. Everything was taking shape and coloring in the picture I'd slowly pieced together bit by bit. "You did it at the prom too, didn't you?"

"I did it intentionally that time," he said, grinning. "Speaking of which, you're a great dancer," he whispered. "Really good rhythm."

I blushed. Was it a real compliment or was he just teasing me? "That's because I used to climb trees a lot," I blathered. Huh? What on earth had made me tell him something like that? I could already imagine him trying to hold back a smile. "In any case, you're not so bad yourself. Dancing, I mean. You didn't step on my toes even once."

Evan laughed out loud. My attempt to downplay things had failed miserably.

"You think I'm silly, don't you?"

"Very," he said, a sparkle in his eye, "but I like it." He looked at me insistently and I hurried to change the topic.

"What about my bike? Are you the one who fixed it?" The question came out spontaneously and, given the circumstances, "fixed" sounded like the wrong word. But it was a mystery I couldn't stop thinking about.

"Ginevra again."

"What else can she do?" This conversation was surreal.

Evan laughed. "It'd be quicker to tell you what she *can't* do."

"And the others? Do they have superpowers too?" I didn't know how else to phrase it.

Evan threw his head back and laughed again. I frowned. What was so funny? No one had ever made me feel so dumb before.

Unexpectedly, he brushed his thumb across my lips, staring at me intensely. Emotion washed over me. Why on earth did he always have to do that to me?

"I'm sorry. We're not used to hearing them called that. We're not characters out of some Disney movie, you know." He winked at me, a smile hiding behind his reply.

At least he knew Disney movies. That was already something.

"So do I need to be careful about what I think when I'm around your brothers?" I insisted, determined to finally pull down all the veils shrouding the truth about them.

"No. We Descendants can't read minds. Not the three of us, at least. That's Ginevra's special ability," he said, looking at the railing in front of him as though choosing his words carefully. He looked at me for a moment, reading my expression, and blurted, "Hers and her Sisters'. Witches can read minds."

"Wha—What?! Back up. Ginevra's . . . a *witch*?!"

I could barely say the word. Part of me was still expecting someone to pop out at any moment and point at the hidden cameras. I couldn't believe this was really happening, that it wasn't a joke or a dream or one of those stories I loved reading. This was *my* world. The world I'd grown up in, where there was a clear boundary between what was real and what couldn't possibly be real. Now that wall was crumbling and everything was blending together—though this wasn't some new world I'd been dragged into. Evan was just helping me to decipher my own world in a different way, to see things with new eyes, eyes that could see past that boundary. *All of this was so insane.*

Evan looked more and more amused by my reaction. "She used to be a Witch, but take my advice: never bring it up around her. She doesn't like to talk about it. It puts her in a bad mood."

"Not a problem," I said, shaking my head. "Thanks for the warning."

The silence that followed seeped into my bones like snake venom. We both knew where the conversation was taking us. The wait for that moment had felt endless, and now that the time had finally come, I was afraid the words wouldn't find a way past the lump in my throat. And yet somehow I had to find the strength to ask him the question. *I had* to force myself at all costs, because I sensed the answer was important, even if deep down in my heart I was afraid it would change everything.

"Evan." I swallowed, avoiding his gaze and trying to keep my voice steady. He sensed how serious I was and looked straight at me, taking my breath away. I managed to continue. "You said 'Descendants.' What are you?" Freed from the burden of those words, I finally looked into his eyes, just in time to see something flash across them.

"I knew you would ask that." His low voice was filled with bitterness again.

For an infinite moment, neither of us opened our mouths. The silence was so oppressive I suddenly wished I hadn't asked. If I'd been able to, I would have rewound time like a tape recorder and erased it. Evan locked his eyes onto mine and stared at me with matchless intensity. "I'm an Angel, Gemma." His voice caressed my name so sweetly that my heart prevented my reason from fully grasping his solemn confession.

Evan stroked the back of my hand, encouraging me to respond. He was probably afraid my mind would get lost in the darkness again, but for the first time I wasn't upset by his confession. Part of me, as though it had always suspected it, told me it couldn't be any other way.

"Does it shock you?" he asked gently, concerned by my silence.

"I don't think so," I said, unsure. "It's just, why are all of you here?" I had no idea why my brain had come up with that question, but my voice had obeyed its command before my lips had the chance to hold it back.

Evan's gaze wavered, as if, of all my questions, this one perturbed him the most. His face filled with sadness. "Well, you see, we're rather special Angels." It was as if an insurmountable wall had risen up, breaking the connection we'd established. I sensed how hard he was trying to get around it, and I couldn't understand why he didn't just knock it down.

"Special? What do you mean, exactly?"

"The race we belong to is a bit unusual. It's our lineage that makes us different, our bloodline."

"I still don't understand."

Evan filled his lungs and looked directly into my eyes, making sure he had my full attention. "I know what I'm about to tell you might sound crazy, but my brothers and I are descended from the children that Eve once hid from God, ashamed that she hadn't yet purified them by bathing them in the sacred river."

As Evan studied my expression I tried to pretend the bizarre story wasn't fazing me. I suspected my irregular heartbeat was giving me away, though.

"When God discovered those children, He decreed that, as punishment, that which had been hidden then would remain hidden for all eternity. That's probably why some people call us Subterranean Angels—they think creatures like us live underground, but actually the name came from our curse. In any case, over the last few centuries no one's talked about us any more, with the exception of a few Norwegian legends that stood the test of time."

"Why on earth should anyone be punished like that? Isn't God supposed to forgive everyone?" I blurted. Then I realized how ridiculous I sounded. Me, talking about God. I still couldn't delve into this new world without the suspicion I was being made fun of.

"Of course," he said sternly, "but even He has His laws. A world, a society, a family without rules would descend into chaos. It would be hell."

"What did you mean by 'hidden'?"

"We didn't fall from grace, we merely . . . descended," he murmured, a grim look on his face.

"What does that mean for you? Is your soul lost?"

Evan laughed to himself, seeing the effect his confession was having on me. "My soul isn't lost. It's just hovering between heaven and hell."

I stared at him, bewildered.

"Here, on *earth*," he explained, smiling. No matter how hard he tried to hide it, I still detected a touch of sadness in his eyes. "All things considered, it's not so bad. We're just halfway between the terrestrial world and Eden."

The look on his face snapped me out of my daze and made me seriously consider what he was saying. Hadn't I already seen proof of his powers? Why should I think he was only kidding?

Like a raging river, the explanations I'd cautiously dammed up burst free and washed over me.

Eden? What was he talking about? Could it all be true?

Angels, heaven, hell . . . *My God.*

I froze, thinking back to our escape on his motorcycle. If he really was an Angel, his opposite must also exist: fearsome demons and who knew what other monstrous creatures. A shudder ran down my spine, making the hairs on my arms stand on end. I began to feel the burden of all that information. It was threatening to overwhelm me.

"Everything okay?" Evan asked, concerned. I hadn't managed to hide how shaken I was and my face must have turned incredibly pale.

"It's not fair, it's not your fault. Millennia have gone by. It's unfair that you should pay for someone else's mistake."

"I like to think it won't last forever," he admitted. "I've always lived with the hope of Redemption." I couldn't tell from the tone of his voice if he was trying to convince me or only himself. "After all, it's not so different for you mortals. You inhabit the earth to atone for someone else's sins too. It's a purgatory for you just like it is for us. You were denied Eden, and that's why you're made to experience suffering and difficulties every day. It's a test, don't you see? God could have cast Eve and her companion into hell like He did with those who were punished for betraying Him, but He gave you another chance. The chance to *choose*. That's why mankind has free will. God doesn't want to force you to love Him, He wants each and every person to freely choose to do so. Only by proving they're worthy, by following His laws, can humans return to Eden, from whence they came. Why shouldn't the same thing be true for me? Why shouldn't I be able to prove I'm worthy too?"

It was the longest, most sincere statement Evan had ever made to me. His voice had grown passionate. In his tone I heard intense hope, but the hint of sadness that lingered in his gaze suggested that wasn't all. Something else was eluding me.

"I'm sure you can do it, Evan," I said encouragingly yet cautiously as I felt doubt rise inside me, pushing to break free. "And when you . . . Um, I mean . . ."

"What do you want to know?" Evan asked, hearing the hesitation in my voice.

"I've seen you in your angelic form. Sometimes I only sensed your presence, but other times *I saw you*, Evan. And you didn't look like a ghost or a spirit. You were flesh and blood. So, well, I was wondering, is your ethereal body somehow *tangible?*"

"Not to mortals," he answered quickly, as if accustomed to answering that particular question, "but you, Gemma, have the power to change that." He looked into my eyes to underline how important that detail was to him. Glancing away, he stared at the floor, as though in some way he felt overwhelmed. "No one had ever touched me before, and the emotion I felt the first time you did was so powerful it made me want to learn more about you."

A gust of wind ran over my skin, ominous yet familiar, making me shiver. Evan looked up cautiously, as if afraid of frightening me. I swallowed with difficulty, my throat dry from emotion. My breathing grew irregular as his eyes, suddenly as gray as molten silver, searched mine inexorably. He'd transformed. The emotion paralyzed me, taking my breath away.

"*Can you see me?*" Evan's voice enveloped me like a warm mantle as our gazes remained silently entwined, exploring the mystery.

"Shouldn't I?" I said hesitantly, almost under my breath.

"You're the only person who's ever looked me straight in the eye."

I sighed, my heart trembling in my chest. "Can I . . . can I touch you?"

Evan slowly raised his hand, palm toward me. Driven by a deep desire, I extended my hand toward his, barely grazing his fingers. He swallowed, and after a moment closed the space between us, resting his hand against mine, palm to palm. "My God." His eyes wavered, as if moved by ecstatic emotion, while a tingle ran over me, a hot shiver that moved from my skin to my heart.

"It's an incredible sensation," I whispered, staring at our hands pressed together.

"Incredible and extraordinary."

My eyes returned to Evan's and found them waiting for me.

"Isn't it?" He smiled and for a moment the complicity of that shared smile united me to him more than a thousand words ever could.

"I have another question," I said, after a moment of silence.

"I'm listening."

"Only if you promise you won't laugh," I warned, embarrassed by what I was about to ask.

"Promise," he said, holding back a grin.

I shifted awkwardly on the cushion and crossed my legs. "This is going to sound stupid—but aren't angels supposed to have wings?"

Evan burst out laughing, making me feel ridiculous.

"You love making fun of me! You promised you wouldn't laugh!" I said, frowning. "I'd like to see you in my shoes." I nudged his arm. The instant I touched him, his face grew serious, as if a violent emotion had struck him.

"Why don't you see for yourself?" he dared me, leaning his back slightly in my direction, a teasing, challenging look on his face.

I blushed, staring at his back, and for a second my heart beat faster.

"Go on, it's okay," he said, looking me in the eye. Touching his hand hadn't been enough to bring down the reserve between us, but then again I'd never been so bold before. And yet I suddenly felt a strange emotion beneath my skin, a mysterious instinctual knowledge that touching him again would carry me into a new world. I knew he was only teasing me, but the temptation was too powerful to ignore.

I reached out hesitantly, seeking his gaze, and in his eyes—suddenly filled with desire—I saw a glimmer of impatience to feel that contact burn on his skin. I swallowed and gently rested my palm on his back.

My hand moved cautiously, searching for anything unusual, as Evan's muscles flexed beneath my fingers. Even his shirt couldn't block the electricity produced by the connection between our bodies.

I felt the overwhelming urge to touch his skin without the obstacle of fabric. Responding to my longing, Evan suddenly turned around, grabbed the hand I'd touched him with and in an instant was on top of me, my body beneath his, pressed down into the cushion as if swept away by an unstoppable wave of pure emotion, an impulse he'd been unable to control. I breathed rapidly against his mouth as my warmth combined with his, his hair brushed my forehead, his fiery gaze locked onto mine as our fingers laced together over my head. My heart skipped a beat and for a second I thought it had stopped forever. His dog tag brushed against my chin and I reached out to grab it, but, like a furious whirlwind dragging me away, I was stunned to discover Evan still sitting in his spot on the cushion beside me, my hand resting on his back. I gulped, utterly bewildered, my breathing still accelerated because of the scene that had dazzled me like a movie shown only in my head; a crisp, clear view of reality that had swept me away. Still stunned by the intense emotion, I couldn't tell whether my mind had been catapulted into the memory of my dream when I touched his body, or if it was just the reflection of my desire for him guiding me.

"Well? Find anything?"

I shook my head, his melodious yet slightly sarcastic voice snapping me out of my daze. Suddenly, doubt gripped me. "Did you do that?" I asked him point-blank.

"Do what?" he said, confused.

"I saw . . . Oh, never mind." I stopped myself from telling Evan about my vision; he definitely would have teased me about it.

Evan shot around and squeezed my arm. "What did you see, Gemma? No, wait, don't tell me." He was shaken, fascinated, his eyes growing wider. "You saw the two of us. I grabbed you and pinned you down to the floor, didn't I?"

My heart lurched. He'd seen the same thing? How was it possible? I'd felt powerful sensations on my skin as if I'd actually experienced it. Could it be that the same was true for Evan? My God. What was happening between us? Neither of us seemed able to understand it.

"You saw it too?" I asked, stunned by our powerful connection.

"It's incredible. It's like we're in symbiosis. Sometimes I feel struck by a strange power when I'm around you. It's a bond between us, some inexplicable alchemy. Can't you feel it too? It's impossible to resist. Or *control*."

That particular detail seemed to disturb him the most.

"But what happened, exactly? Did you project those images into my mind?"

"I didn't do anything. It's like our minds joined together for a moment, connected in some parallel world where we followed our instincts, our desires, despite the fact that our bodies were here. When you touched me, I felt an irresistible desire to touch you and I imagined doing it."

"I imagined it too. But it felt like we actually did." I blushed; I hadn't meant to say that.

"Yeah." Evan was frowning, absorbed in the new mystery, as if nothing so fascinating had happened to him for a long, long time. "It's incredible, it's like my powers get stronger when you're around, but I'm not even sure it depends on me." He studied me for a few seconds, amazed, and smiled with that hint of mockery I was starting to get used to. "So, what about those wings? Manage to find them?" he asked, grinning.

"Very funny."

"You can always try again." He raised an eyebrow and his smile grew sly. "I don't mind. Why don't you take a closer look? Maybe you'll be luckier this time."

I gave him a push, making him turn back around. "Don't make me feel any dumber than I already did asking you!"

"You're never dumb," he said, his face unbearably sweet, before smiling to himself and adding, "Okay, I admit it: all that stuff about the wings, just kidding. It's only a legend. We don't need wings to move from one dimension to the other. They're parallel worlds and we're souls, essences as pure as air, so we can cross through them. If it weren't like that, even mortals would need them to be able to cross to the other side after they die."

I had to admit his explanation made sense. "Are there many others like you? How can you be recognized?"

"We can't. And there are millions of us around the world. We blend in with people and nobody ever notices us. No one knows who we really are. There's just one difference that manifests in our natural form compared to our human form, but no one even sees it because we're invisible to mortals in our natural form."

"Your eyes," I said, beating him to it.

Evan nodded. I was shaken by the recent memory of his silvery gaze lost in mine. But now his eyes were darker than the night.

"In our physical form, they go back to the color they were during our mortal existence. But when there's no physical body to mask them, our eyes are gray, like liquid silver. The soul casts off the body, revealing its colors: pure and transparent, like ether. But when that happens no one can see us."

"No one but me," I reminded him.

"Yeah. It's so strange."

I ran a hand down his arm where the tattoo wrapped around it. He followed my movements with his eyes.

"And then there's that," he said, a touch of melancholy in his voice. "You can see it, can't you?"

"I shouldn't be able to, should I?" I said.

Evan smiled. "That's the sign of the children of Eve, a constant reminder of who we are. We each get one right after we die. It's our curse."

"Does it hurt?" I asked.

"Not as much as the burden of having it," he admitted. Seeing that it saddened me, he smiled. "Any more questions?" he asked eagerly. He seemed to be teasing me again. Or, more likely, he was just happy to finally be getting it all out in the open.

It didn't take me very long to think it over; an endless list had already formed in my mind, but one question stood out against all the rest, driven by a frightened, trembling, little voice in some dark corner of my mind. I couldn't silence it. "You said I was in danger. Why?"

Evan tensed. He clenched his jaw, his hands balled into fists on the cushion beneath us. I seemed to have asked him the one question I shouldn't have. The only one he would never have wanted to answer.

And yet he had to. I had the *right* to know. "Evan, you've got to tell me." I stared directly into his eyes with a determination

I didn't even know I had. "What was that shadow? I *saw* it as it was chasing us."

Something was keeping him from answering, something inside him. He'd already told me who he was. What else could he say that was so shocking? What was he hiding?

"Evan, answer me!"

"What you saw—" He hesitated.

"What was it?" I insisted.

"An Angel of Death," he blurted. "An Executioner."

The whole world fell apart at my feet. *An Angel of Death.*

What did it want from me? The answer came in the form of a shiver that ran down my spine.

Angels, heaven, hell . . . What was really going on? As I stared into space I felt Evan's gaze seeking mine. Unable to react, I'd done the only thing I could do: detach myself from everything and hide away in a warm, cozy shell behind the inaccessible doors of my mind. I could barely hear Evan's voice lingering in the air, as inarticulate and muffled as an echo.

"He's come for you. You shouldn't still be here, Gemma. I'm sorry," he said, confirming the terrible suspicion that had left me frozen in its icy grip. My heart skipped a beat when I heard him say it aloud.

"You mean—" I stammered.

"Your time was up the minute that semi came at you. Death was waiting for you."

I shuddered like never before. "You saved me," I said, finally understanding the importance of those words. *My time was up.* "So it was you who healed my head and my ankle? You hadn't really gone away. That warmth came from *you!*"

Evan nodded.

"Amazing," I whispered to myself. "You changed my fate."

"I only got in its way, I'm afraid."

I looked up at him. "Where is he now?" I forced myself to ask, gripped by a terrifying new fear.

"He'll come back looking for you, but don't worry, he won't come close as long as you're with us. I won't let him."

"Are you here to protect me?" I asked, caught between gratitude and uncertainty. "Is that your mission?"

His eyes darted around, as if my question had made him uncomfortable. He bowed his head and hesitated a moment before answering. *"Tvaddhetunā sarvaṃ saṃçayasthaṃ karomi sarvaṃ tu sahasrakṛtvaḥ punar akariṣyam."* His voice was grim yet mesmerizing, sending a shiver through me.

"What does that mean?" I whispered.

"That I'm risking everything for you, but I'd do it again a thousand times." Another smile spread over his face. "You're safe here with us, don't worry," he whispered, gently touching the tip of my nose. I had the impression he'd put on a mask, that he wasn't being completely honest.

The deep feeling of protection only Evan could provide flooded through me. Even so, that frightened little voice was making its way through my thoughts, trying to resurface. I tried to push it down.

He turned toward me, an intense look on his face. "Don't struggle against your fear. It's normal. It isn't wrong to feel it. You'd be wrong *not* to feel it."

What he said hit me like a blast of air. How could he know my exact emotions? "How— You said you couldn't read minds. How can you know what I'm feeling?"

He smiled. "I've learned to recognize your body language, Gemma. I can decipher the look on your face." For some reason his expression turned sly. "Your unconscious can reveal secrets that you yourself aren't even aware of. It goes where thoughts can't, plucks inaccessible strings. It's hard for me to interpret at times, especially when it comes to you."

"You can read people's unconscious?" I asked, stunned.

Evan nodded and looked at me, very focused. "I can see inside you, Gemma. I can read your most hidden emotions through—"

"—dreams," we both said at the same time.

"My God! So . . ." Suddenly everything was clear. It hadn't been a coincidence that I remembered those dreams so vividly I couldn't tell them apart from real life. There was a reason, even if I hadn't been able to understand where the dream ended and the real world began. "It was real. It was all real! I didn't just imagine it, you were *actually* there."

"It was all real," Evan said, stifling a smile, one eyebrow slightly raised.

My heart reacted by flooding me with heat and sending an alarm signal to my brain. Agitation rose in me as I realized what it meant. My cheeks instantly grew flushed and my heart throbbed violently in my temples. Instinctively I raised my fingers to my lips and felt them tremble, exulting.

Evan and I had kissed.

The weight of his gaze was on me, impatient to meet my own, but I was sure he had an impertinent little smile on his face and I didn't know if I could handle it. Meanwhile, my heart wanted to leap out of my chest for joy. For some time now I'd suspected my emotions had been too intense for the dream to have been simply a figment of my imagination.

Evan and I had kissed. The clear image of that kiss rose up in my mind again, coloring my cheeks.

A memory.

With a mix of embarrassment and euphoria, I made myself break the silence. "So you like the constellations."

Evan laughed at my awkward attempt to change the subject. "The origins of the constellations are ancient, you know. Since the dawn of time, man has observed the sky and drawn imaginary lines connecting one luminous spot to the other. Each culture composed its figures using its own imagination. What to the Greeks was a bear was a wagon to the Romans, a hippopotamus to the Egyptians, and a dipper to the Chinese. Like it is here, can you imagine?" His explanation made me smile. "But I've always found it interesting how the Greeks, in particular, turned the sky into a stage on which heroes and gods performed, led by the imagination. In my mind, the stories make the sky a sort of giant picture book, and every night for thousands of years its characters have come to life before our eyes. All you need to do is look at them." His voice had softened to a hush as a whirlwind of emotion filled his eyes, which had rested on me the whole time.

"Can you . . . can you make me dream whatever you want?" I whispered, embarrassed and tripping over my words.

"It's your mind, Gemma. Dreams are mirrors that reflect your soul, your true essence. They reveal your fears, your anguish, your *desires.*" With this last word, he stopped and stared at me. "It's your unconscious that comes out, I can only try to interpret it."

"And are you able to?" I asked, suddenly filled with the fear of what Evan might be able to read inside of me.

"Not always," he admitted regretfully. "With you it's harder. That's another way things don't work like they should with you."

"Don't work? What do you mean?" I found the courage to meet his gaze.

"I've never come across a soul like yours before. It's complex, different. Almost indecipherable. When I'm in your dreams, it's like your mind creates interference and won't let me hide from you. It feels like there's an irresistible power between us, a giant magnet that pulls me towards you."

I gulped, amazed that his feelings were so similar to mine.

"My powers are complementary. Through the unconscious, I can fully read anyone I want. It's kind of like having the key to a complex secret code. I can interpret the symbols, limitations, and weaknesses, and bend a person's will as I please when I'm connected to them. I'd never been in someone's dreams more than once; generally all I need is one night to create a detailed map of the person. But then I met you. You shouldn't be able to hear my voice. That is, the conscious part of you shouldn't, only your soul should. See why I'm so fascinated by you?" His expression turned into a grin. "Drake says I'm drawn to you like a bear to honey." He smiled at the joke and then grew serious again. "Looks like I just can't resist you."

"Ah, so you're . . . a bear?" I said, raising an eyebrow before I could keep the question from leaving my lips. Only from his warm breath on my neck did I realize Evan had moved closer to me. My heart trembled in my chest as his lips grazed my skin, resting gently on the curve of my neck. "You can't be meaning to pounce on me."

"Why not?" His whisper filled me with heat.

I half closed my eyes and instinctively parted my lips, savoring the memory of his mouth on mine. Evan brushed his lips over my neck, moving slowly up toward my chin. I felt a hot shiver every time his mouth touched me.

"Do you feel what I feel?" he whispered as his lips moved sweetly toward my ear.

"What do you feel?" I whispered back, entranced by this hypnotic enchantment.

Evan ran his lips up the curve of my chin, moving them in a slow search for my mouth as my heart raced like never before. He delicately brushed the corner of my lips, leaving me burning with desire, consumed with anticipation. Without moving away he raised his eyes slightly to meet mine, hesitating as if seeking my consent in them, permission I'd already given him even before he'd asked for it.

"This," he whispered, his voice enveloping me like warm silk. Slowly his mouth touched mine, ever so slightly, with endless tenderness, as my lips moved imperceptibly to follow his. "You are my dark paradise," he murmured to himself. My breathing seemed to have abandoned me. Languid heat spread over my eyes, forcing me to close them as I let myself be borne away on a wave of emotions, longing for Evan to finally kiss me.

"*A-hem.*" Someone nearby cleared their throat a second before Evan could fully press his lips against mine. "Am I interrupting something?"

Ginevra.

Evan's irresistible scent lingered on me like a mysterious spell from which I couldn't awaken. I was so bewitched by the warmth of his lips so close to mine that for a second I considered ignoring Ginevra, grabbing him by the shirt and pulling him back toward me. There was nothing in the world that could make me want to stop. As I forced myself to hold back the urge, Ginevra let out a little laugh.

I felt my face go pale as I realized what she found so funny. *I'd forgotten she could read my mind.* How I wished the earth would swallow me up then and there. But Ginevra intervened before I could say anything stupid. "Hello, lovebirds." She smiled to herself.

"What's so funny, sis?" Evan asked, puzzled by the look on her face.

Perfect. I stole a glance at Ginevra, wondering if she was planning to betray me. What a ridiculous turn of events: I was going to end up taking care of my fate myself by jumping off the terrace out of shame.

Ginevra looked at me out of the corner of her eye, a crafty smile on her face as she walked up to us. She leaned down next to Evan until her mouth was right by his ear. I trembled.

"It's a secret," she whispered, gazing steadily at me as she did so.

Evan studied my expression as I heaved a sigh of relief, trying hard not to show how nervous I was. Puzzled, he turned to look first at me and then at Ginevra. "What's up, you two?" he said, narrowing his eyes, a little smile on his face.

I looked at Ginevra, who winked at me before standing up again. Reassured, I shrugged and raised my eyebrows, pretending not to understand. It seemed to be Ginevra's little way of making up for interrupting us right when Evan was about to kiss me.

She turned to him. "That was fast. I knew there was no way to stop you—you were bound to do it sooner or later."

"She had the right to know," Evan replied.

"This whole thing is getting more and more complicated. I still don't know if we'll be able to handle it," she said, worried.

"We'll find a way. There's always a solution." Evan glanced at me, alluding to what I'd said to him that night under the stars. "We just need a plan. And we need it fast, before—" He stopped mid-sentence, looking at me. "We have to be one step ahead of him, no matter what."

I shuddered at the words he hadn't been able to say. I was still trying to process all the information I'd received, and I felt shaken and unsure what effect this new world was actually having on me.

Ginevra's eyes on me distracted me from my thoughts. "Don't worry," she said in a low voice, stroking my elbow, "we're not going to hurt you." She'd read my fear through my thoughts.

"You're trembling," Evan said, surprised and frustrated that he hadn't noticed my state of agitation as Ginevra had. "Are you afraid?" he asked, worried.

"No," I blurted.

Ginevra stole a glance in my direction and was about to contradict me. I still wasn't used to watching what I thought when she was around. I would have to learn to.

"I wish I weren't but I can't help it," I was forced to admit.

Evan stroked my cheek and stared at me intensely. "Trust me," he whispered, "nothing's going to happen to you. You just need to trust me."

I couldn't bring myself to answer him. I nodded, still shaken.

The embarrassing growling of my empty stomach broke the silence. Once again, I considered throwing myself off the terrace.

"Sorry," I said, embarrassed, biting my lip.

"Evan! This isn't like you!" Ginevra snapped. "Have you forgotten Gemma needs food to survive?"

"Forgive me, I'm not used to thinking about things like this," he said, mortified.

"Don't apologize, I'm not hungry," I lied, but my stomach betrayed me again by growling as I said it.

Ginevra took me by the hand and led me inside. "Come with me, we'll get you something to eat," she insisted as she pulled me down the hallway.

My mouth watered at the thought of food and at a faint aroma I thought I smelled in the air, as if there were a home-cooked meal somewhere nearby. I couldn't remember the last time I'd eaten anything.

Thanks, I thought, speaking to her through my mind. Ginevra turned toward the stairs, casting me a friendly look to show she'd heard me. *For everything.* I hadn't yet had the chance to thank her for saving me at the prom. If it hadn't been for her, the chandelier would have crushed me. Nevertheless, knowing that the monster would come back looking for me left a lump in my throat.

What else would I have to go through to escape my fate? I wasn't sure I could hold out for very long. Maybe I wasn't strong enough. Was I really sure Evan would manage to save me every time?

No one could answer that question for me.

Without turning around, Ginevra squeezed my hand tighter to reassure me. I looked back, but Evan wasn't with us any more, even though he hadn't passed us. I hurried to follow Ginevra down the stairs, driven by the longing to see him again.

29

REFLECTION IN THE MIRROR

Walking into the kitchen from the living room, I immediately found Evan on the other side of the table, smiling at me encouragingly. *Handsome as a god.* He escorted me to the table, gallantly pulling out a chair for me, then, with a flourish, showed me the table piled high with all kinds of food.

I gaped. "Evan . . ."

"I wanted to make it up to you," he said, smiling.

"Don't take all the credit," Ginevra retorted scornfully.

"Thanks." I looked at them. "To both of you, but it's too much, really! I could never eat all this, not even if I hadn't touched food for a whole week."

"Don't worry about that," Evan reassured me. "Go ahead and eat whatever you want. Ginevra will polish off the rest." He hid a smile as Ginevra shot him an angry look.

I stared at the table, amazed at the incredible amount of food. "How did you manage to come up with all this in only ten seconds?" I exclaimed.

"Magic," Ginevra said, winking at me. She'd meant it as a joke, but it didn't come across that way. She looked amused at my expression. I touched a piece of bread to make sure it was real and Evan laughed, making me glare at him.

"It all looks great. Thanks," I said quickly, downplaying my reaction.

"Ginevra tends to overdo it sometimes," he said.

"I didn't know what she liked to eat," she said in her defense. "She loves all kinds of food!"

I blushed, embarrassed. She'd clearly read my mind during some of my more "passionate" flirtations with food. I became a bottomless pit when I was nervous.

"You two have a lot in common then," Evan said.

"Shut up," she warned. "Gemma, you skipped dinner, and it's almost time for breakfast now."

"I'll make up for it," I said, feeling hunger pangs. The aroma of the food wafted through the air and tickled my nose. Unable to wait any longer, I sank my teeth into a slice of pizza topped with French fries and washed it down with ice-cold orange soda.

When the meal was over, I felt my belly would burst. I couldn't remember the last time I'd gorged myself like that. Though the first few bites had curbed my hunger, I'd eaten a lot to avoid disappointing Ginevra, who watched me enthusiastically every time I took a taste of something different. I looked around at the kitchen for the first time. "Don't you guys eat?" I blurted, realizing only then there wasn't a stove.

Evan and Ginevra exchanged brief glances before answering.

"My brothers and I don't need food," Evan said, studying my reaction.

"But you can eat," I said. "You ate blueberry crumble when you came to the diner."

He smiled. "That was an excuse to see you, Gemma," he admitted with a sensual smile. "Besides," he said, grinning at Ginevra, "she eats enough for all of us."

She shot him a withering look and a sharp knife rose into the air, hovering over the table and pointing at Evan threateningly. My chair screeched against the floor as I jumped in my seat, terrified.

Evan's expression, however, seemed more amused than scared. "Don't tell me you mean to eat me now!"

"Yes, but first I'm going to carve you up," she said, a fierce look on her face, and the knife zoomed toward him on its own at the speed of light. I jumped in my chair again, frightened, only to see the blade stop inches from his face.

Evan let out a laugh, reaching up to grab the knife handle as I stared at them, stunned. "Where are your manners? We have company," he scolded her. A smile on his lips, he leaned over to whisper in my ear. "I told you it was best to avoid irritating her."

"Um, I'm right here?" Ginevra reminded him, laughing. "Don't worry, Gemma. We're just kidding around."

I looked at Evan, dazed and still terrified, and he winked at me. Would he ever stop teasing me?

"Don't count on it," Ginevra said in response to my thought.

"You'd better get used to it."

I tried to smile, but the effort it took me was plain to see.

"You look tired," she said.

Now that she'd pointed it out, I could barely keep my eyes open. How long had it been since I'd last slept? It felt like days.

"You should get some rest," Evan said. I heard his melodious voice, but suddenly I couldn't see his face any more. I was on the verge of collapsing. "You've been through a rough day and we don't know what's in store for us tomorrow. I'll take you upstairs."

"No!" I replied quickly.

"I'll give you my room," Evan assured me sweetly.

"Gemma, there's nothing to be afraid of," Ginevra said, sensing my concern.

"Nothing's going to happen to you here with us," Evan added.

"Okay, but I'd rather stay down here. The couch is fine. It looked comfortable. Besides, all I need is to lie down and close my eyes for a few minutes and I'll be as good as new."

"Sure, of course you will!" Ginevra said with a sarcastic grin.

"What time is it, anyway?" I asked, suddenly worried by how much light was already filling the garden.

"Quarter past seven. And in any case, there's a clock right over there. It's that round thing with the big moving hands." Poking fun at how tired I was, Ginevra pointed at the wall behind her, on which was a large clock I hadn't noticed before. The hands moved slowly as my eyelids drooped, and I thought about how my parents would already be at the diner, working the Sunday brunch shift.

I noticed Evan and Ginevra exchanging silent glances. They seemed to have heard something that had put them on guard. The thought that the evil being might have found me woke me up, leaving me not the least bit sleepy.

"What's wrong?" I asked, panicked.

"Don't worry," Evan said, trying to calm me. "It's one of ours."

Ginevra's eyes opened wide as she spotted something behind me. "Drake, wait!" As I turned around, she groaned, "Too late."

Utter shock left me breathless, speechless, devoid of thought. My mind was suddenly blank, wiped clean by the image my eyes were sending my brain. "What the—"

In front of me stood an exact replica of me, staring back at me like my reflection in a mirror. For the first time, I had the horrifying suspicion I was dead and on the outside now, looking at the body I'd just abandoned.

I touched my chest impulsively to make sure I was there. Everything was in its place. I wasn't dead, I was still in my body, alive and well. I stepped closer, drawn by the urge to touch it and make sure it was real, that it wasn't a figment of my imagination. But I hesitated and stepped back again as my brain struggled to choose between running away and passing out. In the end I found myself halfway between the two, gaping as Ginevra and Evan looked at me apologetically.

"I tried to warn you," she said to my twin ruefully.

"Everything okay?" Evan asked with concern, stroking my arm as I started to feel I'd permanently lost my power of speech.

"Sorry, Gemma," Ginevra said. "This really is too much," she added in a low voice to Evan before turning back to me. "We should have warned you. This is Drake," she explained, pointing at the other Gemma, who in the meantime had been carefully studying my every movement.

"Hey!" my double chimed, flashing a funny-looking smile that wasn't very flattering to my face.

Hearing that voice, identical to my own, made me shudder. I felt like my body didn't belong to me any more, like I was seeing it from a distance. It was a surreal, utterly illogical sensation. I had the urgent need to look at myself in a mirror. I glanced down at my hands and was relieved to recognize them as mine.

Ginevra went over to her, her footsteps silent. "Drake, would you mind?" she whispered in my double's ear, nodding in my direction.

"Oh. Right! Sorry, babe," the girl replied in my voice. "I'll give you your body back."

Suddenly her candid, innocent face changed shape and became rugged . . . and *handsome*. Even more dangerous than Evan's. He smiled at me with a slightly ominous gleam in his eyes and his face relaxed.

I stammered something unintelligible as I tried to process what I'd just seen. What parallel world had I ended up in? What had happened to the peaceful, monotonous life I was accustomed to?

"It was hit by a truck," Ginevra quipped in response to my thought. "A red one, in fact, just like the car." She glanced at the dress I was wearing. "I'd pick a new outfit if I were you. Red is *definitely* not your lucky color." She grinned at me as I tried to smile back at her, but couldn't.

I looked over at Drake again. Instead of my small, frail body, now his physique was vigorous, trim, and muscular. Very muscular. He looked even brawnier than Evan and seemed a few years older than we were.

"*This* is Drake," Ginevra said, walking to his side.

"The fun one," he added, raising his hand.

Evan had been right when he'd said my parents wouldn't notice the difference. So I had to thank him as well, and I would have if I hadn't been left speechless. Drake had turned into an exact copy of me and taken my place at home so my parents wouldn't notice I was gone. Such a kind thing to do. It warmed my heart.

"Is he an Angel too?" I asked hesitantly, finding my voice again.

Evan and Drake glanced at each other.

"He's one of us," Evan said. "He'll take your place whenever we need him to. I told you there was nothing to worry about."

It was comforting to think someone would replace me if anything happened to me. My family being spared the grief was at least a partial consolation.

"That's not an alternative," Ginevra said, reading my mind. "Not any more. Nothing's going to happen to you, that's a promise." I wasn't so convinced.

"Man, my ears are still ringing," Drake groaned, rubbing them as Ginevra started laughing. "That pain in the neck of a dog of yours wouldn't quit yapping all night long. Your dad came to check on you four times because of it. I wanted to strangle it."

My eyes went wide with concern. "You didn't hurt him, did you?"

"Relax," Evan reassured me softly, "he'd never do anything like that."

Hard to believe. Judging from his build, he probably could have crushed Irony with one hand.

I couldn't stop staring at them all. I felt like a fly in a room full of butterflies. I was definitely the only one there suffering from an inferiority complex. Ginevra was radiant and Drake looked like a Greek god, although Evan was even handsomer.

Drake's head was shaved, but his hair was definitely dark, judging from his complexion. His eyes were also dark; at that moment they were as black as coal, but I knew they wouldn't be the same color if I saw him in his true essence. He stared at me steadily, his gaze piercing. I'd felt a shiver of terror when I looked into them for the first time, but I knew the feeling was totally unjustified. The three of them weren't the bad guys, though I wasn't even sure why they were continuing to protect me.

Drake looked like a military type. Everything about him made me think he was a soldier. His prominent cheekbones framed his face, as did his slightly square jaw. The Subterranean tattoo stood out on his muscles. There was something about him—I couldn't explain what it was, but it made me uneasy. An instinctive reaction.

"Believe me," Drake said lightheartedly, "I came pretty close to doing it." There was a hint of sarcasm in his voice.

They all laughed at his joke, which only I didn't understand. Evan leaned over and whispered in my ear. "For the record, Drake's the one who brings all the girls here. You're my first."

My heart skipped a beat. He took my hand and gazed into my eyes as I looked back into his. He was so close it made me dizzy.

"Wasn't someone here about to get some sleep?" Ginevra asked, glancing my way.

"Actually, I've never felt so awake in my life," I admitted. There was no longer the slightest trace of the sleepiness I'd felt up until a minute ago. "Is there anyone else I should meet?" I asked Evan. "I thought you said there were four of you."

"Simon," Ginevra replied, her expression turning sweet. "We were in the workout room, but he got a . . ." Her voice trailed off. I looked at Evan just in time to glimpse the odd look he was shooting at his sister.

"He had some things to sort through, I think," she corrected herself, still staring at her brother with a strangely reproachful look.

"Try calling him, Evan," Drake said. "It's meet-and-greet time."

"Drake's right," Ginevra added. "He should be finished by now. We need him here. There's a lot for us to talk about and we need to come up with a plan."

Evan nodded before turning to me. "But after that you'll get some rest," he ordered me firmly. "I'll try to contact Simon." He closed his eyes and concentrated for a moment as we watched him in silence. He was calling his brother mentally.

"Simon's my boyfriend," Ginevra whispered in my ear pointedly, hiding a half smile.

"Oh, I didn't know," I replied, although what she said didn't really sink in. I was still too stunned and confused by the whole bizarre situation.

I suddenly heard Evan's entrancing voice in my mind. I looked up and discovered that his eyes were still closed and his lips sealed.

Simon, where are you? You have to join us. We need you, he whispered mentally. I stared at him, too bewitched by the sight of him to look away. When he noticed, he smiled at me and winked.

This time he hadn't lost control, he'd wanted me to hear him. He'd given me permission. I felt a warm glow of gratification.

"What's up, guys?" The timbre of a stranger's voice broke the silence.

"Finally! Where you been, dude?" Drake said impatiently. He was the only one of us who'd been entirely excluded from the conversation, so he'd been waiting in silence. Not only I but also Ginevra seemed to have heard Evan through his thoughts.

Simon, the only family member I hadn't met, had materialized right in front of Drake, his back turned to me. I was surprised to see how much he looked like Evan, seen from behind. His hair was a lighter shade, but their hairstyles and the cut of their shoulders were incredibly similar; anyone could easily have mistaken them.

"It wouldn't be the first time," Ginevra whispered in my ear.

"I was wrong!" I exclaimed, stunned, as I remembered the kiss I'd seen. Ginevra nodded, a little smile on her face. "So he's—"

"My boyfriend," Ginevra said, finishing my sentence as she slid her arm around Simon's waist.

I finally connected the dots. I hadn't seen Ginevra kissing Evan in the garden, she'd been kissing Simon. And to think I would have been spared a world of grief if only I'd known!

"Well, there's one thing you should always remember to do before jumping to conclusions," she told me.

"What's that?" I said, curious.

"*Ask*." She grinned. "I tried to stop you." She winked at me and pulled Simon closer to her. "I would have told you sooner or later," she said, throwing her arms around her boyfriend's neck. Now that he was standing beside her, he didn't look so tall any more.

A few moments had passed since Simon had appeared in the room and only then did he turn to look at me, a puzzled expression on his face.

"If Drake's over there," he said, pointing at his brother, "then you must be Gemma. Were you guys going to introduce me or do I have to do everything myself? Hi, I'm Simon." He smiled, holding out his hand, his voice velvety and kind.

"Nice to meet you, Simon," I replied, trying to hide my amazement. Looking him in the face, it was ridiculous to have thought he resembled Evan. They were like night and day, although both were gorgeous.

Simon had a more angelic face than the others. It inspired trust. His features were soft and his hair a very light brown, almost blond, while his eyes were closer to sky blue. I wondered if all Angels were so irresistibly fascinating. It couldn't have been otherwise.

"Where on earth have you been so long? You know I don't like to wait. It makes me foul-tempered," Ginevra said, teasing.

"More than usual, you mean?" he shot back with a smile.

She threw a piece of food at him but Simon dodged it and pinned his girlfriend to the wall.

"Hey! No fair," she purred.

I looked away.

"Just trying to make up for it," Simon replied, grinning. Ginevra let herself go in a passionate kiss that made me a little uncomfortable, probably because Evan was standing next to me and I had the almost irrepressible longing to do the same thing with him. He was so close his arm was brushing against mine.

He looked at me out of the corner of his eye before leaning over and whispering in my ear. "They do this all the time," he said, sounding apologetic, though a smile danced on his lips.

"Don't mind them. You'll see a whole lot worse around here," Drake said, smirking.

"No problem, it's okay," I replied, my voice hesitant from embarrassment. "How long have they been together?"

"Practically an eternity!" Evan exclaimed, smiling, skillfully dodging the question. I quickly looked away from him, confused. I didn't know what he meant by that, or how old all of them actually were.

"An Angel's heart is difficult to penetrate, but once you're inside it, there's no way out," he whispered, seeking my gaze.

I started at his allusion, the sweetness in his voice making me melt. Then I turned to look at Simon and Ginevra. I felt an overwhelming desire to have the same kind of relationship with Evan that they had. I wanted Evan more than anything else in the world.

"Gemma, I really think you should get some sleep," he suggested, a touch of regret in his voice. "I'm afraid things are going to be difficult when you wake up."

His words made my fear resurface. I had no idea what was in store for me and I was terrified by the thought of facing that infernal creature. That Angel of Death was there for me and soon he would come to take me, because one way or the other I had to die. It was my fate, and who was I to defy it?

Death, if it came unexpectedly, might be cruel but it wasn't frightening, because you didn't have the chance to realize what was about to happen. Knowing your own fate in advance, on the other hand, was a terrifying form of torture, maybe even worse than death itself. A prelude to madness.

Fearing the shadow of death with each breath was an agonizing countdown that left you exhausted and sapped your will to fight, until its echoing whisper faded into an icy silence that deprived you of everything. It was like a deadly poison that took effect silently, draining your energy, battering your mind's defenses until you ultimately wanted to give in to its comfort, letting it shroud you in its dark mantle so the fear itself wouldn't kill you . . . slowly.

"Gemma, did you hear me?" Evan insisted, stroking my shoulder.

"Yeah, you're right," I said, holding back tears. I couldn't accept it. Why me? Why me, of all people? I wasn't ready to let everything go. I wasn't ready to give up Evan. Not so soon.

"Is this all right?" he asked me, leading me to the couch, which he'd made up with a pillow and a quilt.

"It's fine," I replied numbly, the listless tone of my voice betraying my fatalistic thoughts. "Evan!" I said, calling him back before he left the room. "Don't leave me . . . please," I whispered in a tiny voice, almost pleading.

He smiled. "I'll be right here in the next room, I promise," he reassured me, walking back into the kitchen.

I seriously doubted I'd manage to get any sleep. It was already late morning and sunlight was pouring in through the picture window, keeping me from closing my eyes.

At that instant, the room went completely dark. Alarmed, I raised my head to check the windows and found the heavy drapes had closed, as if they'd obeyed my command. Ginevra peeked into the room from the kitchen. "Need anything else?"

"N-no, thanks," I managed to say, still shaken.

But with the darkness, my fear returned, even stronger than before. Evan was right. I hadn't been given the keys to enter another world; I'd just learned to see the one I'd always inhabited with new eyes. And everything that lurked within it.

I peered at the perimeter of the room, nervously scanning every corner. It was so dark I couldn't even see my own body, but I hoped I'd be able to detect any kind of movement, even the tiniest one, so I'd have the chance to call for help if I needed to.

There was no hope of my falling asleep. I started to feel neurotic, a step away from hysteria. I struggled to keep my eyelids from closing but, realizing I really needed to get some rest, I grabbed a corner of the blanket and pulled it up over my head. Hidden beneath the cozy fabric, I felt safe for the first time. I took a deep breath of the air trapped under the heavy quilt and a delicate scent filled my nostrils. I could still smell Evan on my skin. I closed my eyes and imagined he was there with me.

Only then, overcome with exhaustion, did I surrender to sleep.

EVAN

30

DANGEROUS STRATEGY

"She asleep?" I asked Ginevra, trying to get over my concern. As my brothers left the room, Ginevra cocked her head, listening for Gemma's thoughts.

"I can't hear her any more," she said after a moment.

"Good. All this has been really hard on her. I don't know if she's wrapped her brain around it yet—or if she ever will," I said, fear rising up from the bottom of the heart I'd rediscovered not long ago.

"There's no denying she's in shock," Ginevra said, "but can we blame her? Who wouldn't be?"

I looked at her sadly as we moved closer to Gemma, lowering our voices to a hush so she wouldn't wake up.

"Let's give her time to reflect. She'll understand, she'll accept you, you'll see," she said, trying to be reassuring.

"Look at her," I whispered, being careful not to wake the little angel I'd fallen desperately in love with. "Isn't she *beautiful?*" I stroked her warm, rosy cheek. "I could spend eternity watching her sleep. I can't take my eyes off her. It's a like a spell. It paralyzes me."

A few locks of hair were strewn over her face. I reached out to brush them back but froze when she stirred at my touch.

"She's restless," Ginevra confirmed, saying aloud what I was thinking. "She can't relax. Look how tense she is. Why don't you visit her in her dream, Evan?" she asked.

"No. I want to give her room to breathe," I said, although it gave me pain not to be near her.

Ginevra was surprised by my hesitation. "Well, I think you should try to ease her mind."

"She needs time, like you said. If I went to her now, I'd just risk confusing her." I paused, filled with a deep sadness. "If she decides to accept me for who I am and wants me at her side, it'll have to be her own decision, hers and her heart's. I don't want it to be because I pressured her."

Gemma abruptly turned under the blanket, making me lower my voice.

"Shh. Let's let her sleep," Ginevra whispered, leaving my side. "She's going to need it."

"I'll be right there," I said softly, wanting to stay another moment longer. When Ginevra had left the room, I stroked Gemma's neck with the back of my hand. "I'm not going to let anyone hurt you, I promise," I whispered, brushing my lips against hers upside down. I looked at her one more time and joined Ginevra in the kitchen, leaving behind a piece of my heart.

"It's so liberating to finally be myself around her instead of being forced to wear the mask we put on day after day. But I still can't stand the thought that she might not accept me or might even be *scared* of me. It's frustrating to have to live with the possibility."

"You have to accept it, Evan. It's the flip side of the coin. She'll get through this, I know she will. What she feels for you is very powerful. She just needs time, trust me."

I hoped she was right, but the reason I was so upset went a lot deeper than that, and I couldn't hide it from Ginevra, no matter how much I wanted to.

"Evan."

I looked up, knowing exactly what she was going to say before she even opened her mouth.

"Why didn't you tell her?"

I didn't reply. I didn't know the answer.

"Don't you see it's only going to complicate things?"

"Why? It doesn't matter any more." I glanced into the salon, worried Gemma might overhear us.

"Of course it matters! What's she going to think when she finds out that *you* were supposed to be her Executioner? That *you* were the one sent to kill her?"

Deep in my heart, I shuddered at the thought. "She doesn't need to find out," I said quietly, overcome with guilt.

"Well, it's a risk you're going to have to take if you want to be with her. She's bound to find out, and it would be better for her to find out the whole truth all at once, no more secrets. It would be better for everyone."

"You think I don't know that? Or that I haven't tried?" I hissed. "I planned on telling her, but then she asked about Amy."

"The little girl you killed in the fire," Ginevra said.

I glared at her for saying it out loud. My sadness grew as Ginevra silently listened to the thoughts she'd already read in my mind before I voiced them. Still, I felt like if I didn't get it all out it would crush me.

"I didn't expect Gemma to ask. It floored me. You should have seen the look in her eyes when she thought I'd saved that little girl. She thought I was upset because I hadn't been able to take Amy to safety. How could I admit I was actually there to *kill* her? It wasn't the guilt consuming me, it was the mask I had to put on in front of her. Ginevra, I couldn't tell her what I was."

"You should have tried, Evan," she insisted, ignoring my frustration.

"No," I said with conviction. "I couldn't. It would have been too much for her. She was so scared. I wanted to hug her, hold her tight against me and tell her I wouldn't let anything happen to her, not for anything in the world." I stared blankly at the floor, drawn back in by the memory of the desolate existence I'd been trapped in before meeting Gemma. "My life used to be empty and I didn't know it. I'm not going to let anyone take her away from me. If anybody even dares come close to Gemma I'll send them straight to hell," I swore, an unfamiliar rage filling me at the thought that anyone would try to hurt her. "She's my heaven," I murmured.

Nobody would touch her. Not as long as I was there to protect her.

"You can count on us, Evan. We'll help you keep her safe."

"No. You guys have risked enough already. I still don't know what price I'll have to pay, but the Brotherhood is going to summon us. I'm amazed they haven't done it already."

"We're a team. One for all. If Gemma's the girl you want, she's one of us now. We'll protect her no matter what."

Thank you, I thought.

"Don't thank me yet. There's something else we need to take care of: our strategy," Ginevra stated firmly. Suddenly she stiffened and peered around.

"What's wrong?" I asked, worried.

"He's here, nearby. I can feel him," she barely whispered, all her senses on high alert.

I was enraged. "He wouldn't dare confront us in our own home," I snarled, clenching my teeth as I scanned the room. Sensing a presence, I spun around, but was surprised to find Drake and Simon, who'd silently appeared behind me. "Oh! It's you." I took a deep breath, trying to quell the blood boiling in my veins.

Meanwhile, Ginevra's eyes remained vigilant. My brothers' appearance hadn't calmed her. Since she was a Witch, she was more skilled than any of us at sensing the presence of an Angel.

"Hey, take it easy, Evan," Simon said, resting a hand on my shoulder. "You're tense. We need perfect focus. Or have you already come up with a plan?"

"You think we could convince him to stand down?" Ginevra asked.

"Impossible," I said. "He's not going to give up until he's killed her. Orders come first. Nothing else matters to him."

"Then how can we keep him from doing it without killing *him*?"

I shot Ginevra a look brimming with rage, almost like she'd insulted me.

"You can't be thinking—" Simon was horrified. "Evan, don't tell me you mean to kill him! He's a Descendant! He's one of us!"

I clenched my fists until they ached. "I'll do it if I have to. *Anything*, to keep from losing her."

"But this isn't his fault!" Simon insisted. "He's just a pawn in the hands of the Brotherhood. He's only carrying out orders, you know that. He's innocent, he'd never do anything to hurt us."

"He wants to hurt *her*, and that's reason enough for me," I snapped. "He's not going to take her away from me, even if I'm forced to sacrifice his life. If it's my last resort, I'll kill him. I need you guys to know that up front." I stared silently at Drake, hoping he'd back me up.

"Evan," he said, "you know it's impossible to kill an Executioner, unless—"

I nodded. "There's only one way to do it. I've already thought about that," I told them, glancing at Ginevra. She seemed shocked by my idea.

"My poison," she whispered, appalled.

"It's the only weapon that can kill a Soldier of Death: a Witch's poison. And we have that to our advantage," I said.

My strategy left my family speechless. They stared at me, horrified, wondering how I could plot anything remotely similar against a member of my own race, united by blood over centuries of successions, sacrifices, and deaths. Their accusing looks filled me with self-loathing.

Under any other circumstances it would have been insane to even think of doing anything like it. But Gemma changed everything, and I had no choice but to consider it. Why didn't any of them seem to understand? I wasn't going to let him lay a finger on her. To protect her I'd kill that Angel and anyone else who came after him. Nothing would stop me.

In Gemma I'd found my Eve, my other half. Though some didn't know it, somewhere out there in the world there was a kindred spirit that completed each of us, and not everybody was lucky enough to recognize that person. It had taken centuries, but I'd found her and nobody was going to take her away from me, much less Death, the coward that had made us its keepers. Sooner or later, I'd come up with a solution. Gemma was mine, all mine. Forever mine.

I turned toward Ginevra. *Do you still have any?* I asked her telepathically.

The look on her face gave her away—she didn't want to answer me. "Evan, you can't really be thinking of using my poison—"

"I have to," I said through clenched teeth.

"It would never work, Evan. Consider the consequences, damn it all!" Drake warned me.

"*I don't care about the consequences*," I snarled, precisely articulating each word. "Gemma's all that matters." My voice sounded cold and hard, even to my own ears. I was desperate, willing to do anything. My love for her overshadowed everything else.

"Calm down, Evan, there must be another solution," Simon pleaded. I'd never seen him so concerned.

"You don't understand!" I howled in frustration. "We've got to stop him, damn it!"

"Evan, Evan, listen to me," Ginevra interjected, her voice calmer as she looked me in the eye. "After him, others would come. This kind of war would never end! Do you really want to force her to live in hiding forever? Think carefully: Drake would have to take her place, and she'd never be able to go back to her life. She'd never see her family again or her friends. Is that really what you want for her? She'd end up killing herself. I mean, the thought's already crossed her mind! What kind of life could she ever have if she's constantly being chased by Death? Living in terror would slowly kill her. No one would be able to bear it."

Somehow, Ginevra's words got through to me in the midst of my wild rage, forcing me to reflect.

"You're right," I admitted, resigned. I couldn't let Gemma be the one to pay the consequences. None of this was her fault.

"There must be another way to keep him from finding her," Ginevra suggested.

I fell silent. Her words echoed in my head, almost hinting at the solution. "Of course," I whispered. "Ginevra, you're a genius!" I narrowed my eyes as my brain rapidly formulated a plan.

"It's perfect!" Ginevra gasped euphorically as she studied the strategy taking shape in my mind.

"What's up?" Drake asked anxiously.

"Evan's found a solution," Ginevra replied, letting me be the one to explain the plan we would implement.

"Which would be . . . ?" Simon sounded impatient but also plainly relieved there was an alternative.

"We hide her," I announced, my heart filled with hope. Simon and Drake stared at me quizzically .

"Hear him out. It might work," Ginevra said before they could criticize me. Meanwhile, her eyes continued to scan the room with unnerving suspicion.

"Gemma's fate is sealed," I explained to my brothers. "She has to die. Fine. So she'll die. We can't change what's written."

Their disapproving murmurs rose up and filled the room, but I smiled, more and more convinced the plan would work.

"You don't want to kill the Angel any more? You want to kill Gemma instead?" Simon asked, bewildered. My new plan clearly horrified him more than the first one. "I don't understand."

I felt like I was radiating a new light, a glimmer of hope that my crazy plan might work and the nightmare would be over forever.

"Well?" Drake snapped impatiently. "Have you gone nuts or what?"

"No, I haven't," I said, vaguely distracted by Ginevra, who continued to look around uneasily.

"Gemma takes the lethal poison, not the Angel. Gemma has to die. It's inevitable, right? No one can change their destiny. No one can fight it. What's written must come to pass."

"Tell them how you would convince her to poison herself," Ginevra said, urging me to explain the details she'd already read in my mind.

"Wha—What? You mean you're going along with this?" Simon asked, horrified. Neither of us paid any attention to him.

"I'll force her if it comes to that," I said, utterly resolved.

No matter how hard and cold my voice might have sounded, there was a new warmth rising up inside me, kindled by the hope of a future with Gemma. I was willing to do anything to get us out of our predicament, even something this extreme. I was becoming more and more convinced that everything would turn out fine, that Gemma and I could have a future together.

"It would be better if you gave it to her without telling her, Evan," Ginevra suggested. "It'd be easier on all of us. Just put a drop of it in her glass and her body will be dead in an instant. We wait for her to wake up, and it's all over. We'll take care of the rest. Believe me, knowing would only scare her. She doesn't have to know about it."

"C'mon, you two! Could you explain to the rest of us what the hell you're talking about?" Drake shouted impatiently.

"Listen, guys. We can't fight destiny, no matter how incomprehensible or wrong it might seem to us. It takes precedence over everything else and it's beyond our control. We can run, but it'll come back each and every time to take whatever it wants, unless . . ."

"Unless what? Cut to the chase!" Drake said, exasperated.

"Unless we turn the tables on it," I said, my heart in turmoil.

"Is this some kind of riddle or are you going to explain the plan?" Drake groaned.

"Don't you get it? The answer was right there under our noses all along! What we needed wasn't an escape plan but a loophole. Gemma needs to meet her fate. Okay, she *has* to die, but that doesn't mean we can't bring her back."

I looked at them impatiently, trying to decipher the expressions on their faces, but it seemed as if they'd gotten lost along the way.

"Are you out of your mind?" Simon bellowed.

Not the reaction I'd hoped for.

"Why not? It might work," Ginevra pointed out.

"It *might*. And what if it doesn't? You thought about that, Evan?" Drake spoke up.

"Why so cautious all of a sudden, Drake? Haven't you always been the one who loves a challenge? I hoped at least *you* would react differently, for God's sake!"

"This decision isn't about me, Evan. I just don't want to see you make a huge mistake. You could lose her forever. Nobody knows better than me what . . ." Drake's voice trailed off and dropped to a hush. "Are you willing to run that risk?"

"I have no choice," I roared.

"It's too dangerous, Evan," Simon interjected, worried. "Besides, what makes you think Gemma's going to agree to your plan? You think she's willing to defy Death? You think she's that brave?"

"I know she is," I answered.

"No one is!" he insisted, more upset than before. "Evan, think about it: this has never happened before. We don't know what we'd be up against. The situation could get out of hand."

"You're wrong. It happens all the time and you know it. There's a halfway point between life and death. People come and go without even realizing it. Lots of people wake up miraculously."

"You're talking about being in a coma! This is different, Evan. Some coma patients wake up again because it isn't written that they're supposed to die yet. Their souls wander until they find their way back, their bodies kept alive by machines in the meantime, but it's only because there's nobody there to usher them to the other side. No Subterranean is there waiting for them. Even if Gemma agreed to run the risk, he'd be there waiting for her."

"That's not a problem. I've already thought everything through. I'll pretend to realize I made a mistake and want to make up for it by killing her. I'll find a way to be sure he sees me when Gemma takes the poison. He doesn't have anything against *us*, Simon. He doesn't want to hurt us. I can reason with him. Once he's seen her lifeless body, he'll let me stay with her one last time. I'll tell him I want to accompany her myself. I'm sure he'll understand. I just hope he can't read minds," I murmured, forcing a smile to ease the tension. Actually, the possibility that he might have that power worried me more than anything else. It would ruin everything.

My brothers looked like they were starting to understand my plan. It would be risky, there was no denying that. If I couldn't convince the Dark Angel to leave quickly, I'd lose her forever. I'd only have a few minutes before she was jeopardized by the lack of oxygen to her brain.

In my heart I knew I could do it, but desperation about that small risk of failure pierced my heart like a flaming arrow. I had to risk it, though. For her. For *us*.

"What if the Angel doesn't trust you? If he's not willing to let you be the one to help her cross over? You'd lose her in that case too. If he insists on doing it himself you'll never see her again, Evan."

The thought turned me into a slab of ice. Wasn't that the very reason I hadn't let the semi kill her when her time had come? I grabbed my hair, overwhelmed with consternation. The cruel destiny our race had been condemned to had never felt so heavy as it did right now. Forced into exile, halfway between life and death, unable to see other souls once they'd crossed over and unable to show ourselves to them. *Hidden.* Forgotten. Abandoned to ourselves, to oblivion. For eternity. I would never see her again.

I took a deep breath, filling my lungs to ward off my frustration. "We'll follow my plan and if something goes wrong I'll pay the consequences," I made myself say with confidence, trying to hide my agitation. My chest ached at the thought of that possibility. "I need to know: can I count on you?"

The guys' expressions were half skeptical, half convinced. Only Ginevra seemed fully convinced the desperate plan might work, probably because she'd sensed the fervor that inflamed my thoughts. I hoped that was the reason—otherwise I'd have to consider another possibility, the doubt that continued to burn in my mind, wearing down my resolve: Ginevra wasn't one of us. Maybe my brothers were right. Maybe I should listen to them more instead of letting my emotions drag me into a decision supported by a Witch who couldn't possibly understand the dedication with which a Soldier of Death carries out his orders. With no reservations. No exceptions. Canceling out all else.

I needed to reflect, but suddenly I couldn't. My mind was drawing a blank. The minute hand on the clock was moving quickly, keeping me from thinking, as if time had decided to put me under pressure. Anxiety crept up again, filling every gap, sneaking into every free space, feeding on my uncertainty.

"Don't torture yourself," Ginevra said in a low voice, resting her hand affectionately on my shoulder. "It'll work. I'm not a Soldier of Death, but I believe in you. I've always believed in you, Evan. Don't let doubts creep into your mind to cloud what you saw so clearly a moment ago. Doubts are like mischievous demons, Evan. You have to drive them out of your head."

"You're right. It's just panic messing with me."

"You shouldn't doubt your plan. It'll be easier if we all really believe in it. If you hesitate, you risk being discovered."

I nodded, regaining control of my thoughts.

Time slipped by quickly. Outside, the sun prepared to disappear over the horizon, as though it too were being chased by demons.

Gemma was still sleeping and as yet, there was no sign of our enemy. Before waking her up, I ran over in my mind what I would say to convince her to follow my plan, but no matter how hard I tried, none of the alternatives I came up with seemed right. Anything I told her would end up terrifying her.

I'd immediately rejected Ginevra's suggestion. I could never poison her without her knowledge. Gemma didn't deserve to be tricked and I was sure she'd be strong enough to face reality.

I was *tired* of lying to her. I wanted her to be a part of my world and that couldn't happen unless I was totally honest. Gemma had to see me for what I actually was. She had to know my dark side. I would surrender to her completely, explain everything, hope that she would understand and trust me. Hope that her heart would choose the real me without reserve. Without secrets.

I'd made up my mind. There was no turning back. Even though I had no need for air, I took another deep breath and got ready to talk to her. She'd had enough sleep. It was time to wake her.

It would all be over soon. Another breath, and I hurried toward the salon. Suddenly impatient, my heart throbbed at the thought of seeing her face again, her sweet, penetrating gaze, her shy smile. I couldn't stand this endless, exhausting wait to hear her voice again. I was *obsessed* with Gemma. Like my entire existence had been one long wait until the moment I met her.

I went through the doorway. My heart, ecstatic only a moment ago, instantly withered.

Gemma was gone.

The whole world came crashing down at my feet. An icy claw gripped my chest, preventing me from breathing as I stared at the empty sofa, my eyes burning violently, my body frozen with terror, unable to react. I felt the energy draining from me and crumpled to my knees, utterly desperate. The light in my heart had gone out.

With everything left in me, I thought of her face and screamed out her name in my head, as though I could somehow bring her back to me, wherever she was. As hopeless as a man sentenced to death, I stared, petrified, at the empty sofa, the covers dumped on the floor. How could I have let it happen? Where was my star? Had that dog found a way to take her?

An obscure impulse like a dark, ominous wave brought me to my feet. Rage and evil took possession of me, banishing everything I'd been before.

I had to find him. I had to *kill* him. I would scour the planet if that was what it took. The fiend didn't deserve to exist. I would hunt him down and slaughter him just for taking her away from me. And if the dirtbag had harmed even a hair on her head, he'd end up begging me to kill him just to end the merciless torture I would subject him to. I was devastated, caught between oblivion and reason. Gemma was my light; without her I'd be lost to darkness. I'd never felt such powerful, uncontrollable hatred before, not for anyone.

I forgot my plan—which had already failed—forgot what mercy was, forgot myself. It was personal now, between me and him. The bastard's days were numbered.

31

FATAL DROP

"What's wrong?" Ginevra rushed into the salon, her voice edged with anxiety from having sensed the desperation in my thoughts.

I stared at the empty sofa, devastated.

"Gemma!" she gasped.

"He took her," I hissed in rage and desperation.

"But how? It can't be, Evan! How could he have?"

"I haven't been able to come up with an explanation yet."

"How did he do it? Evan, how could he have slipped into our house without my sensing his presence? No, wait. I did. I sensed something unusual, but it seemed too ridiculous to believe. I detected a presence, but it wasn't here! I checked! That's why I didn't bother telling you. How do you explain something like this?"

"Not a clue. We don't even know what to expect because we don't know what powers he has, damn it!" We both found it inconceivable that he could have come in and taken her away without our noticing.

"He couldn't have been here, it's impossible. I rule that out. So how'd he do it?" Her expression darkened as she thought aloud. Something crossed my mind.

"Yeah, you may be right. If he wasn't here, he must have convinced her to leave! I am such an idiot. Why didn't I think of it before? He's like me," I exclaimed. "He can read inside her. He must have gotten into her head while she was sleeping and convinced her to run away from us."

"But why didn't I hear her thoughts when she woke up?" Ginevra wondered, stricken with guilt.

"He must have blocked you. He wanted to get her out of here. If only I'd listened to you. Fuck!" A furious roar escaped me. I'd gladly burn in hell for the chance to go back and visit her in her dream.

"You wanted her to rest, Evan. You didn't want to disturb her. Don't feel bad."

Deep in my heart, I knew Ginevra was right. Then why did it hurt so horribly? It was all my fault. If I'd gone to her in her dreams I would have kept him from touching her. Instead I'd left her all alone with him. With that *monster*.

The pain grew sharper at the thought of how terrified Gemma must have felt when she found herself facing that demon all alone. And all because of me, because I wasn't there to protect her.

An unstoppable surge of rage boiled deep down in my gut, exploding with devastating power. I smashed my fist onto the crystal coffee table, shattering it before Ginevra's astonished eyes. As I ran my hand through my hair, something hot trickled down my face and dripped onto my forearm.

Ginevra's arms gently encircled my shoulders.

"It's all my fault, don't you see? I was supposed to protect her!" I snarled, overcome by a desperation I'd never known before. "I don't know what I'll do if I don't find her in time."

Actually, I knew perfectly well what I would do if I lost Gemma. Without her, nothing would mean anything any more. Gemma had become my light. I wasn't willing to go back into the darkness. What sense would there be in existing for all eternity as an empty shell? It was sheer agony.

"You know I would never let you." Ginevra had found her way into my thoughts, no matter how hard I'd been trying to hide them from her.

"It's my decision," I said firmly. "Besides, you won't be able to stop me. Sooner or later I'll get exactly what I want."

Silence fell. A gray, devastating silence as grim as death.

"You haven't answered my question," I reminded her as my eyes lit up with the fire burning behind my pupils. "Do you still have some?" My teeth were clenched as I pronounced those bitter words. It was almost as if the poison I was talking about had slipped into my mouth.

"Not if you have any intention of using it on yourself."

"I won't lie to you: that's beyond my control. But I still have one more chance, if we act fast."

Ginevra scrutinized me.

"My guess is you kept a little back in case you needed it one day." I raised an eyebrow and looked her in the eyes, encouraging her to admit it. I was sure Ginevra had saved a little poison, given her natural propensity to be always in control.

Her body suddenly vanished in a puff of mist, like fog dispersed by the wind. I stared at the spot she'd disappeared from, confirming my theory, and my eyes narrowed as I realized I was right. Filled with new determination, I went upstairs to join her.

Strange as it was, I'd never gone into her room before. I'd never stopped to wonder why none of us were allowed to walk through her doorway for any reason. Except Simon, naturally. Ginevra had been very clear about that rule. Despite the powerful connection between her and me, she was the only female among three males, so I'd always deemed it proper to respect her privacy.

But even under these extreme circumstances Ginevra was clearly reluctant to let me in. I began to suspect she was hiding something.

At first sight, the room looked like it had been arranged with maniacal attention to detail. There was a disturbing number of mirrors on the walls. Stacks and stacks of books filled the bookshelves. They emitted the same ominous aura that always surrounded Ginevra. To my surprise, the walls were painted in bright, even brilliant, colors, and the light was multiplied by the mirrors. Set into one of the cream-colored walls was a massive vault door in elegant dark gray.

What was a vault doing inside her bedroom? And why didn't I know anything about it?

"Don't be mad at me for keeping this hidden from you, Evan." Ginevra suddenly seemed worried, almost like she was afraid of how I would react.

"What are you talking about, Gin?" I asked cautiously, trying to curb my suspicions. What the hell was Ginevra hiding behind that door? My mind was riddled with confusion.

"I did it for all of you. It was too dangerous. I had to keep it as far away as possible."

Why did she suddenly seem guilty? And about what? "Ginevra, what's going on? Whatever you've been hiding isn't important, not right now," I assured her, my voice firm. "If what's in there can save Gemma, open it up, for God's sake! We haven't got much time."

She hesitated a second, checking my thoughts to make sure I was being honest, but I hadn't lied to her. Her secret didn't matter to me at all. I wouldn't even have bothered wondering about it if it hadn't been necessary. But it was.

"Ginevra, what are you waiting for?" I said, frustrated.

She glanced at me one last time, a look of weary resignation on her face, and raised her arm, her palm pointed at the sealed door. A moment later, a shiver spread through my bones, as cold as a last breath escaping death's lips, as a light shone in Ginevra's eyes, turning them a stronger shade of green. Her irises narrowed into vertical slits, like a snake's. It had been a long, long time since I'd last seen her like that, and the memory of that time made me shudder. She rotated her wrist counterclockwise. There was a click and the vault door swung open with an ominous groan.

"Follow me." Her voice had grown colder, as though dominated by some dark force.

I crossed through the doorway immediately after Ginevra, feeling a disturbing sensation of cold that seemed to be coming directly from my bones. Semidarkness enveloped us inside the tiny room. Even my sharp senses struggled to penetrate it and send information to my brain. Something wasn't right. Dark, evil energy swirled around me, withdrew and advanced again. It was a blood-chilling sensation I couldn't explain, but inside me it triggered remote yet familiar instincts buried by time. I'd felt that sensation on my skin before.

As if to ward off the agitation that had struck me, Ginevra lit up the room with a sudden wave of her hand. And I realized I'd been wrong.

It wasn't a cramped room. We were in a garden, a lush, narrow glade where branches and plants swayed over the verdant terrain. A little corner of paradise. Amazed, I stifled a gasp and wondered what else Ginevra was hiding from us. The voice of my instinct insisted I pay attention to the chill that had washed over me, but I ignored it, dismissing the ridiculous notion. Ginevra would never go so far.

Seconds later she stopped in her tracks and gestured for me not to move. The mysterious anxiety within me fought harder to emerge, overwhelming me, freezing every muscle, as I discovered what Ginevra had carefully hidden from us for so long. The focal point, the origin of all that dark energy.

I'd been wrong again, it wasn't a corner of paradise. It was a corner of hell.

I stared at the glass case in front of me, feeling like I was trapped in a slab of black ice. *Ginevra!* I wanted to scream at her, but even my thoughts were frozen. It was like every part of me, subjugated by primitive terror, suddenly refused to obey my command.

There was no need for an explanation. I already knew what the glass prison contained. Inside it Ginevra had hidden her serpent. The only adversary an Angel of Death ever had to fear. The only creature capable of annihilating us.

The moment it sensed my presence, the serpent writhed and shot from one corner of the case to the other, gripped by the relentless instinct to sink its fangs into my flesh and corrode my blood with its lethal poison.

"Shh," Ginevra said, trying to calm it down, but the hatred its very nature harbored for my race wouldn't let it. "Everything's okay. Easy, now. I'm here with you."

Like a mysterious spell, Ginevra's voice somehow soothed the animal's instinct. I forced myself to look into its eyes, losing myself in the darkness lurking there, and for the first time I understood the earlier instinct that had tried to warn me. In that creature dwelled pure evil, and my essence was interfering, clashing with it.

"You kept it," I whispered, my voice brimming with contempt.

"You were never supposed to find out," she said, her expression a mix of shame and determination.

"We thought you'd killed it! Damn it, Ginevra! How could you?" I shouted.

"I couldn't do it, Evan! He's a part of me. You can't understand. A Witch forms a special, inseparable bond with her serpent. My thoughts are his thoughts. My flesh is his flesh. Could you ever kill a part of yourself, no matter how evil its nature might be?"

"Does Simon know about this?" I asked, absolutely infuriated, ignoring her excuses.

Ginevra nodded, hanging her head guiltily. "I made him promise not to tell you. Please don't be mad at him. It was too dangerous to get you and Drake involved. Nothing was going to happen as long as you weren't allowed into my room," she said, trying to reassure me. She failed.

I froze at the thought of what *could* happen. It wouldn't affect me because I'd already chosen my fate, but I was worried about my brothers. The unspoken war that since the dawn of time had been waged between the two mortal enemies, Witches and Angels, had never subsided. The evil nature intrinsic to each Witch drove her to hunt down mortals who'd inherited the gene of the Subterraneans—in whose veins ran the blood of our race—to prevent them from becoming Angels of Death and carrying out the mission of ushering souls to heaven. That way, humanity would eventually lose itself in hell, the Witches' realm.

It was a battle for souls. When a new Subterranean appeared on earth for the first time, a Witch was already there, ready to try to corrupt his soul. By reading his mind, she could know whether he was close to surrendering or if he had no intention of being seduced. In the latter case, she would disappear before the Angel had the chance to slay her. But if he wasn't strong enough to resist the temptations she laid before him, if the Witch managed to beguile him with her bewitching, sexy, irresistible beauty, she would kill him with her poison. Witches were the most enchanting creatures in existence, and also the most dangerous. All it took was one drop of their poison to annihilate a Subterranean for all eternity. No one knew what happened to his soul. Everyone assumed it wound up in hell. But not even that worried me. To me, no hell could be worse than having to bear an existence without Gemma.

We'd all thought Ginevra had gotten rid of her serpent when she'd renounced her Sisters to be with Simon. She told us she had. She'd betrayed them for him, and because of it they wanted to annihilate her. She was prepared to make that sacrifice, but she was saved thanks to her close relationship with the eldest Sister, who'd spared her. Since then, the Witches had kept a constant eye on her, and the forces of darkness had returned from time to time, trying to tempt her, but they always failed. Her love for Simon was too powerful for her to give in to evil ever again.

I could understand the bond Ginevra had with her serpent, but I couldn't get over the fact that she'd exposed Simon to such a risk.

"Simon is safe," she told me now, following my train of thought.

"How could you not see how dangerous this is? You were supposed to get rid of it, like you've made us believe all this time. Only you can kill it, Gin. If any of us tried, even if we avoided its venomous fangs, it would end up killing you in the process."

"Forgive me. I couldn't bring myself to kill him. I was on the verge of doing it. Simon stopped me when he saw how agonized I was, how much pain it caused me to even think of giving him up. Simon forgave me for not finding the strength to end it."

"But why aren't you thinking of Simon?" I accused her angrily.

"Simon runs the least risk of all of you, you know that. I would never let anything happen to him. He means more to me than anything else," she insisted.

"Well, what if the door was accidentally left open and that thing slithered out into your room? Ever imagine that?"

"He'd know what to do," she replied coldly. "I've ordered Simon to kill him."

I knew Simon was capable of doing it. Like all Angels, he could control the elements, and while a Witch's poison was the one effective weapon against a Subterranean, an Angel's fire was the same against a Witch.

Cruel fate had amused itself by bringing their two enemy souls together, not to battle, but to fall helplessly in love, forcing them to live on the razor's edge day after day.

"You know he would never do that to you," I said, looking her in the eye.

"He swore he would. An Angel's promise must mean something, I suppose."

"What difference does that make? He would never kill your serpent, because he knows it would kill you too! He'd rather die."

"No! I'd never allow him to," she said, her voice tinged with the tears that the notion had brought to her eyes. "Our bond is a lot stronger than that. I'd sense the danger and be there to help him. Simon never runs risks—none of you do. Trust me, Evan. I've kept the situation under control for a long time and will continue to do so. My serpent won't hurt any of you. A Witch's word means something. Besides, Evan, we should talk about this some other time. Don't forget why we came here: *Gemma.*"

Hearing her name made everything else disappear.

"Do it," I ordered, clenching my jaw.

Ginevra stepped inside the case, closing the door behind her, and looked down at her serpent. Its small size didn't convey how lethal it was. She lifted it from the tree trunk it was coiled around. I could tell from the way they were staring so intently at each other that they were communicating.

Ginevra raised her free hand toward a panel that opened up in the wall on the far side of her room, outside the door of the vault. Not wanting to break the connection between them, she opened it with a flick of her wrist without taking her gaze off the creature. Holding my breath, I watched a tiny vial dart toward her like a nail drawn to a magnet. The vial went right through the glass wall of the case, so strong was her magic. Ginevra showed it to the serpent who in the meantime had wrapped itself around her arm, hissing every time it met my gaze. She stared straight into its eyes and the creature suddenly relaxed its grip and slithered down to her hand so swiftly it made me back up, even though the glass pane between us assured my safety. But the beast wasn't interested in me, it was under Ginevra's control now. It scared me to think my sister had such a powerful bond with such an evil creature.

The serpent reached the vial that Ginevra was holding in her hand and pierced the cap with its fang, as sharp and pointed as a needle. A sparkling droplet, crystal clear and fatal, fell to the bottom of the vial.

One drop was enough.

Ginevra whispered something to the serpent that, despite all the languages I spoke, was incomprehensible to me. She pulled it away from the vial and put it back on the branch.

"We can go now. We're done here," she told me, her voice cold. It seemed like a part of the creature had seeped into her when they'd established their connection, just as Ginevra had controlled it a moment before.

I followed her out of the room, looking over my shoulder at the case. Free from her control, the serpent wouldn't stop hissing, infuriated by my presence.

Ginevra sealed the vault door carefully and walked straight to her desk as though she'd done this many times before. I watched as her eyes returned to normal, ridding themselves of the darkness. She opened the drawer and pulled out a dagger. "You're sure you want to do this?"

"Never been so sure of anything in my life."

She nodded, never taking her eyes off me. "There's no way you can get him to drink the poison. You'll have to stab him," she warned, her voice grim, as though the idea of killing the scumbag might scare me.

"I can't wait," I hissed, a growing rage lashing at my heart. I was burning with the longing to face the damned Angel. Ginevra opened the little vial and tipped it, making the poison slowly slide down the glass wall. She held the dagger underneath it and the droplet fell onto the sharp blade.

"Be very careful not to cut yourself, Evan." She slid the dagger into a leather sheath and handed it to me.

I tied it firmly to my belt and stared at her, on my face the look of someone ready to kill. "That's not going to happen. At least not accidentally," I confessed. I knew what I'd do if it turned out I was too late to save Gemma.

Ginevra nodded again, grief-stricken. She realized that in that case neither she nor anyone else would be able to stop me. "So how do we find her?" she asked sadly, her voice weary. She seemed sure the Executioner was somehow hiding Gemma from us, just like he'd managed to lure her away from our protection.

"I don't know." Frustration seeped into my voice. "I've been trying to reach her with my thoughts, but I can't find her." We didn't know exactly how long ago she'd disappeared. We didn't know where he'd hidden her or why Ginevra and I weren't able to perceive her.

Usually all I had to do was focus on her, the same as with anyone else, to materialize at her side. So why couldn't I sense *anything* now? An impenetrable void surrounded her, concealing her behind absolute silence. No matter how hard I tried, I couldn't perceive the aura emanating from her soul. It was like she was dead. I instantly shoved the thought from my mind, angry at myself for even thinking it.

"Try again," Ginevra said encouragingly, reading my frustration. "Call to her, Evan. Keep on calling to her. I'm sure she'll hear you."

I concentrated on Gemma again. No results. All I sensed was silence. Again and again. It was like an insurmountable wall was keeping me from going to her. I tried to get past it, as desperate as an insect banging against a window to reach the light, but every attempt failed. Anguish closed in on me as the seconds went by until I felt suffocated.

"I can't find her," I admitted, devastated. "Search for her thoughts, Gin!" I begged, a slave to desperation. "You've got to find her! Listen for her voice. Please."

"You think I haven't been trying? I can't hear her. I'm sorry. There's silence all around her, it's like—"

"Focus!" I barked. "You've *got* to hear her. Focus!" I screamed, unable to bear the weight of the words I'd kept her from saying. "Please," I implored her, agonized. I couldn't stand the idea that the silence might be the icy halo of death that had already descended on her.

Ginevra closed her eyes and her face instantly tensed. I waited a few moments, even holding my breath so I wouldn't break her concentration.

"I sense something. *It's him.*"

The air left my nostrils in a snort of rage.

"He's very powerful."

"Where is he? Tell me where he's keeping her!" I snarled, blinded by the longing to kill him.

"I can't—I can't reach them. I'm sorry. He can sense me too, and he's blocking me."

Hatred for that worm burned my very soul. I clenched my fists, ready to pour out all my fury on the first thing I could take a swing at, but Ginevra stopped me before I could vent my anger. "Calm down, Evan, we need to concentrate!"

"I swear he's going to pay for this." My eyes felt like they were burning in some mysterious pyre. "He can't keep me from her. I'm going to find her and I'm going to show him no mercy." Anger consumed me, seared me like fire. "I'm going to plunge this dagger into his chest and send him straight to hell! And if it turns out I'm too late, I'll follow him there. I hope the poison's enough for both of us."

"That's not going to happen," Ginevra reassured me as I sat down on her bed, my eyes hidden behind my fists. "We'll get there in time. Focus, Evan, think of Gemma. Think of her like you've never thought of her before."

I closed my eyes as Ginevra's voice dispelled the rage clouding my mind.

"There's an inexplicable connection between the two of you. I can sense its power. It's intense, indissoluble, it's something not even death can break." Her voice was growing more and more persuasive, like a spell, drawing me inside it, calming even my breathing. "Follow it, Evan.

Follow that cord that connects you to Gemma. Reach her through that connection. Only you can sense the soul inside her. Somehow it's connected to your own. Look for her inside yourself."

Her voice had softened to a hush that led all the way to Gemma, to the infinite love I felt for her, to the alchemy that united us. *Gemma, where are you?* I shouted in my mind, my voice breaking with desperation, hoping my words would find their way to her. *Where is he hiding you? I can't find you! Gemma. My angel . . . Jamie.*

For a split second, like a lightning bolt piercing the sky, she was there.

"I found her!" I shot to my feet, filled with new hope. The hope that it wasn't too late.

GEMMA

FOUR HOURS EARLIER

32

THE ANGELUS

The light illuminated the room softly, like candlelight. A sweet melody filled the air, and although everything around me was calm and peaceful, my heart was racing wildly.

I looked at my feet, noticing that my body was moving to the rhythm of that sweet sound, swaying in someone's arms. Peter smiled at me as I raised my eyes, holding me tighter as though he wanted to keep me there. I looked around, confused. Why was he here at the prom? What had happened to Evan?

The room was full of people dancing as the band on stage played our song. "I bet you're thinking of him." Peter's voice sounded almost threatening.

"No, no. I . . . Pet, where were you? You disappeared."

To my surprise, a hint of sadness suddenly darkened his face. "I didn't disappear, Gemma. *You're* the one who can't see me. You only have eyes for him and you never notice me. I wish he would disappear!"

His accusation, though true, left me puzzled. "Where is he?" I blurted, unable to escape the anxiety weighing on me.

His expression instantly hardened into a bitter glare. "Him! Him! Him! Enough! I can't take it any more! Is Evan the only person who exists for you?" Despite his tone, it hadn't been a question but another accusation.

I let out a dejected groan. Peter had never lost his temper with me like this before. He seemed blinded by anger. Deep-rooted anger toward Evan. "What's gotten into you, Pet? Stop it, you're scaring me."

"*I'm* scaring you? It's not me you should be scared of, and you know it."

"W-what do you mean?" I stammered, following my instinct to defend Evan at all costs. "Who told you that? What do you know?" I said accusingly, my voice growing firmer.

Peter stopped dancing and grabbed me by the shoulders. "Gemma, listen carefully. There's something *evil* about that guy. You can't trust him," he warned, the look on his face so intense it left me breathless. There was something different in his eyes, as if they weren't really his. "*You can't trust him,*" he repeated slowly, so I'd take in his message.

I stared at him for a minute. His echoing words pierced my protective shell, reawakening fears I thought I'd buried. By now I knew what Evan was hiding from everyone. I knew the mask he was forced to wear, so why did I still feel agitated, as if a voice were continuing to whisper into my ear, hinting that there was even more to know?

Peter's face became more and more blurred. I tried hard to focus on his features, but he slowly disappeared, fading like a ghost as the echo of his voice grew fainter, repeating that I couldn't trust Evan.

He vanished completely, and everything around me seemed to turn gray. The light grew cold and dull, like in a black-and-white picture. I could just barely make out a few details surrounding me.

I looked around, suddenly shocked. There was no one else in the room. I was alone.

A sinister shudder of anxiety gripped my body. Piles of streamers and empty paper cups littered the floor. Even the music had stopped and all I could hear was my own breathing. I couldn't explain what had happened or where all the others had gone.

In the bone-chilling silence, a gust of freezing-cold air suddenly hit me, rushing through my hair. The blood in my veins turned to ice. Not because of the cold air, but because of my absolute certainty that someone *was* there, after all, lurking in the shadows. Terror had come back to torment me.

It had to be him. The Reaper Angel. *He'd found me.*

I looked around desperately. Where was Evan? Why wasn't he there to protect me like he promised he would? The thought of having to face that infernal creature all on my own made me shudder. How could I defend myself? Me, a useless, insignificant mortal, how could I battle an Executioner? How could I keep him from killing me without mercy?

My heart lurched, answering my question: there was no way I could.

It was the end.

I took a deep breath and prepared to face him. "I know you're here!" My trembling voice echoed through the empty room. "Don't hide!" I shouted, forcing myself to steady my voice this time.

Like a bolt of lightning, a dark figure shot across the room from one patch of shadow to another. I started with fright, trying to follow it with my eyes so it wouldn't sneak up on me from behind. Again and again it moved, finally stopping beside the dark wall in front of me.

My breathing stopped. I panted, gasping for air, struggling against the panic that threatened to overwhelm me.

The shadow remained hidden, shrouded in darkness, watching me until my brain finally regained control over my body. My panic subsided and I narrowed my eyes, trying to penetrate the darkness in which the figure was hiding. A whimper escaped my lips. He looked so *human*.

"I know who you are," I hesitantly made myself say.

An unexpectedly alluring voice issued from the gloom. It was low, penetrating. "You think you know all there is to know, but you're wrong."

His voice.

Astonished, I struggled to resist the effect it was having on me, destabilizing me to the point that it kept me from grasping the meaning of his words. It was as if I were momentarily bewitched. A leg appeared, moving slowly out of the shadows. Taken by surprise, I flinched and took a step back to maintain the distance between us, but the second my foot touched the ground, a stabbing pain shot through my heel. I stifled a shriek and looked down. Not far from me, the giant chandelier lay on the ground, destroyed. Thousands of pieces of broken glass covered the ground. The sharp crystal shards threatened my every move.

"Careful, wouldn't want to hurt yourself." His voice rose up, hypnotic and entrancing. I could just make out his grin through the darkness. It told me he was enjoying witnessing my desperation.

Meanwhile, the pain in my foot grew stronger, making me wonder how deep and how serious the wound was. I stole a glance at it and found that a large shard was embedded in my heel. Blood was gushing out and forming a pool on the floor. The blood-spattered prisms sparkled as they reflected my image like a dark omen.

I forced myself to ignore the lacerating pain, forgoing the chance to pull the glass from my flesh, and darted my eyes around, searching for my assassin. I couldn't afford to lose sight of him.

"Does it hurt?" he asked, pleased. It was hard to believe such a cruel monster could be lurking behind such a deep, alluring voice. It was clear from his chuckle that the suffering I was undergoing now would be nothing compared to what I would soon have to endure. Containing a rush of frustration, I struggled to keep silent and hide the grimace of pain on my face.

The monster took another step forward, coming into the light.

While my voice had threatened to abandon me when I'd first heard him speak, now that I saw his face, I was paralyzed. He wasn't a shadow, he was a man, a young and incredibly attractive man. No scythe in his hand, no black hood over his head. His appearance wasn't the way I'd imagined it in my worst nightmares. Just the opposite: this Reaper Angel was *gorgeous*.

He wasn't very tall. His hair was short, but his sideburns narrowed into a thin line that framed his face, joining with a dark goatee. And his gray, gray eyes . . . Eyes of ice. They glimmered, bewitching me, glowing in the dim light. They were strangely familiar . . . No. It couldn't be. Was it possible Death could take on an angelic appearance? For a moment I let myself be mesmerized by his fascinating aura, so terrified and enchanted I forgot why he'd come.

"You look surprised." My body tensed. I had to keep my emotions from showing. "What were you expecting? Did you think I'd be a monster? Is that how they described me?" He smiled, his voice as soft as black velvet.

"I know who you are," I repeated, finally able to speak again. "Evan told me about you." Like an antidote, the sound of my own voice snapped me out of the spell he'd poisoned me with. And when I remembered who I was actually facing, I couldn't hold back a cold shiver.

"You're trembling," he said. His voice became darker, with a sharp edge. "Are you afraid?"

"No," I was quick to reply, aware that my expression was giving me away. It was a lie: I'd never been so terrified in my life. Actually, I was *frozen* with terror, hibernating beneath a slab of ice that kept me even from breathing.

"Hmm." He shook his head, drawing closer. "You'll learn soon enough that you can't lie to me."

I flinched, suddenly afraid he could read my mind.

"I can sense it, you know," he whispered, pacing in slow, ever-diminishing circles around me like a vulture. "Your fear." I squeezed my eyes shut and swallowed, trying not to make a sound. "I don't blame you for that—you should be scared," he whispered directly into my ear. "But I see that's not everything."

He smiled as if something had surprised him. "Well, I wasn't expecting *this*," he added, grinning like a wolf with its jaws locked around its prey. "I don't know if I should be offended or amused. I'm not the only one you're afraid of."

"You're wrong!" I lied again, amazed at how quickly I'd reacted. Deep in my heart, I knew I was the one who was wrong. The little voice in my head that I thought I'd buried had suddenly reappeared, feeding on his words, growing so strong it escaped my control. Peter's voice echoed in my ears: *Evan. You can't trust him. He's dangerous.* I shook my head to drive it away, but every attempt just made it stronger.

With sorrow, I realized it wasn't Peter's voice that was tormenting me. It must have been my conscience, the survival instinct that had always urged me to run away from Evan, the voice my heart had always prevented me from obeying.

I tried with all my might to suppress my suspicions of Evan. He'd been honest with me, revealing his deepest secrets, so why should I still have any doubts about him?

"If that were true," the Angel went on, responding to my suspicion, "where's your hero now? Why doesn't he come save you? Wait—wait. Let me rephrase that." He smiled, a strange, evil gleam in his eyes. "Are you still sure he wants to save you?"

"Stop it!" I shouted. "I'm not afraid of Evan." But my voice inevitably grew faint, belying my words.

"Wrong. I've already told you, you can't lie to me. You need to know that."

"Why would I be afraid of him?" As I voiced the question, I realized I wanted to know the answer myself. "I know who he is. And I know who *you* are," I said accusingly, my voice firm. "Evan told me everything."

"Hmm. Wrong again." Like a mischievous ghost, this Angel of Death was having fun torturing me.

I couldn't figure out why I was growing more and more confused with every word he spoke. My head felt foggy, as if I were slowly losing control of myself. He had bewitched me. His words were slowly poisoning me, hiding behind that mesmerizing voice like an evil spell.

"Are you really sure Evan told you everything?" he insisted, his eyes narrowed in a wicked smile.

I recoiled. What was he insinuating?

"As I imagined," he said, smirking when he noticed the surprise painted on my face. "I'm willing to bet he didn't mention he was sent here to kill you."

His blood-chilling words struck me like a bolt of lightning, piercing my chest, killing something inside me. I wanted to deny it, refute it, refuse to accept what he'd said, but my brain instantly registered it as absolute, unquestionable truth. For some bizarre reason, I felt it really was a fact. Maybe part of me had always suspected it. I couldn't even open my mouth to speak.

"He tried to kill you," he said, mocking my expression, which had been reduced to a blank gaze.

"That's not true," I forced out in a stubborn attempt to contradict him, my voice trembling as I stared into empty space.

"Are you sure? When the semi was about to run you over on your bike, how do you think Evan managed to show up at the right place at the right time? Why do you think he was there, Gemma?"

Like an earthworm, his voice dug its way toward the very last part of me that stubbornly resisted. My heart ached.

"He was there for you, he'd come to take your life."

His words corroded my skin like acid. And yet, on the razor's edge between reason and madness, the thumping of my heart gave courage to that little part of me that was still trying to fight back. "But he didn't," I heard myself say, as if in the voice of another. I felt like I'd lost contact with myself, connected to reason only by a fragile bond that continued to struggle, desperate to survive. I tried to bolster it, but it was no use.

"Not yet, but he will soon. You're kidding yourself, thinking you can live a life that no longer belongs to you. He can't change his nature. What you need to realize, Gemma, is that none of this depends on him. Or on me. Your fate is sealed. There's a time for everything. A time for each of us. Death has sent its Soldiers to claim your soul, and it will continue to do so until it's taken you. Imagine this as a game of chess where we're just pawns being moved by someone else. And you're his target. I'm sorry. Evan simply went through a period of distraction. Of weakness. It happens to all of us sooner or later, but loyalty to what we are is deeply rooted in each of us. I bet he's already had a change of heart and at this very moment, while you and I are here talking, he's deciding how to kill you, Gemma. He wants you dead so he can redeem himself."

"That's impossible," I whimpered, holding back tears. I refused to believe his cruel words, but my awareness that he wasn't lying was increasing exponentially. "What does his redemption have to do with me?" I asked, devastated, fearing the answer.

The Executioner raised his left hand, revealing his forearm. My eyes widened as a grin spread over his face. "Because he's like me! What did you think he was? He's an Angel of Death, Gemma—and he came for you."

A shiver ran down my spine, my eyes glued to the mark of the Children of Eve. I shook my head. No. No. No! It couldn't be true, he was tricking me! And yet, his eyes . . . They were identical to Evan's.

"Death wants you at its side, and we're its reapers. We're shadows of fate. Ferrymen of souls. Accept it."

"Enough!" I shouted through my tears. "Why should I believe you?"

"Oh, you already believe me. I can sense it. Evan's the one who killed the man they found in the woods."

"No!" I screamed, begging him to stop.

"Evan started the fire and took the little girl too. He killed her, Gemma, let her burn to death. Mercilessly. You never wanted to accept it, but a part of you has always known. Unconsciously, you even avoided asking yourself the right questions—because you're mortal, weak, and in love with Evan. Whereas he *betrayed* you, Gemma. He only wants to kill you."

"Stop it! Enough!" I shrieked, covering my ears with my hands so I wouldn't hear anything else. Tears continued to stream from my eyes, which were now puffy, keeping me from seeing where my legs were suddenly carrying me as my mind desperately attempted to deny his words. How did he know exactly what I felt? How had he managed to dig deep inside me, uncovering the things I'd been trying to hide even from myself?

I tried to make it to the door across the room but the Angel blocked my way. "It's hard to accept, I know," he said in a low voice, flashing an entirely false look of sympathy.

"Why don't you just kill me now and get it over with?" I groaned, giving up.

The Angel considered my suggestion before speaking, as though choosing his words carefully. "I have something to confess to you— a *secret*," he whispered, putting his face close to mine. "I was sent in only to kill you, but I don't know if I'm going to follow orders this time, because that would be doing you a favor. Maybe I'll let your Evan be the one to do it while I sit back and enjoy the show. In fact, I should be grateful to you. This little game is amusing me even more than I'd hoped.

"Poor little Gemma, the only person you've ever loved betrays you, deceives you. All this passion of yours, all this suffering . . . they've relit a fuse inside me that went out long ago. They've reawakened the Angelus in me, liberating the pain I'd repressed. Fortunately I can take all of it out on *you*.

"For far too long I carried out orders without experiencing any emotion. Now I feel alive for the first time in many, many years. Once my name was Faustian. Then that part of me died, leaving behind only the demon. Now I'm simply Faust," he said, his lips twisted in a sadistic grin.

"You're a monster!" I shrieked with all the voice I had left.

"A monster?" he hissed, cocking his head, his expression pure evil. "Why's that? You've never been anyone to me. Why should I spare you? Or feel compassion for you? Can't you see who the real monster is?" He studied my face. "Evan lied to you, tricked you, and is ready to turn his back on you. Well? Which one of us is the monster? Him or me? Answer me!" he bellowed. "Who's the monster?"

I was shattered, devastated. I wasn't sure my body could contain so much desperation and frustration. *Faustian*: such a sweet-sounding name for such a cruel creature. Faust was definitely more appropriate.

He scrutinized me. "You must love him a lot if part of you is still fighting for him." His statement left me even more stunned. Could he read my feelings? "But it's weak; I can feel it fading. It's about to surrender."

I hoped with all my being that it wouldn't. Inside of me, I still wanted to believe there was hope—even just a glimmer—that Evan didn't really want to kill me.

I grabbed hold of this dream and clung to it tightly, but it slipped through my fingers. I couldn't get it back. I felt mired, as if my mind didn't belong to me any more. I tried to make myself think clearly, but I just couldn't reason.

"You're stubborn. I wasn't expecting that," he said, still studying me. Suddenly, something caught his attention and he cocked his head, as if listening. His face twisted into a smirk of evil satisfaction.

"I'm curious to see how far your stubbornness will go. Let's see if you still have your doubts after what I'm about to show you," he said, a wicked smile on his lips.

I stared at Faust, puzzled, wondering what he meant, but before I could ask, he answered my question. "You'll see it with your own two eyes."

Could he really prove it to me? But the worry that frightened me the most was: if Faust was right, was I really prepared to face it? Deep down in my heart I knew the answer.

No. I never would be.

33

BETRAYAL

Before I could understand what the Reaper Angel was talking about, our cold, eerie surroundings were replaced by a warm, reassuring light. I looked up, quickly recognizing the unusual hazel- and chocolate-colored walls.

We were in Evan's kitchen. Just then, someone talking caught my attention.

"Oh! It's you," Evan said, his voice agitated. For a second, I thought he was talking about us appearing, but realized I was wrong when Simon responded.

Simon. Drake. Ginevra. They were all there. I studied their faces, bewildered. None of them seemed even to care about our presence. But most importantly, why wasn't anyone alarmed by the sight of the Executioner next to me?

Evan finally seemed to notice me and headed straight toward me. But something was wrong. The look in his eye was strange. Absent, detached. He looked so grim it left me confused—and scared. I found myself panting from the sudden fear that gripped me. A strange sensation stirred in my chest. A hostile, dangerous one.

Was he really about to kill me? Was it really time for me to die? As Evan strode toward me, I decided I wouldn't put up a fight. I didn't care about dying any more if it was Evan who wanted me dead. I didn't care about living any more either, for the same terrible reason.

My heart pounded with his every step as he came toward me quickly, without slowing his pace. There wasn't a hint of hesitation in his face. I filled my lungs with a long, agonized breath, thinking it was my last.

When Evan was inches from me, I shut my eyes, resigned to dying for him. At the same instant, a strange energy suddenly washed over me, taking my breath away. It was like a train coming at me full speed or a cascade of ice-cold water, as violent as a hurricane, as painful as a punch.

For a split second, I had the strangest sensation: I felt drained and filled at the same time. Something wasn't letting me breathe. It was as though a waterfall were pouring down onto me.

When I emerged, I whirled around, gasping for air, unable to believe what had just happened.

Evan was behind me. My body hadn't stopped him. He'd passed through me as if I didn't exist, as if I were . . . a *ghost*. An icy shudder gripped me. I peered down at my body, still trembling, wondering what was happening to me. Doubt entered my mind: was I already dead?

A cruel, familiar snicker tore me out of my delirium.

"Faust, what's going on?" I asked, bewildered. "Why aren't they noticing me? Am I dead?" Had it really been that easy? For a second I almost felt relieved.

But Faust's malicious laughter told me I was wrong, mocking me yet again. "You're not dead," he said, chuckling, "not yet."

I looked down at my body again, more confused than I'd ever been. My hands, my feet—nothing seemed to have changed. Everything was in its place. So what was going on?

"Why can't they see us?" I asked him, exasperated. I walked over to Evan and stared straight at him, but his silver eyes looked right through me. He couldn't see me. I heard his voice as though in the background, the sound too low for me to make out what he was saying. It was as if someone had picked up a remote control and hit the mute button.

"They can't see us because we're not really here," Faust said, answering the question burning in my mind. But for every answer, more doubts and more questions arose. What did he mean? I was there, standing right in front of Evan, but he couldn't see me.

Simon, Drake—neither of them sensed my presence. Only Ginevra looked somehow anxious. She had a wary look on her face and kept nervously scanning the room, but couldn't see us.

"If we're not here, where are we?" I asked, confused.

Faustian smiled. "Try to concentrate, Gemma. What's the last thing you remember?"

At first, I didn't understand what the ridiculous question meant, but there was no point in stubbornly trying to follow his logic. By now, my life had been turned upside down and there was no logic to it any more.

I tried hard to remember, but it was all so confused and distant, as though months or years had gone by since my last memory. It was all so *faded*.

"I was here, with Evan and Ginevra. Then the others arrived."

"Keep going," Faust encouraged me, enjoying this new game. "What else do you remember?"

"I was sleepy, exhausted. It was dark and I was afraid to close my eyes." That terrible sensation was a clear memory. It was vivid in my thoughts and still terrified me. "I was trembling," I admitted. "I was afraid, and then—"

"And then you fell asleep," Faust said, adding the words I wasn't able to find myself. At the mercy of the befuddlement clouding my mind, I still didn't understand. "Come," he ordered me, a trace of kindness in his voice.

I stepped toward him. When I looked into his eyes, searching for answers, he nodded toward the salon, prompting me to look.

The room was shrouded in a ghastly darkness. I couldn't see my hand in front of my face. Only after a moment did my eyes begin to grow accustomed to it. I noticed a movement at an unusual height a bit farther into the room.

Someone was there, hidden in the dark. My eyes narrowed to slits. Suddenly, like a revelation, I remembered that was where the couch was.

Evan, Drake, Simon, and Ginevra were all in the kitchen, so who could it be? Whoever it was, their troubled breathing made it clear they were sleeping, if restlessly.

I moved closer. Just then, the blanket covering the person slid to the floor, revealing a face.

I started. It was me on the couch. *And I was asleep.* Drops of perspiration beaded my forehead as my eyes darted nervously behind my closed lids.

I couldn't believe it was all true. I had no choice but to accept it, but it was *too much.*

"It's me," I whimpered, my voice breaking with emotion.

"It's you," Faust confirmed. "We're inside your mind."

"Am I dreaming, then?"

The Angel nodded, though through the darkness I could barely see it. "Let's say it's more of a nightmare than a sweet dream," he said, snickering.

"I don't need you to tell me that, I already know it's a nightmare. The worst one I've ever had, if it makes you happy!" I shot back bitterly, surprised I could still find a sense of humor.

Faust burst out laughing, apparently reassured by the fact that no one except me could hear him. "Ah . . . it certainly will be soon. Don't forget what we came here to do. I still have to show you something." His words sounded more like a warning than a reminder.

Just then, the others' voices reached us from the kitchen, echoing against the walls of the salon as though someone had pointed the remote at them and turned the volume back up.

Judging from their animated voices, they seemed to be arguing. I walked back toward the kitchen to find out what they were talking about. Evan was speaking. I quickened my pace, impatient to feel comforted by the sound of his voice, but his words froze me in the doorway: "Gemma's fate is sealed. She has to die. Fine. So she'll die. We can't change what's written."

Excruciating pain pierced my heart as my soul slowly died. I didn't know words strong enough or tears bitter enough to express the intensity of the emotion ripping through me: a massive wave that pushed me underwater as I thrashed, unable to breathe. The walls closed in around me, suffocating me. I could never have imagined a death worse than the one I was feeling now deep in my heart. I was anguished, devastated, racked with unbearable torment. I felt I would stay there forever, motionless, frozen in my tracks, paralyzed by the pain. I couldn't accept the truth even though I'd heard it with my own two ears.

It was too painful. Far too painful.

A voice replied to Evan's, though I couldn't tell for sure who it belonged to, deafened as I was by my suffering. "You don't want to kill the Angel any more? You want to kill Gemma instead? I don't get it."

My gaze lingered on Evan's face for a moment. He seemed so determined, so proud of his plan. He wanted to kill me. I couldn't believe it. Faust hadn't lied. Even more terrifying than what Evan was saying was the gleam in his eyes. It was as though they were sparkling.

He wasn't being forced. No, he'd decided to do it, and actually seemed excited about the idea.

If only death would take me then and there, cradling me in its comforting silence. Living and bearing such pain was intolerable. It hurt too much. Thousands of needles lanced my heart, threatening to kill me with every breath.

I wished I could hate him for the pain he was inflicting on me, hate him for deceiving and betraying me. But I couldn't. I loved him. I loved him more than anything in the world, more than myself. But I had to give him up.

Racked with pain, I grasped only snippets of what he was saying: "Gemma will be the one to take the lethal poison. Not the Angel. Gemma has to die. That's inevitable, don't you see? No one can change their destiny. No one can fight it. What's written must come to pass."

It was all so absurd, so impossible.

"Tell them how you would convince her to poison herself." Ginevra's calm voice rose up in the silence.

Her too, I thought, horrified. How could she be so cruel after pretending she and I were friends? Had she been faking it all along? I felt doubly betrayed as I listened to Evan and Ginevra plotting to kill me.

"I'll force her, if it comes to that," Evan stated, clearly resolved.

His every word was a knife thrust mercilessly through my heart. I had heard love couldn't kill you but right then I felt it was on the verge of doing just that. His voice was hard and cold, detached, as if he couldn't wait to get it over with.

I shuddered, thinking of what Faust had said: *Which one of us is the monster?* My instinct hadn't betrayed me, it had been right all along. But no matter how incredible it might seem, no matter how hard I tried, I couldn't see Evan as a monster, even though I'd heard him condemning me to death.

Simon tried hard to make Evan see reason. I would need to thank him for his mercy if I had the chance, though by now I doubted I would. There seemed to be no way out for me. I was done for. One way or another, I had to die. If Evan didn't kill me, Faust would. In any case, my minutes were numbered.

I looked wearily at the couch I was lying on, perfectly still, and stared at my fragile, defenseless body awaiting its demise.

Faust's voice echoed in my head, mocking and cruel: *What are you willing to sacrifice when the only person who can save you is the same one who has to kill you?*

An uncontrollable impulse to rebel rose up inside me. I couldn't, I *didn't want* to give up just because they'd made that decision. Not at that price. I wasn't going to sacrifice my life. I had to resist. I had to fight back. I had to at least try. They would wait until I woke up, so I had a small advantage. Maybe if I got a good head start they wouldn't find me. Was there really a place where I could hide from Evan?

An incredible rush of energy washed over me, giving me the answer. It was my survival instinct pushing me to react. There was no time to waste. Faust had disappeared. His presence probably wasn't necessary any more, given that Evan had changed his mind and decided to kill me. I could still barely stand to think of it. Accepting it would be impossible, but I had to do something.

I had to wake up. I rushed over to my unconscious body, unsure how to awaken it.

A new feeling arose amid the previous ones: *power*. I'd never felt anything like it in my whole life. For the first time I realized I was in a dream and could access powers that the real world couldn't offer me. I tried to focus on how to put an end to the nightmare and escape from the house where they were plotting to kill me. I had to run away, as far away as possible, in the hope that no one would find me.

Suddenly, like a bolt of lightning illuminating my mind, I remembered the times I'd woken up in a cold sweat, breathless, feeling like I'd been drowning, unable to swim back up to the surface. Or when I was falling into empty space and would wake up a second before hitting the ground. I looked around the room, dismayed to discover there wasn't any water nearby. Was the thin trickle of the water wall beside the staircase enough? I couldn't risk it. Dismissing the first solution left me with no choice but the second one. I at least had to try.

My first and most immediate instinct told me to hurl myself through the picture window that was covered by heavy drapes. I was on the ground floor, but the impact just might work to wake me up. After all, I was inside my head; the actual height should be irrelevant. I took a deep breath and got ready to run, certain that neither the drapes nor the glass would be enough to stop me. Just like what had happened with Evan's body, I would pass through the window and find myself outside, unharmed. The feeling of falling would wake me up, I was sure of it. I was already breathless at the thought of the terrible sensation I would experience.

Closing my eyes, I tensed my muscles and rushed toward the window with total confidence. A second before my body touched the cloth, though, my surroundings suddenly changed. In the blink of an eye the drapes disappeared, leaving in their place the dusty glass of an old window, and beyond it, empty space. I wasn't in Evan's house any more. Something in my dream had changed, transporting me to the old house on the lake. I felt a pang of terror as a dark force hurled me outside. The impact was far more violent than I was prepared for.

My brain was instantly obscured by the deafening crash of the window shattering into thousands of pieces, and a second later the void swallowed me up, along with hundreds of shards that rained down in a shower of glass. I tried to scream, but the ground below me raced inexorably closer and I couldn't make a single sound.

I knew it was all in my imagination, no matter how real it might seem, and yet I couldn't repress a wave of panic that left me breathless. The air lashed at my face. But the sharpest ache came from my heart. For a second, I wanted to slam into the ground and put an end to that unbearable pain that pierced my heart like poisoned thorns.

I surrendered to that desire, and my body hit the ground with brutal impact.

I opened my eyes, gasping desperately for air, my body drenched in sweat. A second later, my mind cleared and began to assemble the pieces of the puzzle that had led me there. Had I only dreamed it all or was it really happening? The pang in my heart gave me the answer, crushing any hope that the nightmare hadn't been real.

From the next room came the family's low voices, making my heart bleed. For a moment, I almost wanted to pretend nothing had happened and go back to sleep, abandoning myself to whatever it was fate had in store for me. But my body ignored my heart and reacted, rejecting the idea of giving up my fight for survival.

I had to run away before they noticed I'd woken up.

34

THE ESCAPE

I looked around quickly in a desperate search for a way out. The only doors I knew of were too exposed; I could never go through the front door without their noticing, and the kitchen, naturally, was out of the question. I assessed my alternatives, trying to do it quickly so Ginevra wouldn't have time to pick up on my thoughts.

Stumbling through the darkness, I tripped and bit my lip in self-reproach as I groped along. To my relief, I soon recognized the staircase leading up and climbed it one step at a time, trying not to make any noise.

The terrace was my only hope, the only way out I knew of. Maybe I could find a way to climb down without being noticed and reach the ground floor unharmed, or at least without any major injuries. It would be ridiculous if, while everyone was out to kill me, I accidentally killed myself.

When I opened the French door and saw the soft light of sunset, I found the solution. The branches of the big oak tree sprawled over the terrace, offering me their protection like strong arms ready to hold me. I certainly wouldn't find anything better.

I took a deep breath, convincing myself I could do it. It wouldn't be difficult. Quickening my pace, I grabbed hold of the largest branch, but a flashback paralyzed me. The intense emotion I'd felt when Evan had brushed his lips over my neck in that very spot on the terrace filled me as if it had just happened and he was still there, smiling at me and whispering into my ear. Whenever Evan touched me, whenever his eyes looked into mine, I didn't want to be anywhere else except with him. But it hadn't been anything but vile deceit, and now, with bitterness in my heart, I was forcing myself to run away from him, of all people. The thought that Evan actually wanted to kill me was still so impossible, so surreal.

The only thing I felt right now was the unalloyed instinct to survive. There wasn't a trace of resentment in my heart that he'd decided to give up on us for his own redemption. I only felt betrayed, deceived. It would have been better if Evan had let me die on the day I'd been destined to instead of tricking me and giving me the fleeting hope of a future with him. Fate had led us back to our roles: the doomed mortal and the Angel of Death. Prey and predator. One against the other in a battle in which I felt I'd already lost everything.

No matter how much my heart refused to give up the love that bound me to him, my only choice was to hide and hope he'd never find me. I awkwardly climbed up onto the branch, clinging to the rough bark. It felt like my entire body was pierced by pins and needles that drove in deeper with every step, but the desperate desire to live made me ignore the pain. Or, more probably, the bottomless chasm of pain devouring me from inside made everything else seem bearable.

I reached the ground with only a few scrapes on my legs. My dress was torn here and there, the oak's final attempt to hold me back. The last rays of sunset lit up the path as if offering me their guidance. I smoothed down my crumpled red dress. Less than a day had elapsed since the prom, but it felt like an eternity since I'd danced with Evan as he held me tight. I banished the thought and broke into a run without allowing myself time to look back. Probably because I wasn't sure the lump in my throat would ever go away if I did.

I reached the gate, banging against its impenetrable bars. Had I really imagined I'd find it open? Desperation threatened to overwhelm me. I couldn't climb over it without their noticing me. The stone wall was too high for me to scale.

I had a flash of inspiration. I knew another way out. The gap in the wall. A self-mocking smile came to my lips when I thought back on how much pain I'd felt that afternoon. A trifle compared to the sharp blades slicing into my heart now.

I tried to get my bearings and remember where the spot in the wall was. The garden was huge and I didn't want to risk wasting too much time looking for it. Then I remembered that from the gap I'd seen the back of the house, which meant I was on the opposite side. Without giving myself time to think, I ran as fast as I could in that direction.

The cool air was fragrant with the scent of the flowers that filled the garden. It whipped at my face, keeping my tears from falling.

I was about to give up when the wooden bench I'd seen from the gap in the wall appeared, bathed in the soft light of sunset. But I still must have been far away, because I couldn't see anything that looked like an opening. Had they repaired it? Advancing cautiously so no one would notice me, I moved closer, taking shelter among the large tree trunks, until I saw the hole in the wall. Hope filled my heart again. I was free.

Only then, when I'd regained my courage, did I let myself cast a fleeting glance behind me. I couldn't fathom how Ginevra could possibly not have heard my thoughts in her mind this whole time.

With difficulty, I began to crawl through the narrow gap. Just as I finally emerged on the other side, someone behind me grabbed the hem of my dress. I froze, breathless.

They'd found me.

A lump in my throat, I spun around to see who it was. Evan? Ginevra? Someone else, there to take me back to my fate?

I exhaled when I realized I was alone and my hem had gotten caught on the rough stone. By now the dress was in tatters. I didn't care if it got any worse, so I yanked it free, leaving a strip of fabric dangling from the wall. I didn't have time to do anything about it because I didn't feel safe. I had to get out of there fast.

I put one foot in front of the other and started running, completely oblivious to where my desperation was leading me. They wanted me dead and I wasn't sure I'd be able to stop them.

The streetlights flickered on as I listened to my brisk footfalls on the asphalt. Only the beating of my heart was louder, and in the background, Lana Del Rey's voice filled my head. My breathing grew labored and I looked back for a second without slowing down. Suddenly, the lyrics of *Born To Die* seemed to have been written for me. It was a relief to see that Evan's house had disappeared behind me. The surge of adrenaline in my blood eased.

Only then did the bottomless pit in my stomach come back to torture me. I slowed down, spotting a thick cluster of trees and shrubs in which I could hide. I'd reached the wood that rose up on the shore of Lake Placid. Without hesitating, I started running again and plunged into it, not caring about the dangers that might be lurking there after sunset. Nothing could frighten me more than the idea that I'd lost Evan forever.

I continued to cling to the idea of the two of us together, even though he didn't want me any more. He wanted me to die, he'd stopped fighting for us. *He didn't want me any more.* I couldn't get the thought out of my mind. How could he do something like that to me? Sobs choked me as tears rolled down my grief-stricken face and vanished in the wind.

Evan wanted to poison me. And that's exactly what he was doing. The pain spread, coursing through my veins like an unbearable venom, killing me slowly. Every part of me was in anguish. *Then why couldn't I hate him? How could I still love him so intensely, ignoring the fate he was condemning me to? Why couldn't I be mad at him?*

I tried to stifle the question that my heart continued to scream, burying it deep inside myself because it was too much to bear. *Why hadn't his love for me been strong enough to keep him from wanting to kill me?*

I knew the answer. He was an Angel of Death. I was just a soul with a sealed fate. It seemed he'd finally realized that. It was my fault if I'd foolishly believed I could have a future with him.

There were no magnanimous Angels of Death. I'd read enough books about myths and legends to realize that. I'd naively hoped I could write a new story, our story, but it was just an illusion. I was the victim and Evan my Executioner.

Although I'd managed to hide, how would I be able to bear the idea of living without Evan and depriving myself of the emotions only he could trigger in me? How could I give him up, his lips, after I'd tasted them? The lump in my throat grew so tight I could barely breathe. Pain flooded every part of me.

The sun was setting behind the horizon. The trees overhead filtered the last faint rays of light as I ran as fast as

I could, leaves crunching beneath my feet. I ran toward the darkness, a mysterious darkness that had nothing to do with nightfall, toward a dark, unknown destiny. Who would come to save me now?

35

THE HUNT

The further the sun sank behind the mountains, the eerier and more lugubrious the atmosphere became. It felt like thousands of eyes were hidden in the forest, watching me. But I didn't care. I'd lost the most important thing of all; what could my life be worth now, in comparison?

The silence of the forest steadied my breathing and my mind lost itself in a thousand conjectures. Memories of times spent with Evan crowded my brain unbidden, as if part of me was still making them resurface. I wasn't sure if my mind was just being cruel or attempting to make me see something I hadn't noticed before. I'd met Evan for the first time right here in these woods. Back then I'd had no idea what that encounter would end up meaning to me. I'd had no idea how it would change my life. My heart had been chained in steel shackles, and yet I sensed that hiding myself in those memories took the edge off the pain.

Faust was right. Death wouldn't be so horrid if I had Evan by my side. Instinctively, I raised my fingers to my lips, summoning the memory of the taste of his, and a tear slid down beside them, reminding me how bitter real life was. Evan had saved me from my fate, but he must have regretted it and decided to do Death's bidding after all. He'd rescued me from the semi, from Daryl's aggression, and from the crazed car, which I now knew had been under Faust's control.

I couldn't figure out *when* exactly Evan had given up fighting for us. After all, he'd always been so protective of me. The thought that he wanted to kill me began to seem more and more ridiculous—*too* ridiculous—despite the fact that I'd had substantial proof of his betrayal.

Suddenly my head felt lighter on my shoulders as though a sense of oppression were beginning to ease. I realized only then that an impenetrable layer of fog had been clouding my mind; it was as if a gentle breeze had come to drive it away.

Could anything have driven Evan to regret what he'd done to the point that he actually *wanted* me to die—so intensely I could see it in his eyes? It suddenly seemed absurd, insane, illogical. I stopped, unsure whether the forest was spinning around me or if it was all in my head.

Could Evan actually have given up the struggle for us? I'd heard him with my own ears as he sentenced me to death—but could there be some hidden explanation?

My heart grabbed hold of the possibility with both hands and clung to it tightly so it wouldn't get away. I regretted now how impulsively I'd run off. Could it all have been a fleeting illusion that my mind had come up with just to drive away the pain?

I needed to sort through my thoughts, so I continued to run, refreshed by the breeze. I was torn. My temples throbbed to the rhythm of my heartbeat.

Which one should I listen to: my body, which had helplessly witnessed the pronouncement of my death sentence; or my heart, which kept crying out his name? Could my own senses have tricked me? Or were my feelings for Evan clouding reality?

GEMMMAAAAA!!!

The heartrending scream exploded in my head, stopping me in my tracks.

"Evan," I whispered, devastated by the anguish in his voice.

Not anger or bitterness because I'd escaped, but *desperation*. Only intense, overwhelming desperation. I blinked and a stream of sweet tears streaked my face, washing away all my uncertainty.

He loved me.

Evan had never stopped loving me. What had driven me to doubt him after everything he'd done for me? I couldn't remember any more. My heart had tried to warn me, but something had prevented me from listening to it. A conviction that I now found ridiculous, because it didn't even belong to me. It was as though someone else had instilled it directly in my mind. Now Evan's voice had uprooted it, dissolving the fog that had been clouding my judgment.

Gemma . . .

I jumped, terrified. The silence had given way to a whisper, as bone-chilling as the hiss of a demon. It wasn't Evan's voice. When I recognized it, I was gripped with pure terror.

It was Faust. He was back.

Gemma . . .

The voice tunneled through my terror and burst into my mind, which began to spin again.

Gemma . . .

The whisper seemed to be coming straight from hell, or maybe it was lurking in my head, or even in the trees. Or everywhere.

I waited for my breathing to slow, trying to reach Evan with my mind and push away the mantle of terror that was closing in around me, distancing me from him. The silence had become so ominous that every breath of wind and every rustling leaf made me jump.

Exhausted by sheer terror, I cried out his name in my head in a desperate attempt to make a connection between my thoughts and Ginevra's mind, but I failed, time and time again. It was like I'd been sucked down into a dark pit, so deep it hid me from the world.

I was alone again. With Faust. But this time it wasn't a nightmare, it was real life. To my shock, I suddenly realized he had been the one who'd led me there. He was a puppeteer pulling the strings that controlled me, his marionette, so I would run away from Evan's protection.

Something moved in the trees. Frightened, I whipped my head to the left. A black shadow leapt out, making my blood run cold, and then disappeared into the foliage before the shudder it had caused could make its way down my spine. Even the leaves seemed to be holding their breath.

A massive rush of adrenaline made me break into a run. The trees took on a ghostly appearance as I rushed past them at a speed I wasn't sure I could keep up for much longer. Still, it didn't matter how fast I ran or how far I got. There was nowhere I could hide from the Executioner whom Death had sent to kill me. His ghastly voice pursued me, whispering my name among the trees, reminding me I couldn't escape.

Nevertheless, I had newfound hope. No matter how my knees were trembling, I knew I could hold out until Evan came to save me. Because he *would* come, I was sure of it. I just had to play for time.

Like a wish granted, the trees opened up, revealing the old lake house. In a last grueling effort, I focused on my legs, trying to channel all the energy I had left into their muscles so I could seek refuge inside.

Although I was aware its walls wouldn't prevent the Angel of Death from reaching me, my heart still hoped I could survive long enough to be rescued. Why wasn't Evan there to protect me? How could I dream of surviving that terrible monster with eyes of ice for long? I couldn't understand why I wasn't getting through to Evan or Ginevra. Why couldn't he sense my soul? Why couldn't she hear my thoughts? Was I wrong after all?

I raced through the rusty gate and threw open the front door, slamming it behind me. Inside, I pressed my back against the wall and slid down to the floor, panting, in the silence and the darkness.

I trembled.

36

HIDE AND SEEK

I couldn't tell how long I sat there, still short of breath from the run and my terror. It felt like hours. It was so dark outside I lost the notion of time.

Just when my body had stopped trembling and I thought Faust might have given up the hunt, the unmistakable creak of rusty iron stopped my breath.

Someone was trying to get in. What reason did Faust have to come in through the door when he could hide from me by using the darkness as his accomplice?

My heart in my throat, I slowly got up from the floor, trying not to make a noise, and cautiously peeked through the window. The gate continued to make that unsettling creak, swinging back and forth as if someone was having fun moving it. It was a ghostly movement that had nothing to do with the wind.

And yet no one was there.

Why hadn't Faust taken my life yet? He could have done away with me in the blink of an eye. What sort of morbid amusement did he hope to derive from scaring me to death? Could he be that evil? Was it possible there weren't laws in their world to keep him from acting like this?

Without giving myself a chance to reflect, I opened the door to the cellar stairs. I knew any attempt to cling to life would be useless, but part of me still refused to stop fighting.

I knew every nook and cranny in the lake house, every dusty old passageway. And I knew that somewhere in the wall downstairs was a door to an underground passageway that led outside. I just had to find it. When I was little I had often hid inside it, just for fun, to keep Peter from finding me.

Out of habit, I groped on the wall for the light switch, but the moment my fingers brushed it, it dawned on me that naturally it wouldn't work.

The worn wood groaned beneath my feet, forcing me to move with extreme caution. An intense smell of mildew impregnated the walls, leaving the air acrid and almost unbreathable. I stopped in the doorway for a second, but a sinister groan from outside convinced me to keep moving, testing each dusty stair with my foot before putting my full weight onto it as I climbed down into the darkness of the dank cellar. Just as I reached the bottom stair, the door slammed shut behind me, trapping me in the cellar, which wasn't as I remembered it. Several years had gone by, but I was sure the place had never seemed as daunting, forbidding, and eerie as it did right now, barely illuminated by a ghostly moonbeam that crept through the tiny barred window. As anxiety gripped me, I threw caution to the wind and quickly left the stairway behind me. With each step I ran into cobwebs, sending a shiver over my skin.

I was utterly discouraged; no matter how carefully I searched the dusty old shelves, I couldn't find the door that would free me from that ghastly trap. All at once, with a glimmer of hope, I recognized the tattered canvas that covered the way out, but a sudden noise behind me made me spin around. My body reacted instantly, leaping to the side a scant second before a huge crash raised a cloud of dust that filled the cellar. I covered my mouth with my hands, coughing and gasping for air. As the dust began to settle, the moonlight mocked me by revealing the massive bookcase that had almost crushed me and now lay on its side at my feet like a sleeping giant. My heart leapt to my throat, ready to surrender, while my knees trembled, threatening to buckle under my weight. I began to be convinced it was impossible to run away from Death.

Like the hissing of a poisonous snake, Faust's blood-curdling whisper came back to torment me, joining me on that sinister stage. *Gemma* . . .

I was horrified to see that the fallen bookshelf was completely blocking the passageway. It hadn't crushed me, but it had buried my last hope. Climbing the steps three at a time, I arrived at the stairway door, where I grappled desperately with the knob. Panic washed over me when it wouldn't open. I was trapped. And Faust was there with me, I could sense his presence. He must have tired of the chase.

A lump rose in my throat as I realized I was about to die. I cried out for help, my voice rising uncontrollably as I pounded on the wooden door. But it was pointless. No one would hear me because no one ever came near the old house. This cellar would be my tomb.

Relaxing my grip on the knob, resigned and defeated, I took a step back and stared blankly at it, my tears ready to flow.

Fate had touched me with its icy fingers, wrapped me in its dark wings, its plumes as corrosive as poison on my skin, as heavy as chains, imprisoning me in a body that was no longer my own. It was only a matter of time. There was nowhere to hide, nowhere to run. Like a hungry falcon, its shadow loomed over me watchfully. I felt the weight of its wings upon me. The wings of death.

I blinked. I was so frightened I could have sworn the knob had slowly moved. With a sinister sound, the door began to open, confirming my suspicion. I stared at the knob, paralyzed with fear, bewildered and terrified beyond all measure.

No one stood in the doorway. Faust was playing with me like a cat with a mouse. I wondered what difference it could possibly make to keep fighting him.

Repressing my fear, I walked through the doorway, my heart in my throat. I ran through the parlor, throwing everything I could get my hands on behind me, driven by the panic his blood-chilling voice produced in me. As if anything could prevent an Angel sent by Death from catching me.

Gemma . . . Where are you running? The whisper filled my mind. He was toying with me. *I'll find you wherever you go. You can't hide from me.*

A shiver ran over me. He was right.

You can't run from me forever.

"You're insane!" I screamed into the empty room.

I reached the long, steep staircase that led to the second floor and began to rush up it. In the silence, a loud creak warned me not to trust the worn stairs, but before I could think to slow down, my foot broke through the rotten wood. A sharp, shooting pain made me dizzy.

I tried to pull my foot out, but it was lodged in the splintered wood that had lacerated my flesh. My panic grew greater when I sensed Faust's presence, though I couldn't see him. Casting a terrified glance around, I used both hands to try to yank my leg out as a blast of freezing air hit me. I struggled with all my might, fumbling in terror, until I finally managed to pull it free.

Unbearable pain paralyzed my leg. I slipped off my shoe to check the wound and was astonished. That gash on my heel—it was so familiar. I had the impression I'd already lived through all this.

I slid off my other shoe and dragged myself up the stairs, limping badly, as a deafening silence filled the house. There was no sign of Faust.

When I'd almost reached the landing I turned around, afraid he might be right behind me. I faced forward again as I placed my foot on the top step and my heart almost stopped cold. Faust stood there, staring at me with paralyzing heartlessness. I lurched back in fright, the empty space behind me making my every movement perilous. I peered up at him, trying to understand his intentions. If he made the slightest move I would tumble backwards down the steep staircase. Death would soon follow the fall. My chest rose and fell rapidly and pure terror gripped me, but I silently held his cold gaze as Death observed me with its eyes of ice. Without warning, Faust's expression turned more intense and furious.

Everything happened in a blur. From the corner of my eye I saw his arm flash out toward me. The next thing I knew I was flying through the air backwards. I made myself keep my eyes locked onto his face, darkened with evil, every instant of my fall.

Then, impact.

The pain was excruciating, paralyzing. I instinctively raised a hand to the back of my head and stared at my shaking fingers, smeared with warm blood.

I couldn't understand the reason for his rage. Was it just that he enjoyed seeing me suffer? Wasn't taking my life enough? Why torture me? Was Faust really so sadistic? I couldn't believe that was all it was. There had to be something more driving him to act so brutally.

I tried to get up, but my body, traumatized by the violent fall, refused to cooperate. Awkwardly, I rolled onto my side. When I looked up again, my vision blurred, Faust was standing in front of me. I raised my head with difficulty, dimly glimpsing an evil smile on his lips. Suddenly, he vanished.

I seized the chance to get up, channeling all the energy I could muster into my arms. On my feet again, frightened by how difficult it was to keep from staggering, I leaned against the banister.

My vision faded in and out and a lacerating pain shot all the way up the back of my neck. I couldn't tell if the room was spinning or if I was just imagining it. When I tried to lift my foot a tremor ran up my leg, keeping me from continuing, as my eyes struggled to focus on the wavering image of my lacerated heel. I attempted to rest my other foot on the first step of the staircase but before I knew it, a devastating force hurled me forward. I was shocked to find myself hurtling through the air and crashing down on the second-floor landing.

I gasped for breath, my cheek against the floor, and tried painfully to open my eyes. Was life about to abandon me?

A monster. Faust was a monster. Like an icy echo, his laughter swept over my soul, grim as the voice of death.

Crumpled on the floor, I felt my heart beating. I wasn't dead yet. Dazed and battered, my teeth clenched, I searched inside myself and found the strength to get up.

I hobbled down the hallway, barefoot, trying to ignore the atrocious pain I felt in every inch of my body. I wasn't sure nothing was broken.

Gemma . . .

My body shuddered every time I heard his cruel, infernal whisper. "Why are you doing this to me?" I screamed, my tears overflowing. "Kill me if you have to!"

I could knock your head off with a single blow, if it weren't forbidden, but that way I'd miss out on all the fun. Faust's wickedness echoed through the room in a sinister laugh.

"What kind of a monster are you?"

I'm sorry. His voice suddenly grew serious and resolute, without a trace of pity or remorse. *But it's a debt that must be paid.*

"Why?" I screamed, dragging myself along. "Tell me why!" I tried to stifle my desperation, but an even more blood-chilling silence filled the old house.

Why kill me slowly? Was he trying to shed my very last drop of blood? What was the point of my sacrifice?

Like a pearl, the moon shone through the window at the far end of the hallway. As I passed them, the ceiling lamps broke free and crashed down, barely missing me. Guided by the soft moonlight, almost as if it were a fairy who had come to rescue me, I focused on the window in a desperate attempt to reach it and put an end to all my suffering.

Maybe that's where I was actually supposed to go. Faust must have slowly led me to the very spot where I was fated to die.

Driven by a last flicker of desperate opposition, I banged on the glass, hoping the window would open. It didn't, so I peered through it, looking for anything outside I could cling to to avoid falling, but there was only empty space below. And the window was so high up.

To my horror, I realized the end had come. I thought of my parents, how they would grieve when my body was one day found there in the old house in the woods where they'd never allowed me to go.

"End of the line." For the first time, Faust's voice reached me loud and clear, free from the ghastly echo that had shrouded it before. He was behind me.

I turned slowly, a defeated look on my face, realizing there were just a few steps between us.

"Tell me why!" I screamed, caught between resignation and desperation. "You're about to kill me—you could at least offer me an explanation." This time it was a demand.

"Why didn't you kill me right away? Why all this hatred toward me?" I shouted, my eyes narrowed to slits as I struggled to hold back my tears.

Faust's face turned unexpectedly serious and his expression grew so sad I suspected he was trying hard to drive a memory from his mind. Despite the atrocities I'd undergone at his hands, I was still amazed by how handsome he was. It was almost as if that somehow absolved him in my mind of all the torture he'd put me through. I shook my head to free myself from his mind control as he stared into space and relived aloud in a hoarse, empty voice the memory that was haunting him.

"Nineteen fifty-three. We were in the car, Penny and I . . ."

He paused, lost in a memory that was clearly devastating for him. "It was pouring down rain, the water crashing against the windshield. I couldn't see a thing," he muttered, making me shiver. "Suddenly, I saw something in the middle of the road—an animal, maybe." Anger was in his voice, his eyes still blank as he lost himself in the moment, reliving the scene as though there were still new details to discover. "I swerved, I *tried* to avoid it, but the road was slick." His features hardened, verging on desperation. "The car skidded out of control. Then there was silence." He closed his eyes as I held my breath. "I don't remember the impact. We were out of the car. I couldn't understand what that boy was doing with us. I was sure I'd never seen him before, but he kept calling me by my name. I took my girlfriend's hand, afraid he was going to hurt us, but his face seemed kind. I remember every second of it. He nodded over my shoulder and I looked behind me. I was shocked.

"The car we'd been in had crashed into a tree.

"I tried to keep Penny from seeing the horrific sight as I peered inside the crumpled wreckage. I couldn't take my eyes off the two bodies caught inside it—mangled, unrecognizable."

A shiver ran down my arms. In the midst of my terror, I felt a touch of pity when I heard the disarming sorrow in his voice. Still, I forced myself to remember that I would be paying dearly for his pain. "I'm sorry. What happened to you is absolutely horrible, but what does all this have to do with *me?*"

When he looked up, his bloodshot eyes brimming with rage and torment wiped away any trace of pity inside me, making me shudder with pure terror. His pupils glimmered with a hatred I couldn't fathom. "*He* was there," he said, gritting his teeth. "I tried to convince him, to persuade him not to separate us, but he took her, he took her! He took her away from me!" His snarling voice broke with emotion and I froze, finally understanding. "We were supposed to be together forever, even after death," he whispered, his face devastated by the memory.

"Evan," I murmured weakly.

"*Him*," he confirmed, rage overtaking him again. "For decades I've waited for this moment, fearing it might never come." He glared at me, determined and ready to kill me. "And now the hour of reckoning has arrived."

I'd been wrong all along. This was a personal vendetta. Nothing would stop him.

"At first I didn't know who you were. You were with the Witch and he wasn't around. When he came to protect you and I sensed how much he cared for you, and you for him, I finally found a reason to fight. Don't you see? This is the greatest challenge of my life. I finally have the chance to repay him the favor. I couldn't stop Evan from taking Penny away and now he can't stop me from doing the same to him. Today Evan settles his debt."

"Evan is going to save me." The words escaped my lips, my voice almost pleading.

Faust stared at me with a shrewd smile, shaking his head. "Is that what you think? Are you really still hoping he'll come to your rescue? Why do you think he hasn't done it yet? I'm sorry—the answer might disappoint you—but your Evan isn't coming."

The assurance with which he said it left me breathless, as if he'd destroyed the very last hope I'd been clinging to.

"He's desperately searching for you, you know." Perversion gleamed in his eye as he stared at me, relishing my pain. "But he can't find you—and I'm not going to let him until it's too late."

"You're underestimating the bond between us," I said heatedly.

"Hmm." He paused, pretending to be taking my threat seriously. "I wouldn't get my hopes up if I were you." A demonic smile appeared on his face. "I've done a good job so far, wouldn't you say? You followed my plan to perfection. You fell into my trap, accept it. You're all alone now. Evan will get here too late. And when he does I'll be able to delight in the agony, the rage in his eyes when he realizes he's lost you forever. That *I* made your soul pass on, just like he did to my beloved Penny's. After that, I won't care what happens to me any more."

Despite all the torture I'd undergone, the look on his face at that moment terrified me more than anything else. He didn't even care about his own fate as long as he could take his revenge. Nothing could save me from him.

"I'm happy the difficult part is over. All that's left is the final act in this tragic story. I must confess I was afraid I'd never have my chance, but everything's gone according to plan. Deep down I should have expected this. After all, you're just a mortal. Vulnerable and fragile, like the rest of them, and too easily manipulated. You're moved by emotions, worked up so easily, ignoring all logic. You let yourselves be carried away by feelings, by *passion*, running around like chickens with your heads cut off when all you really need to do is stop a moment and think."

In silence, I took in his every word as the suspicion I'd had in the forest became a certainty.

"But what would you know about that?" he said with a sneer, sounding vaguely accusatory. "He challenged everyone and everything to keep you alive. He was willing to give up his soul, though his punishment would be never-ending, because by choosing not to kill you, he lost the chance to redeem himself. He even stood up to the Màsala, for which he's going to pay dearly, I can assure you. And all because you were more important to him than everything else. I know the feeling, I know it well. You, on the other hand, fell into my trap so easily! You think you love him more than your own life, and yet it took so little to convince you not to trust him."

"You brainwashed me," I gasped, a tremble in my voice. "It was *you* who made me run away from Evan," I whispered, shocked and overcome with guilt. I'd already realized my mind had been poisoned by Faust, I just hadn't understood how, exactly.

He peered at me, smiling. "Did you really not understand? I was toying with you, Gemma, from the very start. When I entered your dream, I still didn't know how I'd be able to convince you to leave their house. You were safe as long as you were there. I couldn't have touched a hair on your head. Can you believe it? But you cooperated with everything so nicely."

His words withered me. What a fool I'd been; I'd fallen for his story hook, line, and sinker.

"I have to admit, at first I didn't think it would be so easy. Then I looked inside you and discovered your most deeply buried fears. They were insignificant trifles hidden in the innermost corners of your unconscious, safe and sound, but I fanned the flames of your fears without your noticing. I fanned them until they were unbearable. You felt betrayed, didn't you? The pain was intolerable. You struggled against it, but you couldn't resist, because I was there blocking your mind, keeping you from reasoning freely." He poured out his confession, smug satisfaction on his face.

A myriad of emotions filled me. I was furious with Faust for using mind control to manipulate me, but part of me was happy to finally know for a fact that my suspicions about Evan were groundless. Why hadn't it dawned on me that Faust might have the same powers Evan did?

He'd read my unconscious, uncovering every secret, reading my soul and detecting each emotion before it surfaced. He'd taken control, prevented me from reasoning, and instilled suspicion in my mind, all so he'd have me in the palm of his hand. My heart, feeling it had lost everything, lashed out at him in a scream of frustration. "You used mind control on me! How dare you?"

"It was necessary," he said mockingly, his voice almost soft and caring. "Besides, soon enough you'll have far more horrible things to blame me for." His mouth twisted into a malicious smile.

I smiled to myself, repressing my rage, because I knew how wrong he was. Having given up hope, I was convinced death would be silent, drab, empty. Black. Where pain doesn't hurt any more. Nothing at all like the red of the bitter emotion that had made my heart ache so when Faust convinced me I'd lost everything. But death couldn't steal everything from me as long as I had Evan's love. The only thing I held against Faust was what he'd tricked me into doing. The rest didn't matter any more.

When Evan told me about his power I hadn't fully understood what it meant. To understand it, I'd had to experience for myself how powerfully your own mind can be torn out of your control, driven by your doubts and insecurities. And yet my heart had tried to warn me. Instead, I'd made a mess of everything. I'd let Faust bend my will. But then again, I really had heard Evan plotting my death. Or was that just another of Faust's lies?

"What about what I heard them say?" I asked, instinctively giving in to the longing to understand.

"Actually I'd already had the opportunity to make you suspicious of him. I just took you there to increase your suspicion even further. I'd intended to trick you into thinking he was betraying you, but then I heard what they were talking about and thought you should hear them too. Everything fell into place quite nicely, don't you think? Not even if I'd whispered the words into Evan's ear could it have gone better! At that point all I had to do was shuffle the cards a little.

"He had a plan. An *excellent* plan," he said, his voice filled with satisfaction. "Actually, your Evan never wanted to kill you at all. I just found a way to make you think he did."

"How is that possible? I heard him say it," I insisted, still confused.

"What you heard was only part of their conversation. The truth is he was trying to save you. He had no intention of harming you. How could he? He loves you more than anything in the world. But I made sure you didn't know that. He loves you with all his heart and at this very moment he's going completely out of his mind because he can't sense your soul." An evil grin spread over Faust's face. He closed his eyes and took a deep breath, concentrating. "I can sense his agony. The Witch is searching for your thoughts too," he whispered, a smug look on his face.

"Why can't they sense me?" I asked, gripped with panic.

Was Evan really trying to track me down? My heart ached at the thought of the anguish and frustration he must be feeling.

Faust smiled again before opening his eyes. "Because I'm blocking them. I've spent the last several decades preparing for this moment. Do you really think it would have been so easy for you to escape from three Subterraneans and a Witch? I concealed your escape and I'm shielding our presence right now, generating a protective barrier no one can penetrate. Not even the Witch can scratch it, despite all her power.

"I still haven't figured out what she's doing with them. You probably don't know this, but Angels and Witches have always been mortal enemies, and she's very powerful. It was hard to keep her at bay, especially when we were so close to her there in the kitchen." He stared into space. "That Witch makes me shudder," he murmured to himself, shivering.

His face lit up again. "But that only helped spice up my plan. In any case, you need to face facts. None of them has managed to locate you. It's just you and me. No one's going to find you in time," he assured me.

The proud expression he wore as he stared at me did nothing but drain me of every emotion except guilt. Evan had found a way to protect me, but I'd ruined everything. Now I would pay the price.

"Well, then!" Faust boomed, shattering the silence, his voice tinged with smug satisfaction. I looked up at him and saw he was studying me carefully. "You're right where I wanted you." He twisted his lips into a malicious grin, his eyes dark and foreboding.

My heart leapt into my throat, sensing the danger in his eyes as I peered through the window at the empty space behind me. I had a flash of déjà vu and my heart lurched. I'd already been here before.

Someone had tried to warn me in my dream, like a premonition.

"No, please . . . Wait!" My voice broke with emotion as desperation gripped my throat, because I'd already seen the shattering glass and knew how this was going to end. I wished I could have held on to a little courage, but the words had come out before I could help it.

Had I really thought I could defy fate? My destiny was already written. Putting it off would only make everything harder. No one could escape death.

Faust's face looked momentarily saddened, as if, despite everything, part of him suffered from my agony. Then, swiftly, he flung out his arm and a devastating force burst out at me as violently as a tornado, hurling me backwards before I had time for a last breath.

I smashed through the window, shoulders first.

As though my senses had sharpened, I felt every inch of the glass as it shattered against my back. The deafening crash swallowed up every other sound, cutting me off from the rest of the world and I found myself drowning in a wild explosion of shards. I imagined the pain Evan would suffer for not having arrived in time to save me.

I tried to breathe, but the glass was dancing in front of my face, threatening to cut my throat. The ice-cold air stung my skin. I gasped and my vision grew blurred. I suddenly felt emptied, as if my body no longer weighed anything. Sound ceased, and everything around me went into slow motion. I wasn't afraid of death any more. Sweet oblivion lulled my senses as I plunged toward the ground. I was so tired of running away.

My only regret was a single name: *Evan*. I couldn't bear to lose him so soon. My mind filled with memories of him as the sharp air stole my breath. I should have felt gratitude for those few moments life had given us, but I couldn't find any trace of that emotion in my body. Mocking destiny had brought us together only to separate us forever.

I closed my eyes, cradled by the wind, and my heart sought refuge in one last thought of him. *Goodbye, Evan*, I whispered in my mind. A tear ran down my cheek.

Gemma, my angel . . . Jamie!

A sweet tingle spread over me. My longing to hear his voice again, even for a second, was so intense that I almost thought I'd heard him whisper my name in my mind.

I opened my eyes again, on the verge of losing consciousness, and they met Faust's. He was staring down at me from above, his lips moving, mouthing something slowly so I could make out the words: *You can't escape fate. Death always wins.*

My body turned over as it plummeted down, and suddenly all I could see was the ground right below me.

It was over.

The impact knocked the breath out of me.

"Not if you have an Angel to protect you."

I blinked, stunned by the sound of Evan's voice. Struggling through the fog that clouded my vision, I managed to focus on his face. He was staring at me with a deep, loving look.

"Are you all right?" he asked tenderly.

My eyes filled with tears. "You're here," I murmured, releasing the anguish I'd been holding in. I wasn't sure if I was all right. My body slowly began to feel again and I discovered I was in his arms.

Evan had caught me a second before I hit the ground. He was holding me tightly, like he never wanted to let me go. He caressed my forehead with tremendous tenderness, brushing the hair back from my face, his gaze never leaving mine. In his eyes I could still see how worried he'd been, but I also saw relief for having shown up just in time.

His expression suddenly changed, growing dark, reminding me that it wasn't over. Evan tensed, his body as hard as stone. He clenched his fists and ground his teeth. His face twisted into a black mask, the look in his eyes thirsting for revenge. The earth beneath his feet trembled from the roar of rage that exploded from his chest. I'd never seen him so furious before. His head shot up, finding Faust's embittered eyes waiting for him. Evan set his jaw and leaned down to gently lay me on the ground, his fiery eyes locked onto Faust's. "Stay here," he ordered, his voice suddenly inexpressive. Before I could reply, Evan was gone, leaving a cloud of dust behind him.

Suddenly everything happened very fast.

I looked up at Faust's face, which now seemed nervous and worried. All at once, a deafening explosion made me cringe and cover my ears as the house's windows all blew out at once, hit by a furious tornado, a black hurricane that screamed for revenge. I covered my head to protect myself from the broken glass that came showering down over my bloodstained hair.

Everything went deathly silent, throwing me into a panic. My heart started pounding again in spite of the stabbing pain that gripped my chest with every breath. I painfully forced myself to my feet, shifting my weight from one leg to the other, my eyes darting nervously from one empty window to the next, looking for a sign of Evan. Despite his order to stay where I was, my heart was up there with him and I couldn't keep my body from following it.

I started toward the door, immediately feeling my leg protesting the decision. The pain in my foot flamed up every time it touched the ground. The contact stung like salt in an open wound.

Overwhelmed with anxiety, I dragged myself to the door and turned the knob over and over again, but it wouldn't budge. In a flash, I understood the immensity of my love for Evan. Only a moment ago, when Faust had hurled me through the window, I'd been resigned to death. But at the thought of losing Evan, every single part of me had instantly rebelled, refusing to give up. I had to reach him at all costs.

By delivering myself to death, Faust would have his revenge and Evan would be safe.

I went over to a boarded-up trapdoor hidden in the ground. I knew the tunnel behind it would lead me directly into the parlor. Dropping to my knees, I pushed away the layer of damp earth that covered it, grabbed hold of the wooden boards, and pried them free. The rusty nails gave way, as did the rotten wood, offering me a way in. I lowered myself into the underground passageway, gritting my teeth against the pain that washed over me again and again, threatening to plunge my mind into darkness. The tunnel grew narrower and pitch black. As the walls closed in around me, I was hit with the powerful stench of rotting flesh, causing waves of nausea I wasn't sure I'd be able to hold down.

Suddenly I was struck by the terrifying sensation that my body was about to abandon me there. I would lose consciousness in that underground tomb where no one would ever find me. The air seemed to be running out.

A clap of thunder brought me back to my senses. No, it hadn't been thunder. I scrambled to reach the end of the passageway as the sound grew louder and louder. Somewhere above me a battle was raging. I instinctively ducked when something banged against the floor above my head. It was like the house was falling to pieces under the blows. I pushed cautiously, again and again, trying to raise the trapdoor that was imprisoning me in the underground tunnel, but failed with every attempt. I could barely breathe. The suspicion that this pit would become my grave started to verge on certainty. I made myself hold back a stream of tears, oppressed by the darkness.

The wooden boards above my head rattled, and a tremor of joy ran from my stomach to my chest. A puff of fresh air caressed my face as the hatch was flung open from above. It must be Evan. Then my heart trembled and stopped.

It was Faust.

He stared at me contemptuously, his lips twisted into an evil grin. An atrocious fear cast me into the blackest panic. If Faust was there waiting for me . . . where was Evan?

"No. It can't be," I whispered, brokenhearted, and sealed my lips tight so my teeth wouldn't chatter. I couldn't believe Faust had defeated Evan. I couldn't accept it. Not when it was my turn to protect him.

"Your dear Evan said to tell you goodbye."

"*No!*" I shrieked.

Suddenly his body was violently flung away, becoming a blur to my eyes. I jumped at the sheer speed with which it had been done. My heart started beating again. Evan was still alive. I was still in time to save him.

Driven by that desire, I forced my body to support me as I pulled myself out through the trapdoor, gritting my teeth. The pain in my foot had irremediably spread to my knee, and my lungs pumped painfully as though my ribs were broken, every breath leaving me in anguish. The fire burning in the back of my head threatened to overwhelm me.

"Gemmaaa!" Two bolts of lightning shot past me, pulling the wall panels behind them in the fury of the battle, moving at such speed that I couldn't make out their bodies.

I flattened myself against the wall, concentrating on their shapes, trying to understand which of the two was winning. After a moment, my eyes managed to make out the punches they threw. They moved in sync in a dark, violent dance, dodging the blows one after the other.

I tried to reach Ginevra with my mind, projecting my thoughts to her as panic consumed me and my tortured body flinched at the violence of each blow.

My heart skipped a beat when Evan grabbed Faust and hurled him against a ceiling beam on the other side of the room. The ceiling collapsed, burying Faust's body beneath a pile of rubble. Evan and I looked each other in the eye for a second, his expression tormented.

"Hide!" he shouted at me, his voice broken with frustration. "Gemma, you have to hide!"

But I no longer had the strength to move my legs. Pain had paralyzed me. A huge crash drew our attention, and a searing pain in my shoulder made me gasp. My fingers quickly closed around the wound and a stream of blood gushed through them as I discovered that, like a fiery arrow shot by an able archer, a large, spike-shaped fragment of wood had torn through my flesh and lodged deep inside my shoulder. I crumpled to my knees, gasping.

Hundreds of these spikes had burst through the air, filling the room with a huge cloud of dust and debris. There was no sign of Faust.

My senses slowed by the pain, I was distraught to see the two Angels fighting again, whirling like ghosts in a battle whose prize was my life.

I couldn't bear the idea that Evan might die in order to save me. My heart belonged to him now and it would die along with his. Besides, Death wouldn't be satisfied with only his life; it would continue to send out its demons to hunt me down, making his sacrifice pointless. There was only one outcome that could quench its dark thirst: my surrender.

The floor shuddered every time their bodies collided.

"Enough!!! Stop it!!!"

The scream came directly from my heart, which trembled an instant later when I realized it had distracted Evan for a split second, long enough for Faust to grab him. My desperation verged on madness.

"No! Let him go, please!"

But Faust's evil heart thrived on my anguish, and he hurled Evan brutally onto the old grand piano, which collapsed beneath his weight. Unharmed, Evan shot back to his feet and the battle resumed, raging nonstop.

Their bodies emanated an energy that pushed everything out of their paths. It was as though the power of the earth was supporting them, as if the elements had come together to help them, a single invisible ally.

From time to time, through all the noise, I heard Evan cursing at Faust. As if the furious roar that rose from his chest increased his power, Evan struck him with brutal force, flinging him to the top of the stairs. I held my breath as Evan rushed over to me, looking anxious.

"Are you okay?" His eyes lingered with concern on the wound in my shoulder, which seemed to be the most gruesome of all my injuries. The wooden spike was still sticking out of my flesh like a stake driven into a vampire's heart. "I have to get you out of here." Without taking even a moment to think, he picked me up and shot forward, but Faust materialized in front of us, blocking our way, and hurled us each to opposite sides of the parlor.

"Gemmaaaa!" Evan's desperate cry filled the room.

I looked up and was shocked to discover Faust behind me, glaring at me with a fierce, twisted grin. "It's true what they say, you know," he said as Evan's enraged glare locked onto him from the other side of the room. "Revenge is a dish best served cold."

Evan turned to look into my terror-filled eyes, clearly not understanding what Faust meant. "I presume you don't even remember me." Faust smiled, seeing the lost look on Evan's face.

Evan weighed his words before answering. "Should I?"

Faust hid the bitterness in his smile by lowering his eyes as he shook his head slowly. "You see, Evan, fate plays nasty tricks on us at times. Because you took my beloved from me, and now at last I have the chance to repay you the favor. The irony of fate: the tables have been turned."

Evan's expression wavered as he realized what was going on. "Faustian!" he suddenly remembered. "There was nothing I could do for her. You know that!"

Faust's chest shook in a silent chuckle. "Then why should it be any different for me?" he asked, his voice edged with sarcasm.

Before I could even tremble, a ferocious roar burst from Evan's chest. "Because I'm not letting you near her!" he snarled, baring his teeth.

But Faust was too close to my battered, defenseless body. He pointed his hand at my head as though he wanted to suck the life out of me from that very spot. I squeezed my eyes shut to avoid his merciless gaze that left me breathless with terror.

"DON'T TOUUUCH HEEER!" A bellow of sheer ferocity swept the room as Evan charged at Faust. At that very instant, Ginevra, Simon, and Drake appeared on the opposite side of the parlor and rushed to my side.

"You okay?" Simon asked, helping me up and looking at me with concern.

"Doesn't look like it." Drake examined my wounds, a horrified expression on his face—although I wasn't completely sure there wasn't a hint of sarcasm in his voice.

"Evan! The dagger!" Ginevra shouted as the two Angels struggled on the floor. I turned around as Evan whipped a knife out of his belt. Suddenly I felt a strange tingle under my skin. Some mysterious impulse made my eyes lock onto the blade. I stared at it, perplexed, as a powerful aroma filled my nostrils, making my head spin.

Evan pinned Faust to the floor and tried numerous times to stab him, but his adversary parried every thrust. Struck by a dark force, the knife flew out of his hand, landing far from them.

"No!" Evan shouted, stopping his brothers, who were rushing to help him. "It's either me or him," he said, his voice reduced to an angry hiss.

He turned toward the dagger. Obeying the Angel's command, it slid back across the floor with a blood-curdling screech. Evan gripped it firmly, skillfully flipped the weapon over in his fingers and plunged it into Faust's chest. The other Angel let out a groan of astonishment and Evan's eyes wavered an instant, suddenly veiled with bitterness. From his remorseful expression, it was clear he'd never killed another Angel before. They held each other's gaze as their silent conversation filled my head.

You killed me. But you're a Subterranean. I didn't think you'd go so far. I just wanted her . . . Meanwhile, the veins on Faust's face began to swell like serpents slithering beneath his skin. *What will become of your Redemption?*

I don't care.

Why not? Faust asked, his voice frail and hoarse.

Evan stared at him intensely before answering: *Because I love her more than anything.*

Then don't let anyone take her from you. The pain is eternal. Faust gasped a last breath before vanishing into thin air.

My eyes lingered, hypnotized, on Evan's tormented face as he stared at the empty floor where Faust had been a second ago, and a sudden burst of heat washed over me. My nostrils filled with a bitter, intense smell—the same one that had risen up and reached my mouth, filling it with the taste of metal. I looked down at my dress. Scarlet splatters drenched the fabric. The floor beneath me bowed, threatening to collapse under my weight. Something hot trickled down my neck and as it dripped onto the floor I watched it with a blank stare.

Blood.

Nausea pervaded me. I reached up and felt the back of my skull, discovering that warmth was once again flowing from the deep wound, spreading languidly through my hair, already matted with congealing blood.

I tried to breathe, but something was obstructing my lungs. I sought the others' eyes, but no one seemed to notice me, not even Ginevra. It was as though time had stopped. Evan was frozen to the spot, bent over the empty floor.

Pins and needles crept up my legs and spread upward through my body. My energy drained away as my knees shook. My heartbeat thumped in my ears, drowning out all else, as if I were hidden away in some parallel world. I heard it falter, pulsing slower and slower.

Boom-boom.

Boom—boom.

Boom————boom.

A cold shiver enveloped my body. *Boom.* One last thump sounded in my chest. Then, silence.

When the pins and needles reached my head, darkness shrouded my eyes. I parted my lips, bothered by the taste of metal, and felt blood trickle out of the corner of my mouth and down my chin.

I glimpsed the blurry floor drawing inexorably closer and felt one last, heavy breath escape me.

"EVAN!!!"

Ginevra's desperate scream reached me on the floor, the last thing I heard before life left me.

37

OBLIVION

I found myself suspended in a dark, impenetrable void, as black as night. I sensed presences but couldn't reach them, as though the darkness had arms that could push me down. It felt like I'd always been wandering in that oblivion, with no thought, completely adrift, swept up in a cloud of peace. I was *certain* I didn't belong to the world any more. The pain had subsided. I felt light, in harmony with everything, filled with a strong sense of wellbeing. Yet the darkness was pulling me further and further down as I surrendered to the silence, sinking into an abyss from which I couldn't resurface, a well without light.

So this was the end.

I looked for a glimmer of light to guide me, but everything was shrouded in darkness and silence. All at once, the buzzing of a thousand insects penetrated that barrier, trying to reach me. I withdrew, wanting to avoid them, but the sound turned into a more comforting hum. I tried to reach out for it, to cling to the familiar sensation it produced in me, to move closer to the sound, but I couldn't emerge from the darkness that had me trapped in its mantle and refused to let me go.

The hum grew stronger and stronger.

Voices.

I tried to recognize them, but my effort made them grow muffled. So I waited, allowing them to guide me through the oblivion in which I wandered.

"She's lost a lot of blood."

Whoever had spoken had tried hard to hide their concern behind a veil of confidence, but somehow I noticed it.

"Think it's too late?"

The concerned voice was definitely Ginevra's.

"Her heart's stopped!" the first voice exclaimed, edged with an anxiety that this time came through.

"I can't find her! Fuck!"

Evan.

I would have recognized his voice even if I'd been buried at the bottom of a frozen ocean. Why had it broken with such frustration? I couldn't bear it. His desperation filled me with the longing to break the icy barrier separating us. It was like he'd cast me a line so I could emerge from the darkness. And finally I was drawn back in by the light.

I found myself at the foot of what remained of the piano. Evan and the others were a bit farther away, their backs to me. I stared at them, puzzled because they were being so indifferent and acting so strangely. I couldn't understand why they were all huddled over the floor.

"This is my fault! Goddamn it!" Evan's voice held a desperation I'd never heard before. He cursed angrily, as if consumed by deep, unbearable pain.

Why was he still suffering like this? Couldn't he see I was safe now?

"Evan . . ." From my lips, the thread of my voice followed his dismay until it reached him. As though I'd screamed it, Evan, Simon, Drake, and Ginevra all turned around at the same time and looked at me. The weight of the world came crashing down on me as their movement revealed what their hunched figures had been blocking from my view.

My body. It was lying on the floor in a scarlet pool, lifeless. The spark of life had abandoned it, rendering it useless. The sight catapulted me into a cold, inaccessible world of shock.

"Gemma—"

Evan's cautious voice tried to penetrate the apathetic state that had petrified me as I stared blankly at the empty, lifeless body. A useless shell that no longer moved. Not a breath. Not a heartbeat.

Death had settled the score.

"Gemma."

I looked up at Evan. His expression confused me. His eyes said he was *relieved* to see me. I studied the others' faces one by one; they all gave me the same impression. It was like my presence had suddenly cheered them up. Didn't they realize I was dead?

Evan tried to come closer, but the look of shock on my face convinced him to do so very cautiously. "Everything's fine, Gemma," he whispered, his eyes locked onto mine, as if he was trying to keep me from looking elsewhere.

I tried to inhale and my eyes wavered when I discovered it wasn't my state of shock that had taken my breath away. My new body couldn't breathe, it didn't need to any more.

"Everything's fine. We feared the worst," he said, taking another step closer, his voice broken by the echo of the agony that had afflicted him. "But you're here now," he said, visibly relieved.

"But I'm . . . *dead*," I whispered, petrified.

"We're still in time," he said in a vain attempt to reassure me.

"In time," I murmured to myself, staring into space.

"I'll bring you back. Come with me. Take my hand," he whispered, still advancing cautiously. He extended his arm. "The others are already healing your body." Evan moved forward, trying to prevent me from looking over his shoulder where his brothers were leaning over the tortured body that lay on the floor, deprived of its essence. The body that until a moment ago had been my own. "There's no need for you to see it," he said considerately.

Ignoring his advice, I stared at Simon and Drake who were kneeling with their palms turned toward my ravaged body as Ginevra paced back and forth, looking nervous.

I reached out to Evan, but a little voice rose up from the bottom of my heart, telling me what I had to do. The time had come for me to save him.

"No. Wait." My hand froze halfway to Evan, before he could take it. I stared at it for a second and then, finding the words, I looked up into his eyes. "You're an Angel of Death."

Evan's eyes darted back and forth in surprise as I studied his reaction. As though he couldn't bear its weight, he hung his head to avoid my gaze. So Faust had been telling the truth.

"I didn't want to lie to you," he said, his voice breaking. "I—I didn't want to scare you," he admitted, his tone trapped in a cage of bitterness. "I couldn't stand the thought that you might be afraid of me."

I wavered, overwhelmed, but forced myself to go on, staring him steadily in the eye so he couldn't avoid my gaze again. "Did you want to kill me?" I asked, my voice breaking from the terror of hearing what Evan might say.

"Gemma . . ." His gaze burned into mine with an intensity I'd never seen before. "I can't change what I am or what I do. Yet I've done it. For you. I never, ever wanted to kill you, not for a second, but I had to. Those were my orders. I'm Death. And I came for you. I can't hide any more," he confessed, racked with desperation, as though afraid of my reaction to his secret.

"But you didn't do it." My heart had sent the whisper to my lips to let the truth sink in for both of us. Evan stared at the floor, shaking his head.

"You should have told me! I would have understood. It doesn't matter to me what you are." I made sure he was looking me in the eye as I said it.

"If there's anything I'm more afraid of than your indifference, it's that you might be scared of me."

"I'm not scared of you," I said firmly, "but I don't want you to pay this dearly for my life. Faust told me you were risking everything for me. You won't be able to save yourself any more because of me. You won't be able to redeem yourself, will you?"

His silence confirmed my deduction.

"Evan," I insisted, trying to make him see reason, "you'll be damned forever."

"Don't say that! Don't even think it!" he said, pulling me closer. "It's not *your* fault. *I* was the one who decided. I'd only be damned if I didn't have you with me any more." His forehead brushed my own, his fiery silver eyes on mine. "I'm not even sure it's possible. No one can even prove there really is a Redemption."

"I don't want to ruin your chances," I insisted.

Redemption was the only purpose of his existence and nothing in the world would make me want to stand in his way. The time had come for *me* to save *him*, to protect him from a mistake that in all likelihood he would end up regretting. My life wasn't worth so much; when would he finally realize that?

As if he'd heard my thought, Evan cupped my cheeks in his hands. A new sensation gripped me as I felt the warmth of his skin light up my face in a flame of pleasure, as if— the physical body no longer in our way—the energy that connected us could spread more intensely, bursting with every contact. I half closed my eyes, letting the warmth fill me.

"Gemma." Evan sank his fingers into my hair, overwhelming me with an intensity I'd never felt before as a wave of ecstasy spread from him to me and back to him, the flow of energy that had always united us now almost tangible in this ethereal form. "It's too late. My world would be meaningless without you. I'd be nothing but a lost soul. *You're* my Redemption. Nothing else matters. Nothing would matter any more if I lost you now," he whispered, resting his forehead against mine again. I was lost, at the mercy of his touch.

"Evan, no." Broken-hearted, gulping down the lump in my throat, I forced myself to try to persuade him. I wanted to cry, but I'd run out of tears. "Take me to the other side, please. You, you'll lose everything because of me. I don't want that to happen. I can't let you do it."

Evan stroked my cheek with his thumb, as if he could see the invisible track of the tears I wished I could shed. Our gazes locked for a long, long moment. "You're my world, Gemma. The only way I can lose everything is if I lose you. I'd rather be damned forever than live an eternity without you," he whispered, slowly moving his cheek closer to mine without touching it, until his lips were brushing my ear. He spoke in a low voice. "Stay with me, Gemma, please. I *need* you."

Half closing my eyes at the infinite sweetness of his whisper, I moved my head back an inch, astonished by the new sensations running through me. I opened my mouth to speak, but at the sight of his tortured gaze I closed it and nodded. He'd changed my mind.

Evan smiled at me with new hope and squeezed my hand in his, leading me to my body, over which Simon and Drake were still leaning.

"We're ready," Simon told him confidently. "It's up to you now."

Evan nodded and let go of my hand to join them. As he knelt down, he looked up at me and smiled. "They did a good job." His gaze softened as he invited me to look at their handiwork.

I peeked over their shoulders with the feeling in my chest that if I'd still had a heart, its beating would have deafened me. My body lay on the ground, intact and unharmed, as if it had never been lifeless. Simon and Drake really had done a fine job healing it.

Without taking his eyes from mine, Evan leaned over the still-empty shell, his hand poised over my heart. For a moment his gray eyes searched mine before closing and surrendering to perfect concentration.

An electric current bore me away. A single heartbeat jolted me. I opened my eyes as a wave of heat pervaded me and found myself lying on the cold, damp floor.

Once again in my body.

EPILOGUE

"It's nice to breathe again." I smiled at Evan as I walked slowly toward him. He'd been waiting for me to join him at the lakeshore and greeted me with a radiant smile.

"To me it's no big deal, just an acquired habit."

I shuddered as I recalled the feeling of stasis I'd experienced. It was a very big deal to me. "Thanks. For the clothes and . . . everything else."

"Thank Ginevra for that." He smiled.

"Honestly, I feel brand new!" I said, enjoying the sensation of freshness that filled me. I felt strangely cleansed, and my prom dress was clean and as good as new. Ginevra must have taken care of that for me before I woke up.

"Oh, I don't think *that's* because of your dress," he said, amused. "After all, it's not every day someone undergoes an experience like yours."

"Yeah," is all I said, biting my lip, still too shaken by what I'd gone through to see the humor in it like he did.

I stepped past Evan to the water's edge, letting my thoughts ripple on its surface. The sun would rise soon. The first rays were already turning the dark horizon to a purplish glow that merged with the mirror of water. Despite the faint light, a pinpoint of brightness had escaped the night and continued to shine: my star. I smiled at the memory that flashed through my mind.

My eyes had never seen anything more radiant and full of hope than that morning. I'd known that place my whole life, but it felt like I was seeing it for the first time.

It was a new day. A new dawn. A new life, together with Evan.

I closed my eyes and breathed in the cool air still heavy with dew, hoping the memory would remain engraved in my mind.

I'd felt the caress of fate. Death had sought me out. I hadn't escaped it, but I'd been given a second chance and I wasn't going to waste a single minute of the new life I had ahead of me. I smiled, my heart suffused with warmth, thinking that Evan would live it by my side.

My eyes still closed, I felt his body touch mine, his hot breath on my neck. He slowly wrapped his arms around me in a firm yet gentle embrace, as if to confirm my thoughts and tell me he would be there for me, that he was there now and would never leave me again.

He sensually swept my hair back, baring my neck, and slowly, delicately, brushed his cheek against it, sending a tingle through me. His chest moved slowly against my back, letting me feel his every breath.

"Evan . . ." An instinct I knew I couldn't control made me ask the question that haunted me. I stared at the rippling water dancing to the melody of the breeze. "Why didn't you let me die the first time?" I was distracted by the warmth of his body against mine. It left me dazed. "I mean, you barely knew me."

His chest rose as he took a deep breath, weighing his words. "I can't lie to you. I spent a long time fighting what I felt. Carrying out orders was all I'd ever known. I'm an Angel of Death, even though I know that scares you. It's true, I should have killed you, but I just couldn't. I couldn't bear the thought of never seeing you again. I'd been watching you, spending time with you, although you didn't know it. All those moments gave me the chance to understand what was changing me. What I felt for you, Gemma. And for no one else. Your gestures, your eyes that could see me, against all logic, the way it made me feel when I touched you and you were so shy you pulled away, the sensations that touching you gave me . . . I realized I couldn't live without them any more." Evan rested his chin on my shoulder, pulling me closer. "No, Gemma. I could never have killed you and given up your smile or that funny face you make when you're trying hard to seem angry and you wrinkle your nose and you don't realize that all it does is make you look adorable." He stroked my shoulder. "Or the way you twirl your hair around your finger when you're nervous and walk with your head down, caught up in thoughts that carry you so far away no one could ever reach you." His lips brushed my earlobe, making my heart tremble. "Watching you sleep drives me out of my mind," he whispered. "What do I care about heaven when I can have an even purer angel?"

My eyes filled with unexpected tears. I was an angel with broken wings whom he'd taught to fly.

"I couldn't let it happen," he went on. "It was like feeling the wind for the first time, seeing colors like I'd never seen them before. I felt *alive*. It would have meant killing a part of me. Before I met you, I thought I had everything, but then I realized I had nothing. I'd never felt the need to be close to anyone. Just the opposite, in fact, I was so sure I'd be alone for all eternity. The thought never even fazed me. Not until I met you and was on the verge of losing you. I'd always been a Soldier, but you took me prisoner. I knew I couldn't lose you and give up my heart that I'd just found again. The heart that you stole. If you had died, it would have disappeared along with you. You're my mate, Gemma. My Eve," he whispered tenderly into my ear.

"Your Eve? You mean I'm your temptation?" I said in a low voice, teasing, as his hands slowly slid down my arms, making me tremble.

"I mean that when I look at you, I see my other half."

I closed my eyes as he laced his fingers with mine. I knew exactly what he meant. I felt the very same way. We completed each other. We were like two parts of a mechanism designed to fit together.

His chin was resting on my shoulder. I slowly turned toward him and looked him in the eye. From so close up, his scent was intoxicating. "Evan." He looked at me so intently that for a moment I paused. "Wouldn't it have been easier for us if I'd just died right from the start?" I made myself ask.

"Not at all. Nothing would be left of us but a memory, and there's no way I could have lived with that. I knew I'd be tormented by regret forever if I lost you."

"Does it have to do with your lineage? I mean, the reason you would have lost me." I vaguely recalled what Evan had said on the terrace, but I hadn't completely understood.

Evan nodded, looking down, and prepared to explain. "Dying is always a shock." I flinched. His words triggered the vivid memory in my mind. "It's always traumatic to see your own lifeless body. Our mission isn't over once we've put an end to someone's life. We have to make sure the soul accepts the loss. Reassure it, so it will let us accompany it beyond this world. Each of us has powers to help us carry out the assignment smoothly. Some are needed to bring people to their deaths, others to guide them to eternal life, showing the souls how to pass on. Plus, in our ethereal form, we can perceive every sensation, so we can read someone's soul without the body getting in the way—a little like in dreams, but more intensely." An almost imperceptible sorrow shadowed Evan's face. "But then, once our duty is done, we're not allowed to see any of them again. That's our punishment. For a Subterranean it's inconceivable that anything could be more important than our mission, and that was true for me too. You changed me, Gemma, and I'm not willing to go back to what I was before. If you die, I'll die too. I'll die inside. That's why I didn't kill you the first time. Even then I couldn't stand the thought of losing you."

"You're not allowed into Eden? Is that what you're trying to tell me?" I struggled to put the puzzle together, but it felt like a piece was still missing.

"I can go in, but to my eyes it's deserted. It's heaven—don't get me wrong—but it's still deserted. I can't see anyone and no one can see me."

I stared at the ripples on the windswept lake, filled with a deep feeling of guilt for depriving him of that hope.

"I tried to explain it to you, remember? That's why we're called Subterraneans. God banished us, exiled us. It's like a layer of ether is hiding us from the others, making us invisible. We can interact with mortals, though." He forced a smile.

"I shouldn't have let it happen," I whispered, torn by remorse for the hint of regret I glimpsed in his eyes despite his efforts to hide it.

"It's with you that I want to be, Gemma," he said, his voice as determined as the look on his face as he stared at me. "Even if I have to go to hell to do it."

His conviction overwhelmed me. It was so comforting to have him at my side, to feel the warmth of his body so close to mine. I breathed deeply and Evan's hands squeezed mine even tighter.

"Any other questions?" he asked, finding a smile again. It was irresistible, the way his smile sweetened his face.

"Just a hundred or so," I shot back, looking at him out of the corner of my eye. "Actually, there's something I still don't understand."

"Ask away."

"When you were in the kitchen, you said I would have to take the poison. I heard you say it. What was your plan, exactly?" I teased, a touch of reproach in my voice. It made him laugh.

"I thought that if I killed you, Death would be satisfied and stop hunting you down. At that point I'd bring you back to life. It was a desperate plan, risky, but the only one that came to mind. I really couldn't be sure it would solve things, but I had to give it a shot, even if it didn't turn out the way I'd planned."

"In any case, everything worked out like you'd hoped."

"Not exactly. I gladly would have avoided killing another Subterranean, but I was forced to. He thought all I would do was fight him, trying to prevent your death. Luckily we had the poison."

"The poison? Didn't you need to use that on me?"

"An ordinary dagger alone wouldn't have been enough to get rid of Faustian, so we tipped it with a special, extremely powerful venom," he explained, following my gaze as I sat down on the shore. "That's the only weapon that can kill one of us."

I shivered at the thought of the bone-chilling sensation I'd felt when the glimmer of the blade had hit my eyes. I'd felt like I'd fallen prey to an evil spell, as though some unexpected force had reawakened from the earth and lunged at me.

"Do you think it's possible I smelled it?" I asked hesitantly.

Evan started with surprise and turned to stare at me, an amused look on his face. "Allow me to remind you what state you were in! No, I don't think what you're saying is possible. Ginevra's poison is odorless. Otherwise I would have been the first one to smell it. Our senses are sharper." He let out the laugh he'd been holding back. "You lost a lot of blood—your brain must have been oxygen deprived," he said, making me shiver again. In fact, I found myself shivering at regular intervals. I hoped my brain would soon let me forget the whole thing.

"Did I hear you right? Did you say it was Ginevra's poison? Are you telling me Ginevra's *venomous*?" I asked, gripped with anxiety.

Evan threw his head back and burst out laughing. I'd clearly misunderstood. "Well, you're not all wrong. I'm not sure she isn't. Anyway, the poison we used came from her serpent."

"Her serpent?" I cringed with fright. I'd never liked snakes, ever since the time one had scared the horse Peter was riding. It had reared and thrown him from the saddle.

"Every Witch has one. Together they form a single being, like body and soul."

"And they use the venom against Angels because they consider you their enemies, right?" I asked.

I'd seen for myself how powerful the Subterraneans were and I found it incredible that a tiny animal could be capable of defeating such powerful creatures.

"Hey, you know a lot more than I thought."

"It was Faust. He explained that you were enemies."

"You mean he found time to strike up a conversation while he was torturing you?" His eyes wavered, filling with hatred. I could see him driving away the thought and focusing on my question. "Witches are the highest, most powerful incarnation of evil in existence. Since Creation, leading souls into perdition has been their sole interest, and we're always getting in their way. They did it to Eve, hoping to initiate her into evil, but God spared her; instead of sending her to hell for her transgression, He condemned her to earth and granted her and her mate a second chance. It was a Witch who sent a serpent to tempt Eve. God cursed the evildoing creatures forevermore, decreeing 'On your belly you will go and dust will you eat.'"

"What does that have to do with Subterraneans, exactly?"

"When they discovered that Eve's banished children had been condemned to taking souls back to heaven, the Witches began to slay them to prevent them from doing it. They're very powerful, but we completely outnumber them. Only one Witch is born every five hundred years, and each one is considered invaluable to her Sisters. We, on the other hand, number in the millions. Still, if they declared war on us, no one would be able to stop them. For now, they're having fun slowly corroding the world."

"So they tempt people and lead them into evil?"

Evan's expression darkened slightly. "They *are* evil."

He said it so solemnly it made me shudder. "What about Ginevra?" I made myself bring up this concern, although I wasn't entirely sure I wanted to face the subject. "She doesn't seem wicked."

"That's because she's learned to control that part of herself. Ginevra isn't one of them any more. She's still a Witch, naturally, but she lives with us now. And that makes her one of us."

"Faust mentioned something about rules," I said, hoping he could tell me about that aspect of his life.

"He couldn't use his powers directly on you. Ultimately it needed to seem like a natural death or an accident, a heart attack, an act of aggression—anything, as long as it didn't raise suspicion. But I think it's my turn to ask questions now, don't you?" Evan's expression grew hard. "What was it Faust told you that managed to lure you away from me?"

I avoided his gaze, gripped with guilt. "I struggled against his mind control," I said, feeling miserable. "Part of me resisted up to the end, refusing to believe what he told me, what he accused you of. But then he took me into your kitchen and I heard what you were all saying. I only heard snippets of your conversation, though, so I had no idea you planned to bring me back to life after giving me the poison."

"So that was why you ran away!" Evan gasped, lost in some memory I wasn't aware of. I could see how devastated he'd been when he found out I'd run away.

"Forgive me, Evan. It was all my fault. I ruined everything. Faust made me believe you wanted to kill me. I don't know how he did it, but I really thought it was true. I wasn't myself, you have to believe me!" I begged him. "When I regained control of my mind, I instantly realized I'd been crazy to doubt you, but by then it was too late."

"Don't worry. I know well the power that took you over. Faust was controlling you, brainwashing you. It's not your fault," he reassured me.

I shuddered, realizing what he'd chosen not to say: Evan had that same terrifying power. I'd discovered firsthand that nothing is more frightening than helplessly losing control of your own mind.

"I'm sorry I didn't keep it from happening." His eyes filled with bitterness, his mind clearly moving backwards, trapped in the memory. "Just the thought of not being able to find you," he said in a hushed voice. "It was unbearable. I felt empty and useless. It was a horrifying sensation. I knew you were in danger and with every passing second I felt like I was dying because I couldn't do anything to help you. I was desperate, afraid each minute might be your last, and the very thought that I wouldn't be there beside you to bring you back made me shudder," he confessed in frustration.

"Then what happened? How did you find me?" I asked, still unclear on that detail.

"I was out of my mind with desperation. I'd never known what real fear was. Never," he stressed, looking me in the eye. "I focused all my energy on you, but I couldn't make a connection. I kept calling to you, but I was blocked, groping in total darkness. Right when I was on the verge of giving up all hope, a connection opened up between us, just for a split second, but it was enough for me to find you. I'm sure it was our alchemy that connected us. I know you can feel it too. The emotion is incredibly powerful."

"I heard you! I heard your voice! That must have been the instant you managed to find me," I said. "And here we are now," I added, trying to calm him and drive away the look of melancholy clouding his face.

"Let's not think about it any more," Evan agreed, following me as I headed toward a big maple tree.

"It's strange," he said to my surprise, smiling to himself. "There's one thing you haven't asked me yet."

"What?"

Evan glanced at me uncertainly, like he found it unbelievable that I still hadn't asked him the question he'd expected me to. "Aren't you curious to know how old I am?"

Because of the tension I saw on his face as he waited for me to answer, I teased him, looking down, biting my lip, keeping him on pins and needles a little while longer. I cast him a sidelong glance, sensing his concern, then looked deep into his eyes, making it clear from my expression what I thought about it. "It doesn't matter to me."

"Aren't you afraid I'm too old for you?" he said, laughing, turning forward again to look at the maple tree we were heading toward.

"At this point, I'm not afraid of anything any more!" I said sardonically.

"Oh-ho! So we've become fearless, have we?" Evan said, smiling. As he waited for me to reply, he glanced my way, assessing my silence before saying: "I'm three hundred and nine."

My heart skipped a beat. I tried to hide my shock, but my eyes wouldn't keep still, blinking spasmodically. "I . . . I s-swear you don't look a day over two hundred and ninety!" I said with a grin, trying to steady the quiver in my voice.

He flashed a smile before growing serious again. "I wanted you to know," he said solemnly, "before you decide."

Leaning back against the maple, I turned to look at him. "Decide what?" I asked uncertainly. In the freshness of the early morning, I could smell the bark's mossy scent.

Evan reached out and rested his arms against the tree trunk on either side of my head, trapping me with his body as a tremble rose up from my middle and made its way to my heart.

"If you want to be with me," he replied, and my heart skipped another beat. With resolute tenderness, he locked his eyes on mine, silently waiting for a reply which, inside of me, I'd already given him the first time I'd ever seen him. And yet, hearing his proposal voiced left me in a daze, flooding me with an indescribable emotion.

"I already told you it doesn't matter to me," I said softly.

"Careful—it'll be forever, you know," he warned me gently, stroking my cheek with his thumb.

I couldn't speak. His touch had deprived me of all control. My emotions were in a frantic whirl, making my whole body tremble.

"Every day . . ." he whispered, slowly leaning forward until his cheek tenderly caressed mine. His movements measured, he sank his fingers into my hair, melting me in a delicious lassitude. " . . . and every night," he whispered in my ear, brushing his lips against it, "for as long as you want."

I longed desperately to shout out my consent, but I couldn't speak. My intense emotions had left me in a trance.

His lips moved down my neck, brushing against my skin with boundless sweetness as his hand cupped my head, immersing me in sweet languor. "You said a world where we could be together didn't exist," I whispered, my skin trembling at his every breath.

"So we'll fight for one. I'll defy the entire universe if you'll fight with me."

My voice broke with emotion that threatened to overwhelm me. "Count on it," I managed to say in a barely audible whisper, utterly under the power of his spell.

My heart fluttered when Evan withdrew his mouth from my neck and looked at me intently, melting me like warm honey. His presence, his voice, his touch—so gentle, so real—everything about him mesmerized me. I felt like I'd been bewitched by some dark spell.

"Then you'll be mine," he whispered, "forever and ever." Slowly, he pressed his lips to mine. I rested my hand on his chest, so firm beneath my fingers, and surrendered to him, losing myself in his soft, luscious kiss as a wave of emotion swept me away, flooding me with a warmth I'd never known before.

Every last part of me was his. I felt I belonged to Evan unconditionally. As if I'd been born for him and he for me.

When our lips parted, he gently rested his forehead against mine, his hot breath on my mouth. I opened my eyes and my gaze fell on the dog tag that glimmered against his gray shirt. I stroked it, turning it over in my fingers, still under the spell of his kiss. Infinite emotion pierced my heart when I saw the writing on its flat surface. Engraved on the steel, our names were combined in elegant lettering.

"Gevan," he whispered, taking my breath away.

"Evan, how—when did you have this done?" I managed to ask, overwhelmed by emotion. He smiled at me, narrowing his eyes, the dimples in his cheeks deepening adorably.

"The first time I saved you, when I realized I'd be yours forever. You're part of me, Gemma."

How could my body ever contain such powerful emotion? I felt like my heart was on the verge of betraying me.

"I have something for you," he said, slipping his hand into his back pocket. The moment he pulled it out, the thin silver chain sparkled, capturing a sunbeam from the dawn light.

I started when I recognized it and instinctively raised my hand to my neckline, finding the skin beneath my fingers bare. It was the pendant I never went without.

"You lost it in the woods," he explained, holding it out on his palm. "May I?" He looked me in the eye, seeking my approval, but without waiting for my answer, he opened my palm and rested the pendant on it, brushing the thumb of his other hand against my skin. The white gold suddenly glowed with an almost imperceptible light.

"What . . ." I tilted my head as I stared at it, perplexed.

"The engraving." He smiled tenderly.

With the fingertips of my other hand, I clasped the butterfly-shaped pendant and brought it close to my eyes. A lump rose in my throat because the engraving on my pendant had changed; it wasn't my name glittering on the white gold any more. Instead, our two names had become one. The unspoken promise that I would never be alone again.

"Are you angry?" Evan asked, searching my eyes, looking guilty.

"Evan, it's . . . I'm speechless. It's so *beautiful*," I sighed. The concern vanished from his face instantly.

"I know you never take it off. This way I'm sure you'll always have a part of me with you. May I?" He took the chain from my hands and swept my hair to one side, inviting me to hold it up.

I did, turning around and baring my neck. His fingers brushed against my skin, lingering for a few seconds on my nape. Another shiver ran through me at his touch, and I knew for certain I'd never grow used to that contact.

"There's something I need to ask of you."

I let down my hair and turned to face him again, concerned by how serious he'd sounded. "What?" His charm left me dazed every time, trapping me in some unknown world. Looking him in the eye as I waited for his question, I knew he could ask me for anything and I would gladly give it to him.

"You need to promise me something," he said solemnly.

I nodded, waiting.

"I don't want there to be any more secrets between us, no matter what. Secrets are dangerous. Look at where the smallest one led us. I want you to be mine, mine and mine alone. And I'll be completely yours, without reserve." His gaze pierced me as he waited to hear my reply.

"I promise," I vowed.

Evan caressed my face and I trembled again, emotion washing over me. I couldn't believe it was really happening, that he was really there, so close I felt the warmth of his breath on my face. He ran his thumb over my lip, his eyes following the movement. I felt I might go mad with desire.

"How intensely can you fall in love with someone in such a short time?" I whispered, my eyes locked on his lips.

"To the point of madness," he replied in a hushed voice, swallowing. Then he kissed me with dark tenderness.

"Evan." I closed my eyes as a new fear rose up to torment me. "Do you think they'll come back looking for me?" I suddenly feared someone might take me away from him.

Evan looked away for a moment, reflecting. "I roamed the earth for centuries in search of something that would bring me back to life. Now that I've found it, I won't let anyone take it from me. I'll protect you at all costs." Despite the firmness in his voice, his eyes betrayed his concern. "I won't lie to you; I can't be sure it's really over, but I won't let anything happen to you, Gemma. We'll be together. And it will be forever."

"My *forever* is a little different from yours." I smiled to myself, because with Evan's gaze on me, every trace of fear disappeared. "But even if Death does eventually find a way to separate us, until that moment, I'll be satisfied with every second offered to me."

Evan lifted my chin sweetly, resting his eyes steadily on mine so I could read the promise there. "Not even time will separate us. If I have to defy the entire universe, I'll find a solution to that too."

His lips touched my forehead, sealing his vow.

ACKNOWLEDGEMENTS

It took me three months to write the first draft of Touched, but the process that brought this book to your hands was a long one, and I want to thank all the people who supported me, kept their fingers crossed for me, and celebrated with me along the way. First of all, from the bottom of my heart, I thank my number one fan, the person who's been closer to me than any other on this journey full of difficulty, hope, and—most of all—emotion: my husband Giuseppe Amore, who relives all the scenes with me every time I write a new passage. Thank you for your infinite trust in me and my project. If I'm able to describe love, it's all thanks to you. I couldn't wish for a better husband. You've always believed in me, supported me, and encouraged me to follow my dream, even when I lost my way. Without you and your constant support, none of this would have been possible.

To Gabriel Santo, because your smiles and sweet looks fill my days with warmth, and because when you were born you changed my world. I love you more than anything.

A huge THANK YOU goes to my entire family for the enthusiasm you've shown and for having instantly loved the characters in Touched. Your support allowed the novel to develop and grow stronger with every passing day. To my sisters, Ketty and Rosanna: Ketty, I thank you for helping me with the most difficult task: reconciling my dream with the countless chores of a mother and housewife. And Rosanna, with your wonderful Facebook page Il Silenzio Illumina L'Anima, for your advice and web support. To my parents, for raising me surrounded by love: my mother, who followed Evan and Gemma's love story from the very start, hiding the manuscript when a customer walked into the diner because I'd asked you to keep it a secret; and my father, who, when I was little, instead of reading me stories every night would invent new ones, introducing me to the world of the imagination. To my pug Bam Bam, who curls up at my feet whenever I'm writing (and who sleeps all the time, just like Iron Dog!).

Now I'd like to thank some people who have a special place in my heart. For the passion and enthusiasm they've shown for Evan and Gemma's story, I owe truly special thanks to the fabulous as well as sweet Cristina Prasso and the incredible team at Editrice Nord publishers in Italy who gave me a warm welcome into their wonderful world. I now know that behind a great publishing house are great people. Endless thanks to my editor, Giorgia di Tolle, for your splendid work on Touched. I couldn't be more satisfied, and most importantly, I never would have imagined editing could be so much fun!

Thanks to everyone who worked on the texts. To editor Paolo Caruso for your valuable advice and for coming up with the title "The caress of fate"! To journalist Luca Crovi for enthusiastically believing in the story and helping to improve it. To the very friendly Barbara Trianni and Laura Passarella in the press office at Nord. To Graziella Cerutti, sales director; to Elena Pavanetto and Giacomo Lanaro in the marketing office; to the fantastic Uti for your careful corrections and for keeping Gemma from getting lost on the streets of Lake Placid; and to the whole team from the Mauri Spagnol Group. The final result—which I adore!—is thanks to the advice and hard work you all devoted to it. During my journey with you, I met wonderful people and scaled unexplored heights.

Endless thanks to Melanie Rostock and Elena Rodríguez García from Oz Editorial for the joy you gave me when you contacted me about publishing Touched in Spain!

Thanks with a capital T to my American editor Annie Crawford who's been supporting me (and putting up with me) for some time now. Annie, you're a wonderful person and—I'll never stop telling you this—your help over the last year has been priceless, not only because you're so skilled at what you do, but because you helped me so patiently during the difficult ascent to achieve my big dream.

To my American translator, Leah Janeczko, I could dedicate an entire page of thanks because you've made my dream come true: Evan and Gemma are finally ready to take the next big step, thanks most of all to you. You managed to grasp the essence of the characters and the soul of the novel, and it's been wonderful working with you. Thank you for involving me. I'm so excited about this new adventure! A warm hug to kind, courteous Michele Piumini, the talented translator who put the two of us in touch. You have my heartfelt thanks!

I cherish the invaluable help I received from Professor Sani, professor of Sanskrit at the University of Pisa. I thank you so much for your translations of this fascinating ancient language that readers will also have the chance to sample in the installments to come.

To sweet Sara Helwe who made the breathtaking covers for the spinoff tales of the Touched saga. Don't miss them!

To Linda Salvia Gangemi, for helping me find the perfect setting. Lake Placid really is amazing! My thanks and apologies to the town's inhabitants; I hope I didn't make any unforgivable mistakes. I've never visited your wonderful little town, but I've explored all its streets thanks to Google Earth, so in a way I feel like I've been there. I hope one day to visit in person. Sometimes I used my imagination, but for the most part I tried to make the places as real as possible. I hope I succeeded, at least a little.

Thanks to Alex McFaddin from Lake Placid for putting up with me over the years, answering all my questions about your town. And thanks to sweet Rhiannon Patterson, who goes to Gemma's school and has been a huge help to me over the last few months. I've dedicated two characters in the book to you two and named them after you.

Special thoughts go to the memory of A.A., a boy I never knew yet who inspired the initial story as I was on my way to work one day. Grateful thanks go to my reading teacher Marianna Spagnuolo; even though I was just a little girl, I've never forgotten the trust you had in me and my stories. You're still in my heart. Thanks to my dear aunt Orietta Strazzanti for getting up at dawn every day to read over the manuscript, and to my dear uncle Gino Strazzanti for his technical support and research into ancient cultures and languages.

Thanks also to the really nice friends at the Mondadori bookstore in Caltanissetta, Alberto and Lia, for giving me moral support and cheering me on. I'd also like to thank James Blunt; you'll probably never know it, but your music has been a constant inspiration for me. And I can't forget to express my gratitude to Lana Del Rey, because I wrote some of my favorite scenes in Touched while listening to your beautiful voice.

A big hug to my dear fellow authors Luca Rossi, Rita Carla Francesca Monticelli, Giulia Beyman, Wirton Arvel and all the members of the incredible group of self-publisher to which I'm honored to belong. Without your advice, this experience would not have been the same.

And now, truly special thanks go out to all my affectionate readers and the wonderful bloggers who've supported me along this difficult path: THANK YOU. Your words helped Touched to evolve. Also, thanks from my heart to all the bloggers who will support Evan and

Gemma in the future. I hope to meet you soon! I began this adventure all alone, but on my journey I've met wonderful people and formed true friendships, and I hope to make many more because they bring me such joy. Thanks to Susy Follero and all the little Witches and Subterraneans in the Touched: The Caress of Fate Fan Club. You're in my heart. Go Touchers! Thanks to Bliss Silverleaf of the Libri per passione blog for all your enthusiasm and affection; to Maria Loreta De Benedettis for the beautiful drawings of Evan and Gemma; to Elena Serboli and her family of Subterranean fishies; to Sangue Blu (Sara) of the blog Il piacere di essere letti for the very first critique (I still remember how my heart was racing!). To Elisa Florio for getting an Evan and Gemma tattoo (I still can't believe it!); to Martina Lo Riso and all the girls who got tattoos of lines from the book. You're fantastic! To Glinda Izabel of the blog Atelier dei libri, where Evan and Gemma first took wing; to Franci Cat of the blog Coffee and Books for the constant support; to Vania Previte of the blog Un libro per sognare for having "Evanized" herself (and for coining the term!); to sweet Beatrice Luzi of the blog BookLovers (I wuv you!); to dear Luna Effy Ferrara of the blog Who is Charlie (Go, TeamDrake!); to Lucia Pannacci of the blog TheLoyalBook. To Stella Ferro for being so excited that we ran into each other (and for making me excited about it, too!). To Valentina Canella for the beautiful T-shirts and other items inspired by the Touched saga (including undies!). To Sophie Newton (Jen) and Consuelo Cedioli for the long talks about Evan and Gemma. And to EVERYONE ELSE who's been there at my side since I self-published, for all the emotions you've inspired in me day after day. It would be impossible to name you all, but you're in my heart. When I began this experience, the path was difficult. I basically had to work my way up from the bottom, but I gave it absolutely everything I had, one step at a time, and in the end I managed to make the dream that seemed so distant come true! That this was possible is also due to all of you who let Evan and Gemma into your hearts.

Above all else, wherever you are, I thank YOU, the person who's reading this right now. I hope you've enjoyed my company and that Evan and Gemma made you feel at least a little bit of the emotion that, day after day, makes my heart beat.

I never would have thought it would be so exciting to write acknowledgements. It's like taking a journey back in time and remembering the road—at times rocky—that led me here, and all the people who accompanied me. Some of you walked at my side for only a short distance while others have been with me since Touched was just a first draft. To all of you, I say thank you from the bottom of my heart. Years have passed since Evan and Gemma first popped into my head, standing on tiptoe to whisper their story into my ear. Since then they've become a part of my life and my heart, giving me the gift of a world of emotion, so special thanks also go to them.

To my son: Never let fear or insecurity make decisions for you. Always follow your dreams and never give up, or they'll turn into regrets. Aim high; that way, if you get lost, you'll always have the stars to show you the way. And believe in yourself. Always. Your choices will also be mine.

And to you, reader: if you have a dream you want to achieve, I urge you: don't wait for it to come find you. If your dream is to write, go out and make it happen! I did.

PRESS

"As seductive as *Meet Joe Black*. As mysterious as *City of Angels*. As powerful as *Twilight*."

"Elisa S. Amore is one of the few phenomena in Italian self-publishing." **Vanity Fair**

"Girls who dream of love, a new novel just for you has come out in bookshops." **Marie Claire**

"*The Caress of Fate* is the literary success of the year." **Tu Style**

"A winning novel that's fresh and interesting, one that belongs on your bookshelf." **Io Donna**

"Italy, too, is seeing the rise of the fantasy genre served with a side of romance. Its undisputed queen is thirty-one-year-old Elisa S. Amore." **F Magazine**

"A sensationally successful debut." **La Sicilia**

"Elisa S. Amore is an unquestioned star of the supernatural fantasy genre." **Metro**

"For those who think emotions shouldn't die out as you grow up, this novel has a lot to offer you." **Vero**

"With *The Caress of Fate,* Elisa S. Amore makes her bookstore debut, but if you look up her name on the web you'll discover a whole world. Elisa S. Amore's narrative skills are clear; it's like reading a classic American-made saga." **Pop Up Literature**

"A truly incredible fantasy novel in which love is masterfully combined with the supernatural. A new saga whose readers are already anxiously awaiting the second—and no doubt spectacular—installment." **Il Recensore**

"A love story that goes beyond the confines of reality to unite two souls as they overcome every obstacle. Recommended for all romantics and everyone who dreams of immortal love."
Gli Amanti dei Libri

"Elisa S. Amore has created a world around her novel, making it something unique." **Lo Schermo**

"A modern version of the Italian masterpiece *Death Takes a Holiday*." **Elena – Goodreads**

"As fascinating as *Meet Joe Black*, but for young adults. And not only." **The Bookworm**

"Following the Italian success of Alberto Casella, another fascinating story about death and love." **R. Fantasy**

Hailed by readers as a perfect mix of *City of Angels* and *Meet Joe Black*, with a pinch of the Orpheus legend.

THE AUTHOR

Elisa S. Amore is the author of the paranormal romance saga *Touched*. She wrote the first book while working at her parents' diner, dreaming up the story between one order and the next. She lives in Italy with her husband, her son, and a pug that sleeps all day. She's wild about pizza and traveling, which is a source of constant inspiration for her. She dreamed up some of the novels' love scenes while strolling along the canals in Venice and visiting the home of Romeo's Juliet in romantic Verona. Her all-time favorite writer is Shakespeare, but she also loves Nicholas Sparks. She prefers to do her writing at night, when the rest of the world is asleep and she knows the stars above are keeping her company. She's now a full-time writer of romance and young adult fiction. In her free time she likes to read, swim, walk in the woods, and daydream. She collects books and animated movies, all jealously guarded under lock and key. Her family has nicknamed her "the bookworm." After its release, the first book of her saga quickly made its way up the charts, winning over thousands of readers. *Touched: The Caress of Fate* is her debut novel and the first in the four-book series originally published in Italy by one of the country's leading publishing houses. The book trailer was shown in Italian movie theaters during the premiere of the film *Twilight: Breaking Dawn—Part 2*.

DISCOVER MORE ABOUT
ELISA S. AMORE
www.elisasamore.com

Would you like to talk to the author about Gevan's love story? Join the Touched Saga community!

Twitter.com/ElisaSAmore
Facebook.com/eli.amore
Instagram.com/eli.amore
https://www.facebook.com/groups/251788695179500/

If you want to stay updated about Elisa S. Amore's latest book releases, join the Touched Saga Newsletter! Copy this into your browser:
http://elisasamore.com/Touched-Sign-Up

Join the conversation about the Touched saga using the official hashtags
#TouchedSaga or #Thecaressoffate.

Visit the official site to discover games, quizzes, book trailers and much more, at:
www.touchedsaga.com

Follow us on:
Facebook.com/TheTouchedSaga
Twitter.com/TheTouchedSaga

If you have any questions or comments, please write us at
touchedsaga@gmail.com

For Foreign and Film/TV rights queries, please send an email to elisa.amore@touchedsaga.com

Printed in Great Britain
by Amazon